PENELOPE - TUDOR BARONESS

THE ELIZABETHAN SERIES

TONY RICHES

COPYRIGHT

Copyright © Tony Riches 2023
Published by Preseli Press

ISBN: 9798397387774
BISAC: Fiction / Historical
Cover Art by Ashley Risk

ALSO BY TONY RICHES

OWEN – BOOK ONE OF THE TUDOR TRILOGY
JASPER – BOOK TWO OF THE TUDOR TRILOGY
HENRY – BOOK THREE OF THE TUDOR TRILOGY
MARY ~ TUDOR PRINCESS
BRANDON ~ TUDOR KNIGHT
KATHERINE ~ TUDOR DUCHESS
DRAKE - TUDOR CORSAIR
ESSEX - TUDOR REBEL
RALEIGH - TUDOR ADVENTURER
THE SECRET DIARY OF ELEANOR COBHAM
WARWICK: THE MAN BEHIND THE WARS OF THE ROSES
QUEEN SACRIFICE

ABOUT THE AUTHOR

Tony Riches is a full-time writer and lives with his wife in Pembrokeshire, West Wales, UK. For more information visit Tony's author website: www.tonyriches.com and his blog at www.tonyriches.co.uk. He can also be found at Tony Riches Author on Facebook and Twitter: @tonyriches.

For my grandson
Alfie Thompson

1

THE KING'S MANOR
FEBRUARY 1578

The carriage rattles over deep ruts in the frost-hardened road, jolting Penelope from her daydream. She'd been imagining becoming a favourite of the queen, like her mother and grandmother before her. After a lifetime of listening to colourful stories of the royal court, she longs for the day she can be one of Queen Elizabeth's maids of honour.

Her breath mists in the cold air and she pulls her fur-lined cape closer, pushing away the nagging sense that nothing will be the same again. She is a woman now, and needs a place at court to make her way in the world. Her mother says the queen likes her ladies to be young and attractive, but warned her of the dangers. The queen can be a jealous mistress.

Penelope peers out at the bleak countryside. The harsh winter has followed a poor summer and a stormy autumn, with worrying talk of people starving after yet another failed harvest. There are rumours of Catholic unrest, and they face the ever-present threat of rebellion.

A row of ramshackle cottages appears and a scrawny dog runs barking at the horses, drawing a shouted curse from the coachman – and a crack of his whip. A thin young woman, with a small child wrapped in a woollen shawl, stares at them from her dark doorway as they pass, followed by their baggage wagons, and servants on horseback.

Penelope raises a gloved hand to the woman, sensing her envy and sadness as they thunder onwards. How different her own life might be if her father, Sir Walter Devereux, had not been Earl of Essex, a man who'd risked everything when chosen by the queen to lead her army against the rebels in Ireland. Her grandfather, Sir Francis Knollys, is a privy councillor, vice chamberlain of the royal household, and a leading Puritan reformer.

Her late grandmother, Lady Catherine Knollys, was a daughter of Anne Boleyn's elder sister, Lady Mary Carey, and a cousin of the queen. She served as a maid of honour to the ill-fated Catherine Howard and Anna of Cleves, before becoming chief Lady of the Bedchamber to Queen Elizabeth.

The carriage creaks on the rutted road. Penelope's mother, Lady Lettice, a once-removed cousin of the queen, was so proud of her carriage, made by the royal coachbuilder, a Dutchman named Guilliam Boonen. With her red hair and fine gowns, her mother bears a striking resemblance to the queen, and was delighted when a crowd cheered as she rode her grand carriage through the streets of Westminster.

Penelope's father, alarmed about the consequences for his career, had ordered his coat of arms to be emblazoned on both sides of the carriage. The once grand red-and-white Devereux crest on the leather side panels is faded, and the gilded ironwork shows signs of rust; yet the carriage, pulled by a fine pair of black horses, is still a symbol of high status.

She glances at her younger sister, Dorothy, sleeping at her side. So similar in looks and age they are often mistaken for twins, yet they could not be more different. Dorothy has been withdrawn and sullen since their world fell apart. Penelope knows she must be strong; at fifteen she is the eldest, and must carry the burden of caring for the others.

She turns to her travelling companion and chaperone, Anne Broughton, sitting opposite. 'I'm surprised Dorothy can sleep on these roads. I fear this carriage was intended for paved city streets, not a long ride across country in winter.'

Anne braces herself as the carriage lurches over another rut in the road. 'She told me she lay awake all night, worrying about the future, yet she will wake as fresh as a daisy, while we arrive in York exhausted.'

Anne's family had been the nearest neighbours to Chartley Manor, in happier times. Well educated, and seven years older than Penelope, Anne had agreed to escort them on the ride north, even though she'd recently married. She was more like an elder sister than their housekeeper; Penelope and Dorothy had even been bridesmaids at Anne's modest wedding in their parish church.

Anne's was not an arranged marriage, but a love match, to a man close to her own age, with good prospects – their young family lawyer, Richard Broughton, a barrister of the Inner Temple. Anne's father is appointed to oversee the management of the Chartley estate, which needs to be let to tenants. Penelope feels a pang of sadness at the thought she might never see their family home again.

After their father's sudden death in Ireland, her brother Robert had inherited the title and became the new Earl of Essex at the age of ten. Their father's wish was for Robert to be a ward of Lord Burghley, the queen's Lord Treasurer, who sent him away to Trinity College in Cambridge to complete his education.

Anne's younger brother, Anthony Bagot, had accompanied Robert as his companion and valet. Before he left, he confessed to Penelope that his father's instructions were to 'steer the young earl on the proper path', and she guessed he'd seen the chance to make his own fortune.

She recalls Anthony's reluctant farewell. They'd been close, and he kissed her on the cheek when he said goodbye. His affectionate concern for her seemed more like that of a suitor, but they both knew she would have to marry well. Penelope is destined to wed a noble lord, with a greater fortune than Anthony Bagot can aspire to.

She frowns at the cruel injustice, and looks across at her youngest brother, Walter, known to everyone as Wat, sitting next to Anne. His face is pale, and he seems younger than his nine years. He'd struggled to understand, protesting when their mother sent them away, pleading to remain in Oxfordshire with her and their grandfather at Greys Court.

Penelope stretches out her leg and nudges his boot with hers. 'Be strong, Wat, and have faith. We need you to watch over us, now our brother is away in Cambridge.'

Wat studies her with doubt in his dark eyes. 'Robert promised to visit when he can, but how will he know where to find us?' The note of sadness in his young voice betrays his feelings.

Anne pats his arm with motherly affection. 'One of your first tasks can be to write to your brother, with directions for how to reach us. I'll help you, if you wish?'

Wat brightens at her suggestion. 'I shall also write to our mother, to let her know when we are all safe.' He returns to scowling out at the snow-covered fields, yet his tone suggests he's beginning to accept their changed circumstances. His childhood cut short, he must learn to adapt and make his way in the world.

Penelope gives Anne a grateful nod. None of them has any choice in the matter, but she believes she understands her mother's plan. She needs them out of the way, and the Earl of Huntingdon provides her with the perfect excuse.

She'd summoned Penelope and Dorothy to explain. 'Catherine Hastings, Countess of Huntingdon, is a favourite of the queen and a sister of Sir Robert Dudley.' Her mother had given Penelope a wry look as she spoke. 'Lady Catherine has no children of her own, so makes it her business to prepare the daughters of others for a life at court. Take heed of her advice. You will find no better tutor.'

Penelope looks across at Anne as a thought occurs to her. 'Mother told me nothing about my father's cousin, Sir Henry Hastings, the Earl of Huntingdon. I hope he is a kindly man.'

Anne shrugs. 'My father said Queen Mary ordered Sir Henry to be locked up in the Tower of London for his Protestant faith.' She frowns at the thought. 'It must have been a difficult time for him, but Her Majesty made him President of the Council of the North, so he is now one of the most influential men in the country.'

Penelope places a soft pillow behind her head and closes her eyes, listening to the rhythmic clip-clop of the horses on the frozen track. With each powerful stride they take her further from her old life, towards the uncertainty of her new one. She reaches out and takes Dorothy's hand in hers, wondering what the future holds for them. At least they have each other.

Flakes of snow drift from the darkening sky by the time they reach the hostelry for their overnight stop. Anne takes charge, leading Dorothy and Penelope up narrow stairs to their musty, low-beamed room. A pair of truckle beds have been made up with warm coverlets brought from Greys Court, and a single candle flickers in the cold draught from the shuttered windows.

They each have a bowl of salty beef stew, with a crust of manchet bread and a cup of watery beer, before combing tangles from their copper-gold hair and changing for bed. After

Anne bids them goodnight and closes the door, Dorothy speaks in a conspiratorial voice.

'I overheard Grandfather telling Mother something which will affect us both.' She glances at the door. 'They were discussing her plans for us, and he said there might be a difficulty with our dowries.'

Penelope is used to Dorothy's intriguing, but not the worried frown on her face. 'Father left us each a dowry of two thousand pounds.' She'd hoped for more of an inheritance, but the vast sum will be enough. 'They must respect his wishes.'

'Grandfather said our father's adventures in Ireland left debts which must be repaid.' Dorothy shakes her head. 'There's not enough to meet what is owed to the Crown. Father sold all the property he could, but Mother may have to surrender our remaining lands, and even offer Chartley to the Crown estate.'

'Then we are paupers?' Penelope sits up in her bed as the consequences strike her. 'Robert joked that he is the poorest earl in England, so it could be he knows something of this?'

Dorothy doesn't answer, but blows out the single candle, plunging the room into darkness. Penelope lies on her back, listening to the muffled sounds of others settling for the night. A door bangs, and a man's deep voice calls out for more ale. She decides the time has come to share her secret. 'Do you remember the time Philip Sidney came to Chartley?'

Dorothy's bed creaks as she turns. 'I'll never forget the royal progress. We had to stay with the Bagots and give up our rooms. It cost our parents a fortune to feed the queen's retinue. They drank the cellars dry – and you spent the whole time trying to catch Philip Sidney's eye.'

'I was only twelve, younger than you are now. It's little wonder he didn't pay me much attention, but I was the age of consent for marriage, and Father promised to consider Philip Sidney as my suitor.'

'You're to marry Philip Sidney?' Dorothy doesn't try to hide her surprise. 'He is handsome, despite his pox scars – but he's a good ten years older than you.'

'Only nine years older, which is not unusual, and he cannot help the scars on his face.' She hears the defensive note in her voice. 'He's the nephew of Sir Robert Dudley, Earl of Leicester, and heir to his great fortune, which makes him one of the most eligible men of the royal court.'

'Why have you not spoken of this before?' Dorothy's sharp accusation hangs in the chill air.

'Mother insisted I must not speak of it to anyone until Her Majesty gives her consent.' Penelope frowns in the darkness. 'If the queen hears rumours of a betrothal, she could forbid us to marry – or worse.'

'Has anyone thought to ask Philip Sidney if he will marry you?' Dorothy sounds sceptical. 'If he is so eligible, he will have the pick of the queen's ladies.'

Her sister's words trouble Penelope for most of the next day's long journey. She doesn't know if people marry well with no dowry, but guesses it is unlikely. She can feel her prospects slipping away, now her father is dead and the family in debt. Yet there is a secret she's not shared with her sister.

Her father's raised voice had echoed up the stairway late one evening at Chartley, waking her. He'd accused her mother of having an affair with Robert Dudley, while he was away fighting in Ireland. Worse still, he said the rumours of her infidelity had reached him even there.

After that, Penelope noted the glint in her mother's eyes and how her voice became softer when she spoke of Robert Dudley. Her absences became longer and more frequent. She said she was taking the waters at Buxton for her health, although Penelope doubted it.

Their father stayed in London that Christmas, and their mother left them in the care of Anne while she attended New Year celebrations with her circle of friends. Penelope suspected her mother planned to marry Sir Robert Dudley, one of the richest and most influential men in England. He was the queen's favourite, and if she approved of the marriage, everything would change for them all.

They reach the city of York and pass through the impressive four-storey gatehouse of the Micklegate Bar. Riding through cobbled streets lined with merchants' houses, they stop at an imposing building with mullioned windows and tall chimneys, where Countess Catherine greets them with stern-faced authority.

'Welcome to the King's Manor. This was the abbot's house of the Benedictine abbey of St Mary, and serves as the head-quarters for the Council of the North. You will attend prayers three times a day, and learn the value of devout and godly lives.' She frowns at Penelope's furs and fine gown. 'Nothing must be allowed to distract you from the word of God.'

Penelope fights the overwhelming despair. 'Our mother asked me to send you her best wishes, Lady Catherine, and to thank you for your kindness.'

Catherine Hastings gives the briefest nod of acknowledgement and beckons waiting servants. 'You will wish to change, and then we will meet in the chapel to pray for your mother.'

The edge of disapproval in her voice stops Penelope from speaking further. Her worst fears have been realised. The countess dresses in black, with no jewellery other than a silver crucifix. Puritans detest finery, singing, and dancing – everything Penelope loves. Instead, they face a life of prayer, drudgery and hard work. She prays the time will soon pass.

Sir Henry Hastings returns later that evening. His grey beard hangs over a starched ruff, and if not for his gold chain of office, he could be mistaken for an overweight merchant. He gives each of them an appraising stare with watery grey eyes, and hands Wat a leather-bound prayer book.

'Let this be your constant companion, young Walter. Your father, my cousin, was an honourable man, and a good Protestant. It is your duty to pray for his soul.'

Penelope senses that their presence in his house discomforts Sir Henry Hastings in some way. Her mother once told her to learn from the way men looked at her. In a flash of insight, she guesses Sir Henry's devout Puritan faith is troubled when she catches his wandering eye examining her tight bodice.

She glances across at the countess. She had not missed her husband's momentary awkwardness. Penelope knows that under her formal exterior, Catherine is a shrewd and perceptive woman. She is also a favourite of the queen, wife of the most powerful man in the North, sister to Robert Dudley, and to the mother of Philip Sidney. Penelope must earn her trust, or risk making a dangerous enemy.

Penelope settles into the routine of life at King's Manor with grim determination. Rising at first light, they dress in plain robes with linen coifs covering their hair, and are in the cold chapel for prayers and the reading of a sermon for the day, before breaking their fast.

Mornings are usually spent in contemplation and copying out passages from the Bible. There are more prayers at midday, followed by an unappetising meal. The afternoon tutorials offer some respite, as the countess recognises the need to continue their education.

There is no shortage of language and music tutors in the sprawling city of York, as well as a fencing master for Wat. Penelope is allowed to play her lute for one hour a day, but only religious music. In return, they must attend endless sermons from dour Puritan ministers, who urge them to fear God and love the Gospels.

Countess Catherine also makes time each day to teach the duties of the mistress of the house. 'A lady is modest, meek, submissive, virtuous, and obedient.' She checks these ideal qualities off on her long fingers, as if they are a self-evident truth.

Anne's husband, the Devereux family lawyer Richard Broughton, arrives in York on business and arranges to visit Penelope and Dorothy. His cheerful manner is replaced with grim seriousness as he explains to the countess he must see them in private to discuss their inheritance. When they are alone together, he checks the door and speaks in a hushed voice.

'I must tell you your mother has married the Earl of Leicester, Sir Robert Dudley. Your father left considerable debts, which meant your mother had to rely on your grandfather's charity, but now her future is secure. Sir Robert is a man of great wealth.'

Dorothy gasps, but Penelope is unsurprised. 'Did the queen give her permission?'

'I expect Sir Robert will have informed Her Majesty of his intention.' Richard Broughton glances at the closed door and lowers his voice. 'Their wish is to keep the marriage secret for as long as possible, which is why your mother asked me tell you in person.'

Penelope's mind whirls with the implications. 'The countess will hear about this from her brother soon enough. We should share our news with her—'

'Your mother would prefer you to delay until the marriage becomes public knowledge.'

'If they have the queen's permission, there's no need for secrecy.' Penelope glances at the door as she realises she's raised her voice.

Richard Broughton frowns. 'Sir Robert's enemies spread false rumours about him at court.'

Penelope recalls her mother warning her how vindictive the gossipers of court could be. 'What are they saying, Master Broughton?'

He hesitates before replying. 'I regret to tell you they say Sir Robert had your father poisoned by an accomplice in his household.' He frowns, as if he has difficulty repeating the words. 'Sir Robert expects that when they learn he has married your mother…'

'How can we be sure the rumours are false?' Penelope hears the tremble in her voice. 'Sir Robert was suspected of the murder of his first wife.'

Richard Broughton looks surprised. 'Where did you hear that?'

'From our mother. She told me the rumours were spread by his enemies, to make it impossible for him to propose marriage to the queen.'

Richard Broughton nods in understanding. 'There was never any proof – and the same applies to the death of your father.' He speaks softly, yet his voice is firm. 'Sir Henry Sidney, as Lord Deputy of Ireland, ordered an investigation immediately after your father's death. There was no trace of poison, and he found your father died of the flux, a common enough affliction in Dublin.'

Doubt nags at the back of Penelope's mind. Her mother told her the queen took note of rumours at court, however unlikely. There could be consequences, particularly if, as she suspects, they've risked marrying without the queen's permission.

'Does this mean we can return to our mother?'

Richard Broughton shakes his head. 'Your mother expects you both to continue your education here until suitors can be found for you.'

Dorothy stares at him in astonishment. 'We have to stay here until we marry?'

'You are legal wards of the Earl of Huntingdon, which means Sir Robert Dudley has no obligation to provide for your care.'

Penelope frowns. 'And our mother – does she also have no obligation for our care?'

Richard Broughton looks apologetic. 'For now, your mother is busy making her new life, but I'm sure she does not care any less for you.'

2

THE ORDER OF THINGS
JULY 1579

Penelope's mind wanders as Sir Henry says his overlong grace, thanking God for their evening meal. She thinks of the two letters which arrived for her that morning. One is from her brother Robert in Cambridge, with yet another promise to visit when he could, and the other is from Anne Broughton.

Anne's letters are welcome diversions from the relentless routine of prayer and study; they are one aspect of her life over which the countess has no control. Anne lives in Blackfriars, London, due to her husband's work as a lawyer of the Inner Temple, and provides Penelope with tantalising snippets of gossip from the city, which give her a subtle power in King's Manor. Everyone, even the countess, wishes to know about the queen's French suitor, the young Duke François of Anjou. A regular topic of after-dinner conversation, people have strong views about the prospect of the queen's marriage to the heir to the throne of France.

Servants bring bowls of steaming mutton pottage, thickened with oatmeal and garnished with herbs. Stale bread, cut into triangles, soaks up the liquid, so nothing goes to waste.

Penelope longs for the sugar comfits they loved at Chartley, but notes how the countess and Sir Henry eat the same as them, so she never complains.

Once, when the countess taught them the skill of book-keeping, she had shown them her own ledger, and they saw payments were being made by their grandfather, but these were for their education, not food. They have no money of their own so, as far as they know, they are reliant on the charity of their hosts.

Sir Henry rarely speaks of politics, but after they've eaten, he offers an insight into the concern of government for the succession. 'Her Majesty has been petitioned by Parliament to marry and produce an heir.' He grunts. 'They make it sound simple enough for her to do but, mark my words, our queen will not be ruled by her ministers.'

Countess Catherine glances at her husband. 'It seems Her Majesty likes to keep us guessing about the truth of her feelings for the Duke of Anjou.' She frowns. 'Parliament should be mindful of the risks of childbirth and the queen's age. I've not forgotten the foolish talk of my own brother as a suitor, yet the gossipers revel in every detail of the negotiations for her marriage.'

Penelope wonders if her reference to Robert Dudley is a prompt for her to confess their great secret, yet she innocently continues the discussion. 'I've learned the duke is twenty-two years the queen's junior, Countess. To many people he must seem more like a son than a suitor, and it's said she calls him her *little frog*.' She smiles. 'She named his envoy, Jean de Simier, Baron de Saint-Marc, sent by the duke to lead the negotiations, her *singe*, or monkey.'

Countess Catherine raises an eyebrow at Penelope's flippant tone. 'Her Majesty presented the French envoy with a gold ring from her own finger, as a keepsake.'

Penelope sits back in her chair. 'Could it be the queen plays games with such suitors, and has no intention of marrying?'

Sir Henry listens to their exchange, and raises his voice for the first time Penelope can recall. 'I pray the Lord will save us all from union with the French!' The room falls silent and all heads turn to him, seated at the head of the long dining table. 'The boy's a papist, and his father burned Protestant ministers at the stake.' He scowls. 'One of the Duke of Anjou's conditions is that he should, after marriage, be crowned our king!' Contempt echoes in his voice.

Countess Catherine stares at him with wide eyes, seeming to be torn between loyalty to her husband and to the queen. She speaks in a calm voice, in contrast to Sir Henry's outburst. 'I suspect the queen does what she can to maintain our truce with France.' She frowns. 'We cannot afford to offer the Catholics a reason to rebel.'

Penelope judges it time to share her information. 'I have received news in Anne Broughton's latest letter. She tells me there was an attack on the life of the queen.' She sees she has their interest and continues. 'Her Majesty was being rowed in her gilded barge on the Thames near Greenwich with the French envoy.' She takes Anne's letter from the pocket in her dress, and glances at the countess, who gives her a nod to read the letter aloud. 'A man named Thomas Appletree fired an arquebus from a small boat, and shot one of the queen's watermen, who sat within six feet of Her Majesty, making him cry out in pain, saying he was shot through the body.' She pauses to look at their shocked faces. 'It's thought the assassin's target was Jean de Simier. Thomas Appletree was captured and condemned to death, but the queen granted her gracious pardon, and delivered him from execution.'

She expects them to be shocked at the surprise ending to her story, yet Countess Catherine seems to understand the queen's decision. 'Her Majesty follows the example of the

Gospel of Matthew. If *you* do not forgive men their trespasses, neither will our Lord God forgive *your* trespasses.'

Penelope sits in the long garden of King's Manor, which reaches all the way to the tranquil River Ouse, out of sight of the countess or her ever-present servants. The sunshine and wildflowers brighten the bleak reality of her life, and the oak bench in the dappled shade of a willow tree is her favourite place, a sanctuary.

The countess accuses her of laziness for spending so little time on household duties, yet Penelope knows how to outwit her guardian's rules. She chooses to study in the garden, explaining that the fresh air is good for her health. She reads a new leather-bound book from Paris, *La Semaine*, written in French by the Huguenot poet, Guillaume de Salluste, about the creation of the world.

A gift from her French tutor, who seems besotted with her, the Protestant poetry meets with the approval of the countess. Penelope smiles to herself at how she encourages her earnest young tutor, who must know her knowledge of the language is equal to his.

Tired of the thinly veiled preaching about the Day of Judgement, she marks her page with a red ribbon and closes her book. Penelope shuts her eyes as the sun creeps lower in an azure-blue sky, casting lengthening shadows. A robin chirps, the only sound other than the calming ripple of the river.

The peaceful silence of the garden is broken by a familiar yet unexpected voice calling her name. She turns in amazement to see her brother, hardly able to believe the change in him. Robert looks six feet tall, despite being only thirteen, and wears a silver dagger at his belt. The greatest difference is in his manner; he speaks and acts like a noble, the Earl of Essex and head of the Devereux family.

'They were going to send for you, but I thought to be a surprise.' He pulls off his cap to reveal a tangle of unruly hair. 'I see my sister is grown into a woman and, some might say, pretty enough for the royal court.'

'My brother is grown into a flatterer.' She smiles, unsure whether she should kiss him, so settles for a hug. 'We were starting to think you'd forgotten us.'

He grins, and sits with her on the wooden bench seat, stretching his long legs in fine black leather boots. 'The ride here took us the best part of a week, and my tutors forbade me to travel to York, for fear I might not return.'

'Have you come to see us without permission?'

He shakes his head. 'The master of my college, Doctor John Whitgift, agreed to this visit after news of our mother's marriage to Sir Robert Dudley became known.'

Penelope nods. 'We learned of the marriage from Richard Broughton. He told us Mother wished to keep it secret for as long as possible.'

'A poorly kept secret.' His voice becomes serious. 'I have heard that the French ambassador, Jean de Simier, told the queen.' He curses. 'The man is a troublemaker, and Her Majesty is furious. It's said she calls our mother a she-wolf, and Robert Dudley a traitor.'

Penelope puts her hand to her mouth. 'Will they be punished?'

'They're banished from court.' He scowls. 'Mother used to warn us that the queen can be a jealous mistress.'

'And what about *us*, Robert? What does all this mean for *us*?'

He shrugs. 'I pray they are soon forgiven.'

'I hoped to be chosen as one of the queen's ladies.' Penelope hears the disappointment in her voice as her plans unravel further. 'Richard Broughton said we will remain here as Sir Henry Huntingdon's wards until we are married.'

'Are you not happy here in York?' He gives her a questioning look, concern in his eyes.

'No – but the fault is not with Countess Catherine, or Sir Henry. I'm certain they both have the best of intentions.' She holds up the book of poetry for him to see. 'I have tutors to continue my French and Spanish, and I'm learning to speak Italian. The countess teaches us how to manage a household, and how to conduct ourselves in society … but the days seem overlong.'

'I look forward to when my time at Cambridge is over.' Robert looks wistful. 'I miss the life we had at Chartley.'

'We all do.' She stops herself from adding that not only is their father dead, but their mother too – at least, she might as well be dead to *them*; she rarely writes, even on their birthdays, and never visits, or invites them to visit her.

'How are Dorothy and Wat?'

'We've each found ways of coping with our new life here. Dorothy immerses herself in her studies.' Penelope gives him a wry look. 'She will make someone the perfect Puritan wife.'

Robert frowns at the thought. 'And how is our little brother?'

'Wat hopes to become a soldier, like Father. He has sword-fighting lessons from a man who fought in the French wars – but I've written to Grandfather asking if he'll sponsor a place for Wat at university.'

Robert raises an eyebrow in concern. 'Father wished Wat to go to Oxford, but I'd not want him to face the insults I've had to put up with in Cambridge.'

'Insults?' Penelope sees he is serious.

'I've had trouble with some of my fellow students. They call our mother a harlot, and say Robert Dudley persuaded the queen to send Father to Ireland, to keep him out of the way.'

Penelope shakes her head. 'You were old enough to recall how much Father wished to go to Ireland. He told me it would be the making of him, and how he planned to make a great fortune from plantations.'

'Worse still, they say Robert Dudley had our father poisoned.'

'Richard Broughton said there is no proof—'

'The name-callers care nothing for proof – or the truth, come to that.' A note of bitterness sounds in his voice. 'I wrote to Father's secretary, Edward Waterhouse, asking for his opinion, and he did not deny it.'

'We will never know, but don't forget Robert Dudley was your godfather, and is now your stepfather. His goodwill is important to us all. We must set aside any doubts and ignore these cruel rumours.'

'I've tried to ignore them, but it's not easy. I suspect our grandfather insisted on the marriage to end the threat of scandal.'

'He will have seen it as his duty – and it's your duty to do what you can to defend our mother's name, and Sir Robert Dudley. Do you have friends who would support you?'

'Some seek me out in the belief I'll be of use to them, pretending friendship, yet only because I have the title of Earl of Essex.' He smiles. 'I have Bagot to watch over me, and my tutor, Master Wright.'

'Did Anthony Bagot travel here with you?' Her pulse quickens at the thought. In quiet moments, she still recalls his embrace, and wishes she could see him again.

'Bagot's taking care of the horses. I believe he's ridden all this way in the hope of seeing you.'

'He might be disappointed.' Penelope looks down at her plain, Puritan gown. 'Countess Catherine has strict rules about everything: how we dress, and who we meet – particularly handsome young men.'

'But you find ways to outwit her?'

Penelope smiles. 'I seek sanctuary here in the garden. I believe her servants spy on us, but it's rare for them to venture down here. And if they do, I will see them.'

Countess Catherine ensures there is no opportunity to be alone with Anthony Bagot, but she cannot prevent him attending evening prayers with them in the chapel, and he stares across at Penelope as if seeing her for the first time. He's grown a well-trimmed beard which suits him, and he smiles as he catches her eye.

He seems to have acquired a new confidence since they'd parted. She can't deny the frisson of attraction, and envies his sister Anne's freedom to marry who she wished. Not for the first time, she thinks of her own circumstances as a curse. She's heard no further news about her betrothal to Philip Sidney, and he might not even consider marrying her without a dowry.

With each passing year the danger of his marrying someone else increases. She hopes Countess Catherine will tell her if he does. Her spirits sink at the thought of being forced into a loveless marriage to someone she doesn't even know.

Distracted from her prayers, Penelope wonders how life would be if she were to rebel against the plans of others. She risks another glance at Anthony Bagot, and wishes she had the courage to follow her heart. As her brother's companion, he stands a good chance of being rewarded with a knighthood. He comes from a well-respected family and will inherit Blith-field Hall, with six hundred and fifty acres of land, close to her former home at Chartley, as well as his father's fortune.

A stab of conscience forces her back to reality. She has no choice, and cannot ask him to risk everything for her. Her destiny is to become a favourite of the queen, and to marry Philip Sidney. She must, for the sake of her family and her reputation – and because the eldest has to set the highest standards.

Penelope asks Countess Catherine to walk with her to York Minster. King's Manor is in the heart of the city, yet the countess will not allow them to visit unescorted. She warns of cutpurses and thieves in the narrow alleyways, and speaks of the sins of the drunkards and wastrels who frequent the inns and taverns.

Penelope and Dorothy once risked visiting the stalls on market day, and became lost in the maze of narrow twisting lanes and alleys of the Shambles. Returning late for evening prayers, they expected Countess Catherine's anger. Instead, she made them pray for God's forgiveness.

They are allowed to attend church, see the celebrations of holy days, and to visit Penelope's favourite place – the towering Minster, a short walk from King's Manor. Stripped of flamboyant Catholic trappings, York Minster has become a place of peaceful contemplation.

Penelope feels it is time to talk to the countess about her marriage prospects, and ask about a place at court. She waits until they are safely out of hearing of the servants, and tries to appear casual as she asks her well-rehearsed question as they walk towards the Minster.

'You must have married quite young, Countess.'

'I was betrothed to Sir Henry at twelve years old.' Catherine sounds wistful, with the faintest hint of regret.

Penelope smiles. 'I expect you were more grown up than I was at twelve.'

'It was the proper age.' She speaks slowly, as if remembering, and this time Penelope hears doubt in Catherine's voice.

'May I ask if you were allowed any say in your betrothal, Countess?'

She raises an eyebrow at the question. 'I suppose I was. There was a clause in the agreement that our match could be dissolved, if either of us refused the other.'

'And you were my age when you married Sir Henry?'

'A year younger than you are now.' She studies Penelope for a moment. 'My father was executed for trying to put a Protestant, poor Lady Jane Grey, on the throne. Sir Henry was a handsome man, with good prospects and, at seventeen, only two years my senior. It never occurred to me to refuse him. To do so would have been to question the natural order of things.'

They walk in silence until they reach Minster Yard. The countess seems in an amenable mood, and the yard is quiet, a good time for Penelope to ask the question she'd debated with Dorothy since they arrived. 'I hope you will forgive me, Countess, but I wonder why you have no children of your own.'

Catherine stares at her, as if making a judgement. 'I never speak of it, but I suffered a miscarriage, thirteen years ago, in the spring of 1566.' She turns to Penelope, sadness in her pale-blue eyes. 'The infant was a boy, and would have been named Henry, after his father. My physicians did their best, but I am no longer able to bear a child.'

Penelope doesn't know what to say. 'I'm so sorry, Countess. That must have been an impossibly difficult time for you and Sir Henry.'

'My faith was tested, yet we prayed for guidance and the Lord told me to dedicate my life to the education of young women, such as yourself.'

Penelope places her hand on Catherine's arm. 'God bless you, my lady.'

A new bond forms between them, now she's been trusted with Catherine's secret. They enter the south transept of the Minster and kneel to pray. Penelope offers private thanks for the kindness of the countess. She has no idea where they would be now, if left to the care of their mother.

After seventeen months in York, Penelope sees there is more she can learn from Catherine Hastings than she'd dared to expect. From now on, she resolves to be more like the daughter the countess never had, and make the most of her time, to prepare for her new life at court.

3

THE ROYAL COURT
JANUARY 1581

Penelope stares at the countess in disbelief. 'Her Majesty has asked to see *me*?' Her heart pounds at the thought.

Catherine smiles. 'What better way to celebrate your eighteenth birthday than to be presented at court?'

Her mind whirls with questions. She looks down at her plain gown, with its frayed hem and unfashionable sleeves. 'What should I wear? Do you think she might offer me a place? What if she asks about my mother? What should I say?'

The countess holds up a hand to silence her. 'You must tell the truth. Always the truth. Her Majesty will not be deceived, and has no doubt made it her business to know everything she wishes to know about your mother – and my brother.'

Penelope frowns. 'Our mother's marriage caused trouble for my brother Robert in Cambridge. It would be unfair if I am somehow held to blame for her actions, or Sir Robert Dudley's decision to marry her.'

'Her Majesty knows it is no fault of yours, Penelope. There is no vacancy among the queen's ladies, but I will accompany you, and together we will discover God's will.'

'Thank you, Countess, that is a comfort to know. Although I've dreamed of a life at court, there's so much at stake that the prospect of being presented to the queen makes me nervous.'

'Remember what I've taught you. Her Majesty was chosen by God, but is also a woman who likes to have new companions.' She gives Penelope a conspiratorial look, and takes a red velvet purse from her pocket.

Penelope laughs as she sees the pendant. On a fine gold chain is a golden frog, set with bright green emeralds and two diamonds for eyes that sparkle as she turns it in the light. 'What if Her Majesty takes offence?'

'If I know the queen, my gift will amuse her.'

'Will *I* be expected to have a gift for her?'

Catherine thinks for a moment. 'Her Majesty has little need of more jewels, but you sing well, Penelope, so your gift for her will be a special performance.'

'Do you know what song Her Majesty might like?'

'*Joyssance vous Donneray*. I have the music somewhere. Your distant relative, her mother, Anne Boleyn, sang it at court when she returned from France. Although the queen rarely speaks of her mother, she will appreciate the reason for your choice.'

'I must rehearse until I know this song to perfection.' Penelope embraces the countess, for the first time. They have come a long way since their first meeting. 'I'm so grateful for your kindness.'

Catherine speaks softly. 'I confess I have my own reason to spend time at court. Sir Henry is owed a great deal of money by the Treasury, and cannot continue to meet the expenses of the Council of the North.'

They walk through the royal Palace of Whitehall, their long gowns swishing on the tiled maze of endless corridors, with walls hung with priceless tapestries. Galleries filled with lifelike royal portraits lead to chambers furnished with ornate furniture, golden clocks, and priceless treasures, guarded by stern-faced yeomen.

Countess Catherine seems at home in such finery, nodding to people she recognises as they pass. 'Whitehall belonged to Cardinal Thomas Wolsey, but the queen's father seized the palace for the Crown when the cardinal fell from favour.'

Penelope stares up at the gilded plaster mouldings on the coffered ceilings. Tudor roses and fleurs-de-lis glow with gold in the light of countless candles. 'The palace is far grander and far larger than I imagined.' She gives the countess a wry look. 'Too grand for a cardinal.'

Catherine nods. 'There have been many changes since Thomas Wolsey's days. The palace was extended to become the largest in the country, four times the size of Hampton Court, and one of the queen's favourite residences. This is where her father died, and we are close to the Palace of Westminster, where Parliament and the courts of law sit.' She smiles as they reach the queen's inner sanctum. 'Truly at the heart of the kingdom.'

Penelope takes a deep breath. The lacing of her new gown is uncomfortably tight, and she worries the queen might disapprove of the shimmering blue satin she's chosen from the best seamstress in York. All the stories she'd heard from her mother rattle through her mind, drummed into her since childhood.

The privy chamber is crowded with courtiers, and the gentle buzz of their conversation reminds Penelope of flies on a midden in summer. Her pulse races as she recognises the familiar face of Philip Sidney. She feels a flutter of concern when he doesn't smile, or show any sign of recognition, but it has been six long years since she last saw him.

She also spots her elderly grandfather, Sir Francis, Vice Chamberlain of the Royal Household, standing at the back with his sons, her uncles William and Henry Knollys. Close by stands her great uncle, Lord Hunsdon, who gives her a nod. Penelope is encouraged to see some members of her family present. They have no doubt come to see what impression she might make on the queen, and will surely report back to her mother and stepfather, who are still banished from court.

She feels all eyes are upon her as they are announced and the countess leads her forwards. The queen sits in a raised high-backed chair, and Penelope bends in an elegant curtsey, as the countess taught her, avoiding looking the queen in the eye. She focuses on the queen's embroidered slippers, and says a silent prayer.

The queen gestures with her hand for them to stand, and the countess speaks first. 'We thank Your Majesty for inviting us to court.' She takes the red velvet purse from her pocket, and bows as she hands it to the queen. 'A small token, Your Majesty.'

The queen opens the purse and smiles at the sight of the golden frog, holding it up by its gold chain for her ladies to see. 'We've missed you at court, Countess, yet understand your duty is to support your husband in the North.'

Catherine nods. 'I have another gift for Your Majesty. I present my ward, Penelope Devereux.'

Penelope looks up at the face of the queen. The portraits flatter her. The queen looks tired, the powder on her face failing to conceal her poor complexion. Her extravagant red wig, framed by a wired gossamer veil, glittering with small diamonds, draws attention to her advancing years.

Her brocade gown, embroidered with gold and silver thread, is festooned with pearls, and too much pale flesh shows at her low-cut front. The countess told her Elizabeth would be forty-eight in September, ten years older than Penelope's mother, yet the queen seems much older. Too old to bear a child without great risk.

Despite her strange appearance, the queen radiates unmistakable power. She has the power to make someone wealthy with a nod, or have them committed to the Tower with a snap of her fingers. The intelligence in her bright, unblinking eyes, taking in every detail, reminds Penelope of her father's hunting hawk.

The queen studies Penelope for a moment. 'You have more than a passing resemblance to your mother, when she was young.' She makes it sound like an accusation.

'I thank you for inviting me to court, Your Majesty. I've been told I bear a resemblance to my grandmother, Lady Catherine, when she was young.'

The queen nods her head in agreement. 'My beloved cousin is sadly missed.' She smiles, revealing uneven teeth. 'Be proud of your Boleyn blood. There are few enough of us left.'

Encouraged by the queen's softer tone, Penelope knows the moment has come. 'I have a gift for Your Majesty. I shall sing for you, if you wish it.'

'We will be glad to hear you sing.' The queen claps her hands. Her courtiers clear a space, and the chamber falls silent.

Penelope glances at Countess Catherine, and is reassured by her nod. She takes a deep breath and sings in a clear voice, as rehearsed so many times at King's Manor, in her perfect French, with no need for accompaniment.

Si pour moi avez du souci
Pour vous n'en ai pas moins aussi,
Amour le vous doit faire entendre.
Mais s'il vous grève d'être ainsi,
Apaisez votre cœur transi;
Tout vient à point, qui peut attendre.

Penelope's heart thumps in her tightly bound chest. She's taken a great risk in making such a performance at her first time in court, but the countess knows the queen well. She takes another deep breath, and continues to sing the verse in English, with more feeling.

> *If you should have a care for me*
> *For you I'll care the same degree,*
> *On this Love will you educate.*
> *But if you chafe that it should be,*
> *With me you need not now agree:*
> *For good things come to those who wait.*

Her eyes meet those of Philip Sidney, who moves into her line of sight. This time he grins, and leads the enthusiastic clapping. The queen's eyes shine as she joins in with the applause. Penelope curtseys, and the applause echoes even louder. Her gamble has paid off, and she gives thanks to God.

Countess Catherine looks pleased with herself. 'The queen has chosen you as a maid of honour, Penelope.'

'I thought there was no vacancy…'

'A vacancy can always be found if Her Majesty wishes.' She smiles. 'Now you will learn how our routine at the King's Manor has prepared you for your new life.'

Penelope doubts it. She's already sensed the undercurrent of flirtatious behaviour in the palace. She knows nothing of the game of courtly love, who to trust and who to be wary of, but her mother warned of the dangers of the gossips of court, and the harm they can do. 'I will rely on your guidance, Countess.'

Catherine nods. 'You sang well, and made a good impression on the queen, but being one of her maidens is not all dancing and banquets. You must swear fidelity, dress always in white, and live in the maidens' chambers. You are expected to be ready to serve Her Majesty at any time, day or night, which means learning patience.'

'Will you be staying here in the palace, Countess?'

'My brother has agreed that Dorothy can be sent for from York, and he's offered us the use of rooms at Leicester House, in the Strand.' She takes Penelope's hand in hers, in a rare moment of tenderness. 'I've come to think of you as if you were my own daughter, and will always be there if you need me.'

'May I visit you and Dorothy at Leicester House?'

'With the queen's permission. Take note, Penelope: from now on, all you do must be with the consent of the queen.'

Penelope finds it hard to sleep in the crowded maidens' chambers, with so much coming and going, and gossiping long after the candles are extinguished. She lies awake, thinking she has much to learn. She's become a new favourite of the queen, who often asks her to sing and play her lute to entertain her.

The countess had been right. Being a lady-in-waiting meant long hours of waiting. The other maids of honour seem friendly enough, and she is learning fast. They pass the time teaching her the steps of new dances, and how to play card games. The queen must always be allowed to win, but not *too* easily, which takes some skill.

Although the newest of the queen's maids of honour, Penelope is addressed by the title 'lady', as the daughter of an earl, while the others are addressed as 'mistress'. She has mixed feelings about being called 'the prettiest of the queen's maidens', and is discovering her new power as the eyes and ears of the queen.

Penelope is granted permission to visit the countess and her sister at the end of her first month. The countess arrives in the carriage to accompany her on the short ride from the palace, and listens with keen interest to the latest gossip from court.

'Another of the maids of honour, Anne Vavasour, has been banished to the Tower in disgrace for conceiving a child with the Earl of Oxford, Sir Edward de Vere.' Penelope frowns. 'I saw him jousting in the tournament, as the Knight of the Tree of the Sun, in gilded armour. He showed no sign of being out of the queen's favour.' She didn't mention how magnificent Philip Sidney had been as the Blue Knight, or that he'd found excuses to attend the privy chamber.

The countess gives her a knowing look. 'The queen shows forgiveness for her favourites, yet deals harshly with any of her ladies who break her rules. Tell no one, Penelope, but my brother, your stepfather, is already back in royal favour.'

'And my mother?'

'Still banished, I'm afraid.' She frowns. 'I doubt your mother will ever be welcome at court.'

Leicester House proves to be one of the grandest mansions in the Strand, with towering gates of wrought iron, and a cavernous entrance hall as grand as any chamber in the royal palace, decorated with family portraits in gilded frames. Dorothy comes down the wide staircase to greet her. She wears a peach gown, with her hair loose, and looks older than her seventeen years.

Penelope hugs her sister. 'I've missed you – and have so much to tell you.'

Dorothy smiles. 'I have news as well. I've learned our mother's great secret.' Her eyes flash with amusement. 'She is with child. We are to have a new little brother or sister!'

Penelope stares at her in amazement. 'Mother made no mention in her letters—'

The countess interrupts. 'Your mother wished to be certain.

Such matters have a way of coming to the attention of gossipers, and soon enough to the queen, once they are written down.'

Penelope understands. 'Her Majesty might not take kindly to the news.' Another thought occurs to her. If her mother gave birth to a boy, he will become the Earl of Leicester's heir, and Philip Sidney will be disinherited.

The procession of gilded royal barges, rowed by red-liveried oarsmen, are an impressive sight as they make their way on the River Thames to Deptford. This is Penelope's first appearance in public at a royal event, and she looks forward to seeing the ship which sailed around the world.

The maids of honour travel behind the queen, all dressed in new gowns and white capes to protect them from the light breeze blowing down the river. They gossip about the exploits of Captain Drake, who is to be knighted for his achievement.

'He gave the queen a golden crown, adorned with fine emeralds, brought from Peru,' Lady Frances Howard tells her. 'Her Majesty wore the crown on New Year's Day, and shows extraordinary favour to Master Drake, spending many hours hearing about his adventures.'

At the quayside at Deptford, the yeomen of the queen's guard, armed with swords and shining halberds, hold back the crowds as Penelope follows the queen, with her ladies-in-waiting. Behind them come the chattering courtiers and richly dressed nobles accompanying the ambassador of France, Monsieur de Marchaumont.

A billowing ship's canvas sail is stretched high over the main deck of Drake's ship, the *Golden Hinde*, in the dry dock at Deptford Creek, and the cross of St George flies from the topgallant. Penelope finds it hard to believe this little ship has been through such adventures, and returned with her captain, and most of her crew, safe and well to England.

The golden hind figurehead is freshly gilded, and the ship's topsides are newly painted in royal red, and Tudor green and white. A row of heavy bronze culverins gleam in the spring sunshine, and even the iron anchors have a fresh coat of black paint. The subtle scent of cloves, her last cargo, drifts on the air, and a light breeze carries the tang of new tar, concealing hasty repairs to the hull.

Crowds of Londoners throng around the ship, chattering and laughing. Eager for sight of their queen, they cheer and applaud as the royal party arrives. Trumpeters play a fanfare, accompanied by a drum roll. The red-and-blue royal standard unfurls from the top of the mainmast, and colourful silk banners stream in the breeze.

Captain Drake removes his hat and bows to the queen. On the scrubbed deck, where sailors once battled storms, stand trestle tables covered with fresh white linen. They groan under the weight of a seafood banquet of oysters and sturgeon, conger eels and lampreys, sweet sugar delicacies and goblets of wine.

The queen takes her place on a throne with a cushion of purple velvet, flanked by her ladies-in-waiting, and seems to be enjoying herself as viol players strike up a melodic tune, accompanied by drummers. A sailor plays a tune on a horn-pipe while a young sailor dances a jig.

Captain Drake kneels while Ambassador de Marchaumont draws his sword and lays it on his shoulder.

'I dub thee knight. Rise, Sir Francis Drake.'

The watching crowds give a rousing cheer, and sailors pour wine and ale, bringing baskets of bread and silver platters of fishes. Another fanfare brings more applause as the centre-piece, a baked porpoise swimming in a sea of small silver fishes, is placed on the queen's table.

Penelope turns at the sounds of rending wood, cries of alarm, and shouts of panic. The gangplank they crossed to board the ship falls with a crash, throwing aldermen and guild masters into the mud of the dry dock. The queen laughs at the sight of them, dressed in their finest clothes, as they curse and scramble to escape up the steep, slippery dock sides.

Her mother's wailing echoes like a ghost through the wood-panelled corridors of Leicester House. Penelope has permission from the queen to visit her mother, yet worries about the consequences when Her Majesty learns the reason.

The child is on the way, and the birth is not going well. Penelope confides to her sister. 'If Mother lives, I swear I will spend more time with her.'

Dorothy frowns. 'It would have been easier, particularly for Wat, if Mother made the journey to visit us in York. He misses her so much.'

'How is our little brother?' She'd almost forgotten him with all the excitement and drama of court.

'Not so little now, and more determined than ever to become a soldier.'

The wailing from their mother's bedchamber stops, and the house falls silent. As they listen at the foot of the staircase, a new wail begins, the unmistakable cry of a baby, shrill but strong. The midwife appears, a towel in her hands.

'You have a new brother. He is to be named Robert, after his father, and will have the title of Lord Denbigh.'

Penelope embraces her sister. 'Now our stepfather has an heir, Philip Sidney will no longer become the Earl of Leicester. He was my father's choice of husband for me, yet now will inherit nothing.' She feels her future unravel like a spool of yarn as she says a prayer for her mother.

4

THE BETROTHAL

OCTOBER 1581

The eldest of the queen's maids of honour, Lady Mary Hastings, takes Penelope, as the youngest, under her wing. She knows intriguing stories about everyone, and has answers to Penelope's many questions on the mysteries of life at court.

Like Penelope, Mary has the title 'lady', as the daughter of one earl, and sister of another – Sir Henry Hastings. Penelope suspects Mary spies on her at court and reports back to Sir Henry. Until she marries, she is his ward, and her success or failure will reflect on his reputation.

Penelope sits on the lid of her wooden chest as they pack their belongings for yet another move. 'It seems Her Majesty is determined to visit every royal palace, from Hampton Court to Nonsuch.' She pulls the leather strap tight. 'Now we're returning to Greenwich, for the second time in as many months.'

Lady Mary agrees. 'I'll wager we'll next be sailing upriver to Richmond. The plague is back in London, so each time we move from palace to palace, an army of men move in to fumigate the chambers.'

Penelope's eyes widen in concern. 'I thought we were free of the plague?'

'We will never be free of the plague.' Mary shakes her head. 'There are many deaths in Kingston, and the Privy Council complains to the mayor that the plague increases in the city through negligence. They are ordered to prevent anyone from London and Westminster from going to Kingston on market days upon pain of Her Majesty's high displeasure.'

Penelope thinks of her mother and sister, and the baby boy at Leicester House, and prays for their safety. The queen's travels make it hard to visit her mother, but she is relieved to see her so soon recovered. She smiles at how her mother refers to her new son as the *Noble Imp*, consigning him to the care of a wet nurse while she resumes her social life.

The summer progress also means less scrutiny of the maids of honour, which Penelope takes as an opportunity to make alliances, such as with the dour, hunchbacked Robert Cecil. Although the same age as her, he wears the black robes of a cleric, and always seems to be in the background, watching and learning.

With few friends, he has resisted her attempts to flatter him with her attention, yet his powerful father – William Cecil, Lord Burghley, the Lord Treasurer – is the queen's chief advisor, and grooms Robert as his successor. William Cecil is over sixty, and his son will be a useful ally – or a dangerous enemy.

The other man she seeks out could not be more different, yet proves just as hard to fathom. Philip Sidney, undeterred by the loss of his fortune, gives her a knowing look when he slips her notes as they pass in corridors. The risk adds excitement to their liaison, and his notes are cryptic sonnets, which Penelope enjoys interpreting.

Privacy is impossible to find in the maidens' chambers, so she flattens the scraps of paper in an innocent prayer book. His latest note is the boldest, and leaves her in no doubt. He's offered her a declaration of his unrequited love. Penelope finds a quiet window seat and opens her prayer book at the hidden note.

> *Loving in truth, and fain in verse my love to show,*
> *That she, dear she, might take some pleasure of my pain,*
> *Pleasure might cause her read, reading might make her know,*
> *Knowledge might pity win, and pity grace obtain.*

She snaps the book shut at the sound of approaching footsteps and looks up to see Lady Mary Hastings. She would love to confide her secret and show her the sonnet, but her doubts hold her back. There is plenty of time, and no need to take unnecessary risks.

Mary glances at Penelope's prayer book with a nod of approval. 'You have visitors. Countess Catherine has arrived with her brother, the Earl of Leicester, and they wish to see you about a private matter.'

She follows Lady Mary down the corridor to an ante chamber used for such meetings, her mind whirring with possibilities. Has something happened to her mother? Could it be to do with her dowry? Do they wish to talk about her betrothal to Philip Sidney?

Robert Dudley forces a smile as she enters. He wears a blue velvet cape over a silver doublet with pearl buttons, with a silver-handled sword at his belt, and has the look of a man who expects trouble. The countess is dressed in her black gown, and greets Penelope with a warm embrace.

Penelope senses their news is not good. 'What's happened, Countess?'

'The moment you've been waiting for all this time draws near. You are to be betrothed, Penelope.'

She feels as if a weight has been lifted from her. No more wondering if she will end up like Lady Mary, the oldest maiden in the palace. 'Thank you, Countess. I've enjoyed my brief time as one of the queen's maids, and learned a great deal about life at court, but I'm ready.'

The countess smiles. 'You've been the best of all my students, and learned your lessons well.' She glances at her brother. 'We have chosen your suitor. Lord Rich is a good Puritan with a great fortune, and only three years older than you.'

'Lord Rich?' Penelope stares at her, and struggles to understand. 'I am to marry Philip Sidney.'

Robert Dudley shakes his head. 'Lord Rich is a better match for you, Penelope.' He gives her a condescending look. 'His fortune will make you one of the wealthiest women in the country.'

'I've seen Lord Rich.' She turns to the countess. 'He is churlish, uneducated – and shorter than I am!' A vision of Philip Sidney in magnificent blue-and-gold armour, riding his white charger, swims before her eyes. 'My father's dying wish was that I marry Philip Sidney. I will never marry Lord Rich.'

'Philip Sidney has no inheritance.' Robert Dudley gives her a stern look. 'The decision is made and you will do what you are told, for the good of your family.' He speaks softly, yet the threat in his voice is unmistakable.

A thought occurs to her. 'I cannot marry, as I have no dowry.'

'Your grandfather has agreed to pay your dowry, and has already made the first instalment of five hundred pounds to Lord Rich.'

She feels giddy, and sits in a chair. 'Has Her Majesty given her consent?' Her heart pounds. She already guesses the answer.

'I was able to put the request through Lord Burghley.' Robert Dudley sounds pleased with himself. 'The queen approves his recommendation, and sends her good wishes to you both.'

Penelope slumps in her chair, defeated. She looks up at Robert Dudley, tears in her eyes. 'What will happen if I refuse?'

'You cannot!' His raised voice echoes in the room. 'You must do your duty, as must we all.'

Penelope embraces Anne Broughton, who has come to Leicester House to help her prepare. 'You look exactly the same as I remember.' She gives Anne a questioning look. 'No little lawyers yet?'

Anne laughs. 'I promise you will be the first to know, *and* my first choice of godmother.'

'It's good to see you again, Anne. I only wish…' Her voice trails off and she feels close to tears.

'You must make the best of the hand fate has dealt you.' She looks Penelope in the eye. 'You are not the first to find yourself in an arranged marriage, and will not be the last.'

'I *detest* Lord Rich.' She hears the bitterness in her voice. 'I caught him staring at me, like a fox watching a chicken, and now I know why.'

'You don't know him.' Anne looks thoughtful. 'You call him uneducated, but he qualified as a lawyer at Grey's Inn, which is how my husband knows him. He told me that, as a second son, Lord Rich never expected to inherit the title or the fortune until his elder brother died last year, and then his father died, last February.'

'I suspect he is the worst kind of Puritan.' Penelope frowns. 'I had a taste of that in York. Sir Henry Hastings preaches one thing, yet does another. They don't like music or dancing, fine clothes or—'

'Yet, from your letters, you seemed happy enough at King's Manor.' Anne puts a calming hand on Penelope's arm. 'A marriage is what you make of it.' Her voice softens. 'Even mine has its challenges.'

'But you had a say over your life, and chose who to marry. You married for love. I'm traded like a brood mare to the highest bidder.'

'My husband is away for days on legal business. Even when he returns, he sits working in his study until late at night.' A flicker of sadness shows in Anne's eyes, then she brightens. 'I've been looking forward to returning as your companion ever since I heard you are to be a baroness.'

'A baroness?'

'Although they call him *Lord* Rich, your future husband inherited his father's title, to become the third *Baron* Rich, and one of the greatest landowners in the south of England, perhaps the country.'

There is a knock, and Dorothy enters, carrying a white nightgown. 'My wedding present. The embroidery is my own.' She holds it up for Penelope to see. 'The buttons are made from mother-of-pearl.'

'It must have taken you an age.' Penelope studies the delicate embroidered flowers, stitched with great care.

Dorothy looks wistful. 'Time is one thing I have plenty of, and it helps pass the hours while I wait to see if I shall have your place at court.'

'Thank you, Dorothy.' Penelope manages a smile. 'I should warn you there is much boredom to endure as one of the queen's maids.'

Dorothy glances at the door. 'I fear I have exchanged one prison for another. The countess will not let me set foot outside the door. She says we must take care, for fear of the plague.' She frowns with concern. 'She told me seventy-five have died of the plague in London this past month.'

. . .

Welcome winter sunshine breaks through grey clouds as Penelope walks in the gardens of Leicester House with her mother. She reminds her more than ever of the queen, with her unpredictable moods. For the first time, she notes the streak of grey in her mother's red-gold hair.

'Tell me about your marriage to Father,' Penelope asks, when they are out of hearing of the servants.

Her mother looks surprised at her question, then becomes animated as she remembers. 'He was the most handsome man at court – and so charming. All the queen's ladies pursued him.'

'Then was it a love match?'

Her mother smiles. 'I suppose it was. My father was most pleased to see me married to a wealthy Protestant, and become a viscountess at sixteen. His Devereux ancestors came to England with William the Conqueror, so even our queen could not find an objection to him.'

Penelope is unsure how to raise her question, so decides to be direct with her mother. 'You seem happier now, than you were with Father.'

'Your father became too eager to please the queen, and risked everything for her. I tried to reason with him but—' She stops herself, and turns to Penelope. 'People change in a marriage. Think on that. And once you have children, you will find you will also change.'

Penelope smiles. 'I'd not thought of children. If I have a girl, I will name her after you.'

She takes Penelope's hand. 'Thank you, that means a lot to me.' Her eyes glisten with unexpected tears. 'I promise to be a better mother from now on, and a good grandmother. I will always welcome you, Penelope, whenever you need me.'

The wedding day arrives with alarming speed, and Leicester House fills with friends and family. Penelope is surprised to see how tall her brother Wat has grown, and how much he reminds her of their father. She is even more surprised to learn her brother Robert seems to know her future husband well.

'He visited me in Cambridge, and took me out for a night in the taverns.' He grins. 'It turned into several nights, and I came close to being sent down for being absent from the college without permission.'

Penelope wonders if Lord Rich had bribed her brother, who wears a new brocade doublet and hose with a flowing silk cape. He beckons a handsome dark-eyed man, who wears the orange Essex livery, with a white sash.

'This is Gelly Meyrick. He's a Welshman, from the household of our uncle in Lamphey.' Her brother smiles, as Meyrick takes her hand in his and kisses it. 'And you remember Bagot.'

She had noticed Anthony Bagot the moment he entered the room. Their eyes meet, and she senses his sadness, despite his smile. This was the man who loved her, the one she would have chosen to marry, if her life had been her own.

Penelope closes her eyes and grits her teeth when the moment comes to say 'I do'. She cannot bring herself to look at Robert Rich, for fear of seeing his smug look at winning her so easily. A sharp pain in her fingers breaks through her thoughts. With a jolt she realises he's taken her hand in his and squeezed with all his strength.

She bites her lip, and tries to find the courage to cry out, 'I will not marry this man!' The moment passes, and the elderly minister, who has probably been warned to expect trouble, takes her silence as a *yes*.

Their Puritan wedding has no feasting, music, dancing, or witty speeches wishing them a long and happy life together. In place of festivities, they endure an overlong sermon on the sanctity of marriage, and a strange numbness overtakes Penelope.

She remembers little until she is led to her bedchamber, where Anne waits to help her. Penelope sits on the wide velvet-canopied bed, and weeps. 'I am no longer in control of anything.'

Anne pours her a silver cup of strong red wine. 'This will help.' She smiles. 'It's a wedding present from your brother Robert – and see, he's had the cup engraved.'

Penelope stares at the Latin motto under the familiar Devereux crest. *Virtutis comes Invidia*. Envy is the companion of virtue. She drains half the cup, and feels the rich warmth in her throat. 'I cannot face what is to come.'

'You know what to expect?' Anne sounds concerned.

'Of course.' Penelope gives her a wry look. 'The maids of honour talk of little else.' She takes another deep drink of wine, and holds out the silver cup for more.

Anne fills the cup. 'Talking of it is one thing, but I promise, the act will surprise you.'

'We had a busy farm at Chartley. We watched the pigs rutting, and stallions serving the mares.' Penelope smiles. 'Now that was a sight. Our mother seemed to think it completed our education.'

Anne laughs, then looks wistful. 'When I first married, I could not believe how beautiful such a thing could be.' She blushes at her confession.

Penelope takes another deep drink of wine. 'I have no choice, so all I can do is pray our Lord has a good reason for this travesty of a marriage.'

'There is much you can do. Lord Rich is a man and can be moulded, like any man. It will take time, but time is on your side. He is young, and no doubt eager to please, and you are one of the cleverest women I know.' Anne takes a small glass bottle from her bag. 'A special perfume, from France, my wedding gift to you.'

Penelope thanks her. The exotic scent lifts her spirits, as does the embroidered nightgown she puts on before climbing into the vast, cold bed. Anne wishes her luck, yet her eyes betray her concern as she closes the door.

The candle burns down to a flickering stump before her husband enters the bedchamber. Despite herself, Penelope closes her eyes, unwilling to look at him. She braces herself, expecting his weight on the bed, but instead, she hears him muttering. Curiosity makes her open her eyes, and she sees him kneeling at his side of the bed, hands clasped in prayer. He speaks softly, and she strains to make out the words.

'As thou forgive us our trespasses, so may we forgive others who trespass against us. Show upon us thy goodness, that to others we may show the same. In the hour of temptation, deliver us from evil. Amen.'

The ropes supporting the mattress creak in protest as he climbs on to the bed. Penelope keeps her eyes closed tight, and tries to remember Anne's advice. *You must make the best of the hand fate has dealt you.*

He shakes her, as if he thinks she is sleeping. 'Will you not even look upon me, woman?' He grabs her arm so hard she is sure there will be bruises. 'You must obey me, and show proper respect!'

Penelope hears Countess Catherine's mantra in her head. *A lady is modest, meek, submissive, virtuous, and obedient.* In that moment, she resolves to refuse him, and prevent the consummation of their marriage, without which, she prays it can be annulled.

Robert Rich pulls back the coverlet and begins undoing the small, mother-of-pearl buttons of her nightgown. Dorothy's fine needlework is too much for his clumsy fingers. He mutters a curse and rips the front open, exposing her breasts.

Penelope holds her breath as she catches the smell of stale sweat, and hears him grunt as he climbs on top of her. Robert Rich is stocky, and surprisingly heavy. She keeps her legs clamped tight together with every ounce of her strength, and her eyes tight shut as she prays for it to end.

'Don't you dare defy me!' He slaps her hard on the face with the flat of his hand.

The sharp sting makes her ears ring. No one has ever hit her, and the sudden shock makes her cry out, the sound echoing. She only relents for a moment, but it is all he needs. He forces her legs apart and begins grunting like the pigs she'd watched, rutting in their sty.

She lies awake on her back long after the candle flickers and burns out, plunging the bedchamber into darkness. Her new husband is at her side, snoring, and she finds herself thinking of what might have been, with Philip Sidney. His words repeat in her head. *Knowledge might pity win, and pity grace obtain.* She should feel anger at her husband's behaviour, yet instead she pities him.

Penelope wakes to find her husband fully dressed, with his back to a warm fire, blazing in the hearth. Servants had been in while she slept, as the shutters are opened, allowing a shaft of winter sun to light up the bedchamber.

He must have been waiting some time for her to wake, and when he sees her eyes open, he speaks like a lawyer in court, with no trace of affection. He takes a deep breath. 'I regret what happened last night, and offer you my sincere apology.'

It seems as if he expects some acknowledgement, but Penelope stares at him like the stranger he is to her. Countess Catherine tried so hard to teach her to be forgiving, yet her bitterness keeps her silent.

'I have a proposal for you, Penelope. I will allow you to return to court.' He manages a smile. 'Our marriage has been overshadowed by the visit of the queen's suitor, and plans for an Accession Day tilt.' He sounds scornful.

The fire crackles, and he turns to push an errant log back into place with an iron poker. Penelope cannot believe her reversal of fortune. She'd thought she might not return to court for many years. Her mind whirls as she imagines the fuss of the young duke's visit. The queen will spare no expense to be sure the Accession Day tilt impresses her guests.

He turns back to her. 'There are conditions. You must swear to never mention what occurred between us. You must promote my interests at court, securing me favour, and present yourself as a loyal and contented wife. Finally, you must provide me with a male heir. Do you agree to my terms?' The pleading look in his eyes convinces her.

'I do.'

5

ACCESSION DAY
NOVEMBER 1581

L eicester House is strangely silent and empty after the commotion of the wedding. Before returning to Wanstead with her half-brother, Penelope's mother and stepfather offer her a suite of rooms, and say she can stay for as long as she wishes. She bears no grudge against her mother, and understands the countess believes she'd acted in her best interests.

Robert Dudley is a different matter. She will never forget the calculating look in his eyes when he'd threatened her. Penelope suspects he's schemed with Sir Henry Hastings to marry her off for the money, without any thought for her. He might not have had her father poisoned, but she was certain he'd encouraged the queen to send him to Ireland, while he entertained her mother.

Dorothy and Wat returned to King's Manor with the countess, and their brother Robert stayed at Greys Court with their grandfather. His years at Trinity College have come to an end with his graduation, but he must bide his time until he reaches his majority, and has yet to decide what to do. He'd told Penelope he plans to visit their uncle, George Devereux, at Lamphey Palace in Wales, where he will learn to joust and fight with a sword.

Penelope sends for Anne Broughton to help her with setting up a new household, and prepare for her return to court. She has no idea how to find servants she can trust, or where to find a good seamstress in London. Anne will have questions that might be difficult to answer. Penelope cannot lie to her closest friend, but she will only tell part of the truth.

As expected, Anne gives her a questioning look when she arrives. 'I'm surprised to see you here. Should you not be with your husband?'

'He has business to attend to in Essex. There is so much happening at court he's agreed I can stay here.' Penelope holds her breath as she watches Anne's face. Her answer is the truth, yet too well rehearsed. There is no need to lie, but this is her first test.

'It seems a strange way to begin a marriage.' Anne seems to have guessed something is wrong. Her voice softens and she studies Penelope with a frown of concern. 'I've known you since you were a child, Penelope. I can tell when you're keeping something from me. What's wrong? What has happened?'

She fights back the desperate need to tell her friend everything. One day she will – but, for now, she must keep her word. 'He sees I'm more use to him at court than hidden away in Essex.' Penelope manages a smile. 'There'll be plenty of time for me to give him an heir. In the new year, I'll move to my husband's manor at Leighs Priory. It's close to my mother at Wanstead, and not far from Rochford Hall, the home of another Lady Rich – my widowed mother-in-law.'

Anne seems to understand, although Penelope knows more questions will come soon enough. In normal times, her return to court so soon would have kept the gossipers busy for a month, but these are not normal times. The queen's young suitor, François, Duke of Anjou, is already at Richmond Palace.

'I've never had money of my own, and there is so much to do.' Penelope looks down at her plain dress. 'I'll need new gowns, as well as servants, and I'll be grateful for your help.'

'I'm happy to do what I can, and I've brought someone I'd like you to meet.' Anne smiles. 'How would you like a French lady-in-waiting?'

'This is all so new to me, I had not thought of having any ladies-in-waiting and have no idea how to find them, but I'll be glad of company when I move to Essex.'

Anne leaves the room and returns with an attractive dark-haired woman of about Penelope's age. 'I would like you to meet Mademoiselle Jeanne de Saint-Martin. Jeanne is a Huguenot, and has come to seek sanctuary in England. My husband is doing some legal work for her family. She shares many of your interests, including playing the lute and singing.'

Jeanne curtseys. 'I am pleased to meet you, my lady.' She speaks good English with a French accent.

Penelope senses an immediate connection as their eyes meet, and can see why Anne suggested her. Jeanne has a natural grace and, though simply dressed, her necklace of fine pearls shows she is no ordinary servant. Penelope answers in her perfect French. 'I'm sorry your family were forced from your country. You are welcome to join my household, if you wish.'

'It will be an honour, my lady.' Jeanne answers in French. 'My family were persecuted in France. We lived in fear of our lives, and had to abandon our house and lands. I hope to return one day, but Madame Anne has shown me kindness, and I am resolved to make the most of my time here in England.'

'You play the lute?'

Jeanne nods. 'Since I was a little girl, my lady, and I know many old French songs.'

Penelope smiles. 'Then we shall rehearse together, and perhaps you will have the chance to perform for Her Majesty.' She turns to Anne. 'We must find servants – and seamstresses. We need new gowns, fit for a queen.'

Whitehall Palace bustles with activity, with people chattering in every corner. As well as the familiar faces, it seems most of the nobility of France have sailed to England with the queen's young suitor. The crowds mean Penelope draws little attention and few questions. Her brief time as a maid of honour prepared her well, as she knows how to blend in with the courtiers, and who will share all the latest news.

Lady Mary Hastings is pleased and surprised to see her. 'Lady Rich!' She smiles. 'I feared I would not see you for a good while, yet here you are, looking every inch a baroness in your new gown!'

Penelope returns her smile. 'My husband graciously allowed me to return for the Accession Day celebrations, but I need your advice, Lady Mary. I have no idea how best to be accepted by Her Majesty back at court, and can think of no one better to advise me.'

Lady Mary blushes at her compliment, and takes her arm. 'Let us find somewhere more private.'

The palace of Whitehall has been extended and rebuilt, but much of the older building remains. Penelope follows Lady Mary into a warren of dark-panelled narrow passageways used by servants. The musty smell makes her hold her breath, and ancient dusty cobwebs hang festooned from the ceiling.

They enter a small room used for storing linen, close the

door and sit on a comfortable window seat, overlooking the busy stables. Penelope rubs at the grimy leaded glass and peers out, watching the horses coming and going.

Lady Mary has a knowing look in her eye as she turns to Penelope. 'The queen has no intention of marrying the Duke of Anjou. She has as good as said so, yet encourages the duke while she awaits her moment.'

'I've long suspected as much, Lady Mary, and there are many who will be glad of it, not least your brother, Sir Henry.' She smiles. 'I recall he opposed the council's plan for the marriage from the start.'

'I worry he grows too outspoken in his old age, but if there is a Catholic uprising Her Majesty will have great need of him in the North.'

'Well, let us pray the queen's plan does not offer the Catholics the excuse they've been waiting for.' Penelope frowns at the thought of Jeanne having to flee her country. 'What is the Duke of Anjou like?'

'He's very young, and a poor match for our queen.' Lady Mary shakes her head. 'He looks more like a son, next to Her Majesty, than a suitor. It's true what they say about his pock-marked face, yet he is no worse than Philip Sidney.'

The mention of Philip Sidney makes Penelope's heart beat faster. He's been on her mind since her travesty of a wedding, and she's been watching out for him since she arrived at the palace. 'Is Philip Sidney here?' She tries to sound casual, but Lady Mary gives her a curious look.

'He is, but I should caution you that Philip Sidney has been quite dour since your marriage to Lord Rich. Enough to set tongues wagging.'

Penelope dismisses the suggestion with a wave of her hand. 'Philip Sidney is a hopeless romantic, yet you should know it's not my marriage that makes him dour. He's lost his inheritance, now my stepfather has an heir, and must make his own fortune.'

Lady Mary seems content with her explanation, and returns to her news. 'The young duke sits with the queen from the time he rises until supper. No one hears what passes between them, but the queen has yet to call a council to decide anything.' She lowers her voice, even though no one will overhear them. 'Three of the queen's ships are being fitted out in great secrecy to take the Duke of Anjou and his retinue back to Flanders.'

'After the Accession Day joust?'

She nods. 'I suspect the Frenchmen know her plan, but carry on as if they believe this country will soon be theirs. Her Majesty is spending a fortune for the celebration of her Accession Day, and it's said the duke is to be the guest of honour at the joust.'

'I want to attend, but how should I make my return known to the queen?'

Lady Mary thinks for a moment. 'Your French is excellent, and Her Majesty will be glad to offer the French delegation some new entertainment.' She smiles. 'I will put a word in the right ear for you.'

The banqueters are raucous from too much rich red wine, yet grow curious as two velvet-covered stools are placed in the central open area of the great hall. Penelope hears people muttering as she enters with Jeanne, both wearing their new silk brocade gowns, with fashionable wide ruffs open at the front and pinned to their bodices.

After much discussion, they'd agreed their gowns should be different, but perfectly complement each other, like their singing. They both carry their lutes, yet need no music as they've spent long hours rehearsing their French songs until they know them by heart.

They approach the queen – who sits flanked by the French ambassador, Monsieur de Marchaumont, and a young noble Penelope guesses must be the Duke of Anjou – and bow in graceful curtseys.

'Your Majesty, I present Mademoiselle Jeanne de Saint-Martin, for your entertainment.'

The queen studies them both for a moment. 'We have missed you at court, Lady Rich, and welcome your return.' She raises an eyebrow. 'You must thank Lord Rich for sparing you so soon.' The note of irony in her voice causes a ripple of laughter, but she turns to Jeanne. 'You are most welcome, Mademoiselle.'

The young Duke of Anjou speaks in French. 'An English rose.' He raises his silver cup of wine to Jeanne, and looks a little drunk. 'And a flower of France.'

They both bow to him, and Penelope recognises the look of defeat in his eyes. Lady Mary was right: the Duke of Anjou is a poor match for the queen. There is little doubt he knows the truth, yet must play along with the queen's dangerous game of courtly love.

They sit on their velvet stools, and the chattering falls silent as they begin to sing, their voices in perfect harmony, with the soft accompaniment of their lutes. Jeanne chose her songs well, as the French stand and applaud, calling for more when they finish.

Penelope scans the English guests in vain. The man she seeks is absent, but on her mind as she begins their final song, reputedly the work of the queen's father.

Helas madame, celle que j'ayme tant
Souffrez que soye vostre humble servant
Vostre humble servant je seray a toujours

Et tant que je viv'ray aultr' n'aymeray que vous.

She keeps her eyes on the queen as she sings, and sees her nod of approval. Her return to court is a success, and the memory of her wedding night begins to fade. She can never forgive her husband, but remembers Anne's advice. *You are not the first to find yourself in an arranged marriage, and will not be the last.*

The bells ring out across London to rejoice in twenty-three years of Her Majesty's reign, and colourful silk banners stream in the chilly breeze. Penelope is glad of her thick fur cape and turns to Lady Mary, seated at her side. The temporary white-painted wooden stands, built specially for the tournament, provide them with the best view, and are close to the tiltyard.

'I've never seen Westminster so crowded.'

Lady Mary agrees. 'Or such an extravagant celebration of the queen's Accession Day. I heard the crowd was so great at the pageant that many people suffered injuries, and a woman died in the crush.' She points. 'There's Philip Sidney, on the white charger.'

Penelope smiles. 'It would be difficult to miss him, dressed in armour of bright blue and gold.' She'd watched Philip since he first rode out, willing him to approach her, but until now he appeared more interested in sizing up his competitors. He doesn't wear his helmet, and his long brown hair is cut short, making him look more like a soldier than a courtier.

He rides up to the stand, and calls out to her. 'Your favour, Lady Rich!'

She doesn't understand, but Lady Mary explains. 'It's the custom to offer him a token. A glove, perhaps?'

Penelope pulls off one of her white gloves, and passes it to him. Their eyes meet, and he touches her hand for the briefest moment as he reaches out to take her glove. In that moment she senses his sadness. Too late, she knows the risks he would have taken for her, if only she'd had the courage to ask him.

'I wish you good luck in the joust today, sir.' Her affectionate tone causes heads to turn, but she cares little for the gossipers now.

Philip Sidney gives her a wry smile as he tucks her glove into his saddle. 'They've come for entertainment, my lady, and that's what they shall have. It's all play-acting – but isn't everything at court?' He gives her one last look of longing, and then urges his charger forwards to the row of canvas tents in the competitors' area, without waiting for her reply.

A sharp blast of trumpets announces the arrival of the queen, escorted by Monsieur de Marchaumont, with the Duke of Anjou. A rousing cheer rings out as they take their place under the purple velvet canopy of state. Swathed in white furs against the cold, the queen looks even older at the side of the young duke.

The mounted competitors ride past on their gaudily caparisoned horses, and salute the queen by raising and lowering their lances. Penelope watches as Philip Sidney takes his turn, and sees the queen's smile as she raises a hand to him in acknowledgement.

With another fanfare of trumpets, the Master of the Rolls announces the first to ride. 'For the honour of the queen's Majesty, whom God of his great mercy long continue to reign over this sinful realm of England. Amen.'

Henry Grey and Henry Windsor take their places at either end of the tiltyard. Penelope knows of them both, but has never spoken to them. Henry Grey's polished silver armour glints in the winter sunlight as he spurs his horse into a charge and races forwards.

The sharp crack makes the crowd gasp as his lance smashes into Henry Windsor's shoulder, twisting him backwards in the saddle. Penelope flinches at the sound of the impact as Henry Windsor drops his lance in surrender, and the crowd rise to their feet, cheering and applauding.

Next comes Philip Sidney against Sir Henry Lee. She says a silent prayer as they lower their visors and charge forwards in a thunder of hooves, bringing down their lances in a juddering clash as they meet. The crowd roars in approval as the tip of Sir Henry Lee's lance breaks in a glancing blow to Philip's shield.

They are both handed new lances and turn for a second run. This time Philip Sidney strikes Sir Henry Lee square in the breastplate, his lance shattering into splinters which fly high into the air, unseating Sir Henry, who crashes to the ground and lies still. For a moment, Penelope thinks he is mortally wounded, but then he lifts a gauntleted hand in salute.

Philip Sidney lifts his visor and rides back to the stands to return her glove. 'I trust I proved worthy of you, Lady Rich.' He smiles, yet his eyes reveal his sadness. On his shield the word *Speravi* – I hoped – is crossed through, a sign his hopes are at an end.

Penelope watches him ride off, and fights back tears at her overwhelming sense of loss. Philip Sidney is the man she should have spent her life with. He is everything she could wish for, and could not be more different from the man she married. A nightmare vision of her wedding night returns. The thought of Robert Rich makes her feel sick, and it occurs to her she might already carry his child.

She is about to pull on her glove, but feels the small fold of paper inside. She looks around. Everyone is watching the next two riders preparing to joust. As discreetly as she can, she unfolds the note in her hand, to read his words.

My love, cease, in these effects, to prove
Now be still; yet still believe me.

Thy grief more than death would grieve me.
If that any thought in me
Can last comfort but of thee,
Let me, fed with hellish anguish,
Joyless, hopeless, endless languish.

6

LEIGHS PRIORY, ESSEX

FEBRUARY 1582

P enelope shivers as she sits alone on the window seat, watching drifting snowflakes through the ancient glass of the leaded window. The queen has sailed with her procession of gilded barges for Northfleet in Kent, and White-hall Palace is left to the care of an army of cleaners and workmen.

The overlong celebrations of Christmas and New Year were overshadowed by the queen's decision to send the Duke of Anjou and his entourage back home. Penelope heard he refused to leave without her agreement to their marriage, and wept like a child when she rejected him.

The queen's gift of ten thousand pounds should have sweetened the bitterness of his departure. Robert Dudley, fully back in royal favour, has the task of escorting the Duke of Anjou, and the queen agreed to accompany them to Rochester, despite the freezing winter snows.

Penelope has chosen this moment as the perfect time for her daring plan. After long hours of dreaming, the time has come to act. The linen storeroom, which Lady Mary showed her, has the advantage of discreet access down the servants' passageway, and a clear view of the stables below.

Her heartbeat increases with the thrill of anticipation. She will have her revenge on her cruel husband. Not by having him thrown down the stairs, or poisoned like her father. She would always be suspected, even if there is no proof, and tainted, like her stepfather. She will roll the dice in her high-stakes game, and live with the consequences.

If she wins, her reward will be more than her new wealth can ever buy, a prize beyond value. If she loses, her reputation will be ruined, and it will mean the end of her life at court. They would call her a sinner, yet Robert Rich had violated her, as if it were his right to do so. His treatment of her deserves to be avenged.

A lone rider, wearing a dark hooded cape against the weather, stops and dismounts at the stables below. He turns and stares up at her small window. She raises a white-gloved hand, and places it against the cold glass, a secret sign. She sees the rider's brief nod of acknowledgement as he leads his fine horse into the stables. She watches him emerge soon after, brushing snowflakes from his cape. Her pulse races as she waits.

There are risks, but she must travel to Essex, so will not be joining the royal progress, and so cannot be missed. The fifty-mile journey to Leighs Priory will be a two-day ride, likely to be delayed by the falling snow. Her husband can have no way of knowing when she leaves London, or when she can be expected to arrive.

The door opens and the caped rider enters, a serious look on his face. 'I don't believe I was seen.' He glances around the room and spots a heavy wooden chest, which he drags to block the door. 'A precaution.' He smiles, and pulls back his hood.

Philip Sidney looks different with the stubble beard he's grown as a disguise. It suits him, and conceals the scars on his face, although he's never seemed troubled by them. He could pass for one of the many workmen, and if challenged has reason to be in the palace.

Penelope takes his hand in hers and looks into his eyes. 'Thank you, for taking the risk.' She kisses him on the cheek, and feels a thrill of desire as he puts his arms around her and kisses her on the lips.

He throws off his cloak. Under it he wears a black velvet doublet and hose, with a fashionably wide lace ruff, open at the front. Penelope smiles as she pulls off her white gloves and begins to unfasten his silver buttons. Neither of them speaks as they undress each other. There is no need for words. They know each other's thoughts.

She runs her hands over his lithe body, fixing the memory in her mind. She will relive this moment many times in her dreams. Toned and muscular from his years of riding with a heavy lance, he bears the scars of a life in the saddle. She kisses him again, more slowly this time, savouring the moment.

No longer feeling the cold, Penelope feels no shame in her own nakedness. He traces her soft curves, exploring her with gentle fingers, kissing her with more passion each time. He pulls a pile of folded linen from the wooden shelves and makes a soft bed in moments.

She'd never seen why such fuss was made of kissing. The maids of honour tried to explain, yet now she understands the power of such intimacy, as their bodies merge into one. He knows her better than she knows herself, taking his time, until her body arches and she calls out, without a thought of who might overhear.

Nothing could have prepared her for the intensity of this moment, and she falls back on the soft linen, her heart pounding. She smiles to herself as she recalls Anne Broughton's words. *I promise, the act will surprise you.*

He lies at her side in silence, as if he is also fixing this moment in his mind. A single tear runs down his cheek, and she kisses it away. 'I've been a fool.' He turns to study her face, sadness in his brown eyes. 'I tried to be clever, and squandered my opportunity.'

'Don't blame yourself.' She silences him with a kiss. 'Others decided, long before we ever had a chance.' She frowns. 'I will never forgive Robert Dudley.'

'He enjoys having such power over us all.' Philip curses. 'He takes advantage of your mother, to spite the queen.'

Penelope shakes her head. 'I've seen them together often enough. He loves her.'

'He knows to play his part well. In truth, he's made a fool of everyone, even the queen – and even me.'

She pulls him closer, longing for his warmth. 'Forget about him. We have little enough time, and I have something important to tell you.'

He looks into her eyes. 'What is this important news?'

'I love you.' She kisses him again, more slowly. 'I am in love with you, Philip Sidney.'

He smiles, a twinkle in his eye. 'And I have a poorly kept secret, known only to the gossips of court. I am in love with you, Penelope Rich.'

'I have dreamed of hearing you say those words.'

They lie together in silence, enjoying the moment, sharing each other's warmth, but then begin to dress, knowing their brief time is coming to an end. He reaches for his discarded doublet, and she watches as he pulls something from his pocket and hands it to her.

'A late nineteenth birthday present.'

'I thought you'd forgotten me.' She turns the pendant in her hand, a golden heart on a fine gold chain. 'My mother and my sister Dorothy were both at Leicester House for my birthday in January. They asked me what I wished for, but I couldn't tell them I wished for you.'

'I was tempted to visit on your birthday, but knew we would not have had one moment alone together.'

'You are right.' She turns so he can fasten the locket at the back of her neck. 'I shall wear this in memory of this day.' She kisses him. 'Thank you.'

'You must take care on the road. The snow is settling, but I expect you'll be in no hurry to see Lord Rich.' A trace of bitterness sounds in his voice.

The mention of her husband brings her back to reality. She puts on her white gloves with unnecessary care, fighting the threat of tears. 'You are supposed to escort the Duke of Anjou.' She pulls him close and kisses him. 'Dover is a long ride from London, and I'll bet you will ride hard to catch up.'

'I've had new orders.' He pulls on his hooded riding cape, and frowns. 'Six houses in Dover are visited with the plague. The progress heads for Canterbury, and I must hurry to embark on the fleet, which waits at Sandwich.'

He holds her close in one last embrace and then is gone before she can reply. Penelope weeps as she watches for him at the window seat. Snow settles on the roof of the stables, hiding his footsteps and obscuring her view. She feels as if she's dreamed the whole thing.

Her hand goes to the gold heart at her throat, proof a miracle has really happened. She reaches behind her neck to unfasten the clasp. Opening the finely crafted locket, she reads the three words inscribed inside. *Omnia Vincit Amour.* Love conquers all. She will never forget this day, for as long as she lives.

Robert Rich seems a changed man as he shows her around Leighs Priory. 'I've heard good things from court.'

She manages a smile. 'Her Majesty asked me to thank you for your kindness in allowing me to return so soon.'

He bristles with pride. 'I heard she mentioned me in front of the Duke of Anjou.'

'In front of the entire French delegation.' Her husband is hopefully unaware that the wife of his fellow lawyer, Richard Broughton, is her best friend. Anne Broughton has agreed to make sure her husband passes on only favourable accounts of her conduct at court.

Penelope's mind drifts, as it does so often, to thoughts of Philip Sidney. She's heard nothing from him since that unforgettable day, but learned that the English escort accompanying the Duke of Anjou sailed in a hired ship, the *Barkway*, and the feared winter storms passed south of the fleet.

Her husband turns to her. 'You know why I've asked you to come here?' His voice lacks any trace of affection.

'You wish for an heir, to inherit your fortune?'

'I've heard Greenwich Palace is not altogether sound of the plague, so you are to stay here at Leighs.' He gives her a cautionary scowl, his old manner showing through the thin veneer. 'You agreed to give me an heir and, with the grace of God, I will pass to our son even greater wealth than I inherited.' He looks pleased with himself. 'The Earl of Leicester has invited me to invest in a venture from which I shall make a considerable profit.'

Penelope bites her lip. Robert Dudley still pulls the strings, using all of them as his puppets. She recalls Philip's bitter words. *He takes advantage of your mother, to spite the queen.*

Penelope spends most of the day exploring the many rooms of her new home with Jeanne, marvelling at the tapestries and portraits, yet they discover evidence of extravagance which seems at odds with her husband's Puritan values.

Jeanne studies an ornate silver salt in the shape of a warship in full sail, surrounded by leaping dolphins. 'Your husband no doubt disapproves, but perhaps sees such craftmanship as an investment.'

'You are right. He values everything in business terms – including me.'

Jeanne stares at her in surprise. 'You are mistaken, my lady. I have seen how he looks at you.'

'Like a man might look at a brood mare, to see if it is ready for a foal?'

Jeanne blushes. 'I meant nothing by it, my lady.'

'I'm sorry, Jeanne, but you know this marriage was not of my choosing. Lord Rich wishes for an heir, and might mellow a little, once he has a son.' She smiles. 'If he does not, I will raise the child to love music and dancing!'

Now, as she sits on her canopied bed, waiting for her husband, the prospect of a child with him is less inviting. She kneels in her nightdress at the side of the bed, and prays for guidance, as Countess Catherine taught her at King's Manor.

The door opens, and she hears a grunt of approval from her husband as he sees her in prayer. He doesn't speak but kneels opposite her, his hands clasped together, and joins her in prayer.

Dressed in a white linen nightshirt, he closes his eyes as he prays. She sees him differently now. He wears his faith like Philip Sidney wears a suit of armour, flamboyant protection, yet underneath he is vulnerable, a boy in a man's body.

Penelope climbs into her bed and lies on her back, dreading what is about to happen. She's learned the futility of resisting. She also learned, the previous month that she does not carry his child. Keeping her word to provide her husband with an heir will be no simple task.

The bed creaks as he lies beside her. She blows out the candle at her side, plunging the room into darkness. She has no wish to see what is about to happen. It will be over soon enough, a small price to pay for the miracle of a new life, growing inside her.

He lies in silence for a moment, as if rehearsing his words, before he speaks. 'I know about Philip Sidney.' His voice sounds flat and ominous in the darkness.

She freezes, her mind racing with questions. Was he having her watched at Whitehall Palace? Have they been seen? How much does he know? What will he do?

He seems unsurprised by her silence. 'I know your father wished you to marry him, and hope I am not too great a disappointment.'

She sees her chance. 'You do yourself a disservice, Robert.' She calls him by his name for the first time. 'You have made me a baroness, and Leighs Priory is as grand as any home I could wish for.'

He turns to face her in the darkness. 'I thank the Lord for his providence.'

Penelope takes a deep breath. 'I've not forgotten our agreement.' She wishes it over. 'I will not resist.'

He rolls on top of her, and surprises her by kissing her on the lips. Instead of the revulsion she expected, she feels nothing. She closes her eyes, and takes her mind away from her creaking bed to the linen store, and the bliss of Philip Sidney's loving embrace.

The letter from Dorothy brings a smile to Penelope's face, and she reads it out to Jeanne. 'My sister has taken my place as a maid of honour, and she writes from court that Lady Mary Hastings looks after her, as she did me.'

'It will be good to have your sister so close to the queen, my lady.'

'You are right, but my sister is eighteen next month. I expect the countess will waste no time in marrying her off.' She looks back at the letter. 'Dorothy says my brother Robert was sent to York. I don't imagine he will enjoy the regime of King's Manor.'

'Could your brother not have a place at court?'

'Robert might be an earl, but he's only fifteen, and must wait until he reaches his majority. I will send him money to travel to our uncle at Lamphey Palace.'

Jeanne gives her a coy look. 'Are you going to tell them your news, my lady?'

'I should tell my husband first. He will wish a service to ask God for his blessing.'

'It's been four months. Your secret will be obvious soon enough.'

Penelope places her hand on her middle. 'I felt the child quickening this morning. I will ask my sister to stay with us here at Leighs when the child is due, and we must visit my mother before I take to my chamber. She will know a midwife of good character.'

'Would your mother not wish to be here during your lying in?'

'My mother lacks the patience. She couldn't wait to hand the Noble Imp over to his wet nurse.'

Penelope fights off a wave of nausea as she lies in her darkened bedchamber. She turns to Jeanne, sitting patiently at her bedside. 'I heard morning sickness means the child will be a girl.'

Jeanne raises an eyebrow. 'You cannot know until the child is born, my lady.'

'I sense it. It's hard to explain, but I *know*.'

The dull ache in her back has worsened through the night, and she grimaces as a wave of pain rolls through her body. 'The baby is on the way.'

The child inside her kicks, a strange sensation, yet it makes her smile. She's prayed this is a love child, conceived before her husband's grunting efforts. She toyed with the idea of composing a cryptic poem for Philip Sidney, but the risk is too great. Her husband could ensure the child inherits nothing, and Philip Sidney would be thrown in the Tower.

She tries not to think of the stories she's heard about the pain and danger of childbirth, yet they keep returning to haunt her. Women bled to death in childbirth, or burned with a fever. Another wave of pain racked through her.

'Where is the midwife?' The sense of panic makes her raise her voice.

'She has been sent for, my lady.' Jeanne's tone sounds concerned. 'I shall have to leave you, to see where she is.'

Penelope clenches her teeth, biting her tongue, yet the deeper pain worsens. 'Be quick.' She takes a deep gasp of breath, holding the air in her lungs for a moment, and letting it out slowly.

The door opens and the midwife enters, followed by Dorothy and Jeanne, with a pile of fresh linen. The midwife wears a coif over her greying hair and an apron over her gown. She dampens a small cloth in cold water and Penelope feels the calming coolness as she lays the cloth across her forehead.

'Not long now, my lady.' Her Essex accent is reassuring.

Penelope gasps as her waters break and the baby begins to emerge. She fights an overwhelming urge to scream and curse.

'Have faith, Penelope.' Her sister's voice calms her as she grips her hand tighter. 'The good Lord watches over us.'

'Now *push!*' The midwife's voice has a new note of urgency.

'How much longer?' She grits her teeth as the hurting begins again.

'All in good time, my lady. You need to push now. Push as *hard* as you can.'

Penelope pushes and cries with pain, worse than she had ever imagined. She grips her sister's hand and sees the look of concern on Dorothy's face. She cries out, as another wave courses through her body. 'Please, Lord, let this be over soon.'

Dorothy smiles at the sight of Penelope holding her new baby. 'Have you thought of a name for her yet?'

'I promised our mother if I had a girl, she would be named after her.'

'Lettice?' Dorothy looks unsure. 'I always thought it a strange name.'

'Lettice was originally French, from the Latin, *Laetitia*, which means joy.' She smiles at her bright-eyed baby and loosens her swaddling to allow a tiny hand to escape. She laughs as miniature fingers reach for the gold pendant, glinting on its chain at her throat. 'I certainly feel joy, now my ordeal is over.'

A flicker of concern shows in her sister's eyes. 'How are you now, Penelope?'

'Tired, and every bone of my body aches, but thank God I have no fever – and my appetite has returned.'

Dorothy looks relieved. 'I pray for you every day, and for the baby.'

Penelope smiles at her sister. 'I know you well, Dorothy, and can see there's something you have to tell me. Is there news from court I won't be pleased to hear?'

Dorothy shakes her head. 'Not from court. I must tell you Countess Catherine has planned my marriage.'

'I knew she would.' Penelope frowns. 'She means well, and believes she does her best for us, but who does she plan to marry you to?'

Dorothy hesitated. 'Philip Sidney.'

Penelope stares at her in amazement. 'You cannot marry Philip Sidney.'

'Our stepfather has the queen's permission, but I will not marry him. I know how he feels about you.'

'*What* do you know?' A growing panic grips her.

'Nothing of any consequence, but you've been a maid of honour.' Dorothy gives her a knowing look. 'They love to gossip about men like Philip Sidney.'

'What are they saying?'

'That he's been bereft since your marriage, because he's in love with you.'

7

AN ILLEGAL MARRIAGE

APRIL 1583

L eighs Priory begins to feel like home. Penelope had doubted that day would ever come, yet little Lettice, now known by everyone as *Lucy*, changes everything. A happy child, she makes everyone smile, and even her dour father shows no resentment at having to wait for a son.

He comes to see them in the nursery. 'I will be away for a week or so, on diplomatic business.' He makes it sound important, and looks pleased with himself.

'I was not aware you were a diplomat.' Penelope cannot resist taunting her husband, and believes he will be poorly suited to the role.

He gives her a condescending look. 'The Earl of Leicester asked me to meet the Count of Laski, and escort him to his chambers in Greenwich Palace, where he is to have an audience with Her Majesty.'

'I've heard talk at court of Count Laski. They say he's an alchemist – and a Catholic. I'm surprised my stepfather supports him.' She frowns. If her husband is tainted by this, she will be too. 'Take care.'

'There is more to this than you need to be troubled with.'

He raises his voice. 'The count is an ambassador of the King of Poland. I am to win his confidence and learn the true reason for his visit. I am honoured to assist your stepfather.' He sounds defensive, yet leaves Penelope in no doubt he underestimates her.

He knows she is better educated, with a better knowledge of the politics of court than he will ever have, yet he will always think himself superior. She will encourage him to underestimate her, and then turn it to her advantage.

'With your permission, I will visit my mother in Wanstead. She has written asking to see our daughter.'

He scowls. 'You must also take our daughter to visit my mother at Rochford Hall.' He makes it sound like an order, yet Penelope can tell he is proud of Lucy.

'Will you not wish to be with us when we see your mother?' Penelope feels unexpected nervousness at meeting the first Lady Rich on her own.

'You will offer her my best wishes. I will return in a week, possibly two.'

She has become used to his long absences, sitting as Justice of the Peace at the quarter sessions in Chelmsford, and is grateful for them. He never visits her bedchamber, and they rarely dine together. Penelope is glad to know her stepfather will be away at Greenwich, although she wonders what he is up to with Count Laski, and why he's involved her husband.

She needs to find some way to stop Robert Dudley's plan to marry her sister to Philip Sidney, while there is still time. Even if she succeeds, little will change, but the injustice of it keeps her awake at night. She refuses to believe her mother can do nothing to help, if only she can be persuaded.

They set out in welcome spring sunshine on the forty-mile journey to Wanstead. Her mother's aging carriage leads the way, loaded with servants and baggage, while Penelope follows in a new one, with better springs, owned by her husband. A post-horse can make the journey in a day, but the slower carriages need to stop overnight at Ingatestone.

Jeanne rides with Penelope, with little Lucy cradled in the arms of her wet nurse, Martha, a cheerful Essex woman. With six children of her own, Martha had also become Penelope's tutor, sharing her years of experience.

'I would not be able to cope without you, Martha.' She smiles. 'Little Lucy is such a handful, yet you calm her in no time.'

'You'll learn soon enough, my lady.' Martha gives her a knowing look. 'As our good Lord says, train up a child in the way he should go, and he will not depart from it.'

'And does the same apply to little girls?' Penelope doubts it applied to her, or her daughter. People were always telling her what she must do, and must not do. For once she'd defied them, and has no regrets. She smiles to herself at the thought.

A long gravelled drive, flanked by an avenue of elm trees, leads to her mother's manor house. Surrounded by a sprawling deer park and the ancient woodlands of Epping Forest, Wanstead House was once owned by monks, and has been turned into a palatial home by successive owners.

Penelope's mother wears a richly embroidered gown with a ruff of wired gossamer framing her red hair and white-powdered face, in an uncanny echo of the queen. She welcomes them, fussing over her granddaughter.

'She is the image of you when you were little, Penelope. I've had the nursery prepared for her, and set aside a suite of rooms for you and your ladies.'

Penelope smiles at her half-brother, little Robert, the Noble Imp, now two years old, dressed like a miniature version of his father in a silver doublet and hose. He stares at Penelope, as if making a judgement, then hides behind his mother.

Penelope walks in the garden with her mother. The well-tended pink and white roses are at their best, and their delicate scent drifts in the light summer air. Her mother has mellowed with age, and Penelope takes her arm. They've grown closer, and Penelope understands her better since becoming a mother herself.

Penelope chooses her moment, once they are far enough from the house to not be overheard. 'I'm troubled at how Philip Sidney is considered suitable for Dorothy, but was not good enough for me.' She makes no attempt to conceal her bitterness.

Her mother looks uncomfortable. 'I understand how you must feel, but these things are complicated—'

'My father wished me to marry Philip Sidney.' Penelope struggles to remain composed.

'Your father wished for many things, and was not to know how circumstances would change.' She takes Penelope's hand in hers. 'You know the decision was not mine, but for Countess Catherine to make. You've become one of the wealthiest women in England, with many fine houses.' She smiles. 'Even this house belonged to your husband, before he sold it to your stepfather.'

'My stepfather is the key to this. It's within his power to decide my sister's future – and I believe if anyone can persuade him to reconsider, it's you.'

'How will that help you, Penelope?' Her mother frowns. 'You're married, with a beautiful daughter, and should forget any thoughts you might once have had of Philip Sidney.'

Penelope fights the urge to confess everything. 'Would you have *both* your daughters condemned to loveless marriages?'

Her mother looks thoughtful. 'You need to know that Philip Sidney is betrothed to Sir Francis Walsingham's daughter, Frances.'

Penelope freezes. She knows Frances Walsingham, and suspects her of spying for her father. Only sixteen, she is always listening to the conversations of others, but keeps her own secrets well. If her mother spoke the truth, nothing could ever come of her love for Philip Sidney.

Her mother gives her a knowing look. 'I should also let you know a great secret. Philip Sidney was not the only one being considered for your sister's hand.'

'Then who?' Penelope's mind races with the possibilities. Robert Dudley is capable of anything, even marrying Dorothy to a man his own age, if he can see a way to profit from it.

'Do you promise not to say a word to anyone?'

'Not even Dorothy?'

Her mother frowns. 'Particularly not Dorothy.'

Penelope curses them all for their plotting. She must know, but cannot promise to keep such a life-changing prospect from her sister. She imagines the discussions about her own fate, with everyone ensuring she would be the last to know, until too late.

Her mother speaks in a hushed voice. 'Secret negotiations are taking place to see if Dorothy can be married to King James of Scotland, who has now come of age.'

'My sister could become Queen of Scotland?' Penelope stares at her mother in disbelief. 'Why did you allow my sister to believe her intended was Philip Sidney?'

'A story to throw the gossips off the scent. Philip Sidney is a plausible suitor, yet we know they would never marry.' She takes Penelope's hand. 'Forget him.'

Her mother is not to know that Penelope dreams of Philip

Sidney every night. A worrying thought occurs to her. 'King James is the only son of Mary, Queen of Scots. That could mean trouble for us all. You know how Her Majesty feels threatened by her cousin.'

Her mother gives her a knowing look. 'We must keep one eye on the future, Penelope. Our queen will not last forever.'

Penelope gasps. To talk of the death of the queen is treason, and now she is involved. Her mother doesn't seem to notice that she did not promise to keep the great secret from her sister. Dorothy needs to know what is planned behind her back, and Penelope resolves to be the one to tell her.

Penelope decides to visit her mother-in-law, the widowed Lady Rich, before leaving to meet Dorothy at Leicester House. They rise at dawn for the thirty-mile ride to Rochford Hall. The coachman says their journey can be managed in one day, God willing, unless rain turns the roads between Leighs and Rochford to mud.

There has been no word from her husband, but he'd wished his mother to be introduced to Lucy, and Penelope's curiosity overcomes her reluctance. Her mother told her Rochford Hall was once the home of her great-grandmother, Mary Boleyn, sister to the queen's ill-fated mother, Queen Anne Boleyn.

Their family connection intrigues Penelope. Her mother claims their ancestor was a mistress to both the King of England and the King of France. Like Penelope, Mary Boleyn was forced into a political marriage, to courtier William Carey, who saw no shame in profiting from his wife's affair with the king.

There is also a glimmer of hope in her great-grandmother's story. After her husband's death from the sweating sickness,

Mary remarried in secret, for love, to a soldier with few prospects, and who was socially beneath her. Penelope likes to believe she finally found contentment, although banished from court, living at Rochford Hall.

The widowed Lady Rich is a little older than her own mother, and dresses in the old style, with heavy brocade gowns, a starched ruff, and a long necklace of perfect pearls. Like Philip Sidney, Lady Rich once suffered from smallpox, yet Penelope sees beyond the cruel scars on her face and guesses her mother-in-law must have been quite fair in her youth.

Lady Rich laughs in delight as her granddaughter reaches for her pearls with a tiny hand. 'She looks like you, Penelope, yet has her father's ways, reaching for anything within his grasp.'

The hint of bitterness in her voice suggests some reason for her husband's reluctance to visit his mother. 'What was Robert like, as a child?'

Lady Rich shakes her head at the memory. 'He was sickly as a baby. The doctors despaired of what to do for him, and I feared he would not live.'

Penelope is surprised to find her mother-in-law speaking so frankly, and senses a useful ally. 'I'm sorry that you lost your husband and eldest son within such a short time. It must have been difficult for you.'

'They were taken before their time.' Lady Rich looks wistful. 'I doubt Robert told you we also lost his other elder brother, Sir Hugh.' She places her hand on Penelope's arm. 'Robert never speaks of him. Hugh was a Catholic, and a favourite of the late Queen Mary. He took part in her coronation, and helped persecute Protestants.'

Penelope understands. 'Robert speaks little of his family, or his past, yet you should know he was keen for me to visit you with Lucy. In fact, he insisted.'

Her mother-in-law smiles. 'You may call me Elizabeth, if

you wish. I confess I find it lonely here now, and my son rarely visits. I have a daughter, Frances, but she lives with her husband in London, and has not been to see me for some time.'

'It can be lonely at Leighs, Elizabeth. You must visit us when you can.'

Penelope recognises the conflicted look of hesitation in her mother-in-law's eyes, seeing that she would dearly like to visit her and little Lucy at Leighs Priory, yet suspects that whatever happened between her and her son makes it unlikely she will ever take up the offer.

'It's well known that King James of Scotland prefers the company of men.' Dorothy looks appalled at Penelope's news, when they finally meet at Leicester House. 'I would be shut away in some Scottish castle and never seen or heard of again!'

Penelope glances at the door. 'I don't trust the servants here, so keep your voice down. We must learn from what happened to me, Dorothy. I could have run away with Philip Sidney and married in secret. There would have been a great fuss, and I'm sure we'd both be banished, but these things have a way of settling down, given time.'

'The queen has forgiven our stepfather, but seems in no mood to forgive our mother, and that was five years ago.'

'Our mother chose to marry Robert Dudley, and always knew the consequences.'

'There is someone I met at court.' Dorothy's eyes flash with mischief, as they had when they were girls at Chartley, up to no good.

'Someone worth risking everything for?' Penelope raises an eyebrow. 'Who do you have in mind?'

Dorothy blushes. 'I am in love with Sir Thomas Perrot.' She speaks softly, as if worried they might be overheard.

'Sir Thomas Perrot is twice your age, and his father claims he is an illegitimate child of King Henry VIII.' Penelope frowns. 'True or not, he displeases the queen.'

'Thomas is only one year older than Philip Sidney, and is not responsible for his father's claims. He fought with bravery in Ireland and was knighted there. His father hopes to become the Lord President of Ireland.'

'How did you meet?'

Dorothy smiles. 'Thomas is a champion jouster. He's chivalrous, courageous – and asked for my favour at the tiltyard in Whitehall.'

Penelope's mind returns to happier times, when Philip Sidney made the same request of her. 'I remember him at the joust in honour of the Duke of Anjou. If you love him, you must marry without delay.'

'I have your blessing?'

'This was sent to me at Leighs Priory two weeks ago. Sir Thomas's style betrays his lack of education, but there is no mistaking his sincerity.' She hands the letter to her sister.

Dorothy reads aloud. '*I humbly beg that you commend my honest service, zeal, and love to my lady, your sister.*'

'Marry now, or regret it for the rest of your life.'

'Without the queen's permission?' Dorothy frowns with concern. 'Her Majesty will surely banish me. You know how she watches over her maids of honour.'

'If you delay, you could find yourself locked away in a Scottish castle.'

Penelope's husband returns grim-faced from a visit to London, and scowls at her. 'Your sister has brought disgrace on us all.'

She tries to look innocent but guesses the reason. 'I've not heard from my sister in weeks. What's happened?'

'Her Majesty is furious, and banished her from court for marrying without permission.' He frowns. 'The scandal is the talk of London.'

Penelope has no regrets about her interference in Dorothy's marriage, yet must keep up her pretence. 'Who has she married?'

He studies her as if suspecting she already knows. 'Thomas Perrot.' He shakes his head. 'They should both have known better. As a maid of honour, your sister had a duty to show loyalty to the queen.'

The letter is delivered by a servant under orders to ensure Penelope receives it in person, and she recognises her sister's handwriting even before she has broken the wax seal. The decision to tell Dorothy their mother's secret was one of the hardest of her life. She'd hoped to save her sister from a loveless marriage, yet holds her breath as she begins to read.

My dearest Penelope, you will no doubt have heard about my predicament. My marriage took place at the home of Sir Henry Coke, at Broxbourne. John Aylmer, Bishop of London, granted a licence, and a vicar known to him performed the service.

Sir Henry did not approve and ordered his servants to break down the chapel door. They shouted and made a great commotion, but we persevered, and were married before God.

As we feared, I have offended Her Majesty and been banished from court, and poor Thomas is imprisoned in the Fleet prison. He makes light of it and says he has been there before, but there is talk of the plague in London and I worry for his health.

I was told Lord Burghley tried to have our marriage annulled, on orders from Her Majesty the queen, but we had six witnesses to testify that our wedding was conducted properly, according to the law of England.

Sir Henry Coke is ordered to keep me here at Broxbourne until my husband is released. When that day comes, we plan to escape to his father's home at Carew Castle in West Wales, a short ride from our beloved brother Robert, who is with our uncle at his palace in Lamphey.

Remember us both in your prayers,

Your loving sister, Lady Dorothy Perrot.

Penelope smiles at her sister's signature. She shares her concerns about conditions in the Fleet prison, but from the stories she's heard, the Tower of London would have been far worse. Dorothy made her choice of her own free will, with full knowledge of the consequences, yet Penelope still resents their stepfather's scheming.

She recalls Philip Sidney's words. *He enjoys having such power over us all.* Her hand goes to the gold locket she always wears. As she has so often, she opens it, and reads the three words inscribed inside. *Omnia Vincit Amour.* Love conquers all.

8

THE NOBLE IMP
JANUARY 1584

Penelope wakes early on her twenty-first birthday, and lies alone in her velvet-canopied bed, watching the tentative glow of dawn light up her high-ceilinged bedchamber. She had told her servants to leave the leaded windows unshuttered, despite the frosty mornings, for her to see the winter sun rising in the east.

She finds herself taking stock of the unexpected twists and turns her life has taken. As a girl, she'd dreamed of having a manor house as grand as this, with a daughter she could be a better mother to than her own had been to her. She'd also dreamed of marrying Philip Sidney, and is troubled by the grief of her loss.

She has heard nothing from Philip since his marriage to sixteen-year-old Frances Walsingham. He'd become the Member of Parliament for Kent, serving on several committees, thanks to his new father-in-law's support. She can't imagine him enjoying the world of politics, but guesses he sees it as a stepping stone in his career.

Her husband divides his time between his legal duties in London and Chelmsford, visiting Leighs like a landlord checking on his tenants. He shows her no affection, and never raises the question of a son and heir. He seems fond of Lucy, but his present for her second birthday was a prayer book.

Penelope regularly visits her mother, and her half-brother, the Noble Imp, now three years old, when they are at Wanstead. Her mother never asks about her part in Dorothy's marriage to Sir Thomas Perrot, although she must have known, with it happening so soon after Penelope learned her secret.

One advantage of her wealth is that she can send money to help her family. Robert wrote from Lamphey Palace to thank her, and told her Philip Sidney visited to teach him how to ride in a joust. She also sent a purse of gold sovereigns to Wat, now fifteen. Still at King's Manor, he will soon be sent to university in Oxford, yet wishes to make his name as a soldier.

Dorothy has less need for her charity. Her husband, released from the Fleet prison, took her to live with his family at Carew Castle in West Wales. She seems content in her letters, and Penelope predicts her sister's next letter will tell her she is with child.

A knock at the door breaks through her thoughts, and Jeanne enters. 'I wish you happy birthday, my lady, and have a gift for you, delivered by a mysterious stranger.' Her eyes shine with amusement as she hands Penelope the present, wrapped in blue silk, tied with a ribbon.

Penelope sits up in bed, and pulls at the end of the ribbon. Inside is a small book, with a monogram of an interlinked A and S in gold on the front. Opening it at the first page, she smiles in surprise. '*Astrophel and Stella*, by Sir Philip Sidney.' She turns to Jeanne, waiting at her bedside. 'I didn't know he'd been knighted, or that he'd had his work published. He was always so modest about his poetry.'

Jeanne smiles. 'The gift arrived with instructions to keep it a secret from you until today, my lady. I had no idea who the sender was, and the messenger was gone before I could question him.'

Penelope scans a few verses, tears filling her eyes. She'd hoped to somehow see Philip one more time, when she next attended court. She turns the page, and begins to read.

On Cupid's bow how are my heart-strings bent,
That see my wreck, and yet embrace the same!
When most I glory, then I feel most shame,
I willing run, yet while I run repent,
My best wits still their own disgrace invent:
My very ink turns straight to Stella's name.

She is Philip Sidney's Stella, and this is a lament of his unrequited love, thinly disguised, yet there for all the world to see. Her mind races with the consequences, and she thanks God her husband is too uncultured to appreciate the coded sentiments. There are those who would take pleasure in explaining the poetry to him, but Philip Sidney makes his feelings allegorical, and easily denied.

~

Her mother's brief note fills Penelope with alarm. Her half-brother suffers with a sweating fever. Penelope recalls the stories she's heard of the dreaded sweating sickness. The doctors know no cure, and in a single day the fever can take the lives of young and old, rich and poor.

She shows the note to Jeanne. 'I worry I will bring my brother's fever back here to Lucy, but my duty is to support my mother, for as long as she needs me.'

Jeanne looks concerned. 'I can stay here, to look after your daughter, my lady.'

'The thought of leaving Lucy troubles me, but it's too great a risk to take her to Wanstead.'

'Your mother needs you, my lady, and I have Mistress Martha to help me keep little Lucy occupied.'

Penelope can't ignore the haunted look in her mother's eyes. 'I'm sorry to hear little Robert is unwell.'

'I fear it is serious.' Her mother looks close to tears. 'Our doctors are at a loss, so all we can do is pray for his recovery.'

'My little brother has been in my prayers, as have you.' Penelope takes her mother's hand in hers. Her gold-ringed fingers feel thin, and raised veins show through her once smooth skin. 'Have faith, Mother. You must remember how soon Wat recovered when he was the same age?'

A glint of hope flashes in her mother's tear-filled eyes. 'We feared the worst, yet his fever broke as if by a miracle.' She manages a smile.

They walk in the rose garden, the perfect July morning marred by the looming black cloud of their concern for little Robert. Her mother stops to pick a white rose, taking care to avoid the thorns. She presents the rose to Penelope.

'You might wonder why it took so long for God to grace us with a son, after nearly three years of marriage?'

'I was away at King's Manor, in York.' Penelope could have added that her mother should have thought to visit, or reply to her letters, but she thought better of it.

'I suffered several miscarriages.' Her mother's voice is cold, her blunt statement concealing the true horror of what must have happened.

Penelope stares at her. 'I had no idea.'

'We bought the silence of our doctors. Your stepfather

wished our misfortune to be kept secret.' Her mother shakes her head at the memory. 'I should have sent for you.'

'I am here now, and will stay for as long as you wish.' Penelope gives her mother's hand a gentle squeeze. 'We shall see this through together.'

She wakes in the middle of the night to a wail of anguish, and guesses the reason. Pulling a gown over her nightdress, she goes in search of her mother, feeling her way down the corridor as her eyes adjust to the dark.

Her mother stares at her with red-eyed despair. 'Your little brother is dead.'

'Dear God, no.' It seems impossible. Her mischievous brother, Robert, Lord of Denbigh, with his whole life ahead of him, is gone.

'His nurse woke me, so I could be with him at the end. He shivered, as if from the cold, yet his skin burned with the fever.'

Penelope feels a stab of panic. 'Do his doctors think it could be the sweating sickness?'

'They are not aware of any other cases.' Her mother's voice sounds hollow. 'I've sent for your stepfather. He is at Nonsuch Palace with the queen. He will be devastated. His last memory of his son was chastising him for defacing a valuable painting at Leicester House.'

The official invitation, delivered by royal messenger, is from her stepfather, and presents Penelope with a dilemma. She has not long returned from the misery of Wanstead Manor, yet this could be her chance to see Philip Sidney.

She shows Jeanne. 'Her Majesty is entertaining a French delegation, led by Ambassador Michel de Castelnau, at a hunt in Windsor, but I need to spend time with my daughter.'

Jeanne looks thoughtful. 'There is no need to leave Lucy behind, my lady. Windsor is a long way from here, but the weather is dry and the roads are good. We could all travel with you as company.'

'I will need mourning dress, out of respect for my late brother, and I must send a message to my husband.' She frowns. 'Do we know where he is?'

'We haven't heard from your husband since you left for Wanstead, my lady.'

They make the long journey to court at Windsor, stopping at coaching inns. Lucy proves a good traveller and has become used to the rumble of the carriage wheels. Penelope is glad to return to the intrigue of court and looks forward to ending her isolation in Essex.

Arriving at Windsor Castle before the queen, Penelope is welcomed by her stepfather on horseback. One consequence of her half-brother's death is her promise to forget her grudge against Robert Dudley. She raises a hand in greeting, and he rides up to her.

'I thank you for comforting your mother. The loss of our son serves to remind me of the family I have.' He looks defeated, his face lined by grief. 'God must be obeyed in all things, for all he does is for the best.'

'Yet in such times God's purpose is hard to fathom, and I am deeply sorry for your loss.' Penelope is unsure how to address him. 'I am grateful for your invitation.'

He nods in acknowledgement. 'I am overseeing the entertainment of the ambassador and his companions.' He glances towards the castle. 'They are resting after the ride from Richmond, and I expect they plan a late evening.'

.   .   .

Her stepfather is right; the crowded banqueting hall buzzes like a wasps' nest with anticipation. An usher calls all present to stand as the queen makes her grand entrance, followed by the French ambassador, a handsome man with a pointed beard. Like Penelope, the queen wears mourning dress. Her former suitor, the Duke of Anjou, has died after a long illness.

The ambassador sits at the queen's right hand, with Robert Dudley to her left. Penelope is surprised to be seated at his other side, a place of honour at the top table. She still isn't used to her position as a baroness, making her one of the senior ladies present.

The gilded chair at her side is drawn back, and Philip Sidney sits down next to her. Penelope's heart pounds as she sees he wears the black doublet and hose with silver buttons she'd last seen at their secret meeting. He's grown a neatly trimmed beard, and looks tanned.

She turns to him. 'I expected someone from the French delegation to be seated there, Sir Philip, for me to entertain for the evening.'

He gives her a disarming smile. 'I saw my chance, and make no apology.' His eyes go to her mourning dress. 'I offer you my condolences, Baroness Rich.'

'Thank you, Sir Philip. My mother may never recover from her loss, but now you will inherit what was due to you.'

He leans closer to her and keeps his voice low. 'I understand your stepfather has chosen your brother, the Earl of Essex, to be groomed for greatness.'

Penelope's reply is interrupted as the queen's musicians begin to sing muted French ballads, to the accompaniment of a lute and flageolet. Servants in royal livery bring wine in silver cups, silver platters of salted venison, and loin of veal covered with a German sauce, with gilt sugarplums and pomegranate seeds.

She sips her wine and glances at the queen, deep in conversation with her stepfather and the French ambassador. 'How is married life, Sir Philip?'

'I've been away a great deal. Her Majesty sent me as her special embassy to France, to convey her condolences to King Henri III on the death of his brother.'

'You had an audience with King Henri?'

He shakes his head. 'It proved a fool's errand, and a costly one. The king was away on a progress, so I was recalled, and instead have been tasked with acting as wet nurse to the embassy from France.'

Penelope looks across at the French delegation. 'They seem an unruly lot, who enjoy a cup of wine.'

Philip washes his fingers and dries them on a white linen cloth. 'And how is married life for you, Lady Rich?'

'No one in my household seems to know where my husband is.'

'Well, motherhood suits you.' He whispers in her ear. 'Our French guests commented on your beauty.'

Penelope feels her cheeks redden, and takes another drink of the rich wine. The queen laughs at a comment by the ambassador, reminding her they are near enough to be overheard. She leans closer, and her arm touches his, sending a frisson of longing through her.

'Our daughter has her father's ways and can be quite a handful.'

Philip's eyes widen, then he laughs. 'I am not the only one to talk in riddles. What words she speaks.'

She smiles. '*Persuades for thee, that her clear voice lifts thy fame to the skies, thou count Stella thine.*'

He raises his silver cup of wine. 'My muse.'

Sixty large bucks are trapped within the netted enclosure, known as the *toil*. The Frenchmen shoot at them with cross-bows as the stags run back and forth, snorting in panic, in front of the raised timber platform. A hit brings a rousing cheer, a miss an insult or a curse, to the great amusement of the queen.

A familiar voice speaks softly in her ear as she watches. 'We should only kill out of nobility and kindness.'

Philip Sidney seems oblivious to the risks he takes to be close to her. She longs to turn, but doesn't dare to. 'Will they continue until all the stags are dead?'

'The wounded will be taken by the hounds. The lucky ones will return to the forest, for this afternoon's hunt.'

'I believed this *was* the hunt.' She feels pity for the magnificent beasts, bred for such savage entertainment.

'If only that were so. There is a hill, overlooking the exit from the toil, for coursing with the queen's hounds.' He frowns. 'Sometimes it takes two or three hounds to bring down a large stag.'

'I hunted at Chartley, but only for the table, not for sport.' The Frenchmen cheer as another stag falls, mortally wounded. Against her better judgement she turns to him. 'I cannot bear to watch any longer. Will you escort me from here, Sir Philip?'

'Gladly, baroness.' He glances at the queen, surrounded by baying Frenchmen. 'I do not believe we will be missed.'

He leads her down the wooden steps and back towards the castle. 'There is a shortcut, through the woods.'

As soon as they are out of sight of the hunting party, he takes her in his arms and kisses her. 'Do you know what I've learned?'

She kisses him back. 'Tell me.'

'When you've been loved, you find comfort from memories, even when there is no hope.'

Penelope's husband clears his throat, like a man about to give a speech. 'Sufficient time has passed since the birth of our daughter.'

Penelope looks up from her book. He'd questioned her about her visit to the hunt at Windsor, and she reported every detail, except for the presence of Philip Sidney. For a moment, his statement confuses her, but then she understands.

'Time for me to provide you with an heir?'

'You recall our agreement.' He sounds like a lawyer again, with no trace of tenderness.

She could refuse, as their agreement was long ago, but his blunt proposal solves a problem nagging at the back of her mind. 'I do.'

She waits in her bed, remembering the long evening of the banquet at Windsor. The feasting had continued until late, with too many courses. She'd been careful not to drink too much wine, and spoke briefly with the queen, exchanging condolences, before making her excuses.

Her bedchamber was in the older part of the castle, and Philip Sidney offered to escort her down the dark passageways. They both knew the great risk they took of being seen together, unchaperoned and late at night. He checked the coast was clear before following her in, closing the heavy door behind him, and sliding the iron bolt across, an unmistakable sign of his intentions.

She watches her husband finish his prayers, dreading what is about to happen. He looks up at her. 'I prayed for a fine, healthy son, who will be named after me, and raised as a good Puritan.' He speaks to her as if she is a child, with no opinion of her own.

'As you wish.' If she has a son, he will be named Robert, for her brother. Her husband will never know.

He blows out the candle before climbing into bed next to her. The cold light of a full moon glimmers through unshuttered windows, casting eerie shadows in the corners of the room. Penelope glimpses his pale body as he pulls off his nightshirt, like a fat side of beef, and turns her face away.

He fumbles with the bow at the front of her nightdress and she struggles to hide her revulsion as he kisses her, but knows better than to resist. The bed creaks in protest as he straddles her, pinning her to the soft mattress. She fails to block his gasps and grunts, but her mind returns to Windsor Castle, where she had been loved.

Once he is gone, Penelope stands by the leaded-glass windows of her silent bedchamber, staring at the full moon. She holds her precious book, which is still revealing its secrets to her, despite having been read so many times. It takes a moment to find the page she has in mind, and she begins to read.

> *With how sad steps, O moon, thou climb'st the skies!*
> *How silently, and with how wan a face!*
> *What, may it be that even in heavenly place,*
> *That busy archer his sharp arrows tries,*
> *Sure, if that long with love acquainted eyes*
> *Can judge of love, thou feel'st a lover's case,*
> *I read it in thy looks; thy languished grace,*
> *To me, that feel the like, thy state descries.*

She wipes a tear from her eye. Is he somewhere, looking up at the same full moon and thinking of her? Does he still love her, or has he found love with Frances, now Lady Sidney? She looks down at her book.

Then, even of fellowship, O moon, tell me,
Is constant love deemed there but want of wit?
Are beauties there as proud as here they be?
Do they above love to be loved, and yet,
Those lover's scorn whom that love doth possess
Do they call virtue their ungratefulness?

9

THE ROYAL MUSTER

APRIL 1585

Jeanne hands Penelope a letter. 'The messenger who delivered this was exhausted, my lady. He said he'd ridden three hundred miles from the far west of Wales. I sent him to the kitchens for a hot meal, and asked him to wait for your reply.'

Penelope's hand trembles as she breaks the dark wax seal, praying it is not bad news. She reads Dorothy's neat handwriting, and smiles. 'My sister has had a baby boy at Carew Castle.' She looks back at the letter. 'He's named Thomas, after his father. She says the birth proved difficult, but the child is healthy, thank the Lord.'

Penelope's hand moves to the child growing inside her. She senses the child she carries is not going to be named after his father. Her sister's talk of a difficult birth hints at the nightmare she fears, an ominous dark cloud in an otherwise clear blue sky.

Jeanne seems to read her mind. 'You were fortunate with Lucy, my lady, and they say the first is often the most difficult.'

'My sister is given to understatement, like my mother.' She frowns. 'If Dorothy admits she had a difficult birth, you can be sure her life, or that of her son, must have been at risk.'

'We will use the same midwife as you did for little Lucy. She has many years of experience and knowledge of delivering babies.' Jeanne looks sympathetic. 'Have faith, my lady.'

Penelope folds Dorothy's letter. 'My faith in the will of God has been tested. But you are right, Jeanne – it does me no good to worry about what *could* happen.'

'You used to worry about your sister after she was banished from court, but she seems content with her new life in Wales.'

'I believed I'd brought nothing but trouble to my sister, but her father-in-law has been made Lord Deputy of Ireland, and Dorothy is the lady of the manor at Carew Castle. Now I am back in favour with my stepfather, I shall see if he is prepared to ask the queen to forgive my sister.'

Penelope stands on the temporary wooden scaffold, built high enough for the noblemen and ladies to view the impressive May muster at Greenwich Palace. By chance, she finds herself next to Lady Frances Sidney who, like her, is visibly pregnant, and looking older than her eighteen years.

Lady Frances turns to Penelope. 'Congratulations, Baroness Rich.' She smiles. 'It seems we are both to have a child.'

Something about her tone puts Penelope on her guard. This might not be a chance meeting. Frances could know about her liaison with Philip. She forces a smile. 'My second. We have a daughter, named after my mother, who is now three. My husband prays for a son, to be named for him.'

Frances nods. 'My husband says he hasn't a care if it is a boy, but if the child is a girl, she is to be named Elizabeth, after the queen.'

Penelope looks out over the ranks of soldiers. 'Is your husband taking part in the muster?'

'The cavalry display.' She lowers her voice, and leans closer to Penelope. 'He says the muster is a waste of time and money, which should be better spent on training the men, but this show of strength is important. Her Majesty's soldiers help keep the peace by reminding the Scots, and the French, of the extent of royal power.'

Penelope understands. Frances seems well informed about matters of state, but her father is Sir Francis Walsingham, the queen's principal secretary, and not-so-secret spymaster. Frances and Philip share his London home, close to the Tower, and she will have discussed the reason for the muster with him.

She watches as an army of pikemen march into view, carrying flags and accompanied by the steady beat of drummers and the shrill whistle of fifes. 'There must be thousands of soldiers here today.'

'Four thousand men, divided into opposing companies. One side is commanded by the Earl of Rutland, Sir Robert Constable, as Lieutenant of the Ordnance – and the other by your grandfather, Sir Francis Knollys, Treasurer of the Household.'

Penelope stares at her in surprise. 'I hadn't realised my grandfather took such an active role in such things.'

Frances smiles. 'He told my father the only way to control the costs is to keep a close eye on the expenses. Even the timber for this scaffold is salvaged from the last tournament in Whitehall.'

A fanfare announces the arrival of the queen, dressed in a magnificent white gown which glistens with diamonds and pearls. She is flanked by the ambassadors of Scotland and France, her ministers following in procession, and the watching crowds cheer as the queen takes her place under a golden canopy of state.

Sir Robert Constable approaches the queen on a fine grey charger, caparisoned with his colours of azure blue, and salutes with his sword. Penelope cannot hear what words they exchange, but Sir Robert turns and raises his sword in the air as the signal to the waiting gun crews.

Cannons roar with such a volley of shot the air fills with a sulphurous smell and billowing grey smoke. The ranks of soldiers engage each other in a well-rehearsed skirmish, shouting curses and pushing forwards with long pikes. Some fire pistols into the air, and musketmen fire continuous volleys over their heads.

After the skirmishing, Sir Robert Constable leads his men in a march past the queen and her guests, to cheers from the crowd. So many men march in ranks, ten abreast, that even the ambassadors cannot fail to be impressed. Penelope is certain a report will also be on its way to the King of Spain before the day is out.

A quintain, with a shield on a swivelling pole, is set up in front of the queen, and the cavalry ride into view with a clatter of hooves on the cobblestones. Penelope spots the familiar blue and gold of Sir Philip Sidney.

She stares in amazement at a rider caparisoned with the orange-and-white livery of Essex. He turns, and she sees the red-and-white Devereux crest on his shield. Her brother had not been wasting his time in Lamphey after all, as he spears the target at his first attempt.

After the display of horsemanship, the cavalry rides past the queen. Penelope's heart misses a beat as Philip raises a gauntleted hand to the spectators high on the wooden scaffold, but there is no way to know if he salutes her, or his pregnant young wife at her side.

The drummers strike up a rhythmic beat, and the fifes play a shrill tune as soldiers armed with pikes and halberds march past the queen in battle order, led by the Lord Chamberlain, Lord Howard, Lord Hunsdon, Sir George Carey, Sir Walter Raleigh, and Sir William Drury, all on horseback, with their swords unsheathed and held before them.

Penelope looks in vain for her stepfather, but feels an unexpected surge of pride as her grandfather, dressed in burnished armour, kneels before the queen to rapturous applause and cheers. The soldiers and gunners fire a final volley of shot and call out, 'God save the queen!', the signal the extravagant royal muster is over.

Penelope meets with her brother at Leicester House, where she has a suite of apartments. She wears a copper brocade gown with wide, slashed sleeves, embroidered with flowers in golden thread. Her pearl necklaces reach to her waist, and a large pearl pendant adorns her forehead.

She embraces Robert. 'It's good to see you again, dear brother. You rode well in the muster.' She smiles. 'How is our sister, and little Thomas?'

'I called to see Dorothy and her son before I returned to London. She said the birth took its toll on her, but she asked me to tell you she is well. But what of you? It seems you've given your husband the slip.'

She gives him an innocent look. 'My husband granted me leave to visit for the May muster, as I will be in my confinement soon enough. The day is too good to stay inside. Will you walk to the river with me?'

He follows her down the gravelled path through the gardens of Leicester House, past ornamental flower beds, a well-stocked herb garden, and an orchard of medlars. The path ends at the watergate and long wooden jetty, where a wherry can take them downriver to Greenwich or upriver to Hampton Court.

A bench seat, shaded from the sun by overhanging trees, with a good view of the river, reminds Penelope of her sanctuary at King's Manor. She turns to her brother.

'Sit here with me. I want to hear all about what you've been up to.' She gives him a questioning look. 'What do you make of our queen?'

Robert grins. 'I've only seen her from a distance, but our stepfather has agreed to present me at court, and says if I play my hand well, he will recommend me to take his place as the queen's Master of the Horse. I've lived on the charity of others since leaving Cambridge, and must make a life of my own.'

She studies his cloth-of-silver doublet and smiles. 'You seem to have done well enough on charity.'

'Even the clothes on my back are paid for by our stepfather, but I fear there is a campaign to do great harm to his reputation.'

'That could have consequences for all of us.' She frowns. 'Who would wish to do such a thing?'

'Our stepfather names Sir Walter Raleigh, for one, but it seems there are plenty at court who resent his return to favour.'

Penelope knows he is right. 'You'll find there is a price for winning the queen's affection. Some will stop at nothing to undermine you for their own gain. I've never met Sir Walter Raleigh, but he has quite a reputation.'

'Our mother said this is bigger than Raleigh. The papists are circulating a document they call the Leicester Common-wealth, which makes cruel accusations against our stepfather.'

'What sort of accusations?'

'They accuse him of driving away the queen's suitors by protesting that *he* was contracted to Her Majesty.' Robert curses. 'The trouble with such lies is they are repeated by those who should know better. They accuse him of procuring the poisoning of our father, and say he had his first wife murdered.'

Penelope raises an eyebrow. 'We've spoken of this, and at one time I was tempted to believe such stories. People love to take a grain of truth, and grow it into a web of lies.'

'Worst of all, they say our stepbrother's death was God's punishment upon his father.'

'This document will upset our mother. Can't our stepfather find the people behind it, and have them charged with defamation of his character?'

He shakes his head. 'They work in the shadows, like the cowards they are, but the Mayor of London has been commanded to suppress as many copies as he can.'

'I had no idea this was going on.' A thought occurs to Penelope. 'How can we be sure the Catholics are behind this document?'

'They implore the queen to recognise Mary, Queen of Scots, as her successor.'

'She cannot. It would be bad for us if the queen's cousin proves as vindictive against Protestants as her sister, Queen Mary.'

Robert looks serious, and pulls a folded letter from his pocket. 'This is from Richard Bagot. You need to read it.'

Penelope frowns as she tries to understand the consequences of the letter. 'He's been ordered to prepare Chartley to imprison Mary, Queen of Scots.' She looks at her brother. 'You can't afford to pay for the changes that would be needed.'

'I pointed that out to Bagot, but he told me it means I can make any repairs and improvements we need to restore Chartley at the queen's expense.'

'That would be a good thing.'

'Our stepfather doesn't agree, and there is a risk I'll never have Chartley back.'

'If the queen has made her decision, you'll risk her anger if you refuse – and then you'll never be her Master of the Horse.'

'I'll take that chance.' Robert looks defiant. 'I've lost most of my inheritance to the Crown. I'm not going to surrender Chartley as well. I might not be able to stop this, but I'll try.'

'Take care, Robert. I doubt the queen came up with the idea on her own. One of her advisors has put her up to it.'

'There is something else I need to tell you.'

'There's more?'

'I am accompanying our stepfather on an expedition to the Low Countries. The Duke of Parma has taken Antwerp, and the queen appointed our stepfather as commander of her army. Dorothy's husband, Thomas, is coming with us, and Philip Sidney is sailing with the advance party, to take up his post as Governor of Flushing.'

Her pulse races at the mention of Philip Sidney leaving, but she knows better than to show her true feelings to her brother. 'Our stepfather should know better than to put you in such danger.'

'He said if we don't act soon the Netherlands will become a Spanish colony and a papist stronghold – the ideal place from which to launch an attack on England.'

'Is the Crown meeting your costs?'

He gives her a wry look. 'I plan to borrow the money, as I don't have my own funds, but see it as a good investment in my future.'

'Like our father did in Ireland?'

Robert scowls. 'Our father never had the chance to make his fortune.'

'Well, I hope our stepfather keeps you safe, Robert.'

'He's agreed to recommend me to the queen as General of the Horse, in command of his cavalry, and I can't let him down.'

'But you've never been in command, and have no experience of fighting, let alone of cavalry.' The enormity of what he plans to do seems overwhelming. 'I beg you to reconsider, at least until you've had more training.'

'This is my chance to make a name for myself, Penelope.'

His eyes flash with ambition. 'I shall return a hero, and restore our father's reputation.'

Jeanne helps Penelope pack for the return journey to Leighs Priory. Penelope knows her so well she can tell something is wrong. Usually talkative, Jeanne folds her petticoats in silence and seems deep in thought.

'Is something troubling you, Jeanne?'

'I'm sorry, my lady. I should have told you earlier, and now it is too late.'

'What is too late?'

'There is a man in the household here, a Huguenot I knew in France.'

'You mean Jean?' Penelope smiles. 'He is the only other Huguenot here.' She gives Jeanne a conspiratorial look. 'He's quite handsome, and well educated too.'

Jeanne brightens at her words. 'He was able to gain a place at Oxford, and worked as secretary to your stepfather.'

'Let me guess. He's asked you to marry him?'

'I dared to hope he was going to, but he wished to tell me he's going to the Netherlands to fight for your stepfather.' Jeanne frowned. 'He's a secretary, and knows nothing about fighting.'

'Few of them do – including my brother Robert.' Penelope frowns at the thought of the great risk. 'Does Jean know how you feel about him?'

Jeanne stops folding clothes and sits on the canopied bed. 'He does, my lady, but it seems he believes there is plenty of time.'

'One thing I've learned is that there is never as much time as you think. If you love him, tell him you will marry him, before he leaves, or you could find you have plenty of time to regret your silence.'

'I cannot, my lady.'

'Why not? What do you have to lose?'

The simple wedding takes place with a special licence in the chapel at Leighs Priory, with Penelope and her husband as witnesses. Jean makes a short speech at the wedding feast and says he owes everything to Sir Robert Dudley, and feels it his duty to support his campaign in the Low Countries.

Penelope watches them with mixed feelings. She will miss Jeanne's company; she's become much more than a lady-in-waiting. She worries about Jeanne's husband. A gentle, studious man, he seems unsuited to the dangers of life as a soldier. She will pray for his safe return, as well as for her brother, Dorothy's husband, and Philip Sidney. Penelope hopes her stepfather will not allow any of them to be placed in danger.

The delicate scent of rose water competes with the honeyed aroma of beeswax candles, their flickering light casting ghostly shadows. The midwife arrives in the middle of the afternoon, yet there seems no end to the birth of this stubborn child.

The concern in the midwife's grey eyes tells Penelope the birth is not as it should be, but she already knows it in her heart. This is different from little Lucy. She fights the panic echoing in her mind. *Something is wrong. It's taking too long. I'm going to lose my baby. The pain is not supposed to be like this.*

She cries out as the baby moves inside her. It seems there will be a price to be paid for this child. She calls out to God as she pushes with all her strength, but is weakened after so many hours. She tries to push again, for the sake of her baby, the effort helping to keep the deep despair from her mind. Is it the Lord's will for this baby to live?

The door opens and Anne Broughton enters, carrying clean white towels. She has travelled from her house in London to help, and forces a smile. 'How are you now, Penelope?'

'All I wish is for it to end.'

She closes her eyes as another wave of pain passes through her body. She promises herself, whatever the outcome, she will accept it as the will of the Lord. She repeats a silent prayer between each deep breath. *Please God, let this soon be over. Let my child live.*

Anne sits at the side of her bed and holds her hand. 'Take deep breaths.'

Penelope gasps. 'The baby is on its way.'

The midwife exchanges a nod with Anne. 'You can start to push again, my lady.'

Penelope pushes, but the pain makes her feel faint. This is much worse than last time. She turns to Jeanne and gives her an accusing look. 'You told me it would be easier this time!'

'The baby's cord is around the neck, so do not push until I say, my lady.' The midwife tries her best to sound encouraging, but Penelope sees her frown.

Anne Broughton, seated at Penelope's bedside, clasps her hands together and begins to pray aloud for her. Time stands still, and Penelope focuses on Anne's prayers. Her mind wanders as her strength ebbs like the tide at the shallow estuary. She recalls hearing that one out of every forty women dies in childbirth, or is it one in every fourteen?

The midwife breaks through her thoughts. 'The baby is right enough now, my lady. It's time to push again.'

Penelope calls out as she puts every ounce of her remaining energy into one last push. 'Dear God!'

Her baby is pulled free by the midwife in a moment of release. Penelope clenches her teeth as she fights the pain. She feels as if her insides have been torn from her body, yet she gives thanks to God. At least her ordeal is over.

'You have another little girl, my lady.'

The midwife's words are followed by the shrill cry of a baby. Penelope smiles at Anne and Jeanne. All the worry ends in an instant. 'Essex.'

Jeanne looks puzzled. 'Essex, my lady?'

'My daughter will be named Essex, after my father. Everyone called my father Essex, and now that's what they will call my brother.'

Anne Broughton looks doubtful, then smiles. 'We can call her Essie, for short. Lucy and Essie. You shall have a house full of young ladies.'

Penelope lies back on the crumpled sheets, still hurting, but relieved the birth is over. Her husband will be disappointed not to have a son and heir, but she doesn't care. She has two wonderful daughters, and they are all that matter in her life.

10

THE BABINGTON PLOT

AUGUST 1586

Penelope calls into the nursery late in the evening to see her daughters. She lives in secret dread of either of them falling ill, and checks on them as often as she can. A virulent outbreak of smallpox in nearby Colchester alarms her, and she is haunted by the thought of her daughters suffering the disfiguring scars.

Little Essie is restless, crying fitfully in the summer heat, but her wet nurse, Martha, has no concerns. 'All babies are different, my lady.' She smiles. 'Your Lucy could never get enough milk, but little Essie is more particular.'

Penelope places her hand on her daughter's forehead, relieved to find it cool to the touch. 'I've not forgotten how easily my stepbrother succumbed to a fever, or what happened with Essie's birth.'

Martha gives her an understanding look. 'It's natural for a mother to worry, my lady, but you've been blessed with two healthy children, and have my word you'll be the first to know if there is any sign of illness.'

Lucy sleeps soundly, and Essie stops crying to stare up at her, as if wondering what the fuss is about. Penelope turns to

Martha. 'My mother has retired to live at Drayton Manor, some twenty-five miles south of Chartley. Is Essie old enough to travel with us?'

Martha smiles. 'Of course, my lady, but we'll need to keep her out of this heat.' She looks down at Essie. 'As the Lord says in Proverbs seventeen, our children's children are the crown of the aged. It's good for her grandmother to see her.'

They travel with Essie in the care of Martha. Lucy, now four years old, is a good traveller and rides in the carriage next to Penelope. Arriving tired and dusty from the long journey on dry roads, Penelope can tell her mother is concerned about something.

'What is it, Mother?' She prepares herself for the worst. 'Is there news from my brother or stepfather?'

'There's a plot against the queen, and I fear we are in peril of being caught up in the middle of it.'

Penelope places her hand on her mother's arm. 'You must tell me about this plot. I want to know everything. But first, there is someone I wish you to meet.'

Martha carries little Essie, and loosens the tight swaddling to free her arms. 'Your granddaughters are good travellers, my lady.'

Penelope's mother manages a smile as she takes her newest granddaughter in her arms. 'She is like her sister, with fair hair, yet their father is dark. Do you think they might take after me?'

Martha smiles. 'Lord Rich asked me the same question, my lady. Some babies have lighter hair at first, but Lucy is already turning darker. I'll wager she'll have your red hair soon enough, Countess.'

Penelope is not so sure. Sometimes she looks at Lucy and sees the echo of Philip Sidney in her blue-grey eyes. There is no way to know for sure, yet the thought nags at the back of her mind. Her mother asks questions and so, it seems, does her husband. The likeness could become more apparent once Lucy comes of age.

She leaves her daughters in Martha's care, and follows her mother into her stepfather's private study. A stern-faced portrait of Robert Dudley, wearing his gold chain of the Order of the Garter, dominates one wall, and his coat of arms surmounts the marble fireplace.

Penelope crosses to the mullioned window, with views across the parkland. The grass is parched like straw by the heat of the summer sun, and the deer have come closer to the house in search of grazing. 'Is my stepfather in trouble with the queen?'

Her mother sighs. 'The queen claims to be offended by his acceptance of the post of Governor of The Hague. He is the obvious choice, as commander of our forces, but his enemies at court conspire behind his back, looking for any excuse to blacken his name.'

Penelope is unsurprised. 'Robert said there's a campaign to harm our stepfather's reputation. He believes Sir Walter Raleigh could be one of those behind it, or the Catholics.'

'Whoever it might be has turned their attention to me. Someone reported to the queen that I was preparing to join my husband in the Low Countries, with a train of ladies and gentlewomen that would surpass Her Majesty's own court.'

'This was untrue?'

'Of course – but it contrived to inflame the queen's anger, and prevent me from visiting him.' Her mother's eyes flash with annoyance. 'I hear I was cursed by the queen with great oaths, and she said she would have no other courts than her own.'

'Is there nothing you can do, Mother?'

'I wrote to my father, protesting my innocence. I hoped the

queen would listen to him, as he is highly regarded at court, but this has been overtaken by a greater worry, closer to home.'

'The plot against the queen?'

She nods. 'Robert told you they moved the queen's cousin, Mary Stuart, to Chartley against his wishes?'

'He was trying to prevent it before he left for the Low Countries, but it seems the decision was already made.'

'I fear there was a reason for the choice of Chartley. Sir Francis Walsingham set a trap there for Mary Stuart, to have proof of her treason against the queen.'

'But surely we could not be implicated?'

'We cannot be sure of anything now. Our enemies seem prepared to stop at nothing, and Richard Bagot rode here from Blithfield to warn me of his concerns.'

'What did he say?'

'Sir Francis Walsingham asked him to find accommodation for one of his spies, a Catholic named Gilbert Gifford, and to replace his steward with Gifford within the household at Chartley.' She frowns. 'When Richard refused, Gifford threatened to implicate him in the conspiracy against the queen.'

'You must write again to your father, and ask him to do what he can to remind Her Majesty that we are all loyal Protestants. I will write to Anne Broughton, and ask her to come here with her husband. I would like to see her again, and I suspect we could have need of the services of our family lawyer.'

Anne and Richard Broughton arrive with news from London. 'There are bonfires in the streets, and all the church bells are ringing to celebrate the arrest of a Catholic, Anthony Babington, who plotted with others to replace Queen Elizabeth with Mary, Queen of Scots.'

Penelope frowns. 'I was at the May muster. The queen has never had so great an army to defend her.'

Richard Broughton looks grim-faced. 'The plotters waited for most of the army to leave for the Low Countries. If their plot had succeeded, we could have faced an invasion by the French, supported by King Philip of Spain, with dire consequences for us all.'

'That doesn't mean Mary Stuart wished to harm Her Majesty.'

Richard Broughton shakes his head. 'Sir Francis Walsingham has proof. Letters, signed by the queen's cousin, approving of the plot to assassinate the queen, were smuggled from Chartley in kegs of beer.'

Penelope glances at her mother. 'We are concerned that the plot was uncovered at Chartley.'

Richard nods. 'I understand, but Anne's father co-operated with Walsingham's men, and he is acting on your brother's behalf, as custodian of the estate.'

'What is to become of the queen's cousin?'

'She's been taken to Fotheringhay Castle, where she will stand trial for treason.' He frowns. 'I understand Walsingham's men did serious damage to Chartley during a search, tearing up floorboards and ripping out much of the panelling. I will meet with Richard Bagot on your brother's behalf to discuss reparations from the Crown.'

'A few repairs seem a small price to pay, compared with what might have happened.'

Richard Broughton agrees. 'Anthony Babington and his conspirators have all been found guilty of treason.' He scowls. 'They are to be dragged from the Tower of London to the scaffold in St Giles's Field, where they are to be hanged, drawn and quartered.'

Penelope recalls what she'd heard of the traitor's death. They would be hanged, and cut down while still alive, castrated and disembowelled, their organs burned in front of them as they died. Even then, their ravaged bodies would be hacked into quarters, the pieces nailed above the city gates, as a warning to others of the consequences of disloyalty.

Penelope's hand trembles as she reads the rambling letter from her brother Robert. There, along with his complaints about the food, the unseasonably wet weather, and stories of drunken revelry in the Low Countries, is a mention that Philip Sidney suffered a serious injury to his leg in a battle.

The letter, already several weeks old, had been brought by ship, then by messengers from the port. In his usual bluff, long-winded way of writing, Robert failed to mention how Philip Sidney was, where he'd been taken, or when he would be returned to England.

Penelope says a silent prayer for Philip Sidney. She'd imagined him living a life of decadence as Governor of Flushing, writing his poetry and dealing with minor disputes. She should have known better. Like any of them, including her younger brother, he would wish to be making a valiant name for himself on the battlefield, not sitting behind a comfortable desk.

She must find out how he is and sits at her writing desk, drafting a carefully worded reply to her brother. There is no need to alert him to her true feelings, so only after the usual entreaties for him to take care, does she enquire after Philip Sidney's health.

Penelope listens while Jeanne plays an old Huguenot lament on her lute, singing of her lost homeland.

'Enough of these sad songs, Jeanne.' She finds herself thinking of Philip Sidney, somewhere across the sea, and wishes she knew how he was. 'You shouldn't worry that we've had no reply to our letters. It could be weeks before we can expect any news.'

Jeanne looks apologetic. 'I am sorry, my lady. I miss my husband, although I know it does no good to worry.'

Penelope picks up her lute and plays a few bars of a lively dance she remembers from her days as a maid of honour. 'I miss the excitement of court, the dancing, and even the gossip.' She smiles. 'The things the queen's ladies spoke of in the maidens' chambers would make a soldier blush.'

'You could return to court, my lady. We can stay at Leicester House, and I will help look after the girls.'

Penelope brightens. 'We'd be more likely to hear news from the Low Countries. I could send for my sister to bring her son to see us. She must miss Sir Thomas.'

'Shall I make the arrangements, my lady?' Jeanne sounds pleased to have something to occupy her.

'I'll need my husband to agree, but he no doubt has some interest he'll wish me to promote at court.' She places her lute back on its wooden stand. 'Is he here today?'

'Lord Rich is working in his study, my lady, although he may have already left for Chelmsford.'

Her husband's frequent and unexplained absences suit Penelope, but she resents having to beg his approval before leaving Leighs Priory. Not for the first time, she is reminded of the hollow sham her marriage has always been.

Unlike her stepfather's richly furnished study, her husband's room reminds her of a monk's whitewashed cell. Apart from two shelves piled high with dusty legal books, the only ornament is a wooden crucifix on one wall. Her husband sits hunched over his desk, cluttered with legal papers, and turns as she enters.

'What is it?' His irritated tone suggests her interruption is unwelcome.

'I must ask your permission to travel to London.' She plays her part well, recalling Countess Catherine checking off on her fingers that the mistress of the house is modest, meek, submissive, virtuous, and obedient.

'For what purpose?' His voice is terse, as if speaking to a lowly servant.

'I would like to see my mother and my sister, Dorothy, at Leicester House. It is also time I attended court, before the queen forgets all about me.'

'Her Majesty is not in London. She is under protection at Windsor, following the plot against her – and you will not return to court until you've given me a son.'

'The good Lord has graced us with two daughters—'

'Do not take the Lord's name in vain!'

His raised voice echoes in the room, startling her, but she will not be bullied by him. 'There is plenty of time to have a son.' She makes the mistake of allowing a note of contempt into her voice.

He crosses the room and seizes her arm. 'Well, there is no time like the present.'

Penelope struggles to break free, but he is too strong. His grip on her arm tightens until it hurts, and he pushes her back hard against the wall. She stares into his face and sees the animal glint in his eye. It seems he enjoys having such power over her.

Her mind races as she tries to stop the rising panic. She could call out for help. She still has one hand free, and could rake his face with her sharp nails. She weighs the risk of increasing his anger, against what might happen if she surrenders without a fight. She takes a deep breath, and prepares to scream as loud as she can.

A sharp knock at the door makes him loosen his grasp on her arm. Jeanne enters, her eyes widening as she takes in the scene. 'Forgive me, my lord, but your daughter is asking for her mother.' She sounds urgent.

Penelope sees her chance and follows Jeanne out through the door before her husband can reply. She rubs her arm and she guesses there will be bruises. She isn't sure how, but she will have to ensure she cannot be treated so roughly by her husband again.

Penelope's brother Robert arrives late in the evening at the head of a band of armed men, who ride clattering into the paved courtyard. Jeanne cries with relief to see her husband among them, and Robert says their sister Dorothy's husband is safe and on his way to Wales.

Penelope smells the tang of stale horse sweat as she embraces her brother, sensing how he's changed. She stands back to look at him. He's grown a reddish beard, and wears an impressive silver-handled sword at his belt, as well as his usual dagger.

'You sailed from England a boy, and return as a man, dearest brother.'

'It's good to be back.' He manages a grin. 'I've been looking forward to some decent English food.'

She smiles, although her question burns in her heart. 'I shall send for wine, and will rouse the cooks to prepare a feast to welcome you and your men.'

'Thank you.' His face becomes serious. 'I made a solemn promise which I have a duty to keep. There is no easy way to tell you, Penelope. I regret to say our good friend Philip Sidney is dead.'

Penelope freezes, his words ringing in her ears. She's lived in hope, praying each day that all of them – her brother, Dorothy's husband, Jeanne's husband Jean, Philip Sidney and her stepfather – would return from the wars unscathed. Part of her was prepared for bad news, perhaps that he'd lost his leg and would be forever crippled. But not this.

Robert takes her hand, leads her to a chair and sits her down, before finding a chair for himself. 'Philip Sidney rode at the head of two hundred cavalrymen, in a mist so thick we could not see more than a few paces. The plan was to attack a Spanish convoy on its way to the town of Zutphen.'

Penelope's serving maid brings wine in silver goblets, and they wait in silence while she pours them both a drink. 'Philip left our camp and met the marshal, Sir William Pelham, who wore light armour. It's believed Philip took off his own leg armour, so that he would be no better protected.' Robert frowns at the thought. 'Some would call his gallantry misplaced, as when the fog lifted, they were confronted by a thousand of the enemy's cavalry. Philip Sidney's horse was killed, but he captured one from the enemy and returned to rescue a fellow knight. The fighting was hard, and we lost a quarter of our men, with many more wounded.'

Penelope takes a deep breath, fighting back her tears. 'You said in your letter Philip was wounded in the leg.'

Robert nods. 'A bullet struck him above the knee, where his armour should have protected him. I don't know how, but he rode a mile and a half back to the camp, and was taken in our stepfather's barge to Arnhem. There was little the surgeons could do. He told me they discussed removing his leg, but the bullet had shattered his thigh bone, and the wound became corrupted, poisoning him.'

'He must have suffered great pain.' She could not bear to imagine how terrible it must have been.

'He fought for life, Penelope, and won the admiration of all who visited him, including me.' Robert unbuckles his sword to show her. 'He bequeathed me this, his best sword, which I shall treasure for the rest of my life.'

'That was when you made your promise to tell me?' Penelope fears Philip Sidney's sense of honour could include a deathbed confession, revealing their secret.

'Philip's wife, Frances, nursed him until the end, often staying up through the night. I came to know her well, and she told me she carries his second child. Frances was the one who made me promise I would travel here before returning to London, so you would hear first from me.'

Penelope shares several bottles of rich red wine as they talk late into the evening, remembering happier times. Robert becomes a little drunk, and confesses he'd taken great risks, but won his spurs and was knighted by their stepfather as his reward.

Jeanne helps Penelope to bed, and she drifts into a fitful sleep. She wakes early, and remembers dreaming of Philip Sidney. He'd come to her in the darkness, casting his armour to the floor, and climbing into her bed. She recalls how roughly he'd kissed her, violating her, as if meaning to punish her.

The truth dawns, like the bright autumn sunlight streaming through her window. One of the mother-of-pearl buttons is torn from the front of her nightgown, and both her arms are marked with blue bruises. Philip Sidney would never treat her so harshly. The memory floods back, despite her wish to forget.

Her brother was not alone in having had too much wine to drink. Her husband had returned late from Colchester in a vindictive mood, meaning to have his revenge, and had taken advantage of her grief.

11

SWEET ROBIN

FEBRUARY 1587

F rances Sidney looks close to tears as she stands with Penelope in mourning dress. The invitation to join her is a surprise, but Penelope understands. Philip Sidney hadn't needed to make a deathbed confession; unlike Penelope's husband, Frances could decipher her husband's allegory, and knew the identity of his Stella.

In keeping with tradition, Frances will not be seen at his funeral, but wishes to witness the procession in remembrance of her husband. They wait together at the upper-floor window of a merchant's house, with a good view of the long road leading to St Paul's Cathedral. The cobblestoned streets are lined with crowds of curious Londoners.

Frances has yet to talk about her husband's suffering in his last days, but speaks of the perilous voyage home. 'We were caught in a fierce storm. Our little fleet was scattered and our sails were torn to rags. I feared we would all be drowned, and I made my peace with God.' Her sadness echoes in her cold voice. 'I lost our second child, a daughter, stillborn.'

Penelope's hand unconsciously moves to the growing bulge under her loose satin gown. 'I'm so sorry, Frances.'

'The will of God is hard to understand.' She turns to Penelope. 'You know this spectacle is planned to distract the people from what happened at Fotheringhay Castle?'

'I confess I hadn't made the connection. I've been out of touch with the politics of court. I didn't believe Her Majesty would agree to sign the death warrant for her own cousin, an anointed queen.'

'She had no choice. My father said—' Frances stops herself. 'For five weeks we'd had many alarms and a general uproar throughout the country. False stories were spread abroad that the Queen of Scots escaped from Fotheringhay Castle and London was set ablaze.'

'I heard that a thousand Spanish invaders landed in Wales, and that certain nobleman fled the country in fear of their lives.'

Frances frowns. 'Some even said Windsor Castle was sacked and burned, and Her Majesty murdered.'

'I was at Leicester House when we heard all the church bells ringing, early in the evening. We sent a man out to learn the reason, and he returned a short time later to say that the Queen of Scots had been executed.'

Frances stares out of the window at the gathering crowds. 'May God preserve us all. There may still be repercussions. The queen cast the blame on her hapless secretary, William Davison. She sent him to the Tower, and banished William Cecil from court for his part in persuading her to sign the death warrant.'

The rhythmic sound of approaching drumbeats interrupts Penelope's reply. They watch the silent crowd below, where every inch of space is filled by the people of London. The women clasp their hands in prayer, and the men pull off their caps, bowing their heads.

The long procession passes with the tramp of marching boots and the clatter of horseshoes on cobbles. Penelope guesses many of the soldiers might have fought with Philip Sidney, and know of others who would have less glorious remembrance after death.

Frances points. 'My father paid for thirty-two poor men dressed in hooded black robes, one for each year of Philip's life, to lead the way.' She frowns. 'He could ill afford it, but likes to see the old traditions upheld.'

Penelope hadn't expected such frankness, and sees her openness as a sign of the growing trust between them. She's always imagined Sir Francis Walsingham to be a wealthy man, but it seems he is not so rich after all. Penelope suspects that Walsingham, like her own father, has been tricked by the queen into running up debts in her service, with hollow promises of reward.

Behind Francis Walsingham's poor men march the queen's grim-faced yeomen, in royal livery, with drums rattling out a sombre beat in the chill morning air. Sixty liveried servants, physicians and clerics follow, with Philip Sidney's fine black charger, ridden by his young page, who carries his master's broken lance and reversed battleaxe.

The royal heralds carry Philip's spurs and gauntlets, and four men hold tall banners with the blue and gold of the Sidney coat of arms. A single tear runs down Penelope's cheek at the sight of the coffin draped in black cloth and carried high on stout poles. She counts seven men on each side, and recognises Philip's younger brother, Sir Robert Sidney, as chief mourner, riding at her stepfather's side.

Her own brother, Robert, rides behind them with Sir Henry Herbert, Earl of Pembroke, and the lords who fought at the Battle of Zutphen. Her grandfather, Sir Francis Knollys, rides with Dorothy's husband, Sir Thomas Perrot, and a stocky, bearded man Penelope recognises as Sir Francis Drake. She sees her brother carrying the fine sword bequeathed to him by

Philip. Their father would have been proud to see him do so well.

Frances must have also recognised him, as she turns to Penelope. 'Your brother Robert has been a comfort to me in these difficult times.'

'He told me of your dedication in Arnhem.'

'Did he tell you he stayed at Philip's bedside all night, watching over him, so I might have some rest?' Frances looks wistful. 'Your brother was the only one of Philip's comrades to show such chivalry and care for him, or any concern for me.'

Penelope recalls her brother's admiration for Frances, voiced after he'd drunk a little too much of her good wine. At least he should be allowed to choose his own wife. They are the same age, and their stepfather will be quick enough to see the advantage of an alliance with the queen's spymaster.

The Lord Mayor of London and aldermen of the city, leading the grocers' guilds in full livery, come into view, and at the rear follow the London bands, marching three abreast. Their shrill fifes sound too cheerful, out of place on such a sad occasion.

There are too many to count, yet Penelope guesses this must be the grandest funeral procession seen in London for many years. A lone voice calls out, 'God rest you, my Lord Sidney!' But otherwise the crowd remains respectfully silent.

Penelope echoes the man's words. 'May God rest you, my Lord Sidney.' She imagines Philip Sidney would have made some wry remark about being given such a funeral, after having to wait since the previous October.

She follows Frances as they make their way to the cathedral, where the once towering spire has not been rebuilt since being struck by lightning. The Catholics say the damaged spire is God's judgement on their Protestant queen. Penelope sees it as reflective of the broken state of religion in the country.

They are seated behind a screen, out of sight of the

congregation. After prayers, a long and mournful sermon, and even longer speeches, Philip Sidney can rest in peace. A salvo of gunshots rings out, making her jump. Penelope says a silent prayer for him, and thanks God he has taken their great secret to his grave. He'd loved her, and she loved him. She will remember her time with him for the rest of her life.

Penelope realises her mistake too late. She'd invited her mother to Leighs Priory, to keep her company during her lying in. She hadn't accounted for the fuss her mother makes, how she orders the servants about, or that she observes all the old traditions.

The windows, which Penelope would have liked open to the spring sunshine, are obscured behind heavy drapes, turning her birthing chamber to near darkness. She soon loses track of the hours, unsure whether it is night or day, and her enforced lying in seems twice as long.

In keeping with tradition, her mother has her servants decorate the walls with faded old tapestries of biblical scenes. Instead of helping Penelope put her faith in God, she finds them bleak and dreary. She longs for the peace to lie in bed and listen to the birdsong in the early mornings.

One unexpected visitor is Frances Sidney, who travels all the way from London to see her. She still wears mourning dress, but has returned to court and is happy to share the latest news when she is alone with Penelope.

'The talk of court is that the Spanish prepare their fleet for an invasion by sea. There is much debate about what should be done to prevent them, while we can.'

Penelope's eyes widen in alarm. 'Is our navy able to take on the Spanish fleet?'

'Captain Drake sunk a good few in his raid on Cadiz.

Some thirty ships are being rigged and furnished with all things necessary, and Drake is appointed as general.' Frances lowers her voice. 'The Spanish outnumber us two to one, but our informers tell us they are not well prepared for us to attack a second time.'

'It seems a great shame to declare war on Spain, after all the efforts the queen has made to avoid it.'

Frances gives her a wry look. 'The queen tolerates the Spanish ambassadors for the sake of appearances, while men like Sir Francis Drake sink their warships and plunder the Spanish gold fleet with impunity.'

Penelope looks at Frances with new respect. There is no doubt she knows more about the secret web of information behind the politics of court than many of the great men of state. She could not blame Frances for marrying Philip, and is glad to count her as a friend – and perhaps, one day, a sister-in-law.

'How is Her Majesty?'

Frances shakes her head. 'All this talk of an invasion unsettles her, and she shuts herself away for long days in her chambers, apparently in mourning for her cousin.'

'I imagine she regrets what she's done, however necessary her advisors thought it to be.'

'Her secretary, William Davison, was tried in the Star Chamber for misprision and contempt, before commissioners including the Archbishops of Canterbury and York.' Frances frowns at the injustice. 'He's been found guilty, fined ten thousand marks, and sentenced to be imprisoned at Her Majesty's pleasure.'

'What news is there of my brother?' Penelope watches Frances to judge her reaction, and is rewarded with a coy smile.

'Your brother Robert has become the queen's Master of the Horse in place of your stepfather, and is a great favourite of the queen since his return from the Low Countries. They are together so often the gossips of court talk of them being lovers.'

Penelope laughs. 'The queen is ten years older than our mother!'

'He plays his part well, as the son she never had, and takes liberties few others would dare. He holds her by the arm, calls her *Bess*, and jokes with her.'

Penelope raises an eyebrow. 'The queen can be a fickle mistress. I shall have to speak to my brother.'

The pain begins in the night, a gentle wave at first, then the familiar cramping that tells her the child is on the way. Penelope rings the bell, her agreed signal. Her servant enters, carrying a lit candle, which she places at the bedside.

'Do you need me to fetch the midwife, my lady?'

Penelope gasps. 'Quick as you can – and rouse Mistress Jeanne. Tell her the baby is on the way.'

She lies back on the bed as another wave runs through her. She prays her ordeal will be easier than with little Essie. Jeanne enters carrying towels, followed by her faithful midwife, wearing a linen apron, and pulls a chair to the side of the bed.

'Do you want me to wake your mother?'

'No.' Penelope grimaces at the thought. 'I'll not disturb her.'

The waves build until she can bear them no longer and her cries of pain echo in the darkened bedchamber.

The midwife tries to calm her. 'Let your body do the work, my lady. Don't fight the pain, surrender to it.'

Penelope lets her mind drift to another place, floating up until she seems to be looking down on her tormented body. She sees the midwife's nod to Jeanne, and the sweat on her own face glistening in the candlelight. The sudden release as the midwife pulls the child free brings her back with a jolt.

'Well done, my lady, you have a little boy – and much quicker this time.'

Penelope watches as the midwife ties the cord. The baby lets out a shrill cry. He sounds strong. After more than five years, she's kept her part of the bargain, and given her husband the heir he demanded. From now on, she will be her own woman, free of his threats. She smiles at the thought of her new future.

Robert comes to visit Penelope at Leicester House, and stares at his new nephew. 'The future Baron Rich.' He grins. 'One of the wealthiest babies in the country – I'll wager he's wealthier than I am!'

Penelope looks down at her sleeping child. 'He's named Robert – after *you*, not his father. I shall always remind him to be proud to be a Devereux.' She smiles. 'We already call him *Sweet Robin* – which is what I hear the queen calls *you*, dear brother.'

He frowns. 'She used to call our stepfather Robin, but has worse names for me when I fall from her favour.'

She turns to him. 'Dorothy was here, and told me that your plan for her to see the queen did not go well.'

'That was our mother's idea, not mine. Although she long since abandoned any hope of being accepted back at court, she keeps a great interest in the comings and goings of the queen. She learned the summer progress would take her to North Hall in Hertfordshire, home of our stepfather's elder brother, Sir Ambrose Dudley, Earl of Warwick.'

'Mother told Dorothy to be visiting Lady Warwick when the royal party arrived.' Penelope shakes her head. 'Mother does not understand the queen, even after all these years. She is more ready to forgive any man than the most innocent of her ladies.'

Robert raises an eyebrow. 'I told her the queen is no fool, and would see through her plan, but she said it was perfectly reasonable for Dorothy to visit her aunt, and it would be up to the queen whether she agreed to see her – or not.'

'Dorothy told me what happened. She said you argued with the queen.'

'She refused to see our sister.' He frowns. 'I suspect Walter Raleigh warned her of our plan.'

'How could he have known?'

'He makes it his business to know, as captain of the queen's guard, and saw his chance to make trouble for me. I asked Her Majesty to allow Dorothy a second chance. I reminded her our sister's only crime was to marry for love, but she began shouting about our mother.'

'What did she say?'

'She called our mother a vixen, and said she was lucky not to be thrown in the Tower for her disloyalty.' Robert scowls. 'I'd had enough of her insults, and thought to leave to join our stepfather. I planned to re-establish my reputation, and make my fortune in the Low Countries. I'm sorry for Dorothy. It seems she will always be banished. Her Majesty will never be persuaded now.'

'You didn't leave the country. What changed your mind?'

'We rode to Maidstone, where we were found by Robert Carey, who brought a message from the queen. She commanded me to return to court.'

'For punishment?'

'Quite the contrary. She's forgiven me.' Robert smiles. 'Another day and we would have been at sea, but Carey said he had orders to pursue me to the Low Countries, if necessary.'

Penelope shivers on the high wooden platform, painted red and gold, built for the queen's Accession Day. Silk banners flap like angry swans in the chill breeze, and the late November weather is not in their favour. Ominous slate-grey storm clouds gather overhead, as if in keeping with the mood of the country.

Lady Frances sits at her side, and has become a trusted companion. Penelope learns much from her, particularly now they face the threat of war. Opinions veer from her mother's alarmist talk of Spanish soldiers rampaging through the streets, to her husband's disinterest, so she is glad to have reliable information.

Undeterred, the queen had commanded her Accession Day celebrations to proceed. Vendors selling ale and pies call out to customers, and a troupe of minstrels adds a festival atmosphere to the occasion. Heavy horses canter down the list as knights make practice runs, and a rousing cheer goes up as the heralds sound a fanfare to announce the start of the tournament.

Leading the procession of riders is Penelope's brother, Robert. Dressed in burnished armour, his charger is caparisoned in Essex orange and white. He canters up to the royal canopy of state, saluting the queen with a dip of his lance, and her ladies present him with a gold button as a token of her appreciation.

The Master of the Joust announces that the Earl of Essex will ride against Sir Henry Lee. Penelope feels a frisson of concern. One of the most experienced jousters on the field, Sir Henry Lee is the queen's champion for good reason, and organised the tournament.

She turns to Frances as her brother is handed his lance and lowers the visor on his helmet. 'I worry for Robert. I don't believe he's had time to practise jousting.'

Frances smiles. 'He was taught by my late husband, and Philip told me your brother has a natural talent.'

Although this is only for show, Penelope's pulse races at the thought of imminent danger, and she says a prayer. The Master of the Joust gives his signal, and Robert charges. His lance wavers, as if he struggles to keep it steady, before Sir Henry's lance crashes into his shoulder. A jagged scar on Robert's armour shows where he's been struck, yet Penelope is relieved.

Frances gives her a knowing look. 'We cannot be sure, and I'm sure he will deny it if asked, but your brother let old Sir Henry Lee win the point.'

'Out of chivalry?'

'He was trained by one of the best.'

Penelope watches her brother pull off his helmet and run his fingers through his long hair. He has taken the place of their stepfather in the queen's affection, and proved himself worthy of Philip Sidney's sword. At last, it seems there is hope for her family.

12

THE SPANISH ARMADA

JUNE 1588

The antique French lute is too large for Lucy, now six years old, yet her little fingers play the tuneful melody with note-perfect confidence. The concert is for her mother, but as the last notes fall silent in the high-ceilinged chamber, Lucy looks to her teacher for approval.

Jeanne smiles and applauds. 'Bravo, Lucy. *Maintenant, inclinez-vous devant votre mère.*'

Jeanne is the perfect tutor for Lucy, and spends long hours teaching her the old Huguenot songs. Lucy began her lessons as soon as she could first talk, and speaks French as fluently as she does English. The lute is Lucy's latest challenge, and this is the first time she has played before an audience.

Lucy bows in a graceful curtsey. Her long hair is the deep copper her grandmother hoped for, and which she takes pride in telling her granddaughter is the red of her Tudor heritage. Her gown of burgundy brocade, with a collar and cuffs of French lace, makes Lucy look like a miniature version of her mother.

Penelope smiles happily and applauds her daughter. 'Bravo, Lucy!' Her children are her world, now she is unable to travel to the royal court. She encourages Lucy to question everything, and finds it hard not to spoil little Essie, after coming so close to losing her when she was born.

A happy and mischievous child, Essie beams her smiles at everyone. She even wins the heart of her surly father, who seeks her out on his infrequent visits. Little Robin is a poor sleeper, keeping his nurse, Martha, busy through the night, yet seems strong and is growing fast.

Jeanne's husband, appointed as secretary to the baron, administers his rents and deals with the tenants of his numerous properties. He lives with Jeanne in an apartment at Leighs Priory, which means Penelope sees even less of her husband. The arrangement suits them all, yet seeing Jeanne so happy reminds Penelope of what she misses.

Her mother has found contentment with Robert Dudley, and Dorothy seems happy with her life in Wales. Even her little brother Wat is marrying for love – an heiress, Margaret Dakins, who he met in the household of Countess Catherine at King's Manor in York.

Penelope dreams of her precious moments with Philip Sidney. She still wears the gold heart pendant he gave her, inscribed with *Omnia Vincit Amour*. Love conquers all. She believed she would never forget that day for as long as she lived, yet even those most poignant memories begin to fade with the passing years.

Her loneliness and longing had unexpected consequences. On a cold winter's night in early January, her husband came to her bedchamber. She encouraged him, and he responded with passion. She'd been surprised by the first sign of tenderness in their marriage, yet he'd not returned to her bed since. Now, six months later, she is heavy with her fourth child.

A young servant interrupts them. He bows to Penelope and hands her a sealed letter, carried on a silver tray. 'Forgive me, my lady, but the messenger who brought this asked me to tell you it is urgent.'

Penelope breaks the red wax seal and recognises Anne Broughton's familiar hand. She frowns as she reads the troubling news. 'An invasion of the country is imminent. They are building a chain of warning beacons along the coast, and she worries about us being so near to the sea.'

Jeanne glances at Lucy. 'Should we take the children to your house in London, my lady?'

Penelope looks down at Anne's letter. The icy dread makes it hard for her to think clearly. Leighs Priory, which seemed so safe, could become a target for the Spanish if they invade, and any Catholic uprising would have dire consequences for her family. She fears more for her children than herself.

'I don't know if anywhere is safe. Frances said the Spanish fleet outnumber our ships two to one.' She frowns. 'I hoped it would never come to this. It's hard to decide whether we should take the children to London – or down to my sister in West Wales. Dorothy told me her husband has raised a local militia to keep her and little Thomas safe.'

Jeanne stares at her with wide eyes. 'It will be too late if we wait until they light the warning beacons, my lady, but there have been reports of Spanish warships before. They all proved to be false alarms.'

'Anne seems sure enough. She says a merchant ship arriving in Plymouth sighted the Spanish fleet heading for England. Every seaworthy ship in England is commandeered for the navy, and men are being brought from the fields to be trained to fight.' Penelope folds the letter. 'Tell the servants to start packing. I fear this is it, Jeanne, and we must be prepared.'

Penelope's husband arrives with an engraved silver breastplate over his doublet, and a fine new sword in a black leather scabbard at his belt, the first time she's seen him armed. His face looks grim. 'All the peers have been summoned to military service, and I am to report to your stepfather, who is now Lieutenant General of the Army.'

His sword looks more of a badge of office than a weapon. As far as Penelope knows, he's never commanded fighting men, yet he has a new air of authority. 'You are going to fight?' She stares at him, finding it hard to believe the change in her husband, and wonders if she really knows him at all.

His eyes narrow. 'My orders are to ride to Tilbury to guard the approaches to the Thames, but Sir Robert agrees I shall remain in Chelmsford to command the Essex militia.' He glances at her bulging middle. 'You will take the children to our house in London, and stay there until I say it's safe to return.'

'I shall, but what about your mother? Rochford Hall overlooks the sands. She has no one to defend her.'

'I've sent a message to my mother, but suspect she will not move from Rochford Hall.' He studies her as if thinking this might be the last time. 'I've told her I will lay down my life before I allow a single Spanish Catholic to set foot in Essex.'

Penelope recalls her husband's words as she shades her eyes from the bright August sunshine. She joins the crowd gathering to watch the royal flotilla depart from the quay at Greenwich Palace. The queen looks magnificent in her gilded barge, and the people cheer her courage, but Penelope hopes the real danger is over.

Rumours and speculation make it difficult to be sure of news of events at sea reaching London, but Penelope has the advantage of reliable information. Frances told her the

Spanish fleet sailed along the south coast in a formation over seven miles long, while the English navy bombarded them from a safe distance, taking advantage of the longer range of their new cannons.

Penelope worries for her brother Robert, who has been promoted to General of the Horse, and commands the queen's cavalry. He has joined their stepfather in Tilbury ahead of the queen, and says he is keen to fight. But if the Spanish land, his little army will not stand a chance.

He'd written to Penelope, complaining they hadn't seen a single Spaniard, and that he'd sunk deeper into debt. As well as buying a new suit of armour, he'd had to recruit and equip his company of a hundred and twenty musketeers and arquebusiers, and some two hundred cavalrymen, in his Essex livery of orange and white.

Part of her brother's reward for his service to the queen is the use of York House, a grand building, once the palace of Cardinal Thomas Wolsey, which forms part of the palace of Whitehall. In his absence, he suggests York House is safer for Penelope and the children than her husband's house in the east of the city.

Penelope places her hand on her bulging middle and turns to Jeanne, who watches the spectacle with her. 'If not for this, I might be on one of those barges, heading for Tilbury.'

Jeanne has been reserved since leaving her husband behind to defend Leighs Priory. 'Her Majesty shows bravery to go to see her troops in person.'

'Frances told me the worst of the danger is over. The southwesterly winds prevent the Spanish ships from landing, and storms are expected to drive them east. Our navy plans to attack them at night with fireships, when they seek shelter.'

'Let us pray Frances is right, as we are poorly prepared if Spanish soldiers land in Essex.' She frowns at the thought.

'There was no time to train the militia, and few have any experience of fighting – including our husbands.'

'Jean served in the Low Countries with my stepfather, so he must have *some* experience.'

Jeanne shakes her head. 'He told me Sir Robert Dudley stayed in The Hague for most of the time, drinking wine with ambassadors, while others risked their lives in reckless battles.'

Penelope thought of Philip Sidney. Like her stepfather, he could have sat out the war in relative comfort as Governor of Flushing. He chose instead to lead their army into battle … and they all live with the consequences.

The high, mullioned upper windows of York House provide a good vantage point from which to watch the victory parade. Frances has come to keep Penelope company, and her daughters, Lucy and Essie, are allowed to watch with Frances' daughter, Elizabeth, now three years old, and a good companion for Essie, who is the same age.

Penelope sees something of Philip Sidney in his daughter, a quiet, sensitive girl. She knows he would have been so proud of her, and promises herself she will tell Elizabeth about her father's poetry one day, and give her a copy of *Astrophel and Stella*, when she is old enough to understand.

Lucy calls for Essie and Elizabeth to come to the window as the parade comes into view. The booming thump of drumbeats, clattering hooves, and the sound of marching men remind Penelope of Philip Sidney's funeral. A cheer rings out as the queen appears in her gilded state coach, escorted by Robert Dudley on his warhorse, his sword held high as a sign of their victory.

Penelope smiles at the sight of the children's eager faces.

'Let us pray you will not see the like in your lifetimes. We give thanks to God we have been spared from our enemies.'

Frances nods. 'It was God's work – and our fireships.'

Penelope studies the cavalrymen following behind the queen, and spots her brother's distinctive orange-and-white livery. She turns to Frances. 'My brother wrote to say they didn't see a single Spaniard.'

Frances gives Penelope a meaningful look. 'God was on our side, as strong winds forced the remaining Spanish ships north, scattering their fleet.'

'They've returned to Spain?'

'Our navy chased them as far as Scotland. They escaped by way of Ireland, but I heard many of their ships were wrecked along the way.' She glances at Lucy, playing a game with her daughter Elizabeth, and sees they aren't listening. 'The Spanish who managed to make their way ashore in Ireland were not treated well.'

They watch as the procession continues to St Paul's Cathedral for the service of thanksgiving. Penelope looks down at her children; Lucy, asking so many questions, Essie, and Philip Sidney's daughter Elizabeth. She says a silent prayer of thanks that they have all been spared.

Penelope weeps as she reads her mother's scribbled message. Robert Dudley has died of a fever at his lodge in Cornbury Park in Oxfordshire. She cries for her mother's loss, and her own regret that she never fully forgave her stepfather.

Too late, she wishes she'd told him she understood. He did his best for her, by making her a wealthy baroness, for their family, for her mother, for her children. She sends for her brother, who arrives having already heard the news.

'The queen is distraught. She's locked herself in her

bedchamber, with strict orders not to be disturbed.' Robert frowns. 'Her ministers argue about whether her door should be broken open, for her own good.'

Penelope shows him the note from their mother. 'I knew our mother was to accompany our stepfather to Buxton, to take the waters there.'

Robert reads the note and looks up at her. 'He spent much of his time at Tilbury in his tent, suffering with what they call the marsh fever.' He frowned. 'We didn't lose a single man through fighting, but many died from the fever. I suspected this visit to Buxton was an excuse not to attend the queen.'

'Why would he not wish to see the queen?'

'There is a dispute at court about the costs of the war with Spain. Our stepfather paid his men from his own pocket, and the Lord Treasurer told him the royal coffers are empty – which is a lie.'

'It seems history is repeated. I remember how our father became indebted to the Crown in the same way.'

Robert scowls. 'The fault is not with Her Majesty, but with her advisors, men like Lord Burghley and Robert Cecil, who see it as their duty to make sure she does not pay what she owes her men, however loyal their service.'

A thought occurs to Penelope. 'You are the head of our family now. You will need to make the arrangements for the funeral, and I will send for Richard Broughton, to take care of the legal consequences.'

'I've seen a copy of our stepfather's will. His wish is to be buried in the Beauchamp Chapel of the church of St Mary, Warwick, but there is a problem. He names his bastard son as his heir.'

'By Baroness Sheffield?' Penelope stared at her brother. 'You will inherit nothing—'

'And our mother's share will be challenged.' Robert scowled. 'Even in death, our stepfather treats us as his puppets.'

Penelope recalls Philip Sidney's warning, so long ago. *He enjoys having such power over us all. He takes advantage of your mother, to spite the queen. In truth, he's made a fool of everyone.*

The stabbing pain makes her bend double and grit her teeth. Her child is on the way, yet they are not ready. The midwife was sent for, and should have arrived days ago, but there has been no word from her. Penelope's mother is still in mourning, and she has not asked either Anne or Dorothy to travel to Leighs Priory.

Penelope shouts for Jeanne. 'Come quick!' She feels an unsettling wetness as her waters break, and braces herself for the next wave.

Jeanne stares wide-eyed as she realises what is happening. 'We're going to have to do this ourselves, my lady. There is no sign of the midwife, and I've no idea where to find one in time – but I've seen what she does.'

Penelope says a prayer for them all as the baby moves inside her. With Jeanne's help she makes it the short distance to her bed. 'We'll need help if anything goes wrong.'

Jeanne looks concerned. 'I'll have to leave you alone while I have the kitchens boil hot water.' She runs into the corridor, calling for servants.

Penelope tries to recall her loyal midwife's instructions as the waves of pain roll quicker. She should have arranged for Anne or her sister to come to York House to help her. Even her mother would have been better than having her baby alone.

She questions her faith. She will not accept it as God's will if she loses this child, but what will happen to her children if *she* were to die? Her husband would no doubt remarry a good Puritan wife, who will resent little Lucy, Essie and Robert. The thought gives her a renewed will to live, and see her new child brought safely into the world.

Jeanne rushes in with one of the chambermaids, and surprises Penelope by taking charge. 'That's good, now push when I tell you to.'

The pain eases a little, and Penelope tries to relax. Her midwife told her not to fight against nature, and her instinct tells her when to push. She feels Jeanne pulling the baby free, and hears her say it's a little girl.

Jeanne has seen what the midwife does enough times, and ties the cord, before severing it with a sharp kitchen knife. The baby shrieks with a reassuring wail as she wraps her in white linen and hands her to Penelope.

She stares into her large eyes. 'She is to be named Elizabeth.'

Jeanne smiles. 'After the queen?'

'After my mother-in-law, the first Lady Rich. It is time she was reconciled with my husband.'

Penelope holds her daughter close, and stares into her large eyes. 'You were too eager to come into this world, little Elizabeth.' She says a silent prayer of thanks to God.

The royal messenger brings an impressive christening gift from the queen, a hundred silver shillings, and her offer to act as godmother. The news is delivered by Jeanne, with a smile. 'You shall have to say your daughter is named for the queen now, my lady.'

Penelope is bemused. 'I can guess the hand behind this. It must be my brother, Robert.' She smiles. 'He's seen another way to please the queen, and told her about my little Elizabeth.'

'The messenger said Her Majesty will send one of her

ladies to represent her at the christening, and the money is intended as a reward for your midwife.'

'Well, my husband will be glad of this when I tell him – and as you served as my midwife, Jeanne, it is only fair that you shall have the reward.'

'It is a great deal of money, my lady.'

'You deserve it, Jeanne, with my gratitude. Where would I be if not for your quick thinking?'

The children's nurse, Martha, wakes Penelope. The lantern she carries casts a flickering yellow light, and reveals the despair on her face. 'I have grave news about your daughter, my lady.'

Penelope takes a moment to understand. 'Which of my daughters?' Her mind races as she hurriedly pulls a gown over her nightdress.

'Little Elizabeth.' Martha glances towards the door. 'It's best if you come.'

'Have you sent for the doctor?'

Martha looks close to tears. 'It is too late, my lady.'

'Too late?' Penelope hasn't worried too much for her daughters, despite her half-brother's death. Yet now she feels the icy dread return. She follows Martha down the dark corridor to the nursery. As she sees little Elizabeth, she understands.

Penelope kneels beside her daughter to pray for her. She stares at the perfect little face, which looks as if she is sleeping, yet her skin is cold to the touch. Her faith is tested as she gives in to the tears and weeps like never before. She cries for her little daughter, taken far too soon.

13

THE SCOTTISH KING

NEW YEAR 1589

The New Year celebrations at Richmond Palace offer Penelope respite from her grief. On an impulse, she sends a messenger to Rochford Hall, inviting her mother-in-law, Lady Elizabeth Rich, to accompany her. To her surprise, her husband decides to escort them.

'It's time we were seen together.' He watches her reaction, like he might when judging an accused man in the dock. 'I know what they say, and we must prove them wrong.'

Penelope recalls Anne Broughton's advice when she first married. *Lord Rich is a man and can be moulded, like any man. It will take time, but time is on your side.* It has taken years, yet her husband *is* changing; he showed rare compassion over the loss of their child. Yet their marriage is irretrievably damaged.

'We need suitable gifts for Her Majesty. I shall give her the silk forepart I embroidered during my confinement.' Her grief threatens to return, but she blocks the painful memory, a defence she's learned to master. 'It took me months, and is the finest work I've done.'

Her husband agrees. 'I shall give Her Majesty a purse of gold, and the same for my mother.' He gives her a knowing look. 'Lord Burghley claims the Treasury coffers are empty after the war with Spain, so it seems our queen has greater need of money than of foreparts.'

Penelope knows the queen better than her husband does. His purse of gold will find its way on to Lord Burghley's list of New Year's presents, but her personal gift will remind the queen of the sender long after the money is spent.

The great hall at Richmond has become an enchanted forest. Trees with gilded branches line the walls, and a thousand candles flicker like fireflies on a summer evening. The royal musicians dress as forest creatures, some in furs, others wearing antlers, and play lively tunes for the dancers.

Servants in emerald green and white Tudor livery carry pitchers of rich red wine, refilling silver cups as soon as they empty. The noisy festivities suggest a great deal has already been drunk by the time they arrive, and Baron Rich frowns in disapproval at the bacchanalian revelry.

Penelope is shocked at the change in the queen, who sits hunched in her chair like a crow on a gatepost, her dark sunken eyes missing nothing. Her orange wig draws attention to the paleness of her powdered face, but her majestic gown of cloth of gold shines with pearls and sparkles with precious jewels stolen from Spanish treasure galleons by men like Drake.

They join the queue of courtiers, and the queen's thin lips, red as blood, part in a smile, revealing browning teeth, as Penelope bows before her. 'Lady Rich. Our condolences on your loss.' She sounds tired, and her smile fades. 'Grief is a heavy cross we all must bear.'

Penelope looks into her dark eyes and guesses she still mourns the loss of Robert Dudley. 'May I present my mother-in-law, Your Majesty, Lady Elizabeth Rich.'

Her mother-in-law bows, and seems in awe of the queen.

Penelope thinks they must be much the same age, yet the queen looks frail as she acknowledges Lady Elizabeth with a nod. The moment passes and they move on, but Penelope's mind whirls with the consequences of what she's seen. The queen, who always seemed invincible, appears weakened by the stress of the past year's Spanish threat.

She is no longer the charismatic *Gloriana*, and looks like a dogged survivor, who should be planning her succession. The Armada is defeated, yet the cost of her conflicts with Spain and in Ireland must be a burden to her. The people grow restless after another poor harvest, and the threat of a Catholic revolt has never been greater.

Penelope takes a drink of wine, and the rich warmth improves her sombre mood. The musicians strike up a lively galliard, and several young men approach. Penelope glances at her husband out of courtesy. She knows his views on dancing, but he's talking with his mother. She prays that whatever happened between them is forgotten, as they are good company for each other.

She offers her hand to the most handsome of the waiting courtiers, who takes her fingers in his and leads her to join the dancers. It has been some years since she took part in a galliard, yet her memory of the steps soon returns, and her partner smiles at her in encouragement as they dance together.

About her own age, he wears his dark hair long, with a fashionably broad ruff, and a doublet and hose of cloth of silver, so must come from a noble background. She notes the affectation of a single large pearl in his ear, another court fashion encouraged by the queen.

The next dance is a volta, and he places his hands on either side of her waist. She puts her hands on his broad shoulders and he lifts her into the air as if she weighs nothing. He moves with effortless ease, and has a gift for anticipating her steps, as if reading her mind.

Onlookers applaud their elegance and skill, and Penelope glances in search of her husband as their dance comes to an end. He has retired to a far corner with his mother. She expects he will have something to say about her public display when they return.

She enjoys the thrill of dancing with a handsome partner, and of being the centre of attention. Her twenty-sixth birthday is in two weeks and dancing makes her feel young again. This night reminds her of her life of intrigue and excitement at court, a life she was forced to abandon too soon.

Leicester House has been seized by the queen in lieu of her late stepfather's debts, run up on her behalf, but her brother has already had it renamed Essex House, and claims ownership as part of his inheritance. Penelope resolves to move back to her apartments there, and to return to court.

Her partner seems in no hurry to leave her, and she follows him to the side of the dance floor. A servant offers them both another glass of wine, and she feels unsteady, placing her hand on his arm for support. The music begins again, and it's hard to speak to him over the noisy chatter of the revellers, so she leans closer.

'Thank you, sir. I cannot remember when I last danced at court.'

He stares into her eyes for a moment longer than is necessary. 'You are the perfect partner, Lady Rich, and it is my honour.'

'You have me at a disadvantage, sir.' She gives him a coy look. 'I don't believe we've met.'

'Charles Blount at your service, my lady.' He takes her hand and kisses her fingers, never taking his eyes from hers. 'I've been away fighting in the Netherlands for some years.'

'I've heard you rival my brother for the queen's affection.'

'That's true. We were introduced at court at the same time.'

He gives her a conspiratorial look. 'You know I challenged your brother to a duel?'

'I do – and that you beat him.' She frowned in disapproval. 'He wouldn't tell me what it was about, but his leg is scarred for life. You could have killed one another, and you both know the queen forbids duelling.'

'We fought over a golden queen, which Her Majesty gave me from her personal chess set, as her favour at a tournament. Your brother called me a fool for wearing it on a red ribbon.' He gave her an apologetic look. 'You are right: I should have known better.'

'So should my brother.'

He smiles. 'Well, you'll be glad to know we are now the best of friends, and are off on a great adventure together.'

'What is this great adventure?' Penelope knows her brother well enough to worry for his safety.

'The queen has agreed to send an English Armada to put an end to the threat from Spain, once and for all.'

Penelope confronts her brother Robert, and sees his eyes shine with ambition. 'You are no sailor, Robert. You are the queen's favourite and Master of the Horse. You should leave this English Armada to men like Sir Francis Drake.'

'I spoke to Captain Drake when he came to Richmond Palace for a meeting with the queen.' His tone is scathing. 'I asked him to give me command of one of the queen's ships, and he had the nerve to refuse me!'

'Taking on the Spanish is a great risk. Captain Drake will wish to have only the most experienced men as his commanders.'

'Drake's fleet has six royal galleons, and sixty armed merchantmen, as well as flyboats and pinnaces – more than enough to finish off the Spanish. The ships which survived their attempted invasion are being repaired in Spanish ports. They're vulnerable to attack, so we must take this opportunity to prevent them returning.'

Penelope understands. 'You still have the problem of convincing Captain Drake to allow you to take part.'

Her brother gives her a knowing look. 'Sir Roger Williams commands one of the queen's ships, the *Swiftsure*. We fought together in the Low Countries and I know Sir Roger will allow me to sail with him.'

A thought occurs to Penelope. 'Has the queen given permission for you to sail with Drake?'

He grins. 'She forbids me to go, but by the time she finds out, it will be too late.'

'You know the queen. You stand the risk of banishment from court when she learns you've disobeyed her, as she surely will – and her displeasure will reflect on us all.'

He nods. 'That's a risk I have to take. I've grown tired of trying to please the queen. The last year left me in debt, and my inheritance from our stepfather is being challenged by the Crown, but we will return with our holds filled with Spanish treasure, and I shall earn my share.'

Penelope sees his mind won't be changed. 'Promise to take care, Robert.' She places a comforting hand on his arm. 'I shall pray every day for your safe return.'

She will also pray for Charles Blount, who has stayed in her thoughts since the New Year's celebrations. He has something of Philip Sidney's mystery, and she knows he is attracted to her. Her pulse races as she hopes he will meet her, in secret, when he returns from their risky Spanish adventure.

$\approx$

Penelope cannot believe her mother's plan. 'You can't marry so soon.' She frowns. 'You are in mourning. What will people say?'

Her mother shrugs. 'I'm long past caring what people say about me, and Christopher sees no need to wait.'

'Christopher Blount was our stepfather's servant. He is a good deal younger than you, and has no prospects.' Her voice is raised.

'He was Master of the Horse, a respected position, and knighted on the battlefield for his courage. He's twelve years younger than me, and keeps me feeling young.' Her mother sounds pleased with herself. 'Your late stepfather made sure I am well provided for.'

Penelope shakes her head in exasperation. Christopher Blount is a cousin of Charles Blount. He is always around her mother – out riding, leading her carriage, and hunting with her. She resents the idea of a man only eight years older than her becoming her stepfather. But another, much greater, problem occurs to her.

'The man is a Catholic.'

Her mother gives Penelope a conspiratorial look, and lowers her voice so as not to be overheard. 'He wishes the Catholics to believe that, but he works for Sir Francis Walsingham, as an informer. He has done so for many years, and helped bring about the downfall of Mary, Queen of Scots.'

Penelope sees there is nothing she can do to persuade her mother, but decides she will ask Frances about Sir Christopher Blount. He may be an informer, but they were too close to the Babington plot for comfort, and it troubles her to know they have a Catholic spy in their midst.

Robert returns from his adventures in an unrepentant mood and, as Penelope expected, without a fortune in Spanish gold. She welcomes him with a jug of her best wine, and is glad to see him safe, and to hear of Charles Blount's safe return.

He sits opposite her, warming his hands on the log fire in the hearth, and takes a sip of wine, nodding in appreciation. 'Drake was furious when we caught up with his fleet. He said I'd displeased Her Majesty, who'd sent our grandfather to bring me back, but he was too late.'

Penelope shakes her head at her brother's recklessness. Their grandfather is seventy-five, and it seems unfair he should pay for her brother's actions. 'I'm surprised Captain Drake didn't send you straight home. The queen could have blamed him if any harm had come to you.'

'He couldn't spare a commander with Sir Roger's experience, and we'd sailed too far.' He sat back in his chair and stretched out his legs, warming his feet at the fire. 'We'd missed the battle at Coruña, where they burned the town and many Spanish ships, but Drake agreed we could join his attack on Lisbon, and said I could be the first ashore, to redeem myself.'

Penelope frowns at the thought. 'He put you in danger.'

Robert nods. 'I had to prove my worth, and we did well, capturing a fort, before I rode to Lisbon with Wat.'

Penelope stares at him in amazement. 'You didn't tell me Wat was with you.'

'For good reason. You would have tried your best to stop him going, but he's a man now, and must make his way in the world.' Robert grinned. 'Wat suffered like a dog with seasickness, but is back safe and well, and has had a taste of life as a soldier, which is what he always wished for.' He takes another drink of wine and stares into the flames. 'Lisbon proved too well defended, with high city walls, and they knew we didn't have enough men or supplies to hold them to siege.'

'You risked your life and reputation for nothing.' Penelope hears the disapproval in her voice.

'It's true we didn't capture Spanish treasure, but we plundered a good many merchant ships, some laden to the gunwales with copper.' He looks across at her. 'Wat and I hope to have our share of the profits from this adventure, once the ships and cargos are sold.'

'And the queen?'

Robert smiles. 'I am surprised to be welcomed back as a hero, and at how easily I'm forgiven by the queen. Despite her threats, she wished to know every detail of my adventures. I gave her an astrolabe I looted from the Spanish fort, and she was as pleased as if it were made from solid gold, rather than brass.'

'You are back in her favour?' Penelope stares at him in surprise. 'I expected there would be consequences for disobeying her so publicly.'

He nods. 'So did I, but I'm back to having to amuse her. Like her pet.' He frowns. 'She refuses to offer me the position of state I deserve. It's her way to punish our mother, through me.'

Penelope decides to share the concern on her mind since seeing the queen at the New Year's celebrations. 'The queen is growing older, Robert. And we must look to the future.'

He raises an eyebrow. 'You mean to talk of the succession?'

'I thought it might be timely to pledge our loyalty to King James of Scotland.' Her words hang in the air like the wisps of smoke escaping from the fire.

Robert shakes his head. 'The time will come, as sure as night follows day, but can you imagine what our enemies would make of it, if they knew we'd done such a thing?'

'Our enemies?'

He sits forwards in his chair, a serious look on his face.

'Robert Cecil watches me like a hawk that's seen a rabbit, and waits for the opportunity to bring me down.'

'I've never liked Robert Cecil, but why would he wish you harm?'

Robert looks at her, his eyes serious. 'The queen surrounds herself with ministers like the Cecils, and rogues like Walter Raleigh, who line their nests in the name of protecting her.' He frowns. 'Something should be done about them. They band together like rats in a cellar, watching and awaiting their chance.'

After her brother leaves, Penelope lies awake, alone in her bed, her mind whirring as she thinks over what she's been told. She's seen with her own eyes how the queen grows frailer with each passing year. She bans any talk of succession, and calls it treason, yet the country will be in disarray if she is too ill to rule.

She's had a little too much wine to drink, but with a flash of insight, she sees what her brother means; the queen's self-serving ministers await their chance to rule the country in her name, and will deal with anyone who tries to step in their way.

An idea occurs to her. Like Philip Sidney in *Astrophel and Stella*, she too can conceal her identity. She will write to King James, but sign her letter *Rialta*, and refer to her brother as *Ernestus*, pledging support for his succession to the English Crown. Jeanne's husband, Jean, will deliver the letter, but can have no knowledge of the content.

Unable to sleep with the excitement of her intrigue, Penelope rings her bell to summon a servant to bring her writing paper, pen and ink. She smiles to herself as she seals her letter with dark wax, glad to have done something for her brother. She chooses *Victor* as her code name for the King of Scotland, who will thank them, one day, for their declaration of loyalty.

14

A DANGEROUS AFFAIR

FEBRUARY 1590

Penelope counts to five before a rumbling clap of thunder follows the flash of lightning, rattling the windows like a bad omen. The winter storms and lashing rain ravage the city, tearing off roof tiles and stirring up the icy waters of the River Thames with waves too dangerous for a wherry.

She visits her husband in his bedchamber, and gestures for his nurse to leave them. His illness started with a hacking cough, then he lost his appetite and the doctor ordered him to take to his bed. She sits in the chair at his bedside, and wonders if he will live.

His death would free her yet, despite all that has happened between them, he *is* the father of their children, and she has yet to tell him she carries another child. They have an understanding: she no longer asks permission to do as she pleases, but she prays for his recovery, and spends long hours at his house, helping his nurses.

Another flash lights up the room and Penelope counts to three before the sharp crack of thunder vibrates the oak boards beneath her feet. The threat of fire is a constant worry in St

Bartholomew's, with many old timber buildings built close together. One lightning strike could mean disaster.

Her husband opens his tired eyes and stares as if surprised to see her. He'd always been so strong and independent, and seemed to enjoy the power he had over her. He has yet to speak of it, but she is sure he hates the way their roles have been reversed.

'Have you eaten today?' She wishes she'd asked the nurse, as her husband doesn't always speak the truth.

'I could manage a little broth.' His voice sounds hoarse and breathless, and his doctor fears his throat is damaged by the illness.

Penelope rings the bell to summon a chambermaid. 'A bowl of warm broth, and a little bread, if you please.'

Her young maid bobs a curtsey and closes the door. Penelope turns to her husband. 'I'm returning to court, and will live in my apartment at Essex House.' She waits for an answer but he doesn't reply. 'I plan to keep the children with me in London, and will need Jeanne and her husband, as well as the children's nurse, Martha.'

'As you wish.' He sounds resigned, as if he no longer has the energy to disagree. He knows there are over a hundred servants at Essex House, yet also knows there is nothing he can do to stop her.

His vulnerability makes Penelope feel a twinge of conscience. 'You are welcome to come and see the children.'

He doesn't answer, but nods in acknowledgement. A shower of hailstones rattles against the leaded windowpanes, breaking the silence. She reaches out a hand and adjusts his feather pillows, so he can sit upright.

Her maid brings a wooden tray with a bowl of steaming broth, a silver spoon, and a slice of manchet bread. 'Chicken broth, my lady, and the bread is still warm from the oven.' She

---

places the tray on the side table and looks relieved to be allowed to go.

Penelope expects to have to feed her husband, but he takes the spoon and manages to eat some broth. She smiles at his small victory. 'I thank God you are doing better, Robert.' She hasn't called him by his name for longer than she can remember, yet it is too late for her to feel affection for him.

An air of sadness hangs over Walsingham House in Seething Lane, close to the Tower of London. Sir Francis Walsingham, the queen's principal secretary and spymaster, has died after a short illness. Penelope calls to pay her respects, and Frances appears with her daughter, Elizabeth, now aged five, both wearing mourning dress.

Frances turns to her daughter. 'Please play in the garden, Elizabeth, while I speak to Lady Rich.'

Penelope watches her go, and sees how Elizabeth resembles her little Essie. The same age, they could be twins, or at least mistaken for sisters. 'I'm sorry for your loss, Frances. I didn't know your father was unwell.'

Tears glisten in Frances' blue eyes. 'Father loved his work, but it cost him dearly.' Her voice wavers as she remembers. 'He has suffered with poor health these past months, and I pleaded with him to rest, but he insisted on working.'

'Her Majesty always placed quite a burden of responsibility on him. She took him for granted, as she did my own father.'

'My father had to meet the costs of his network of agents from his own pocket. He worried about having so little to show for more than thirty years of loyal service. He was buried in haste, at midnight, to outwit his creditors.' Frances frowns. 'I expect the Treasury will seize this house to repay his debts. I will have to take Elizabeth to live with my mother, at Barn Elms.'

'I'm sorry, Frances. You are welcome to come and stay with us at Essex House, if you wish. We have plenty of room, and I will be glad of your company.' She smiles. 'Elizabeth is good company for Essie, and they can share tutors.'

Frances nods. 'I have much to do here, sorting out my father's affairs, but thank you.' She leads Penelope into her late father's study and closes the door. 'There is a troubling matter I have to tell you about.' Her face becomes serious. 'My father discovered your secret, and told me, so I could warn you.'

Penelope's first thought is that she refers to Philip Sidney, then her pulse races as she guesses it must be her more serious secret, which could have her locked up in the Tower, and her brother as well. She holds her breath as she waits for Frances to tell her.

'I cannot believe you took such a risk, writing to the King of Scotland.' Frances gives her a look of disapproval. 'It seems your code fooled no one.'

Penelope is glad of the chance to explain. 'You have seen how frail the queen is now, Frances, but she is never going to name her successor. We must think of the future. I wrote those letters not for myself, but for my brother. My code was a simple precaution, and if anyone is punished it should be me.' She looks up at Frances. 'Do you know who your father told about my letters?'

'No one, as far as I know. I found his notes before Robert Cecil's men came for the rest of his papers.' She glances at the stone fireplace. 'I burned them, just in time, as they searched the whole house from the attic to the cellars, and took everything away.'

'I owe you a debt, Frances.'

'I am afraid this might not be over yet, Penelope. Robert Cecil has taken control of my father's entire network of informers, and could discover your correspondence with King James. If he does, he's sure to find some way to use it against your brother.'

'I'm grateful for what you have done to keep my secret. I dread to think what the queen would say.'

'I should tell you I have another motive.' Frances manages a smile. 'I have fallen in love with your brother, and would be glad of your blessing.'

'Of course you have my blessing.' Penelope feels a weight lifted from her, and smiles. 'I can think of no one better for my brother.'

The look of sadness returns to Frances' eyes. 'I wish the queen would say the same. I fear she will refuse to give her consent. I'm not of noble birth, and cannot even raise a dowry.'

Penelope shakes her head. 'The queen would refuse permission for whoever my brother asks to marry. I shall speak to Robert.' She gives Frances a knowing look. 'It will not be the first time he's risked Her Majesty's displeasure – or the last.'

Penelope has learned her lesson, and decides not to remind her mother her child is due. The windows of her bedchamber are open to the mild breeze from the river, a blessing in the August heat. She imagines her husband, far away in Essex, on his knees in the chapel at Leighs Priory, praying for another son.

He has recovered from his winter illness. He takes more interest in the workings of Parliament than of court, and visits to see the children, but never wants to see her, or asks how she is. They keep up their pretence of marriage to the world, but not to each other.

She thinks of when her other children were born. Lucy, the difficult first one, Essie, and Robert, born in the middle of the night. She tries to put the sad memory of her little daughter Elizabeth's short life from her mind. Her sister Dorothy cannot be with her, as she has a new daughter, and has named her Penelope.

Anne Broughton will also not be with her this time, as she is blessed with a longed-for daughter, named Mary. As expected, Frances is with her mother at Barn Elms, in Putney. Only her loyal friend and companion Jeanne is here, as well as her faithful midwife.

This time there is to be no fuss, no rushing or worry. Penelope tries her best to relax, and closes her eyes. She says a prayer for her unborn child, and promises to trust in the will of God. She hears the church bells ringing to call the faithful to vespers, and knows it is late afternoon.

Her midwife is here, and Jeanne sits at her bedside. Penelope trusts Jeanne as she would a sister, and will miss her when she returns to France with her husband. She takes Jeanne's hand in hers, and they know there will not be much longer to wait.

For once, the child comes quickly, and they are ready. She knows to let her body do as it will, and not to fight the pain, which seems less severe than she remembers. The midwife encourages her, and she is rewarded by the sudden cry of her fifth child.

Exhausted but happy, Penelope holds her baby and stares into his large eyes, with the special love only a new mother can feel. Her husband's prayers have been answered with a fine healthy boy. The midwife waits to bind him in linen swaddling and hand him over to his wet nurse.

'What name have you chosen for him, my lady?'

'Henry.' Penelope smiles. 'My little Henry Rich.'

Jeanne leans closer and lets the baby grasp her finger with his tiny pink hand. 'Henry must work extra hard, as a second son, my lady.'

Penelope nods. 'As a second son he will find it easier to marry who he wishes, and will no doubt have a happier life than little Robert.'

The black-robed minister sounds nervous as he asks in a hesitant voice if anyone knows of good reason why Sir Robert Devereux, Earl of Essex, and Lady Frances Sidney, should not be joined in holy matrimony. They wait in silence for an answer.

The echoing chapel is empty except for Penelope, Frances' mother, Lady Walsingham, their trusted family lawyer, Master Richard Broughton, and Robert's loyal friend, Anthony Bagot, who have come to witness their wedding.

Penelope knows of a good reason to stop the wedding. Like so many before him, her brother decided not to risk the queen's refusal by asking her permission. There will be consequences, but they have decided their marriage must be a secret for as long as possible. By the time the queen finds out it will be too late.

Penelope smiles at Frances, who holds one hand over her middle, another secret. Only Penelope and the widowed Lady Walsingham know Frances carries a child, too small yet to be visible under her loose gown. Frances told her they have planned to name him Robert, after his father – or Ursula, after her mother, if the child is a girl.

As she watches them together, Penelope cannot help wondering if she has witnessed a love match, or a marriage of convenience. Robert needs an heir, and Frances needs someone to care for her now her father is gone. Her brother could have his pick of the queen's eligible ladies, and she suspects he chose Frances out of loyalty to Philip Sidney.

Penelope is enjoying improving her apartments at Essex House, her main home now the lease is finally in her brother's name. She's been saving her husband's generous allowance, and has bought a new bed, canopied with black velvet, edged with gold and black damask, with gold and silver filigree ornaments.

Luxurious hangings of silk and velvet, trimmed with gold lace, replace the dusty tapestries and paintings left by her late stepfather. Rich carpets, imported at great expense from the mysterious East, cover the ancient oak floorboards, deadening the sound.

Robert and Frances are to have her mother's former apartments, as she remains at Wanstead since her unpopular marriage to Christopher Blount. Frances' daughter, Elizabeth, has also moved in with Lucy and Essie. Jeanne and her husband deal with the running of the household, now numbering over a hundred servants, including grooms and gardeners.

The celebration banquet after her brother's secret wedding is held in the great hall, where Robert Dudley once entertained the queen. Many of Robert's close friends and companions stay in the guest apartments, and Penelope is pleased to see Charles Blount is among them.

He takes her hand as he bows, and kisses it. 'Her Majesty once said of your mother she would have no other court than hers, yet it seems you have a new one here at Essex House, and you are its queen, my lady.'

She smiles at his flattery. 'Treasonous talk, sir, but you can be sure you are among friends here, where our secrets are safe.'

Charles Blount sits at Penelope's side at the wedding feast and, for once, neither feels the need to hide their true feelings.

No one present disapproves, and they make the perfect couple. When the servants clear the tables for dancing, there is a new connection between them and they never once take their eyes from each other.

As the evening draws on, Robert's wedding guests grow rowdy, and Charles suggests they find somewhere they can talk. Penelope leads him to the privacy of her apartment. She pours her best French wine into two perfectly matched Venetian glasses, and hands one to him, a twinkle of mischief in her eye.

He raises his glass before he drinks. 'I would like to propose a toast. To a fresh start.'

She raises her glass. 'A fresh start.' She smiles. 'I'd not thought of it, but that's exactly what I need.' She takes a sip of her wine. 'I wish to put the past behind me, and make the most of the time we have left.'

Charles Blount looks serious. 'I cannot promise you much, other than my complete devotion, and my true love.' He takes a blue velvet bag from his pocket and hands it to her.

Penelope reaches inside and takes out a miniature portrait of him, inscribed with the words *Amor Amoris Premium*. Love the reward of love.

'You must have guessed how this evening would end.' She laughs. 'This is the work of Nicholas Hilliard. He is more than a little in love with me.'

'He named his daughter Penelope, in your honour.'

'I am her godmother – and he painted a miniature of me, which I sent to King James of Scotland.'

Charles raises an eyebrow. 'What was his reply?'

'I only know he seemed pleased to have my brother's support.'

'Your brother knows of this?'

'I should tell you I have no secrets from my brother.'

'Even about your feelings for me?'

She nods. 'I don't wish for a furtive affair, but an open one.' Penelope raises her glass. 'A fresh start.'

'My only income is from the queen's grant of Keeper of the New Forest, and my pension. My father squandered the family fortune in the foolish pursuit of alchemy, and my elder brother, William, inherited his title. As a younger son, I expect to inherit nothing of consequence.'

'I'm married to one of the richest men in the country, and he's taught me that to be happily in love is worth more to me than anything.'

'I would also like to have a son, one day.'

This time Penelope raises an eyebrow. 'I've found providing a son can take a little longer than you might expect, but I'm only twenty-seven, so time is on our side.'

'What about your husband?'

'Have you noticed how similar my Essie looks to my brother's stepdaughter, Elizabeth?'

'Are you telling me they share the same father?'

'Who can know?' She smiles. 'I can tell you it is a possibility, which my husband is no doubt aware of, although he's never spoken of it.'

She leads him into her bedchamber and he stares at her new bed in amazement. 'I've never seen one like it.'

Penelope smiles. 'My brother teases me that it doesn't look at all like a matrimonial bed, but a lover's bed … which it is.'

He closes the door and turns the key in the lock, then takes her in his arms and kisses her. Penelope feels his passion, and returns his kiss with all the longing that has built up since their first meeting at Richmond Palace. She undresses him, savouring every moment. His body is more muscular than she'd imagined. The physique of a man well used to fighting and riding hard.

She traces the line of a jagged white scar on his thigh with her finger. 'Was this from jousting, or from your duelling?'

'A bullet wound, from the Battle of Zutphen.'

'Zutphen? You fought in the same battle as Philip Sidney?'

A shadow passes over his face, then he smiles. 'The wound was deep, but God saw fit for me to live to see this day.'

Until now, any mention of Philip Sidney has brought a flood of memories, but this is her fresh start, and time to move on. As they climb into her luxurious bed, Penelope has no sense of guilt, and is without a care for who knows, or what they might say. She surrenders to Charles, and they begin their new life together.

15

LIFE AND DEATH

JANUARY 1591

St Olave's Church was chosen for the christening, being just across the road from Walsingham House, within sight of the Tower of London. The oily scent of tallow candles blends with the musty smell of the pews, and relentless rain drums on the rafters as they gather around the ancient stone font.

The future Earl of Essex cries out as the stern-faced minister plunges him into the cold water of the font, and names him Robert Devereux, in the name of the Father, the Son, and the Holy Ghost. By tradition, Frances is absent, recovering from her ordeal, but her mother, Lady Ursula Walsingham, looks proud of her new grandson.

Their grandfather, Sir Francis Knollys, pleased to act as the child's godfather, hands Robert the gift of a leather-bound prayer book. Penelope suspects her brother would rather have a purse of money, as he is still deep in debt, but their wealthy grandfather's Puritan belief is that they must make their own way in the world.

For the sake of appearances, Robert has invited Penelope's

husband to be a godfather. This is the first time they have been together in public for many months, but few would guess they lead separate lives. There are only three years between them, but his greying beard and black robe make him seem much older than Penelope.

As the short service ends, she wraps her fur-lined cape closer, and slips away to visit Frances across the road at Walsingham House. Their lawyer, Richard Broughton, has managed to transfer the lease to Lady Walsingham, despite the efforts of her late husband's creditors to have it sold to pay his debts.

She finds Frances sitting at her fireside. 'Your son is baptised, although we could hardly hear the minister over his wailing, and the hammering of the rain.' She pulls off her wet cape, and takes the empty seat opposite Frances.

The well-worn leather arms suggest the chair has seen much use, and she guesses it must have been Sir Francis Walsingham's favourite. The shadow of his presence still haunts this house, but Frances will join them at Essex House once her father's affairs are finalised.

Glad of the heat of the crackling log fire, she warms her hands and looks across at Frances with a frown of concern. 'How are you feeling?'

Frances manages a smile. 'I am still a little weak, but I'm glad it is over.'

'My brother tells me the queen banished you from court, which is a shame. But court is not what it was.'

Frances looks resigned. 'I have my liberty, and it's a relief to know neither of us is to be sent to the Tower.' She gives Penelope a wry look. 'I'm sure the new baby will keep me busy enough.'

Penelope agrees. 'Others have not been so lucky. My sister Dorothy's husband, Thomas, was sent to the Fleet prison.' She shakes her head at the memory. 'Robert said he has never seen the queen in such a rage. She accused him of conspiracy, by keeping the truth from her.'

'We believe Robert Cecil was the one who told her. He knew from the day we first married, but it's something of a mystery why he chose to keep silent about us for so long.'

'Robert Cecil does nothing without good reason.' Penelope frowns. 'I suspect he planned to use his knowledge to put pressure on my brother for some purpose.' A thought occurs to her. 'Do you think Robert Cecil has a spy in our household at Essex House?'

'I'm certain of it.' Frances stares into the fire for a moment. 'No doubt he has more than one, as there is plenty of opportunity. You have so many servants, it's impossible to be sure of them all. We could not keep our secret forever, so it was really just a matter of time.'

'Well, your secret was kept for long enough.' Penelope smiles. 'My brother isn't known for his discretion, and has been celebrating the birth of the future Earl of Essex with his companions in every tavern in London. I hoped becoming a father would change him, but he still acts like a single man.'

'Do you think he's grown tired of me?' Her sharp question hangs in the air, like a glowing ember with the potential to destroy all it touches.

Penelope hesitates. This is not the moment to tell Frances that Robert is having an affair with one of the queen's maids, Elizabeth Southwell.

'You know how impetuous he can be, Frances. He struggles to keep his mind on anything for long, before he's planning some new adventure. He was always like that as a boy, and has yet to learn it's no way to live his life as a man.'

~

Charles Blount lies sleeping next to Penelope in her bed in their new home at Wanstead, now owned by her brother Robert. Her mother no longer lives at the manor house, which has too many memories for her. Close to London, Wanstead suits Penelope, offering more privacy, with forty acres of walled fields and forests. Wanstead is also a day's ride from Leighs Priory, where her children have returned to live with their father.

Penelope's husband could have made life difficult for her, yet seems to understand he's lost her to Charles Blount. He allows her to visit their children whenever she wishes, in return for her keeping up the pretence of their marriage, and pays her a generous allowance – as if nothing has changed.

Charles is more relaxed at Wanstead Manor, and has proved well suited to Penelope. In his quiet way, he is as literary as Philip Sidney, and shares her interest in French poetry, which he reads to her on long winter evenings. Also like Philip, he is a champion jouster and wears Penelope's favours with pride, even at the queen's Accession Day tournament.

Penelope shakes him awake, and he gives her hand a drowsy kiss. 'I want to talk to you about my brother's latest plan.'

He stretches and turns to face her. 'His expedition to Normandy?'

Penelope nods. 'I wish to support my brother's ambitions, but wonder if becoming the chief supporter of King Henri of France is ill-advised – dangerous, even.'

Charles lies back on the bed. 'I thought the queen would forbid him from going to France, yet she's made him Captain General of her army.' He smiles, and turns to look at her. 'I am a little jealous of how she favours him, despite the way he disrespects her.'

Penelope gives him a stern look. 'I hope you're not thinking of going to France with him?'

He laughs, and glances at her middle, their well-kept secret – for now, at least. 'I have good reason to stay safe at home, and Her Majesty insists I remain at court.'

'Richard Broughton told me my brother instructed him to sell off Keyston Manor to reduce his debts, but I suspect he plans to use the money to equip an army in his new livery of orange and gold.'

'I hope this campaign isn't the ruin of your brother, as it was for your father. I'll bet the queen hasn't agreed to pay him.' Charles frowns. 'He should spend the money he has on weapons and supplies, not fancy clothes. The Catholic League will not be impressed by his finery.'

'What do you think I should do?'

Charles thinks for a moment. 'His cause is the defence of Protestant France against the scourge of the Catholics. There are plenty of wealthy Protestants who would sponsor his campaign.' He gives her a wry look. 'Your husband, for one – and have you asked your grandfather, Sir Francis Knollys?'

Penelope smiles. 'You are right. And I have nothing to lose by asking them both.'

The letter from the port of Dieppe bears her brother's Essex seal. Penelope smiles as she reads his laboured style. Their grandfather and her husband have helped to meet the costs, but she worries for Robert's safety, and for their brother Wat, who again wishes to make a reputation for himself, fighting at Robert's side in France.

In their own way, both her brothers are determined to restore the reputation of the Devereux name, and she wants to help them. The problem is that, as with their father, the lure of fame and fortune seems to obscure the practical issues of campaigning in another country.

Her brother writes that it took longer than he expected to raise three thousand soldiers, and some four hundred cavalrymen. Easterly winds kept them waiting in Dover harbour for conditions to improve. After a risky crossing in heavy seas, they'd arrived in Dieppe, but they'd been waiting for three weeks for King Henri to agree the queen's treaty.

Penelope wishes she had stopped him going, as he's ended up like their father: paying his men to do nothing. He writes that their camp is in fields outside the town, which the rains turn to muddy marshland. Supplies are running low, and the men are growing restless.

He makes no mention of their brother Wat, but seems in good spirits, saying that once he's taken the city of Rouen, there will be reward enough for them all, and they will return as heroes. Penelope folds the letter and says a prayer for them to return home safely.

Robert Cecil's summons to see him in Whitehall offered no clue as to the reason, yet Penelope senses it cannot be good news. His office reminds her of her husband's austere study. Papers are piled high on his desk, and there is no decoration on the walls, only shelves with rows of dusty, leather-bound ledgers.

Many years have passed since she first tried to charm Robert Cecil, and since then they've had a wary truce. He stands as she is shown in, his chair scraping on the tiled floor. He wears the black robes of a lawyer, with a starched ruff and a black hat with a brim that looks too big for his head. His reddish beard is trimmed to a point, and she finds it hard to believe they are the same age.

He gestures for her to sit. 'Thank you for coming to see me,

Lady Rich.' His face is stern. 'I shall come straight to the point. Our informer in the court of King James of Scotland has made me aware of your correspondence.'

Penelope sees the calculating way Robert Cecil studies her. He is planning something. There is no point in denying what she's done. Her pulse races; he could call the queen's guards and have her arrested for less. 'If you've seen my letters, you know they are innocent.'

He raises an eyebrow. 'You present me with something of a dilemma, Lady Rich, but I have a solution which will benefit us both.'

Penelope sits back in her chair, and tries to appear calm, but her mind whirls with the possibilities, none of which are good. She hardly dares to ask what price must be paid for his silence. 'What do you propose?'

'That you write one more letter.' He holds up a finger to emphasise his point. 'It seems King James appreciates your support, so I would like you to tell him he can also count on mine.'

Penelope stares at him in amazement. Then she remembers: the queen calls him her *pygmy*, ridiculing his hunched back. She's seen how others mock him too. She doesn't trust Robert Cecil, the newest member of the Privy Council, who helps his father act as Secretary of State. She knows from Frances he is also the queen's new spymaster, and controls Walsingham's network of informers. Robert Cecil is a powerful man.

'*Exitus acta probat*. The outcome justifies the deed.'

He gives her an appraising look, and the ghost of a smile appears on his face. 'Ovid. Let us hope the outcome *does* justify the deed, Lady Rich, but you can be sure that if anything of our discussion becomes known, I shall deny it.'

❧

Robert Carey arrives at Wanstead Manor having ridden hard from France. A good friend of her brother, Robert Carey commands one of his regiments, and is the queen's trusted messenger for good reason. The haunted look in his eyes puts Penelope on her guard. There must be good reason for him to stop at her home on his mission to deliver an urgent message to the queen.

'It is my sad duty to tell you that your brother Walter has been killed in battle, Lady Rich.' He stares at the ground. 'I am sorry for your loss. He was a good man, and a good friend to me.'

Penelope feels unsteady on her feet as memories flash before her of Wat begging their mother not to be sent away to York, and of his beaming smile as he learned how to fight with a sword. She'd promised to protect him, and now he was dead. She brushes a tear from her cheek and fights to remain composed.

'How did it happen?'

Robert Carey hesitates, as if trying to think how much to tell her. 'He died a hero, at the siege of Rouen.'

Penelope shakes her head. 'I deserve to know the truth, not the tale you will tell the queen.'

Robert Carey nods. 'Wat was within four miles of Rouen, leading a skirmish to test the resolve of their defences. He was hit in the face with a musket shot, and died instantly. You have my word he showed great courage, and saved the lives of many others by making the enemy reveal their positions.'

'Was he buried in France?' Her voice sounds cold.

Robert Carey looks uncertain. 'That is the normal practice but, in truth, I don't know.'

'I wish my brother's body brought back to England for burial.' Another tear runs down her face. 'I owe him that much.' A thought occurs to her. 'How is Robert?'

'He asked me to tell you he is returning soon. He has been summoned by the queen to explain why he disobeyed her orders, but is beside himself with grief, and had succumbed to a fever, so I have come in his place to plead his case to Her Majesty.' He frowns. 'We worried he might die, but he is strong, and is making a good recovery, thank God.'

After he leaves, she kneels in prayer for her youngest brother and is overcome by her grief. She prays for Robert, who will no doubt blame himself, and for Wat's new wife, Margaret, who she's never even met. Her only comfort is that Wat didn't suffer at the end – if Robert Carey told the truth…

Her brother Robert arrives late in the evening and sends her maid to wake her. He embraces Penelope, and speaks in a whisper. 'The burden of responsibility for our brother's death weighs heavily on me, dear sister.' Despair echoes in his voice.

She holds him close in a moment of shared grief. 'Robert Carey told me. He said our brother died a hero.'

'He was fearless.' Robert looks close to tears. 'He would still be alive if I hadn't allowed him to come with me to France.'

'You cannot blame yourself.' Penelope studies him and frowns. 'You've lost weight. Robert Carey told me you suffered with a fever, and they feared you might die.'

'I sent Carey back to plead for me. Do you know if he saw the queen?'

'He called to see me on his way back to France. He said she flew into a rage when she saw your letter, so I am surprised to see you.'

'I was too hasty to return to England. No doubt Robert Carey is arriving in Rouen now, to tell me I have permission to stay.'

'Don't be too quick to throw your life away in some heroic gesture, Robert. You're my only brother now, and you have two sons to think about.'

'Two sons?' He stares at her in bewilderment.

'Do you not know your mistress has given you a son?'

'You mean Elizabeth Southwell?'

'How many mistresses do you have?'

Robert frowns. 'As God is my witness, I had no idea Elizabeth carried my child.'

'There was quite a scandal at court. Thomas Vavasour took the blame, and is imprisoned in the Tower for his sins.'

He stares at Penelope in disbelief. 'I must do what I can to have him set free. Thomas Vavasour fought with me in the Low Countries. Why would he risk his career to protect my reputation?'

She gives him a knowing look. 'You had better ask that question of your mistress.'

'Is she here?'

'I felt sorry for her, and sent her to our mother in Drayton Basset. She was certain you are the boy's father.'

'But the queen doesn't suspect?'

'If she did, it is *you* who would be languishing in a cell in the Tower of London.'

'She plays her games with me as if I were a court jester!'

Penelope smiles. 'There are worse positions at court.'

'Do you mock me?' Robert scowls.

'Jesters get away with saying whatever they wish and, in my experience, are never quite as foolish as they seem.'

'I deserve better. Her Majesty seems determined to ruin me, even though I yield to her will.'

Penelope places her hand on his arm. 'You might be the Captain General of the queen's army, but you are still my little brother and should listen to my counsel. Be glad you have what you want. She has allowed you to return.'

'It's the manner of her doing it…' Robert curses.

'Don't you see? Her list of grievances to the King of France is her way to save face. She wishes you to have a second chance, and you must seize it with both hands, for Wat. His death cannot be without reason.'

16

THE TOWER

JANUARY 1592

The snow continues to fall as the passing bell tolls for Wat's funeral, the first time Penelope's family have all been together since they left Chartley. Her mother, swathed in black furs against the cold, is there with Sir Christopher Blount, who bows to Penelope.

Dorothy has made the long journey from Wales, despite the dangers of icy roads. She arrives without her husband, Sir Thomas Perrot, but is escorted by their uncle, George Devereux, from Lamphey Palace. She hugs Penelope and looks tearful. 'My husband has been imprisoned without charge. I hope you can help.'

'Of course.' Penelope glances at their family lawyer, Richard Broughton, who is there with his wife Anne. 'There must be a reason, and we should take comfort that there is no charge, but we must get to the bottom of this as soon as we can.'

They stand in the arched doorway of the old church, sheltering from the sleet as they welcome the mourners. Penelope's husband arrives, a grim-faced stranger, dressed in black. She hasn't seen him since his mother's funeral, before Christmas. He avoids her eye, glancing instead at her broadening middle, evident despite her thick winter cape. He says nothing.

She was never close to his mother who, like her husband, was too Puritan. But they were bonded together by marriage, and Penelope helped reconcile her with her son, so will miss her. One of her worst fears is that she will end up like Lady Elizabeth Rich, a lonely widow, watching her children becoming estranged from her, or dying, one by one, like ripe fruit falling from a tree.

Penelope's grandfather, Sir Francis Knollys, is seventy-eight and looks frail as he escorts Wat's young widow, Margaret. He wears a heavy black cloak and walks with a stick, his back stooped. Wat was a favourite of his, and he insists on reading from the Bible at the service.

Margaret stares at Penelope with cold, questioning eyes as they pass, as if she somehow holds her responsible. Margaret is back at King's Manor with Countess Catherine Hastings, who will no doubt be seeking a new husband for her, too soon.

Penelope's brother Robert arrives without Frances, who has given him another son, named Walter, in memory of their brother and father. He should be celebrating, yet the dark sorrow in his eyes reveals how deeply he feels the loss, and the unwitting part he played in Wat's death.

He speaks quietly to Penelope. 'I swore to avenge our brother, but the queen ordered me to return before my work was done.' He scowls. 'I wished to carry Wat's coffin into the city of Rouen and hold his funeral in the great cathedral there, where Richard the Lionheart is buried.'

Penelope shakes her head. 'Wat would have preferred to return home, so we can all say farewell.'

He nods. 'After the service, we will escort his coffin to St Peter's Church in Carmarthen where he will be laid to rest beside our father.' He glances at her middle. 'I do not expect you to come, but Dorothy is returning with us, as well as Sir Christopher, and Charles Blount.'

Penelope hugs her brother, to show she understands he carries the burden of their brother's death. His campaign in France is over, and although they halted the advance of the Catholic League, it is considered a failure. Their siege of Rouen was lost without King Henri's support, and Robert received a terse note from the queen, summoning him home, saying it did not befit an earl of the realm to be used on so futile an errand.

Robert's Welsh retainer, Gelly Meyrick, now Member of Parliament for Carmarthen, wears a sprig of rosemary in his hatband, in the old tradition, and bows to Penelope and Dorothy. 'Your brother was a fine man, my ladies. We shall all miss him, and will not see his like again.'

Richard Bagot has ridden from Chartley with Anthony Bagot. Penelope hasn't seen either of them for some time, and their greying beards remind her of the passing years. Anthony Bagot catches her eye, and the old connection flickers like the bright flame of a candle – still there, despite all she has been through.

The mournful clanging of the church bell stops, and her brother Robert takes their mother's arm and leads her up the tiled nave to where the coffin, draped in black, waits on a trestle. They stop to look at Wat's sword and helmet on the coffin, then take their place in the front pew, next to Wat's widow, Margaret.

Penelope and Dorothy sit behind them, and she sees how Robert stares at their brother's coffin as the service begins. This could have been *his* funeral, but for luck and the grace of God. At least Wat's death was so sudden he would not have suffered. The minister calls them to prayer, and Penelope clasps her hands together and thanks God for that small mercy.

Anne Broughton arrives at Essex House to help Penelope and, once they are alone, gives her a questioning look. 'Is this Charles Blount's child?'

Penelope nods, feeling defensive about Anne's critical tone. 'I don't expect your approval, Anne, but my husband knows, and the child shall have his surname.'

'I'm not sure that makes it any better, but I count you as one of my oldest friends. I cannot leave you to cope alone at such a time, particularly as your sister Dorothy cannot be here to support you.'

'Dorothy wrote to say she cannot leave her home for fear of looters.' Penelope frowns. 'I know her husband is in prison, but it seems the local people have become judge and jury, and await their chance. It's unjust for Dorothy to be punished, especially as her Thomas has yet to be charged with any crime.'

'Richard told me there is talk in the city that her father-in-law, Sir John Perrot, faces a serious charge of treason against Her Majesty, and is locked up in the Tower of London.'

'Treason?' Penelope recalls the chilling threat of a traitor's death. Not for the first time, this feels too close to home. 'What is Dorothy's father-in-law accused of?'

'Richard believes his actions as Lord Deputy of Ireland have finally caught up with him, thanks to Sir Christopher Hatton, who accuses him of boasting that he was King Henry's son, and of saying immodest words about the queen.'

Penelope frowns at the thought. 'I remember an allegation that he seduced Sir Christopher Hatton's daughter, Elizabeth. Could this be him taking his revenge?'

Anne nods. 'The rumours ruined his daughter's reputation, so let us pray Sir Thomas has only been arrested as a precaution.' She looks thoughtful. 'Have you considered giving your mother another chance? There is time to send for her, if you wish.'

'I know better than to invite my mother to come here and help me. In any event, she seems content with her life in Drayton Basset with Christopher Blount. I confess I have missed Jeanne since she returned to France with her husband. It seems it is just the two of us now.'

Penelope is back in her luxurious bed, canopied with black velvet, edged with gold and black damask. Her brother Robert spoke the truth when he called this extravagance her *lover's bed*. Paid for from her husband's allowance, this is where her child was conceived, so is an appropriate place for her lying in.

She tries to escape the pain by drifting into another world now that her baby is ready to be born. She imagines rising out of her body and looking down at herself, as others try what they can to save her life and that of her child. This is the time of greatest danger for them both, yet she trusts her loyal midwife, who knows more about delivering babies than any doctor.

An old worry nags at her, though, like an itch that cannot be scratched. She feels sure Anne Broughton will not be the only one to disapprove, and when the queen finds out, her world of privilege will be swept away. This is Charles Blount's child, and one day soon she will know whether there are to be consequences for them all. If Anne already knows the truth, then so do others – others who might wish to make mischief for her, or for Charles.

It seems simple when Charles Blount tells her he wishes for a son, which it *is* for him, but not for Penelope. For now she will have two families. The only answer is for the world to believe this is her husband's child, given his name and brought up as his own. She thanks God that, for now at least, he seems prepared to go along with her pretence.

In a rush, the child is born and waves tiny arms in the air as the midwife cleans it with a towel. Penelope tries to sit, but is too weak and collapses back on to her bed. She calls out to the midwife. 'Is it a boy or a girl?'

'A girl, my lady.' She wipes sweat from her brow and looks at Penelope with kindly eyes. 'A good healthy girl.'

Penelope senses history repeating itself, as it seems to do for her. She'd warned Charles Blount that providing him with a son might be no simple matter, but she stares at her new daughter and thanks God her birth has been without incident.

She never takes anything for granted, and should be happy now the long wait is over, yet cannot put a new fear from her mind. Frances had a perfect, healthy boy – named Walter, after his grandfather and in memory of his uncle – yet he'd been found cold and dead in his cot one morning, having shown no sign of illness.

Anne brushes damp hair from Penelope's forehead. 'What are we going to call this little one?'

Penelope frowns as she recalls her discussion about names with Charles. 'It may seem an odd choice, but I've agreed to name her after myself, so she will have to be my little Penny.'

Anne smiles. 'Some would say the world is not ready for more than one Penelope Rich, but Penny is a good name.'

Charles Blount arrives with a look of concern. 'There is a new scandal brewing at court involving Sir Walter Raleigh. Bess Throckmorton has borne a child, and it's said he is the father – and that he married her in secret, without the queen's permission.'

Penelope raised an eyebrow. 'When the queen knows of

this, he'll be imprisoned in the Tower, and probably poor Bess as well.'

'Walter Raleigh is conveniently away at sea, but he has a talent for making enemies of men like your brother Robert, so it is only a matter of time before someone with a grudge against him informs the queen.'

'I know Bess Throckmorton. She told me her father was an ambassador, but died when she was a child. She had no fortune, or money saved for her dowry, and expected she would serve the queen for the rest of her life.' Penelope smiles. 'It seems her destiny is quite different, but I would never have thought to match her with an adventurer like Walter Raleigh.'

Charles nods. 'I know her brother, Arthur Throckmorton – a good man, and I count him as a friend. The problem is that if our secret comes out now, the timing could not be worse, and the queen could make an example of us.' He kissed her. 'The plague has returned to London, so you must take our daughter to Essex until this matter has died down and it is safe for you to return.'

Penelope stares at him in surprise. 'I've been away from court far too long and was hoping to return. But you are right. They say out of sight is out of mind, and I've no wish to stay in the Tower, or to see you sent to prison. I will take our daughter to see my mother at Drayton Basset, then go to Essex to see my children. But first, we should show support to poor Bess Throckmorton.'

'What do you have in mind?' He sounds wary.

'We cannot live our lives in the shadows for fear of upsetting the queen and incurring her anger.' Penelope smiles. 'We shall invite Bess and her child here. We have much in common, and it's time my brother and Walter Raleigh set aside their differences.'

Bess Throckmorton is a gentlewoman of the chamber, a favourite of the queen, and two years younger than Penelope, who greets her as she arrives at Essex House. At Penelope's insistence she brings her small entourage of servants, including her wet nurse, carrying her infant son, the cause of so much trouble.

Bess looks relieved to see her, and grateful for Penelope's offer of a suite of rooms. 'I've been hiding myself away at my brother's house in Mile End. It's far enough away from court, and he has been very kind to me. His wife, Anna, is good company, but I worry I will cause them difficulty when the queen finds out what I've done, which she surely will.'

Penelope smiles as she looks at Bess's little son. 'Has he been baptised?'

Bess shakes her head. 'His father is away, and I have no idea when he might return.' Concern echoes in her voice. 'He promised to write, but so far I have heard nothing.'

'I've spoken to my brother, and he has agreed to act as godfather, if you agree. We can have the service at St Clement Danes Church, close to here. The minister is discreet, and your brother Arthur and his wife can also be godparents.'

Bess smiles for the first time since she arrived. 'I don't know how thank you, baroness.'

'Well, you can start by calling me Penelope, and I hope you can think of me as a friend.'

Penelope wonders whether her mother knows her poorly kept secret as she welcomes her new granddaughter to Drayton Manor. 'Another Penelope Rich.' There is a wry note in her voice, yet she smiles. 'It is a favourite name of mine.'

'The wife of Odysseus.'

Her mother raises an eyebrow. 'Penelope's commitment to her husband means her name is the embodiment of loyalty.'

Penelope could have plenty to say to her mother about loyalty, but this is not the moment. 'We call her Penny, to save confusion.'

'Another granddaughter is always welcome.' She leads Penelope to her parlour. 'I hear the plague has returned to London, and the queen is at Hampton Court, in the hope of escaping it.'

Penelope nods. 'The summer progress is cancelled, as are the Accession Day celebrations.'

Her mother looks unsurprised. 'A distant cousin died of the plague.' She frowns. 'An unpleasant way to die, but the queen will find it not so easy to avoid, with so many servants and visitors. You must stay here with me, Penelope, until we're sure the threat of the plague, or of your secret being discovered, has passed.'

'You know?'

'A mother knows these things. Particularly when she has a son like Robert.'

'It's good to know he has no secrets from you.' Her voice carries a note of irony.

'I presume Charles Blount hoped for a son?'

'I tried to tell him it's not so easy.'

'One child can sometimes be explained. We are only human, after all. But if you have another by him, it looks deliberate, and will be much harder to explain.'

'To the queen?'

Her mother frowns. 'The queen enjoys the power these situations give her. Do not underestimate her, Penelope. She takes her own failures out on those closest to her.'

≈

Anne Broughton arrives at Leighs Priory with news from London. 'My husband was able to have Dorothy's husband Thomas freed from prison, but her father-in-law, Sir John Perrot, was convicted of treason and attainted, and has died in the Tower of London, before the sentence can be carried out.'

Penelope stares at her with wide eyes. 'By his own hand?' She imagines that would be preferable to the nightmare of a traitor's death.

'My husband suspects Sir John was poisoned, but there is no proof, only that it is probably best for all concerned.'

A worrying thought occurs to Penelope. 'Does the attainder mean Dorothy and Thomas will inherit nothing?'

'My husband is helping Thomas Perrot to place a claim for his father's estate, although it will require an Act of Parliament. We will need all the support you can muster.'

Penelope understands. 'I will speak to my brother and grandfather.' She also thinks to speak to Robert Cecil, but need not mention this to Anne, for now.

'There is also bad news about Bess Raleigh.'

'The queen has learned of her marriage?'

Anne nods. 'Sir Walter Raleigh and Bess have both been sent to the Tower, for their sins.'

'What about her little son?' Penelope curses the queen for her cruelty, and can only imagine what it must be like for Bess Raleigh.

'He's been taken in by relatives, but we should not be surprised. We knew what the queen would do when she found out.' Anne shakes her head. 'You always said the queen can be a jealous mistress.'

Penelope frowns. 'There is nothing I can do to have Bess released, but I heard conditions in the Tower can be improved if enough money is paid.' She opens a drawer in her bureau and hands Anne a purse. 'Will you ask your husband to get this to Arthur Throckmorton. He will know how best to use it.'

Anne feels the weight of the purse. 'There must be a fortune in here.'

Penelope nods. 'I was saving it for emergencies, but see this as a small price to pay if it makes life a little easier for poor Bess.'

That night, as she says her prayers, Penelope prays for Bess and her little son. The unfairness of the queen's punishment leaves a bitter taste in her mouth. She knows, but for the grace of God, it could be her and Charles Blount in the Tower. Not for the first time, she wonders if the country would be a better place under the rule of King James.

17

AMBASSADORS OF FRANCE

FEBRUARY 1593

The long winter means there is hope the plague is less virulent in London, but those who can have abandoned the city, including the queen. Penelope remains at Leighs Priory with her children and, now her thirtieth birthday is passed, she no longer wishes to make the journey to Essex House until the weather improves.

One disadvantage of life at Leighs is that she cannot see Charles Blount, who travels from palace to palace with the queen as she tries to escape the pestilence. They agree it is too great a risk to write letters, so Penelope must rely on her brother to relay brief messages.

She welcomes a letter from Bess Raleigh, released from her prison in the Tower before Christmas, but is saddened to learn of the death of her infant son. Bess writes that the hardship of the past year has changed them both. With typical unfairness, the queen released Walter Raleigh three months earlier, and rewarded him with Sherborne Manor House in Dorset.

Penelope thanks God that, for now at least, her secret seems safe from the queen. She imagines people find it hard to believe her husband is so ready to pass another man's child off as his own. The worry still nags at the back of her mind, but less so with each passing month.

A log fire crackles in the hearth, and little Henry and Penny sleep in the nursery while Essie and young Robert watch Lucy, now eleven, play her lute. Essie will be eight this year, and speaks fluent French. She has spent less time with Penelope, and seems a little in awe of her. Robert will be six years old in June, and reminds Penelope of her brother Wat when he was the same age.

Lucy sings one of the old Huguenot songs Jeanne taught her. Penelope worries about Jeanne and her husband; there has, as yet, been no reply to her letter, and France seems to be in disarray. King Henri of France is converting to Catholicism, and no one can be sure what that means for the Huguenots.

She smiles as her daughter finishes her song. 'Would you like me to teach you to dance?'

Lucy frowns. 'Father says we are not to dance. Dancing can lead to sin.' Her father's harsh tone echoes in her young voice.

Penelope is going to say that her father speaks nonsense, but thinks better of it. 'I will speak with your father. One day you will be presented at court, and you'll be expected to know how to dance.'

Lucy looks at her with wide eyes. 'I never thought I would meet the queen.' She frowns. 'I shall be quite scared of her.'

'The queen is old, and loves to surround herself with young ladies, to make her feel younger. She will like you to play the lute for her, and sing in French, as I did when I was young, and your grandmother before me.' She smiles. 'The queen might make you one of her maids of honour.' Even as she says the words, Penelope feels misgivings about allowing her eldest daughter into the strange and dangerous world of the royal court.

Penelope's brother Robert visits, and has a new swagger since achieving his ambition of a place on the Privy Council. He wears a new doublet and hose of black and silver, no doubt paid for with more loans. He has a silver sword at his belt, and a white ostrich feather in his cap, the latest fashion at court.

'Now they must take me seriously.' He raises his glass of Penelope's best wine in a toast. 'To democracy, and the end of political corruption.'

Penelope doesn't believe he cares about democracy or corruption in government, unless it's to his advantage. She doesn't trust her brother's new friends and advisors, Anthony and Francis Bacon, cousins of Robert Cecil, engaged to tutor him in the art of statecraft and help plan his future as a privy councillor.

She raises her glass of wine in acknowledgement. 'And what are you going to do to change the world?' She regrets the note of mockery in her voice. Her brother's rapid rise is remarkable, and she hopes he has finally grown up.

'Parliament meets for the first time in four years to discuss funding for war with Spain. This is my chance to make my name as a statesman – and an adventurer.'

'You wish for war against Spain?'

He grins. 'That's how I intend to make my fortune. The Spanish no longer see us as a threat, so this is the perfect time to prove them wrong. Lord High Admiral Charles Howard is the only other member of the Privy Council with experience of leading an army and keeping them fed, equipped and paid. We will work together to triple the Treasury subsidy – and *I* shall be the one to benefit the most.'

Penelope takes another drink of the rich red wine, savouring the taste as she considers the consequences of her brother's plan. 'You risk making an enemy of Lord Burghley. He advocates a peaceful settlement with Spain, and tells the queen she can't afford another war.'

'Lord Burghley is an old man, suffering with gout, and represents all that is wrong with the queen's advisors.'

'His son waits in the wings, and could prove to be an even greater enemy at court.'

He takes a deep drink of his wine. 'Robert Cecil asked me to send you his best wishes.' He gives her a questioning look. 'I didn't know the two of you were close?' This time it is *his* voice which carries a note of mockery.

She cannot tell him about Robert Cecil discovering her letters to the King of Scotland. 'I see no advantage to either of us in making an enemy of him.'

'I don't trust Robert Cecil, and believe he spies on me.' Her brother scowls. 'He seems to know my plans better than I do.'

'Frances must have told you Anthony and Francis Bacon worked as informers for her father?'

He frowns. 'Frances said they are Robert Cecil's cousins, through his late mother, but Anthony Bacon has no love for his cousin. He confessed that he once joked about Robert Cecil's crooked back, and he's never forgiven him.'

'All I am saying is be careful who you place in your trust. And how is Frances?' Penelope notices he has not mentioned her since he arrived.

'I'm pleased to tell you Frances is once again with child, and has taken my stepdaughter, Bess, and little Robert to Barn Elms, her mother's house in the countryside.' He sounds as if he could not care less.

'You should bring her back to Essex House, and her mother could be with her for her lying in. I can join them when her time comes, if she wishes.' Penelope smiles. 'God knows I have enough experience of bearing children.'

Her brother shrugs. 'As long as Frances is happy, she can stay where she likes. I'm having Mother's old home at Wanstead redecorated, and a hunting stand built in the deer park. I am to entertain a diplomatic mission sent by King

Henri of France.' He drains his glass. 'You are welcome to join us, sister. You can dazzle them with your perfect French.'

Penelope fails to see her brother as a diplomat, and knows he will need her help. 'If they are sent by the French king, they should be received by our queen. I've not forgotten how she insists there shall be no other court than hers.'

He looks pleased with himself. 'The queen asked me to entertain the delegation. She is hidden away at Oatlands, after one of Lord Lumley's maids died of the plague at Nonsuch Palace.'

Penelope frowns as she thinks of Charles Blount, who'd been with the queen at Nonsuch. 'I hoped the plague had run its course.'

He shakes his head. 'It grows worse.' His face becomes serious. 'Fourscore and eleven have died in London in the past week, six more than the week before.' He curses. 'There is no cure or certain way to avoid it, so all we can do is pray we are spared such an ignoble fate.'

Wanstead has never been busier as an army of servants prepares for the reception of the ambassadors from France. Sounds of sawing and hammering drift from the woods as workmen build the new standing for the hunt. Servants arrange long trestle tables around a central open area in the great hall, ready for the banquet, and the smell of fresh paint mixes with the warm scent of beeswax polish.

Penelope has her mother's old suite of rooms, where a portrait of Robert Dudley watches her with an accusing stare. She picks up a silver hairbrush from the table in the dressing room. It has strands of her mother's red hair, as if her ghost still haunts her rooms.

Her brother wears a gold chain, and has a new air of confidence. As she'd predicted, he has made enemies of the Cecils with his plans for war with Spain, but has succeeded in ensuring a special Act of Parliament is approved by both Houses, providing Dorothy's husband with his late father's estates, except Carew Castle, which is seized by the Crown.

He nods in approval at her expensive gown of dark crimson silk, which she wears with an elaborate winged ruff of shimmering silver lace. 'How is your Spanish?'

Penelope smiles. 'I've had little enough chance to speak it, but my tutor in York was one of the best.'

'Good. You will be my secret weapon against those who think they can outwit me in this game of diplomatic bluff.' He grins. 'The French delegation is led by the Vidame de Chartres, and he brings with him a man who once served as the King of Spain's Secretary of State. I need you to find out whether I can trust him. His name is Antonio Pérez.'

'I'll be glad to. I confess I've missed the intrigue of court, and at Leighs Priory my only challenge was to outwit my husband.'

'I should tell you Her Majesty disapproves of Antonio Pérez. She says any man who betrays his *own* sovereign might have little compunction about betraying another.'

'The queen is right.' Penelope has an instinctive distrust of the disloyal Spaniard. 'I've told you before: be careful who you trust.'

'Maybe so, but if you think I *can* trust him, I plan for Antonio Pérez to help me set up a network of informers to rival any working for Robert Cecil. Francis Bacon says knowledge is power – and I intend to have both.'

The French delegation canter into the courtyard with an army of supporters, laughing and joking to each other in ribald French. They seem in good spirits, yet Penelope feels a frisson of nerves as she stands at her brother's side. She has not been involved in diplomacy, and plays a high-stakes game, representing the Queen of England.

She has no trouble spotting Antonio Pérez. She guesses he is about sixty, with a well-trimmed dark beard. He wears a cape of black velvet, and has his cap at a rakish angle. He stares at her with intelligent, sensitive eyes as she offers her hand for him to kiss. 'Baroness Rich, sister to the Earl of Essex.'

'Don Antonio Pérez of Aragon at your service, my lady.' He speaks English with a Spanish accent, and has the presence of a man used to dealing with royalty.

She smiles, and replies in her best Spanish. 'You are welcome to our home, Don Antonio, and I look forward to hearing about how you became an ambassador of the King of France.'

He answers in Spanish. 'I will tell you, but must warn you it is a long story, my lady, and I might use it as an excuse to spend more time with such a beautiful English rose.' There is a twinkle in his eye as he holds her gaze for a moment longer than is proper.

'You flatter me, Don Antonio. I shall ask my brother if he will seat you at my side at the banquet.' She speaks softly, and guesses only he will understand her Spanish, an easy bond between them.

She feels a strange attraction to this man who is old enough to be her father, and realises she hasn't thought about her father for many years. His early death left a void in her life. Something about this charming Spaniard reminds her what she is missing.

Penelope excuses herself from the hunting, as her brother brags he has penned in the finest stags in the forest for the delegation. A half-forgotten memory of Philip Sidney's familiar voice in her ear returns as she remembers the laughing Frenchmen at the queen's hunt, long ago. *We should only kill out of nobility and kindness.*

In the absence of Frances, she assumes the role of lady of the manor, directing the servants and checking every detail of the banquet. She makes sure all the servants wear her brother's livery, and that the right number of places have been set. She welcomes the queen's minstrels and tells them of her plan for the evening.

The sun is setting by the time her brother returns with the noisy huntsmen, and they take their places around the trestle tables. The queen's minstrels play familiar French songs, and Penelope's nervousness returns as she hears the delicate sound of a lute. She has kept her secret from everyone, including her brother, and prays she has made the right judgement.

Don Antonio Pérez has changed into a black velvet doublet and hose, with silver buttons and a Spanish style white collar in place of a ruff. He takes his place at her right side, and her brother sits at her left with the young Vidame de Chartres, Prégent de la Fin.

Penelope washes her fingers and dries them on the linen towel, then leans towards Don Antonio and speaks in Spanish. 'The Vidame seems young, for such an important position.'

Don Antonio nods. 'He is chosen not for his diplomatic skills, but as the son of the resident French Ambassador, Jean de la Fin, Sieur de Beauvoir.' He gives her a conspiratorial look. 'That is why I am here, to ensure this mission succeeds.'

'I understand you are seeking loans from our queen, but what do you offer in return?'

He smiles. 'A treaty with King Henri. We share the desire for peace, and must unite to keep the Spanish from our doors, but after talking with Lord Burghley we have little hope of returning to France with money.'

A servant fills their goblets with wine and Penelope takes a sip. She recognises it as her late stepfather's best claret, and smiles to herself at her brother's resourcefulness. The queen takes advantage of him to save her own expenses, yet her brother learns well, and achieves a great deal at little cost to himself.

Servants, in her brother's new livery of orange and gold, carry silver platters of steaming venison, basted in sweet butter. She cuts a slice with her knife and savours the taste of cinnamon and ginger, with a hint of rosemary and the scent of precious cloves.

She turns to Don Antonio. 'You come from Aragon, like the mother of our former queen?'

'I was born in Madrid, but my father, Gonzalo Pérez, who was Secretary of State to King Charles of Spain, was from Aragon, where I spent my childhood.'

'Forgive me, but does it trouble you to side with France against your own country?' She sees the flicker of hesitation in his eyes.

'When my father died I became Secretary of State to King Philip. For many years I was his main advisor, but you cannot do such work in Spain without making enemies.' He frowns at the memory. 'I was accused of having an affair with the king's mistress, Ana de Mendoza, the Princess of Éboli.' He helps himself to a small portion of venison, and nods in approval.

'What happened?'

He sits in silence for a moment before he answers. 'I was arrested by the Inquisition, as were my wife, Juana, and my sons. I managed to escape to France, but my family are in prison in Madrid.'

'I'm sorry to hear that.' Penelope frowns. 'Are they safe?'

'I pray they are, my lady, and live in hope of their release. They are innocent, as am I.'

Penelope doubts Don Antonio is innocent, but finds she likes him more than she expected. She sees the diners grow restless, and decides it is time for her surprise. She touches her brother on the arm, and speaks softly in his ear. He nods in agreement, and she smiles to Don Antonio and leaves.

She finds Lucy and her governess waiting in a side chamber. 'Are you ready?'

Lucy nods. 'Yes, Mother.' She looks pale, but there is a glint of anticipation in her eyes.

The great hall falls silent as they enter, carrying their lutes, and take the two gilded chairs in the central area. They play a Huguenot song, singing together in perfect harmony, and she sees they have the rapt attention of every member of the French delegation. Penelope also sees the look of admiration from Don Antonio, and hopes she can know him better before he must return.

18

THE SPANISH VISITOR

APRIL 1594

Penelope is back at Essex House, in her black silk and velvet canopied lovers' bed, with Charles Blount sleeping at her side. London is clear of the plague, for now at least, and she is preparing to return to court. The rumours of the queen's death proved false, but have given them all reason to think again of the succession.

Dorothy is coming to visit, with her children; her husband, Sir Thomas, has recently died after a long illness. Her sister suspects this was a consequence of his imprisonment, as he'd never been in good health since his release. Dorothy has inherited his estates, and chooses to live at her late husband's west London home, the former abbey, Syon House.

Penelope persuaded Frances – who has a new daughter, named Penelope in her honour – to join them at Essex House, but her brother prefers to sleep elsewhere. He spends little time with his new family, and is away most nights. Penelope believes she knows the reason.

She shakes Charles awake as a worrying thought occurs to her. 'I need to ask you something.'

He turns, rubbing his eyes, and kisses her on the cheek,

then frowns at the troubled look in her eyes. 'What's the matter?'

'Frances told me my brother is trying to prove a conspiracy involving the queen's physician, Doctor Lopez. He claims the doctor was planning to poison the queen.'

He nods. 'He told me about this suspected conspiracy, but it's complicated, and I'm not sure you will want to know the details.'

It takes her a moment to realise he is teasing. 'Tell me what you know.'

'There's a rumour Doctor Lopez was treating your brother for the pox.' He shakes his head. 'He promises me it's untrue, but you know how they love to gossip at court – and how damaging such a rumour is to your brother's reputation.'

Penelope lies back in silence for a moment. 'I've known Doctor Lopez for years; he was my stepfather's personal physician. I thought of him as a good man. Why would he wish to harm the queen, having tended to her health with such care?'

Charles puts his arm around her. 'He is the son of the physician of the King of Portugal, and was raised as a Catholic.' He kisses her on the cheek. 'Who can know what is in the mind of such a complicated man?'

'I recommend his potions to others. I can't believe he's involved in a conspiracy.'

'That is your brother's problem. The gossips of court will say he is trying to silence Doctor Lopez, and half the Privy Council considers him to be their personal physician.'

Penelope frowns. 'I hope my brother knows what he's doing, and isn't being led astray by someone.'

'Francis Bacon?' His voice has a note of disapproval.

'How did you know I was thinking of him?'

'Because that's where your brother has been spending so much time: in Francis Bacon's chambers. I presume he's trying to gather evidence against the doctor.'

'What else have I missed at court?'

'Do you know Frances Drury?'

'She's one of the queen's youngest maids of honour, and her mother, Lady Stafford, is one of the ladies of the privy chamber.'

'There is another scandal. Someone told the queen that your cousin, Sir Nicholas Clifford, has married Frances Drury.'

'Without the queen's permission?'

'The queen has not given permission to *any* of her maids of honour to marry, for as long as I can remember.'

'Are they banished?'

'Worse, I'm afraid. Young Frances Drury has been sent to the Fleet prison, and Sir Nicholas is locked up in the Tower.'

'That's awful. I must see what I can do for Frances Drury. Bess Raleigh said they improved her conditions after her brother paid her warders.'

'It's not Frances Drury I worry about.'

'It's us?'

He puts his arm around her, and pulls her close. 'You've said it before: Her Majesty can be a jealous mistress.'

The Spanish diplomat, Don Antonio Pérez, arrives at Essex House. He looks confident and prosperous, with a gold chain over his fur collar, and cuffs and a ruff of fine white lace. His doublet is embroidered with gold thread, and he could be mistaken for a noble. He bows as Penelope greets him.

'Don Antonio, my brother is not here, and I've no idea when he will return.'

'It's not your brother I came to see, my lady.' He speaks in Spanish. 'I have persuaded the French king to allow me to remain in England as your brother's guest. I have a business proposition for you to consider, and promised to tell you the story of why I turned my back on Spain, and became an ambassador of France.'

'I have not forgotten, Don Antonio.' She replies in Spanish, and cannot help being intrigued by his mysterious proposal, but thinks it wise to have a witness, as well as a chaperone. 'My brother's wife, Lady Frances, is here, and would like to meet you. You are welcome to join us.'

'That would be an honour, my lady.'

Penelope sends one of her servants for spiced wine, and leads Don Antonio into the parlour to introduce him to Frances. She's told Frances about him, and knew he'd remained in England, but hasn't seen Don Antonio since their first meeting at Wanstead Manor.

He sent her a pair of fine leather gloves, with a covering letter in overly familiar Spanish. She'd been disturbed to find the gloves were made from *piel de un perro*, which she translated as *the skin of a dog*. She doesn't know enough about Spanish culture to tell if this is true, or a joke at her expense – but she never wore them.

Don Antonio bows to Frances. 'It is my pleasure to meet you, Lady Essex. I was sorry to hear of the passing of your father. I never met him, but knew him by reputation.'

Frances nods in acknowledgement. 'I heard your delegation was finally granted a meeting with Her Majesty. Was the Vidame pleased after his audience with the queen?'

She sounds as if she doubts it.

Don Antonio gives her a wry look. 'It took a long time to arrange the meeting, my lady, because of the plague in London, but little came of it, apart from Her Majesty's gifts.' He smiles. 'They were unusual.' He counts them on his fingers. 'A basin of silver gilt, and a pair of gilt vases, for the King of France. A pair of gilded Hanse pots, and five gilded bowls with covers, as reward to the Vidame for his trouble.'

Penelope raises an eyebrow but is not surprised. 'Gilt pots

and vases seem a small reward for such efforts, and travelling all the way from France.'

Don Antonio nods. 'Her Majesty does not approve of the conversion of the King of France to the Catholic faith, and so there is no treaty.'

'Then the mission was a failure.'

'Not for me, my lady.' He smiles. 'For me, the mission has been a great success.' There is a twinkle in his eye. 'I've transferred my loyalty before, and now do so again.'

'You are working for my brother?'

He smiles. 'I have information which is of value to him, as well as many useful contacts.'

Penelope studies him, trying to decide if he is loyal to her brother, the French king, Spain – or whether he has only his own interests at heart. 'I don't want my brother to underestimate the Spanish. He thinks they will be unprepared for an attack from the sea.'

Don Antonio looks serious. 'The sea is the only place the King of Spain *expects* an attack, since Sir Francis Drake trapped the Spanish fleet in the port of Cadiz. He prepares accordingly, and spends a great deal on refitting his war fleet. He also protects the harbour at Cadiz with powerful cannons which can sink a ship with a single shot.'

Frances looks thoughtful. 'You were arrested by the Inquisition, Don Antonio. Few survive the experience, so I am curious to know how you escaped to France.'

He nods. 'You are right, Lady Essex. The first time, I risked my life by jumping from a high window. I sought asylum in a church, but the king's men broke down the doors and arrested me.' He frowns. 'I was given a death sentence, but was able to make my escape when they moved me to the prison in Madrid. I had help from accomplices, and dressed as a shepherd.'

Penelope's servant arrives and pours them each a cup of spiced wine. She tastes a sip, and feels its warmth in her throat.

She knows Frances well enough to see she has doubts about Don Antonio, but she finds him intriguing and exotic, and knows there is more to his story than he is telling them.

'How did you persuade the King of France to send you here as his envoy?'

Don Antonio has a sip of spiced wine before replying. 'Everything I owned was confiscated by King Philip of Spain, so I had no choice but to make my living selling what I know. I found it easy enough to make myself useful as an advisor to the young Vidame, Prégent de la Fin.' He smiles. 'And now I find myself at the heart of the English court.'

'You said you had a proposal, Don Antonio?'

He takes another drink. 'Your brother spends much time at Anthony and Francis Bacon's chambers at Gray's Inn. I suggested he makes Essex House his centre of operations, and spends more time with his wife and child,' he nods to Frances, 'and his sister – who, like the Spanish, is not to be underestimated.'

Penelope gestures to her servant to refill their glasses. 'I agree that would be preferable, and we have the room here, but why did you need to see *me*?'

'Your brother is deep in debt, and is not able to pay for me to join his household, my lady. I therefore offer my services as your secretary and will be happy to escort you, whenever required.'

Penelope sees Frances raise an eyebrow, but has missed Jeanne and her husband since they returned to France. The idea of having Don Antonio Pérez as her secretary would never have occurred to her, but it has a certain appeal. There will be much to do at Essex House if her brother makes it his headquarters, and her present secretary, Master William Downhall, was the Earl of Leicester's retainer, and is overdue retirement.

'I shall engage you on a trial basis, Don Antonio, and

your first task is to arrange for my brother to establish himself here in Essex House, with whoever he needs to support him.'

After he leaves, Frances looks concerned. 'Don Antonio Pérez worked for my father as an informer, but I don't trust him – and neither did my father. He's charming, but also an unscrupulous rogue, and is prepared to sell his soul for the right price.'

Penelope smiles. 'He is a survivor, and Robert needs to understand what he will be up against before taking on the Spanish fleet. His life might depend on it.'

Penelope cannot wait to tell Charles her news. She is certain she is with child again. There is no doubt he is the father, and she senses that the child she carries will be a boy, the heir he longs for. He returns from a meeting with his lawyer, looking grim-faced.

'I regret to tell you my brother William has died at the Bishop of London's house by St Paul's.'

Penelope embraces him. 'I'm sorry. I only met your brother once.'

'He was not the most sociable of men, and rarely showed his face at court.' Charles frowns. 'I visited him before he died, but he hardly spoke. I'm not sure he knew who I was.' A note of sadness carries in his voice.

'Did he remain unmarried?'

Charles nods. 'He left no heir, so I inherit the family estates in Dorset, as well as his house here in London. I believe there is a good income from rents.'

'And the title, my lord.' She manages a smile.

'That's right. I never expected to have the title, or the estates. My brother was only two years older than me, and I expected he would marry. I have become the eighth Baron Mountjoy, and will have a seat in the House of Lords.'

'If I am free to marry you, I will still be a baroness.' A plan forms at the back of her mind. She pushes the thought away, for the sake of her children, but knows her husband is a pragmatist.

He takes her in his arms and kisses her. 'When you *are* free, I *will* marry you, even if it means waiting for the rest of my life.'

Dorothy surprises them all with her betrothal to Henry Percy, Earl of Northumberland, and one of the wealthiest peers of the court. The ceremony takes place in the old chapel at Syon House, once the heart of the great abbey where King Henry VIII's coffin rested for one night before continuing to his burial place in St George's Chapel at Windsor Castle.

Once again, their family is reunited for the occasion. Her mother wears a magnificent gossamer ruff framing her red hair. Their stepfather, Sir Christopher Blount, smiles as he looks on. He has supported Penelope's brother at every vote in Parliament, and they've become close friends.

Penelope and Dorothy turn heads in matching gowns of shimmering golden silk as they arrive. Lucy, now aged twelve, Essie, aged nine, and her cousin, Frances' daughter, Elizabeth, act as Dorothy's bridesmaids, and follow in matching silk gowns, with their hair long, carrying bouquets of white roses.

The ceremony is overlong, and the minister delivers a sermon on the sanctity of marriage. Penelope wonders how many know her marriage is a sham. At first, only her immediate family knew her great secret. She worried what would become of her if it became more widely known, particularly by the queen. Now she will be glad if something would happen to force her husband's hand.

At the reception banquet she sits at Dorothy's side. 'Who would have thought my little sister would be Countess of Northumberland.' She raises her glass. 'Here's to a long and happy marriage.'

Dorothy smiles. 'I could not face the rest of my life as a lonely widow, and the girls need a father.' She glances at her new husband, deep in conversation with their brother. 'I know you all think I rushed into this, but I saw my chance and could not take the risk of delaying.'

Penelope says a silent prayer for her sister, who has not married for love, or for money, but has the approval of the queen. Her new husband is the same age as her, but has something of a reputation for his interest in alchemy and astrology, which he shares with his close friend, the court astronomer, Doctor John Dee.

After the banquet she finds her brother also has concerns. 'They say Henry Percy is a secret Catholic. His father was a supporter of Mary, Queen of Scots.' Robert scowls. 'He protested his innocence, but was locked up in the Tower, where he committed suicide.'

'No one can be sure it was suicide.' Penelope glances across at their sister. 'I worry for Dorothy, and fear she has rushed into this new marriage for the wrong reasons.'

Robert nods in agreement. 'Did you hear about Doctor Lopez?'

'He suffered a traitor's death.' She tries not to shudder at the thought.

'Her Majesty surprised us all by summoning Doctor Lopez out of prison to treat her, and he took the opportunity to tell her his confession was extracted under torture.'

Penelope no longer knows what her brother is capable of, and gives him a questioning look. '*Was* it?'

'It suited his purpose to claim they tortured him, but he made a full, written confession of his crimes as soon as he saw the manacles.'

Penelope speaks softly. 'I don't blame him for trying to avoid a traitor's death.'

Her brother scowls. 'Hanged, drawn and cut into quarters, thanks to proof in letters provided by Don Antonio Pérez.'

Penelope frowns. 'I didn't know Don Antonio had played such an important part in his conviction.'

'The doctor professed his innocence to the end, but it was the evidence provided by Don Antonio that condemned him – and your husband who judged him guilty of treason.'

Penelope shakes her head. 'It seems you saved our queen from an early demise, although I doubt she will admit she owes you her life.' She sees the flicker of uncertainty in her brother's eyes, and doubts she can continue to trust Don Antonio Pérez.

19

THE INFANTA ISABELLA

JANUARY 1595

Penelope stares at her new daughter and knows she will have to try again. She cared little if people thought it improper for her to appear in public while pregnant, as she'd done so before, but this time she did nothing to jeopardise the life of her unborn child, and made great sacrifices.

She'd missed seeing her brother and Charles ride in the joust at the first Accession Day tournament at Whitehall Palace since the plague. She stayed away from court, was absent from the Christmas and New Year's banquets, and celebrated her thirty-second birthday with only Frances for company.

Frances smiles as she holds the newborn child, swaddled in white linen. 'She's perfect. What are your thoughts on a name for her?'

Penelope lies back, exhausted, on her soft pillows. She gives thanks to God they both survived the ordeal, but feels a pang of disappointment. She'd been certain she carried a boy, and had suggested he could be called Charles. If that didn't spur her husband into action, then she wondered what it would take. 'I like the name Isabella. It's another form of Elizabeth.'

Frances looks surprised. 'A Spanish name?'

'Italian … but popular in Spain.'

'Do you think Charles will be disappointed?'

'If he is, he'll hide it well – but, God willing, we will be due a boy next time.' She gives Frances a meaningful look. 'God has a way of resolving such things.'

The character of Essex House has changed now Penelope's brother uses it as his base. He spends more time with Frances at Walsingham House in Seething Lane, but eight of the rooms on the first floor of Essex House are used by his staff. Visitors are always coming and going at all hours, but Penelope enjoys the variety and keeps a sisterly eye on her brother.

She visits Anthony Bacon, who has chosen the former wood-panelled library as his apartment. She is surprised at his choice, as the room is at the top of the stairs leading to the third floor. Although only five years older than Penelope, he suffers from severe gout, so must find the staircase a challenge.

He rarely goes out, and helps Penelope keep an eye on the Essex household in lieu of rent. He is literate and witty. She finds Anthony Bacon good company, and does not need a chaperone at their private meetings. He was Sir Francis Walsingham's man in France, so they often speak in French, and he has useful contacts in the court of King James of Scotland, who Penelope is keen to cultivate.

He uses a stick to stand as Penelope enters. He wears an elaborate lace ruff and his black doublet is embroidered with silver.

'My lady.' He bows. 'How can I help you?' His tone is subservient but his dark eyes have the glint of someone with news to share.

'What progress you are making with setting up my brother's network?'

'We have an intelligence service to rival that of Sir Robert Cecil.' He smiles. 'Your cousin, Sir Nicholas Clifford, has joined us, my lady, and Sir Anthony Standen has returned from imprisonment in France.'

Penelope frowns. 'I am glad my cousin is with us, but Anthony Standen served Mary, Queen of Scots.'

Anthony Bacon nods. 'He was invaluable to Sir Francis Walsingham, and has his own network of agents in France and Spain. We need to secure the support of men like him, my lady, if only to ensure he doesn't transfer his loyalty to the Cecils. Antonio Pérez is summoned back to France by King Henri, but promises to return with useful news from the continent.'

Penelope understands. 'We shall miss him – although my brother won't miss his extravagance.'

Anthony Bacon agrees. 'Henry Wotton has agreed to become your brother's secretary, and your stepfather, Sir Christopher Blount, has also joined us.'

'And your brother?' Penelope has not got on well with the articulate lawyer Francis Bacon, who seems to disapprove of her open liaison with Charles Blount.

'My brother hopes to become Attorney General, with your brother's support, but I fear Robert Cecil will have to die first.'

Penelope stares at him in amazement, then realises he is using black humour. She thinks to mention her deal with Robert Cecil about her letters to the Scottish king, but it is still too early to be sure if she can trust either of these scheming brothers.

'Have you seen a copy of the new book about the succession, my lady?'

Penelope shakes her head. 'I've heard talk of it, but would have thought to even own a copy is too great a risk.'

Anthony Bacon holds up the leather-bound book for her to see. 'I saw it as my duty to acquire a copy, and obtained this from my contact in Amsterdam. I had to see for myself if the rumours I'd heard about your brother were true, my lady.'

'What rumours?' She finds it irritating that Anthony Bacon likes to reveal his secrets in riddles.

'You should read the dedication, my lady.' He hands her the book.

The title page reads: *A Conference about the next Succession to the Crown of England, by R. Doleman.* The formal dedication is several pages long. Penelope reads the first page, and looks up at Anthony with concern in her eyes. 'My brother is mentioned by name.'

Anthony Bacon nods. 'The author claims he has done him favours.'

Penelope's pulse races as she thinks of the implications. 'Who is this R. Doleman? Who wrote this?'

'The author is Robert Parsons, a Jesuit writing under a pseudonym. Although English, he is an advisor to King Philip of Spain, and founded a seminary in Madrid. He is promoting the claims of the Infanta Isabella of Spain, and says he met your brother during his campaigns in France.' He shakes his head. 'Your brother has no recollection of him, but there is no way he can prove he had no part in this book.'

Penelope puts her hand to her mouth in alarm. 'There is a real danger someone will alert the queen, and there will be consequences for us all if she believes he's involved in some way. By chance, I've named my daughter Isabella, but those who wish to cause trouble will make a connection where none exists.'

Anthony Bacon nods. 'Some are drawing the conclusion that your brother is, at the very least, a patron of the author. We have no idea how many copies have been printed and distributed. This appears to be a deliberate attempt to discredit your brother, my lady.' He takes back the book and reads aloud from the foreword.

'*No man is in a more eminent place than yourself, or in favour with your prince, or high liking of the people, and consequently no man can like to have a greater part in deciding this great affair, than your honour, and those that will assist you are likeliest to follow your fame and fortune.*'

'Robert Cecil will call that treason.' Her words hang in the air.

Anthony Bacon looks sympathetic. 'The book sets out a balanced argument, but is disparaging about the suitability of King James of Scotland, and predicts a civil war in England after the death of the queen.'

Penelope frowns. 'What should we do?'

Anthony Bacon closes the book. 'I advised your brother to see Her Majesty as soon as possible, and swear he had nothing to do with the book, or the author – whoever he might be.'

Penelope chooses the Shrove Monday masque at Whitehall Palace for her return to court. For the sake of appearances, she is escorted by her husband, who seems to have mellowed with age. He looks distinguished, with a trace of silver in his beard, plays his part well and never asks about Charles Blount, or the girls.

She has chosen a plain, well-fitting gown of peach satin, with a necklace of pearls and a ruff of filigree lace, open at the front. The worst mistake she can make is to upstage the queen in any way, as her mother did. She still turns heads as they make their way through the crowd to the queen, and worries that there might be good reason.

They join the queue of courtiers being presented, and when Penelope's turn comes, she cannot help noticing how much older the queen looks, despite her thick make-up and extravagant red wig. She has rehearsed this moment many times since she left court, yet her well-chosen words desert her.

Instead, it is her husband who pays the queen an insincere compliment. She studies him with sharp eyes, as if making a judgement. For an anxious moment Penelope worries the queen is about to ask a question neither of them will wish to answer, but she nods in acknowledgement.

'Welcome, Baron Rich.' She turns to Penelope and manages an unconvincing smile. 'It is good to see your wife has recovered from her ordeal.'

Her husband bows. 'Your Majesty.'

The moment passes and they move on, yet Penelope senses a missed opportunity. Her husband has enhanced his status at her expense – the price, she supposes, of her infidelity. She looks forward to the succession, when everything will change. Her brother has a letter from the King of Scotland, which gives them hope that the great risks she took have finally borne fruit.

The highlight of the evening is a performance in the great hall by the boisterous young lawyers of Gray's Inn of *Proteus and the Rock Adamantine*. A narrator reads a lengthy introduction to the masque, sounding more like he's defending a case in court as he explains about nymphs and Triton. He bows to Queen Elizabeth, and says she is the attractive virtue which draws all hearts.

A man swathed in a cloak of fish scales, as Proteus the sea-god, strikes a 'rock', made from grey painted canvas. A small choir emerges to sing a lusty hymn in praise of Neptune. They are followed by seven burly men dressed as knights, led by dwarves carrying bright, burning torches.

Each knight selects a lady from the audience, and one takes Penelope by the hand. The queen's minstrels play and she dances a galliard, pleased at how the memory of the steps returns. The other dancers stand aside and she becomes the centre of attention at court.

The choir sings another hymn as a finale, and the audience

applaud and cheer. Penelope's husband gives her a look of disapproval, but her heart pounds from the exertion of the galliard, and she knows she cannot be blamed. She smiles as the queen thanks them all for the performance, and knows whatever happened in the past is forgiven – for now.

Penelope hears the church bells clanging in alarm before her brother shouts for the servants to lock the gates and barricade the doors. She rushes down to the entrance hall, where she finds him wearing a sword and dagger, looking grim-faced.

'What is it? What's going on?'

Penelope's brother is restless, pacing the hall. 'Rioters, in great numbers, heading this way.' He frowns. 'They set fire to a wagon in the street, and have started looting.' He takes a pair of pistols from their box and sticks one under his belt, while he loads the other with powder. 'I doubt they will try to break in, but we must be prepared if they do.'

'You cannot shoot at them.'

'I have the right to defend my family and property.' The glint in his eye suggests he is enjoying the commotion.

Anthony Bacon joins them. 'I'm not surprised to see disorder and riots in London. The apprentices have had enough.' He peers through the window. 'There are a good many, and now they've been joined by out-of-work soldiers and masterless men.'

Penelope flinches at the sharp crack of gunfire, echoing in the street. 'They shout about the council, but it's no one's fault. We've had three poor harvests due to the wet summers. It's little wonder there is a shortage of food and prices are so high.'

'They've been campaigning against the Lord Mayor, Sir John Spencer, who sent many protestors to jail.' Her brother gives Penelope a knowing look. 'They put up a scaffold outside his offices and threatened to hang him.'

'They cannot be allowed to riot in the streets.'

'The previous rioters were punished by pillorying and whipping, but that led to another riot, involving some two thousand men. The queen will have to proclaim martial law, which will make these gatherings a treasonable offence. But, for now, we must look after ourselves – and not only from rioters.'

'What do you mean?'

'The Spanish have landed warships in Cornwall.' He curses. 'They caught us unprepared at dawn, and burned houses in the towns of Penzance and Mousehole, as well as a parish church.'

She tries to calm him, but shares his concern. 'Is this the start of a new invasion?'

He shakes his head. 'Only four galleys made landfall, but there are reports of up to forty ships seen to seaward. They sailed off before we could do anything, but they mock us.' His voice is raised in frustration.

'This is for men like Sir Francis Drake to deal with.'

'Drake and Sir John Hawkins are preparing to go westward, but I fear the queen will not permit me to sail with them.'

Penelope joins Anthony Bacon at the window. 'The rioters have passed, and without trying our gates.' She turns to her brother. 'You look disappointed, but this is a sign of the times we live in. Even the queen can no longer take anything for granted.'

November rain threatens to ruin the Accession Day celebrations at St Paul's Cross. The special pulpit in St Paul's Churchyard has been repaired and painted, and Dr Fletcher,

Bishop of London, is soaked by the downpour as he preaches a long sermon in praise of the queen.

Penelope is glad of her hooded riding cape as she joins the prayers of thanks for Her Majesty, with the Lord Mayor and aldermen of London in their best liveries. As the sermon ends, a shrill trumpet sounds and a choir sings an anthem.

The deep rumble of cannons sounds as the men of the Tower of London fire a salute, and the church bells ring in happy celebration.

Penelope has never seen such crowds gathered for the Accession Day tournament, and guesses there must be over a thousand spectators crowded into every available space around the tiltyard. Her brother is in charge this year, and decides he will be first to ride, against Sir George Clifford, Earl of Cumberland. Penelope thinks Clifford, champion of many jousts, an unwelcome influence on her brother, for his notorious gambling.

She is among the chattering ladies, all wrapped in thick furs against the cold, with her sister Dorothy. The queen watches from a high window, flanked by the Lord Admiral, Sir Charles Howard, and Edward de Vere, Earl of Oxford, the Lord Chamberlain. She seems in good spirits, and laughs happily at some comment, no doubt another unwarranted compliment.

Dorothy points as their brother rides into view, with a tabard of dazzling white over his armour, carrying a twelve-foot lance, painted white with a gold coronal on the blunted tip, designed to shatter on impact. He wears a white ostrich plume on his helmet as a sign of knightly purity, and rides to the window where the queen shelters from the weather, then dips his lance in salute. Penelope feels an unexpected surge of pride, then recalls how her brother has treated Frances.

She turns to Dorothy. 'How is your new husband?'

'I see him so rarely I suspect he forgets we're married.' A note of bitterness echoes in her voice. 'He tells me he is busy, but I fear he wastes his time looking for the secret of alchemy.'

'We seem to have a talent for making poor marriages.' Penelope frowns. 'Our mother seems content for our stepfather to spend more of his time at Essex House than he does with her. My marriage has run its course, and yours has yet to start.' She watches her brother canter past. 'As for Robert, it seems he married poor Frances out of some misplaced sense of duty towards Philip Sidney.'

She feels a pang of loss as she mentions his name for the first time she can remember since his death. She wears his gold pendant, but has never opened it since meeting Charles Blount; her copy of *Astrophel and Stella* is kept safe in her oak chest, yet many years have passed since she last read it.

The crowd cheers as the tournament begins, and Sir George Clifford canters down the list, resplendent in his gilded armour, with a golden lance. His charger is dressed as a red dragon, and pounds the sawdust-covered cobblestones with heavy hooves. He wheels and halts in front of Penelope, and asks her favour.

She suspects her brother is behind the gesture, to prevent Charles Blount from making a public display of their liaison. She hands Sir George a red silk ribbon, which he ties to his saddle, before dipping his lance to her in salute. Yet again, Penelope has unwittingly become the centre of attention, and sees the queen is watching.

A fanfare sounds, and both riders prepare to joust. Her brother knows horses, and has chosen well. On the signal, his powerful stallion takes off like a charging bull. As if to reassure the doubters, the winter sun breaks through iron-grey clouds and flashes from Sir George's magnificent gilded armour. Penelope says a silent prayer for her brother. Good men have been crippled and even killed at the joust.

She holds her breath as they charge in a clash of lances against shields. To a rousing cheer, Sir Robert Devereux, Earl of Essex, unseats the champion, shards of broken lance flying into the air. The queen applauds and shouts her congratulations. Penelope stands, and calls out with the others.

'Long live the Queen! God save the Queen!'

20

THE AZORES VOYAGE

MAY 1597

Penelope leaves her children in the care of her husband and makes the long journey in her carriage from Leighs Priory to her mother's home at Drayton Manor, with only her servants for company. She had thought to bring Lucy, now of marriageable age at fifteen, yet her mother's brief note which summoned her is mysterious about the reason for urgency.

Having stopped at a coaching inn overnight, she arrives as the sky is glowing with a brilliant orange sunset. Her mother greets her, wearing a magnificent embroidered brocade gown with a high, gossamer ruff and a necklace of pearls that would not look out of place on the queen.

Penelope is pleased to find Charles Blount is also there to welcome her, looking handsome in his black doublet and hose, with a cape of dark blue velvet over his shoulders. She has important news for him, and has not seen him, or even been able to exchange letters with him, since she left Essex House.

He kisses her. 'I know you don't like me coming to see you at Leighs Priory, and I wanted to tell you my news in person.'

He smiles. 'I am to be a Knight of the Garter, together with Thomas Howard, George Carey, and Henry Lee.'

She embraces him and returns his kiss, unconcerned about her mother or any servants watching. 'The queen has finally seen fit to reward your loyalty – and you must have friends on her council, as any one of them could have stopped your nomination.' She smiles. 'I have news of my own.' She puts her hand to her middle. 'I am with child again, and believe this time it *will* be a boy.'

Her mother gives Penelope a disapproving look, and leads them into the great hall where a table is set for supper, with tall beeswax candles flickering in silver candlesticks. Her stepfather, Sir Christopher Blount, sits in a leather chair by a welcoming log fire, which blazes in the hearth.

He stands as they enter, and smiles as he sees Penelope. 'I expect Charles has told you?' He gives him a knowing look. 'First a baron, and now a Garter knight.'

Charles grins. 'It's something of a mixed blessing. There's to be a cavalcade of Garter knights-elect, marching twenty-five miles from London to Windsor. I'm expected to outfit my men in blue coats, each with a plume of purple ostrich feathers in their hats, and my gentlemen are to wear chains of gold.'

They take their seats at the table, and Penelope washes her fingers in a silver bowl of warmed rose water, drying them on her linen towel. 'My father was a Garter knight, and my brother joined the Order of the Garter when he was only twenty-two.'

Her mother smiles. 'I remember your father was so proud. He was Viscount Hereford at the time, and the same year was made the Earl of Essex.' She smiles at the memory. 'We held a banquet at Chartley Manor, with dancing and a mummers' play.'

Penelope nods. 'I remember that banquet well. I was nine, old enough to know life would change for us all – as it did.' She hasn't thought of her father for some time and feels his loss as she recalls how happy he'd been that day, with his whole future ahead of him.

Servants bring platters of capons in plum sauce, and engraved silver goblets of sweet Rhenish wine. The centrepiece is a roasted suckling pig on a large silver dish, and Penelope realises they've been waiting for her arrival.

'I sense there is something else…' She looks across at her mother, then at Charles Blount, who nods.

'There is to be a voyage to the Azores. Your brother is made Lieutenant General, and Governor of the Army and Navy – he will lead us against the Spaniards.'

Penelope frowns. 'I'm surprised the queen gave her consent after what happened in Cadiz. He had a fleet of a hundred and fifty ships, half as many again as sailed against the Armada, yet they destroyed only four warships in Cadiz harbour, and missed capturing the Spanish treasure fleet by days.'

'That was no fault of theirs.' Charles sounds defensive, and helps himself to a plate of capon and plums. 'The Spanish set fire to their own merchant ships in Cadiz harbour, rather than allow them to be captured.'

Penelope shook her head. 'I wish Robert would learn from his adventures abroad. He always says they will be the making of him and secure his fortune, yet Anthony Bacon told me his last venture cost the Crown some fifty thousand pounds, with little to show for it. I suspect my brother is deeper in debt now than he ever was.'

Her mother holds up a hand to silence her. 'Robert told me he'd been hit by bullets twice, and was only saved by his armour. He showed great courage in the attack on Cadiz, yet the queen unfairly blames him for their failure. He was so upset he threatened to exile himself to Lamphey, until the queen called him back.'

Penelope is unconvinced. 'I would prefer he secured his place on the council, rather than risking his life on these reckless attacks on the Spanish.'

Charles Blount shakes his head. 'Our informers report that the Spanish war fleet is preparing to sail to Ireland, to establish a base for the invasion of the West Country. Our new expedition will aim to intercept them, and more than pay for the expenses by capturing their treasure ships, returning from the Indies.' He grins. 'We'll return as wealthy men, laden with gold and precious spices.'

Penelope raises an eyebrow as she cuts a slice of capon. 'You said *our* expedition. Will the queen allow you to sail with my brother?'

He nods. 'We set sail next month, and the fleet is already assembling in Plymouth. Her Majesty made me Lieutenant General, and gave leave to Henry Wriothesley, as well as your stepfather.' He nods to Christopher Blount. 'And … Lord Rich.' He gives her a mischievous look, and his words hang in the air as they all wait for Penelope's reaction.

'My husband is going on this voyage?' Penelope stares at him in amazement. 'He's told me nothing about it, and the last time he set to sea he was so sick he said he thought he would die.'

'Your husband is one of the main investors in the mission. He has advanced one thousand pounds and wishes to see the Spanish treasure fleet for himself.'

'None of you are sailors – or military commanders.' Penelope hears the exasperation in her voice.

'The queen has made Sir Thomas Howard Vice Admiral, and Sir Walter Raleigh Rear Admiral. They both have experience of sailing to the Azores, and have their own ships, with experienced crews.'

A thought occurs to Penelope. 'The Spanish have their secret agents watching our ports, so there is little chance of you taking them by surprise.' She sees the concern in her mother's eyes, and looks in turn from her stepfather to Charles. 'I shall worry about you, and will pray for you all until you return.'

Penelope visits Frances at Walsingham House to see if there is any news from her brother. His flagship, the *Due Repulse*, sailed from Plymouth on the tenth of July at the head of his fleet, in stormy weather and heavy seas. She'd heard nothing from him since, or from her husband.

At the last minute before they sailed, the queen ordered Charles Blount to remain and strengthen the defences of Portsmouth harbour. Penelope still worries about him. If the Spanish attack he will be directly in the firing line.

Frances looks pale and tired, but relieved to see her. Her two small spaniels appear, and one bounds up to Penelope for attention, licking her hand, its tail wagging. The other dog stares at her, as if making up its mind whether she is welcome, until Frances calls it to heel.

Frances glances up at the clear blue sky. 'We could take these two for a walk along the footpath which follows the bank of the river, if you like?'

Penelope agrees. 'That would be perfect.'

Frances pulls a light cape over her gown and puts on a pair of white gloves. The river is a short walk from her home, and busy with wherries and tall-masted sailing barges. They pass through the people queuing for wherries at the Tower jetty, and once they are alone she turns to Penelope, her face grim.

'I should tell you that I have suffered a miscarriage.' She frowns. 'It seems God doesn't wish me to have another child.'

'I'm so sorry, Frances, I had no idea.' Penelope had planned to tell her she is with child again, but decides her news can wait for now.

'Your brother doesn't know. I decided not to tell him, but it was a nightmare.' Frances frowns at the memory. 'I'm better now, but my doctors have said I might not be able to have any more children.'

'What do the doctors say about little Penelope?'

'She's a constant worry to me. They seem at a loss to know what is wrong.'

'I can pay for the queen's physicians to examine her.'

'There is no need—'

'I want to, as her godmother, and I know how Robert's adventures only increase his debts.'

'I've heard nothing from Robert, although that's not unusual with these long sea voyages.'

Penelope stares out at the tall masts of ships, moored at the wharf downriver. 'Robert promised to send a note at the first opportunity. I worry they should have waited for the weather to improve. He was never much of a sailor, or good at listening to the advice of those who know better, but I'm sure he will send a message when he can.'

Lord Rich sits propped up on pillows in his bed. Penelope hasn't been into his bedchamber before and finds it cold and unwelcoming, like her husband. The whitewashed walls are bare of any decoration, and the windows are shuttered, despite the summer sunshine. The only light is from a tall church candle at the side of his bed, which casts dancing shadows as it flickers.

He does not look pleased to see her. 'Your brother and his crew are safe, for now at least. After leaving Plymouth we were blown off course, and forced to land for repairs at the port of Falmouth.' He scowls. 'I was not sorry, as I was confined to my bunk for most of the time, and was little enough use to anyone while we were at sea.'

Penelope says a silent prayer of thanks, although she knows this is a temporary respite. 'They plan to set off to sea again, once repairs are made?'

He nods. 'Your brother knows he will be blamed for setting out in bad weather. He is determined to prove himself to the queen, but has no idea how many ships and men are lost, or whether they will be able to continue after repairs to the damaged spars and rigging are made.'

'Well, I for one pray they cannot.'

He stares at her swollen middle and scowls, his old manner returning. 'You should be ashamed of yourself, woman.'

'*I* should be ashamed?' She hears the contempt in her voice. '*You* are the one who should be ashamed, after how you've treated me.'

He glowers at her. 'Do you think I'm weak, to say nothing about your infidelity?'

She cannot answer without provoking him further.

'You must believe I don't care. Well, I *do*. I have tolerated your wanton behaviour for the sake of our children. Your *legitimate* children.' He shakes his head. 'Go, and don't come back. I disown you.'

The midwife places a cool cloth over Penelope's forehead. 'Not long now, my lady, God willing.'

Penelope manages a smile of gratitude. She has chosen not to invite her sister, or Frances, both of whom have lost children – or her mother, with her well-meaning childbirth traditions. Her good friend, Anne Broughton, has been a regular visitor during her lying in, yet cannot be here now.

She misses Jeanne, who wrote from France to say she and

her husband are well, and have a boy of their own. The future for Huguenots is uncertain, and they might have to return to England. Penelope sent her money, and the names of two associates of Anthony Bacon who can help them, if they need to escape the threat from the Catholics.

She says a prayer that her child will be safe and healthy, and promises herself she will not be disappointed if it is another girl, although in her heart she hopes this time she will give Charles the son he wishes for. She's had enough of staying away from court, and wishes a rest from the seemingly endless cycle of childbearing.

Her lying in also means she hasn't seen Charles Blount since he left for his duties in Portsmouth, but he's written, hinting of a good return on his modest investment in the Azores voyage. He does not mention that her brother has yet another failed mission to his credit.

The Spanish fleet of some sixty warships was scattered by the savage autumn storms. The threat of invasion is over, the treasure fleet has eluded them, and Robert could delay no longer. He'd failed in his mission. He'd risked the queen's ships, and the lives of all his men, yet the Spanish escaped to fight another day.

He'd given the order for the fleet to return to England. Gales scattered their ships yet again and, battered by storms, they limped home with little more than spices to show for their venture. Penelope suspects they returned with something of more value, but must keep it secret from Robert Cecil, who would confiscate it in the name of the Crown.

A wave of pain brings her back from her daydream, and she calls out. 'Please God, let it be over soon!'

Her maidservant, Mary, a mother of several children herself, joins the midwife and together they urge her to push. Penelope closes her eyes and imagines how pleased Charles Blount will be when he sees he has a son. She tries to ignore the waves of pain, but this time feels everything as the child is pulled from her.

She gasps, and holds her breath. The silence is broken by a sharp cry. Penelope raises her head to see the midwife's look of serene satisfaction of a job well done as she cleans the baby with a towel. She has learned to read the woman's face, and knows the signs are good.

'A fine boy, my lady.'

Penelope falls back on to her crumpled satin pillows, her hair matted, breathless with the exertion of her delivery. She smiles to herself as she thinks of telling Charles, but the memory of her husband's stern admonishment returns. *You should be ashamed of yourself, woman.*

She is not ashamed. He told her to go and not come back, although she cannot, for the sake of their children. If God graced her with a boy, she'd planned to name her child after his father. She knows it will cause a scandal, yet will not be enough to make her husband wish to leave her.

The midwife hands her the new baby, swaddled in white linen, with only his little face showing. Penelope is over-whelmed with relief, and speaks to him, oblivious of whatever her midwife or maidservant might think.

'You are the new little Mountjoy, and that's what you shall be named.' She smiles at the thought of what the world will make of her choice.

Penelope returns from court to Essex House, and is greeted by Anthony Bagot. 'Does my brother still languish in his bed?'

'I fear the strain of the islands voyage has taken its toll on him, my lady. His fever has returned.'

She raises an eyebrow. 'Will you rouse him for me? Tell him to get dressed, for I have news from court he will wish to hear.'

Anthony Bagot has a twinkle in his eye. 'I trust it's good news. Your brother is in no fit state for another berating by Her Majesty.'

Robert appears after a short while. Penelope knows his curiosity will win over his fever. He wears a warm coat over his nightgown, and groans. 'I've had enough of Queen Elizabeth's games, and the gossiping of her self-serving courtiers.'

'You have more lives than a cat!' She smiles. 'It seems you are back in favour with Her Majesty.'

'How can that be?' He scowls.

'That's what I said.' Penelope gives him a mischievous look. 'How can my errant brother redeem himself so easily?'

He brightens. 'Tell me what you've heard.'

'One of your commanders, Sir Francis Vere, returned to court and was summoned to provide his account of your conduct. I only have it second hand, but it seems he paints quite a different picture from the others, and walked with the queen in her garden. He told her the storms you encountered were the fiercest he'd ever seen, and far from treating Sir Walter Raleigh badly, you showed true leadership and understanding.'

'The queen likes to play us against each other. I never liked Francis Vere. He sent the press gangs out in Plymouth without my approval, and resented Charles Blount's appointment.'

'That's why the queen trusts Sir Francis Vere's word. She knows he wouldn't lie for you.'

'I'll not return to court unless I'm ordered to.' Her brother shakes his head at the thought. 'The queen rewarded my greatest critic, Lord Admiral Charles Howard, by making him Earl of Nottingham – for sitting safely at home!'

'Lord Admiral Howard is an old man, at the end of his career.' She places her hand on his arm and gives him a comforting squeeze, as she had when he was a boy. 'Return to court while you can, and make the most of this opportunity.'

21

ST VALENTINE'S DAY

FEBRUARY 1598

Penelope's mother presides over the festivities like a queen surrounded by her courtiers. It was her idea to recreate the feast of Lupercalia, the original Valentine's Day celebration. The great hall of Essex House has been decorated to resemble a Roman villa, with pillars painted to look like marble, and a raised wooden balcony.

The men dress as senators, with tunics and togas, and the ladies in high-waisted gowns, with colourful sashes. Minstrels play on lutes as servants wearing togas bring sugared delicacies and ewers of wine. The tables surround an open area for the highlight of the evening: a special performance of a new play by the Lord Chamberlain's Men.

Penelope sits between Charles Blount and her mother, who has Christopher Blount in a white toga at her side. She makes an attractive Roman lady, with a sash of scarlet silk and a gilded laurel wreath in her hair. Charles looks impressive as a Roman centurion, wearing a black leather breastplate, with a red velvet cape fastened with gilded clasps over his shoulders.

She is pleased to see that her brother is back with Frances, although he talks too loudly, and seems already a little drunk.

He tells anyone who will listen that he has been made the queen's secretary, but Penelope knows the appointment is temporary, until his nemesis, Robert Cecil, returns from his diplomatic mission to France.

Penelope chooses a heart-shaped sugared comfit from her plate and offers it to Charles Blount, who takes it with a smile. Neither of them worries about what the gossips might say. She has heard nothing from her husband since he sent her away and her family lawyer, Richard Broughton, says her marriage can only be dissolved if it is proved the union has never been valid. Despite this difficulty, she feels a special bond with Charles since the birth of little Mountjoy, their strong and healthy son.

Charles places his hand on her arm, and speaks softly. 'I see your sister is here on her own.' He frowns. 'I worry for her. Henry Percy is proving to be a poor husband. He should be here with her, but the man is a hopeless dreamer. He cares only for staring up at the stars, and wastes his money on his study of alchemy.'

Penelope glances across at Dorothy. 'Did you know she's carrying his child?'

'No, I didn't – but that might be a good thing. The responsibility of a child could be the making of Henry Percy.'

A drum roll demands their attention before Penelope can reply. Master Will Kempe, narrator of the Lord Chamberlain's Men, steps into the centre of the floor. Dressed as a Roman senator, he makes a flamboyant bow to Penelope's mother. 'My lords, ladies and gentlemen, we present for you this evening a tale of two households, both alike in dignity.'

Penelope enjoys the play and finds herself thinking that her Lucy would have made a better Juliet than the sallow boy who calls from the wooden balcony. She glances at Frances, and sees a tear glisten on her cheek. The tragedy of the ill-fated lovers has touched her, but it could also be a worrying sign her marriage has gone the way of the others in the Devereux family.

The darkened room feels oppressive, and there is not enough light from the candles for Penelope to read her book. She suspects her mother's well-meaning influence, as she looks at the tapestries of religious scenes blocking the light from the shuttered windows. But this time it's not Penelope the midwife has been called for.

With typical stubbornness, her sister Dorothy will not be persuaded to leave Syon House. Penelope finds the former abbey cold and haunting, yet the journey from Essex House is short enough by wherry, and Dorothy is grateful for her company.

'She will be here soon.' Penelope smiles to hide her concern. 'I sent Anne Broughton with my carriage for her, to be sure she isn't delayed.'

Dorothy nods. 'I was going to send for my midwife from Wales. She served me well in the past, but it's too far to travel, and she has a family of her own to care for.'

'My midwife is the best in London. You will be safe in her care.' Even as she says the words Penelope hopes she isn't tempting fate. Dorothy lost her last child, and the doctors could not explain the reason.

She changes the subject to her sister's errant husband. 'Do you know where Henry is?'

Dorothy looks resigned. 'I've not heard from him since I began my lying in, but that doesn't surprise me. Henry is not the most affectionate of husbands, and has many interests to occupy his time.'

'Why did you marry him in such haste?'

'A better question is why did *he* marry *me*?' Dorothy flinches as the pain troubles her, but the question seems to take her mind from it. 'He is eighth in the list of presumptive heirs to the Crown. The Catholics spread a rumour he planned to declare for their faith, and strengthen his claim by marrying Lady Arbella Stuart.'

'He married you to prove the rumours wrong?' Penelope sees that such rumours would ruin Henry Percy at court. The gossipers would not care if they were true or false, and someone would inform the queen.

'It is possible, but who can know?' Dorothy gives Penelope a wry look. 'I suspected he wanted Syon House because Doctor Dee lives so close by.'

'Charles said Henry spends much time at Doctor Dee's house discussing mystical ideas. He said they call him the *Wizard Earl*.'

Dorothy nods. 'I had no idea when I married him, but he's addicted to smoking pipes of tobacco, and gambles away our money like a fool.' She winces with the pain of her contractions, but manages a smile. 'He makes our brother look careful with his money.'

Penelope glances at the door. The midwife is late, despite being sent for at the earliest signs. The prospect of having to deliver her sister's baby fills her with dread, but she tries to appear calm. 'I'm concerned about our brother. He plays a high-stakes game, and is reluctant to listen to my advice.'

Her sister tries to sit up, but another contraction overwhelms her, and she groans. 'Robert has no talent for the politics of council, but has a gift for making enemies of men like Robert Cecil and Walter Raleigh.'

'There is nothing we can do for him, Dorothy, other than pray.'

The door opens and Anne Broughton enters, followed by Penelope's midwife and one of Dorothy's maids with a pile of clean towels. Penelope feels a sense of relief as they take charge. All she can do now is hold her sister's hand.

'I'm sorry to be late, my lady.' The midwife ties a white apron over her gown. 'I was delayed by an emergency.'

'I'm glad you are here.' Penelope gives her a relieved smile. 'I was beginning to worry that I would have to do your work.'

Dorothy cries out as the pain increases, but there is no sign of her child. She lies back on the bed and turns her head to face Penelope. 'He seems reluctant to make his way into this world.'

Penelope brushes a strand of damp hair from her sister's forehead. 'He?' She smiles. 'You seem sure this baby is a boy.'

'That's – what – I've – prayed – for.' Dorothy gasps between words, a look of alarm in her eyes. 'If anything – goes – wrong…'

Penelope gives her hand a reassuring squeeze. 'You will be fine, but rest assured I promise to always look after your girls.'

The midwife interrupts before Dorothy can reply. 'Not long now, my lady.'

Dorothy cries out, a worrying sound in the darkened bedchamber. 'Dear God!'

Penelope studies the face of her midwife, and sees she looks unconcerned. She feels unexpected guilt at her relief that it's her sister who suffers this time, and not her. She takes Dorothy's hand and says a silent prayer for her.

The midwife prepares to deliver the child. 'Push now!'

Dorothy groans and her face contorts with effort as the baby emerges. She grips Penelope's hand so hard her nails dig in, then relaxes and falls back on to her pillows.

The baby bawls as the midwife washes it clean. 'Another girl, my lady.'

Dorothy stares at her in disappointment. 'I was sure it would be a boy. I haven't thought of a name for a girl.'

Penelope smiles. 'You are young, and time is on your side.'

She gives her sister a mischievous look. 'You could name her after our mother. She would like that.'

Dorothy shakes her head. 'You already have a daughter named after her. But I do like the name Lucy.'

'Lucy Percy has a ring to it.'

Dorothy nods. 'I shall leave the decision to her father. It might help him take more interest in her.' She smiles as she holds her baby in her arms. 'I must be grateful for God's mercy in delivering her safe and well, and pray she lives longer than —'

Penelope sees the tears form in her sister's eyes, and guesses she is remembering the sudden death of her last child. She hopes a new daughter will bring an end to her grieving for her loss. Dorothy has been withdrawn since the death of her last child, and it will be good to see her happy once more.

Penelope knows her brother well, and recognises the signs that something has gone wrong. 'What troubles you, Robert?'

He strides around the room as he speaks, stopping to peer out of the window, as if he suspects someone is coming for him. 'I've been drawn into a row about who should be the new Lord Deputy of Ireland.' He frowns. 'I told the members of the council I suspect the previous deputy, Lord Burgh, was poisoned.'

'Like our father?' Penelope keeps her voice low. 'They used to say Robert Dudley had our father poisoned, so who do you accuse?'

'I'm accusing no one, but have my suspicions.' He gives her a conspiratorial look. 'Robert Cecil could be behind it, but he's too clever to be caught out, and, like our father's murder, I can never prove it.'

'Why would Robert Cecil wish Lord Burgh dead?'

'Lord Burgh complained that Lord Burghley kept back money meant for our men in Ireland. Robert Cecil continues his late father's penny-pinching, and plans to put his own man in charge.'

'You can't believe that's enough reason to have someone murdered?' Penelope doubts even Robert Cecil's ambitions reached that far, but a worrying thought occurs to her. 'Do you hope for the post yourself?'

'I nominated Sir George Carew, who has experience of fighting in the Desmond rebellion, and proved himself worthy in Cadiz.'

'Well, even Robert Cecil couldn't object to that. He chose Sir George Carew to accompany him on his mission to France.'

Her brother scowls. 'The queen accused me of wishing George Carew out of the way.'

Penelope struggles to understand the problem. 'It doesn't sound like much of a row to me.'

'I made it into one by asking the queen to tell me why my opinion matters so little to her.'

'What did she say to that?'

'Your opinion serves only your ambition!' He grins at his parody of the queen's arrogant tone. 'I said to her: why ask for my counsel if you plan to ignore it?'

'After all this time at court, it seems you've learned nothing about how best to handle the queen. You need to ply her with subtle compliments, and choose your moment well. You should know there will be consequences if you challenge her judgement.'

'You soon forget the way she insulted our mother, banishing her from court, and ruined our father.' His raised voice has a sharp edge. 'She told me to go to the devil, but when I turned to leave, she struck me on the face and shouted: do *not* turn your back on us!'

Penelope imagined he would hardly have been able to keep his self-control. 'What did you do?' She spoke softly, hoping for the best but fearing the worst.

'Charles Howard stepped forwards and saved me. I saw the satisfaction in his eyes, which infuriated me.'

'It seems you owe him a debt of gratitude.'

'I found the whole business infuriating, and told the queen I would not take such insults from her father.'

Penelope puts her hand to her mouth. No wonder he looks anxious. This row was more serious than she'd imagined. 'She did not take kindly to that?'

'She yelled at me, that I should be taken out and hanged for my insolence.' He scowls. 'I am ruined. In all my time at court, I've never seen the queen strike anyone.'

'I have never heard of her being spoken to with so little respect.' Penelope shakes her head in disbelief. It will take a miracle for her brother to redeem himself.

His boots thump the tiled floor as he continues pacing, his brow furrowed and his hand on the hilt of his sword. He peers out of the window again, then turns to her. 'I decided to come back here and wait to learn the consequences.' His eyes have a haunted look, like the stags in the hunting pen that know their days are numbered. 'What should I do?' He sounds like a little boy again.

'Beg her forgiveness, and pray being her favourite still means something.'

He frowns at her suggestion. 'Francis Bacon suggested a solution to my difficulties. The situation in Ireland is worse than ever. I might be able to redeem my fortune.'

Penelope feels a stab of concern. 'You are so like our father. Ireland is a dangerous place. I heard two thousand men have been killed in the fighting, and many more are injured or have deserted.'

He nods. 'I've lost the will to fight for our queen, but I am still the Lord Marshal of England. I shall put my name forwards to lead the new campaign in Ireland, clear my debts, and finish what our father started. What is there to lose?'

Penelope stares at him in silence for a moment. 'All who try to deal with the Irish have failed, including our father, and everyone since. You were fortunate to get away with what happened in Cadiz, and again in the Azores, but if you fail in Ireland you could pay with your life.'

He has a glint in his eye as he summons up the old bravado, as he used to when they were children. 'I shall ask the queen's consent to lead the greatest army ever seen in Ireland.'

Penelope's eyes widen in concern. 'Charles said the rebels gained control of Ulster, and will soon be at the gates of Dublin. They will not be easily defeated now they've tasted victory, and you will need money.'

'Charles has agreed to buy Wanstead from me. He says it's perfect for him. Private and close to Leighs Priory.'

Penelope can see he won't be dissuaded. 'Well, if you are determined, you must write a letter of apology to the queen, or your problems will only be worsened.'

She doesn't hold out much hope, even though he's always been the queen's favourite. With a wave of her hand, she can grant his wish, or order his arrest, and have him locked up in the Tower dungeons. She sees her brother regrets his outburst, but the queen will not forget his behaviour.

Penelope wakes in a sweat. Her head aches, and her muscles have a dull numbness. She rings the bell for her maidservant, a blunt-speaking woman named Bessie. She cannot afford to be ill, as she must spend more time at court if she is to return to the queen's favour, for her brother's sake.

Her maid opens the wooden shutters and fixes them back,

flooding the bedchamber with sunlight. She turns to speak to Penelope. 'My lady—'

'I don't feel well, and would be glad of a little warmed milk with some honey.' She can see her maid looks uncomfortable. 'What is it, Bessie?'

'You have a rash on your face, my lady.' She frowns. 'It reminds me of the smallpox, which my poor cousin Catherine suffered with.'

'Bring me my Venetian mirror, if you will, Bessie. It's in the middle drawer of my dressing table.'

As she waits, she prays Bessie is mistaken. Wishing a pox on someone is a terrible curse, and she despairs of what she can have done to deserve this. The sense of dread makes her hand tremble as she holds the mirror to catch the light and stares at her reflection.

A gift from Don Antonio Pérez, the little oval mirror has a gilt frame, and serves its purpose well. She can see why her maid wishes to leave. A rash of angry red spots covers her face and neck, and she knows her plans must change.

The queen suffered with smallpox. Like her, it began with a fever, and it was feared she would die. God saved her, but Philip Sidney once told her his mother, Lady Mary, nursed the queen and caught the illness. He'd said his mother was terribly disfigured by the scars, becoming a recluse through shame.

Penelope looks up at her maid, who waits at the foot of her bed. 'What happened to your cousin?'

Bessie hesitates to answer. 'I'm afraid to say she died of the pox, my lady.'

The doctor keeps his distance but seems certain of his diagnosis. 'I regret to say you most definitely have the small-pox, my lady.'

Penelope feels her pulse race. 'People have died from this…'

He nods. 'Most survive with no ill effects, but you should know the disease is fatal in about a third of cases.'

'And the scarring?' Her voice wavers as the full implications dawn on her. All her life she has been used to compliments about her perfect complexion, and she was once called the greatest beauty at court.

Her doctor's face is grim. 'You deserve to know the truth. Many smallpox survivors have permanent scars over large areas of their body, especially their faces, my lady. Some are left blind.'

'Thank you for being so direct.' Penelope frowns. 'What do you suggest I do?'

'Isolation is best, until it has run its course.'

'Is there a cure?'

'I pray for one, my lady, but whatever people may tell you, little is known about how to treat this disease, or how to prevent it.'

Penelope turns her face from him, and weeps. She fears what will become of her children if she is not there to protect them. For now, they will all have to stay away from her, as must everyone she cares about. She must fight to survive, as they cannot be left to the mercy of her husband.

22

THE IRISH REBELLION

MARCH 1599

'These are the cards I've been dealt, Penelope. I have to play them.' Her brother sounds as if he has mixed feelings about his new position as Governor General of Ireland and the commander of the queen's army there.

'I heard she danced a galliard with you. Is that how you persuaded the queen to let you go?'

He smiles at her teasing tone. 'I told her the Irish believe they have the better of her, and I see it as my duty, as her Lord Marshal, to assert her sovereignty over Ireland.' He grins. 'I've been granted an advance of twelve thousand pounds to begin the preparations, and plan to raise six hundred cavalrymen.'

'It seems you are learning how to deal with Her Majesty.' A thought occurs to her. 'Have you said farewell to Frances?'

He frowns. 'She is annoyed with my plans for my step-daughter, Elizabeth.'

Penelope nods. 'You should have consulted Frances before choosing a husband for her daughter.'

'Frances can hardly object to Roger Manners. He is the Earl of Rutland, and a loyal friend. He will be a good husband for Elizabeth, and she will be a countess, like her mother.'

'She is only thirteen.' Penelope gives him a questioning look. 'Can you not wait at least until she is of childbearing age?'

'Elizabeth has a good education, thanks to her mother, and acts older than her years. She will be fourteen soon enough, and Roger Manners is only ten years older than her, which is not unusual.' There is an edge of irritation to his voice. 'He's coming with me to Ireland, so you will understand I must have this marriage settled before we sail.'

'Is that the real reason for such haste?' Penelope knows him well enough to doubt it.

He holds the hilt of Philip Sidney's sword at his belt, and hesitates to answer, then looks up at her with a glint in his eye. 'I owe it to her father's memory to see his daughter married well, while I can.'

The mention of Philip Sidney brings back a flood of poignant memories from her past. She still wears the gold locket he gave her, but has not opened it for many years. She can imagine the promises her brother made to him as he lay dying, and guesses providing for his daughter Elizabeth was one of them.

He studies her, his eyes resting on the faint scars on her once flawless face, visible despite the pale ceruse she uses. 'I prayed every day for you, Penelope. Mother warned me we must prepare for the worst news, but I always had faith in your recovery.'

'I confess I feared I would die, and it proved to be one of the harshest winters anyone can recall. My time in isolation at Leighs Priory tested my faith, as well as my resolve, but God must have heard your prayers, Robert. None of my children, or any of the household there, contracted the disease.'

Penelope stares at her brother, fixing him in her memory. 'I want you to take this.' She hands him the charm. 'Don

Antonio Pérez gave it to me. It's a bezoar stone. He swears it's the only way to protect against poison.'

'It will take more than superstition to protect me, dear sister.' He grins. 'I have an invincible army, and shall return a national hero.'

'Then carry this stone with you to remember that I pray for you, and I beg you not to put yourself into needless danger.' She fights back tears at the prospect of never seeing him again, and takes some comfort as she sees him slip the bezoar stone into his pocket.

Charles returns to Essex House with worrying news from court. 'A messenger arrived from Ireland. Your brother negotiated a truce with Hugh O'Neill, the rebel Earl of Tyrone, against the queen's orders, and is returning, also without her consent, to explain himself.'

Penelope hears the concern in his voice. 'In his last letter, he said he suffered with a fever in Dublin, from which he has not fully recovered.'

Charles nods. 'I cannot say if the fever is real or an excuse to return. He had no easy task. The rebels outnumbered our army two to one, and had a new resolve. We have underestimated them for far too long. They live off the land, waiting to ambush us at every turn, but I expect the queen will not take kindly to his disobeying her orders – and *some* will say it's a surrender.'

'What are we to do, Charles?'

'I need to protect him from himself. You know how he argues with the queen.' He frowns. 'The court is at Nonsuch Palace, where your brother has his own chambers. It will be easy enough for me to see him in private, to remind him how to conduct himself, *before* he is granted an audience.'

'I'll come with you.'

'Your presence will draw too much attention. I will be discreet, and after I've seen your brother I shall try to be present when he is summoned to the privy chamber.'

'But he will listen to me—'

He holds up a hand to silence her. 'You must wait here, Penelope. There is nothing you can do.'

She stares at him, surprised at this authoritative side to him, which she has not seen before. 'There must be something. I feel so helpless.'

'Say a prayer for your brother, and you should visit his wife. Her child must be due soon.'

He returns late in the evening, his face grave. 'Her Majesty summoned the Privy Council to an urgent meeting to discuss your brother's conduct in Ireland.'

Penelope fears the worst. 'They will never give him a fair hearing. Robert Cecil will make sure of that.'

'He believed he might be forgiven, but told me he is not surprised that his enemies at court see their chance.'

'How was his audience with the queen?'

'She wanted to know every detail of his adventures in Ireland, and he didn't hold back. He described the stinking streets of Dublin, the dreadful state of the castle, and the churlish attitude of the council. He said the rebels fight like savages, with bows and arrows, throwing spears as they ambushed his army in the forests.'

'How did the queen treat him?'

'She said little enough, and at dinner sat with Robert Cecil and Walter Raleigh.' He frowns. 'They were deep in conversation about some serious matter. I hope it was not about your brother's future.'

'So, all we can do now is wait.'

He nods. 'I told Robert to take care with what he says to the Privy Council, as they are as likely to set up an ambush as any rebels in Ireland. Francis Bacon is attending the meeting, and agreed to come here to let us know what was said.'

Penelope feels a sense of misgiving. 'I've never trusted Francis Bacon. He is an ambitious man, and still blames my brother for not securing him the post of Attorney General. I would not be surprised to find he has been working for his cousin, Robert Cecil, all this time.'

'We have no choice but to trust him, Penelope. We need all the support we can get.'

Francis Bacon arrives from the meeting of the Privy Council the next afternoon, dressed in his black lawyer's robes. 'The Earl of Essex is charged with being in contempt of Her Majesty's instructions, in returning to England without permission.' He glances at Penelope. 'He is also charged that his letters from Ireland have been presumptuous, that he was over-bold in forcing entry to Her Majesty's bedchamber, and that he created an unjustified number of knights.'

Charles shakes his head. 'He told me he didn't intend to surprise the queen in her bedchamber, and she seemed pleased to see him.' He curses. 'You list many charges, Master Bacon, but the Earl of Essex will have a good answer for them all – *if* he's granted a fair hearing.'

'I only report what I have heard, Sir Charles. Nothing more, and nothing less.'

Penelope's mind races with the consequences. 'What is to happen to my brother?'

'He has been taken to York House, where he is detained under guard in the care of Sir Thomas Egerton, the Lord Keeper, at Her Majesty's pleasure.' His voice carries a hint of satisfaction. 'The Earl of Essex will be tried by his peers who, I am sure, will listen to his answers.'

Penelope hasn't seen Frances since the tragic funeral of her little daughter in June, now resting with her two infant brothers, and feels a stab of conscience when she finds her new baby has been born. She folds back the coverlet to reveal a sleeping child.

'This is your new niece, Frances Devereux. She is a strong little girl, thank the Lord.'

Penelope smiles. 'I am so pleased for you, Frances. Have you been able to tell my brother?'

Frances frowns. 'I wrote to the queen to plead for his release, or for permission to visit him, but Her Majesty has not replied, and banished me from her court.'

'Then I shall see her, and put your case.'

'I will be grateful for anything you can do, but fear the queen is being advised by Robert's enemies, who know this is their chance to be rid of him.'

'But she gave him an impossible task.'

Frances nods. 'I see now it was all part of Robert Cecil's plan to have him sent to Ireland in the first place.'

'Do you know how Robert is coping?'

'His man, Gelly Meyrick, was allowed to see him, and came to visit me here. He says Robert has lost weight, and still suffers with the fever which he caught in Dublin. He claims he is too weak to rise from his bed, but when the queen sent her doctor he refused to take his potion.'

An idea occurs to Penelope. 'I will send our family doctor to York House, and tell him not to be sent away. We've seen my brother like this before often enough.'

'At least he should be able to find out if this fever is real or imagined.' Frances has a note of bitterness in her voice. 'Did you know there are rumours in the taverns of London that he has died?'

Penelope makes sure none of her servants can hear and speaks softly to Frances. 'I fear he will be committed to the Tower, so I've written to King James of Scotland.'

'I'm not sure that will help. In fact, there is a danger you will be drawn into this mess.'

'That's a risk I have to take, Frances.'

Penelope chooses her black gown. One of her plainest, she wears a modest ruff and none of her expensive jewellery. The last thing she wishes to do is upstage the queen, after all that has happened.

Despite herself, she feels a frisson of nerves as she enters the presence chamber. So much is at stake – her brother's liberty, even his life, if she can handle this well. She says a prayer, and takes a deep breath as she enters. The queen is not there. Instead, Robert Cecil waits to greet her.

'Lady Rich.' He studies her for a moment; she sees his eyes going to the ceruse on her once flawless cheeks. 'Her Majesty declines to permit you an audience.'

Penelope must think fast. 'All I ask is that my brother is allowed to see his wife, Sir Robert.' Her tone is as deferential as she can manage, despite her dislike of the man he has become.

'Her Majesty is offended by his actions, Lady Rich, and calls him a traitor.'

Penelope stares at him, her eyes wide. 'He is no traitor, sir. He risked his life for the queen every day in Ireland, and only returned to explain his actions. I've been told he is not well, and is unfit to command an army.'

'He has dispersed his army in Ireland, and many have

returned, against the orders of the queen.' There is an air of finality to his words, as if he wishes her to leave.

She knows he is enjoying this moment of triumph over her. He is clever, yet so is she. 'As I cannot speak to the queen in person, I beg of you, Sir Robert, to use your influence to allow my brother to be set free, pending a fair trial, where he can give a proper account of his actions.'

She notices his eyes twinkle at her flattery. She doubts he has many compliments, and under all his status is a lonely widower. Penelope places her hand on his arm. 'I shall be forever in your debt, Sir Robert, and thank you for your great kindness.'

'I will ask Her Majesty to permit his wife one visit, if only in remembrance of the service her father provided – and I shall visit him, to see for myself whether he is well enough to stand trial.'

Charles wakes Penelope with a kiss. 'We cannot let your brother be taken to the Tower.' He puts his arm around her and pulls her close. 'You recall what happened to poor old John Perrot?'

Penelope struggles to think for a moment. 'He was accused of treason, and didn't even have a chance of a trial. There was talk he was poisoned in his cell.'

'That's right. The warders at the Tower are paid little enough, so it's easy to persuade them to slip something into a prisoner's food or drink, and impossible to prove.'

Penelope sits up in the dim light and studies his face. He has that serious look which she sees often now. 'What are you suggesting?'

'I was thinking that few enough people have escaped from the Tower of London, but it would be quite a different matter to free him from York House. I spoke to Gelly Meyrick, who says he is not well guarded.'

Penelope stares at him. 'I cannot let you take the risk. If you are caught you could both end up in the Tower.'

'There is no need for me to be involved. Gelly Meyrick has any number of men loyal to your brother who would risk their lives for him.'

'What would he do, if he's set free?'

Charles thought for a moment. 'He could become a mercenary in the Netherlands, or even ride to King James of Scotland, where he might find some sympathy.'

Penelope wasn't so sure. 'He might be able to live under an assumed name in Wales, and at least I would be able to see him again.'

Charles turned to her. 'We could seize control of court, and oust troublemakers like Cecil and Raleigh.'

Penelope kissed him. 'Now I know you are dreaming, Charles. That would mean taking on the queen's guard, and everyone loyal to her scheming councillors.'

'That might be less risky than what the queen has planned for me.'

'Don't tell me she is sending you to Ireland in my brother's place?'

He curses to himself. 'She gave me her glove at the Accession Day tilt for good reason. The queen sees me as your brother's replacement.'

Penelope feels a familiar sense of dread. 'That would suit Robert Cecil. Frances believes he persuaded the queen to send my brother to Ireland to have him out of the way.'

'If I were to succeed in defeating the rebels, it will be at your brother's expense, and if I fail...'

Penelope lies back on her soft pillows wondering what will become of them all if her brother escapes. The thought of Charles being sent to fight the Irish rebels fills her with dread, but in her heart she knows he is right: there is nothing she can do to prevent it.

Frances calls after visiting Penelope's brother at York House. 'I've come to thank you. Robert Cecil was as good as his word, and saw my husband after you spoke to him. He agrees Robert is too ill to stand trial, and asked me to nurse him back to health.'

Penelope places her hand on her arm. 'Is he really ill?'

'He has a mild fever, but I am more worried by his deep melancholy.' Frances shakes her head. 'He's lost the will to defend himself, and I fear what will happen if he is committed to the Tower.'

Penelope looks to see none of her servants can overhear. 'We cannot allow him to go to the Tower, and if it means having to free him—'

Frances stares at her with wide eyes. 'We must not, Penelope. He would be a fugitive for the rest of his life, and what do you think would become of me, and the children?'

'If we have Robert Cecil on our side, there is hope of a fair trial.'

Frances looks thoughtful. 'I've been banished from court, but you have not, and neither has your sister. The queen is usually in a better mood at Christmas time, so you could try again to gain an audience. If you see her, she will listen to what you have to say.' She produced a silver brooch set with emeralds. 'This was a gift from my late husband. He would approve of it being used to help your brother.'

Penelope holds the jewel in her hand, seeing how the emeralds glint in the light. Frances is right. Her gift will catch the queen's eye and could ensure her prisoner may be out of sight, but not out of mind.

23

THE VERDICT

JANUARY 1600

Penelope risks the freezing snow and icy roads to visit Richmond Palace with her sister Dorothy. They avoided the Christmas and New Year festivities of court, and both dress in mourning black. Their brother's illness worsens, and the bells of St Clement's Church, opposite York House, tolled for him while his enemies at court danced and feasted.

He claims a fever, but Frances believes his real illness is in his mind, and they plan to ask the queen's permission to see him before he might die. None of Penelope's letters of petition are graced with a reply, despite her gifts of jewels. Dorothy is granted a brief audience with the queen, but dismissed as soon as she mentions their brother.

In her heart she fears the worst, yet Penelope tries to remain positive, for her sister's sake. 'Frances said the queen was generous with her New Year presents. She gave her young daughter Elizabeth twenty pounds in gold to mark her becoming the Countess of Rutland.'

'I wish she showed the same generosity to me.' Dorothy

looks wistful. 'I had nothing from the queen this year, thanks to our brother.'

'Everyone knows your husband is one of the wealthiest men at court. I expect she believes you have no need of her charity.'

'Henry spares me as little as he can, and saves the rest for his betting at games of cards with Sir Walter Raleigh, which he generally loses, and his pointless experiments in alchemy, which come to nothing.' The note of bitterness echoes in her voice.

Robert Cecil greets them as they approach the queen's chambers. His beard is more pointed, and his deformed back more hunched than Penelope remembers. He touches the brim of his hat and turns to Dorothy.

'Forgive me, Countess. I need to speak to Lady Rich in private about a matter of concern to Her Majesty.'

Dorothy gives him a questioning look. 'Of course, Sir Robert.' She turns to Penelope. 'I will wait here for you.' She nods to Robert Cecil. 'Good day, Master Secretary.'

Penelope's mind is a whirl as he leads her to his wood-panelled office, where a warming fire blazes in an iron grate. He sits behind a polished oak desk, and gestures for her to take the chair opposite. She hopes for good news, but his grim expression tells her he is uncomfortable with what he has to say.

'I must ask you to stop writing to the queen.' He studies her face as if not sure what to do. 'I fear it does nothing to help your brother's case.'

Penelope sits back in surprise at his directness. 'I am at a loss to know what else to do. Her Majesty has not granted me an audience for me to ask her in person.' She gives him a coy look. 'I owe it to my brother to petition the queen on his behalf.'

'Her Majesty showed me your last letter, which you will agree is more than a petition, Lady Rich.' Robert Cecil frowns. 'You will not be surprised to learn she is offended by your accusation that your brother's enemies poison her mind against him.'

Penelope struggles to recall what she'd written, and curses her naivety. Even a cursory read of her letter will be enough for Robert Cecil to know he is one of those subjected to her criticism. She has often warned her brother about the dangers of making an enemy of such a man, and now it seems she has done so herself.

'That was not my intention, Sir Robert.' Most men could be charmed by her demure tone, but Robert Cecil is not like most men, and it seems she's dealt him an unbeatable hand.

He takes a silver key and unlocks a drawer in his desk, which makes a scraping sound in the silent room as he pulls it open. He produces her letter, which he unfolds on the desk in front of him, smoothing the creases with unnecessary care. 'Would you like me to remind you?' He studies her letter and reads aloud.

'My unfortunate brother… who would vouchsafe more justice and favour than he can expect of partial judges or those combined enemies that labour on false grounds to build his ruin, urging his faults as criminal to your divine honour, thinking it a heaven to blaspheme heaven; whereas by their own particular malice and counsel they have practised to glut them-selves in their own private revenge, not regarding your service and loss so much as their ambition and to rise by his overthrow.'

He gives her a glance of disapproval. Penelope cannot look him in the eye. She imagines the discussions in the privy chamber, with the queen waving her letter in the air, and knows he is right. Her words do nothing to help her brother's case, and play into the hands of his enemies. He skips a few lines and continues reading, his tone like that of a witness providing evidence in a court of law.

'I have reason to apprehend that if your fair hands do not check the courses of their unbridled hate, their last courses will be his last breath, since the evil instruments that they by their officious cunning provide for the

feast, have sufficient poison in their hearts to infect, the service that they will serve will be easy to digest till it be tasted.'

Penelope bows her head. 'I regret my poor choice of words, Sir Robert, and humbly beg forgiveness.' Her voice is soft, but she sees his eyes narrow as he judges her.

'It's too late to beg forgiveness, Lady Rich. I must tell you the queen is shocked that a lady such as yourself, a baroness, is so bold to write in such a style to her.'

'Should I write an apology to Her Majesty?' Penelope is close to tears at the thought that her actions have made her brother's predicament worse.

Robert Cecil holds up his hand. 'You've done enough with your letters, Lady Rich. You should return to your husband and await the summons.'

'Summons, sir?' A pit forms in her stomach.

'You are like your brother.' He sounds dismissive. 'You should know such actions have consequences. You will be summoned to appear before the Privy Council to explain yourself.'

Charles holds her close. 'I was hoping for some reply from King James, but I've delayed this moment for as long as I can, and the queen leaves me no choice.'

Penelope embraces him and holds him tight, as if she can stop him going. She kisses him, not caring about the servants. 'This is the worst time for you to leave. My husband plans to marry Lucy to Sir George Carey, who is twice her age, and there seems to be nothing I can do – but I understand, and will pray for you.' She stares into his eyes. 'Come back safe, and write when you can.'

He kisses her one last time, and fastens his riding cloak over his shoulders, then pulls on his gloves. 'God willing, I'll be home before Christmas. There's nothing worse than an army of discontented men in winter.'

She watches his young groom bring his horse. The men who are to travel to Ireland with him are mounted and waiting, and Penelope sees how their faces betray their true feelings about this venture. She knows from her brother what they can expect in Ireland.

On an impulse, and to delay their departure a little longer, she calls for her servants to give each of them a cup of wine. One of them shouts out a brave toast to the queen and victory over the rebels, and they all raise their cups of wine in acknowledgement.

Charles swings into his saddle, and manages a smile. 'Show deference to the Privy Council, but stand by what you believe is right, Penelope. They are good men at heart, and cannot punish your loyalty to your brother – or to Her Majesty.'

She slips him a sealed note. 'Read this when you reach Dublin.' It is a declaration of her love, and her promise to marry him one day, even if it must be against the law.

Penelope takes the wherry to the watergate at Essex House, where Frances waits to meet her. In her note, Frances warns that the house is out of bounds to visitors, but she has persuaded Robert's new jailer – Sir Richard Berkeley, the white-bearded former Lieutenant of the Tower – to permit them to meet in the gardens.

Frances is expecting another child, and looks more at ease than she has for a long time. 'Your brother is not allowed out while you are here, Penelope. No one can speak with him, except for myself, and Sir Richard's servant, Porter, but he sends you his love, and thanks you for coming.'

Penelope walks up the gravelled path from the river with her. 'Has he recovered from whatever ailed him?'

She nods. 'Robert is back to his old self, cursing the Privy Council when the public hearing set for the Star Chamber in February was cancelled, and he was given no reason.'

Penelope nods. 'I heard there was quite a commotion, as a good number turned up, not realising there was nothing to see.'

'He suspects a conspiracy to drive him to madness, but I told him to be grateful he's not locked up in the Tower of London.'

'Did you know I was summoned to be questioned by the Privy Council?'

She gives Penelope a look of sympathy. 'I suppose it was to be expected, but I heard there is to be no punishment.'

'Appearing before the members of the Privy Council was punishment enough. I confess I was quite nervous by the time they called me in; they'd kept me waiting for hours.'

Frances stops to admire the roses, planted by Penelope's mother in happier times. 'What did they ask you?'

'They told me to explain my letter to the queen, and tell them who I accused. I told them the truth: that I wished to do what I could for my brother, and meant what I wrote.'

'I'm surprised you were let off so lightly. I expected you would be banished from court, like your mother.'

'I had an anxious moment when they told me they knew about my letter of apology, which I sent against Robert Cecil's advice. Fortunately, I asked the queen to burn the letter after she'd read it, which it seems she did.'

'Well, I for one am relieved no one tried to set your brother free.' Frances glances over her shoulder to be sure they are not overheard. 'Gelly Meyrick has a plan to help him escape by boat from the watergate, but Robert says Sir Richard Berkeley has shown him kindness, and fears he will pay the price if he escapes.'

'But that would be better than being committed to the Tower?'

'It will mean risking everything, so is a last resort only.'

Penelope agrees. 'Charles was ready to help, as was my stepfather, but only with the approval of King James.' She frowns. 'My new problem is that someone published a letter I wrote to the queen, and copies are circulating abroad. I suspect Robert Cecil, but any member of the Privy Council could have had a copy.'

Frances puts her hand on Penelope's arm. 'You don't need to worry. You've answered the Privy Council's questions, so is that not the end of the matter?'

'They have summoned me again, and I fear it's to accuse me of having my own letter published.' She gives Frances a wry look. 'It seems I am the only person in London who does not possess a copy.'

Frances thought for a moment. 'You can follow your brother's example. Tell them you are unwell, and go to the country until this matter has passed.' Frances smiles. 'I plan to stay with my mother at Barn Elms for my lying in, so you can join me there. Mother will be glad of our company, and it is close enough for you to see your children whenever you wish.'

'Thank you, Frances. I will go to see my children at Leighs Priory first. I've been away for far too long, and I know my husband will arrange a marriage for Lucy, who is eighteen now, or Essie, who will soon be sixteen, so I will take them both to visit my mother.'

The hot summer by the Thames at Barn Elms should be idyllic, but the ever-present danger to Charles in Ireland, and her broth-

TONY RICHES

er's forthcoming trial are never far from Penelope's mind. She
prays for them both every day, and lives for the visits of messengers
from Charles, and Gelly Meyrick with letters from her brother.

Charles sent her a letter when his ship, the *Popinjay*, reached
Dublin after a stormy crossing from North Wales. He'd found
his army in disarray, with many sick or injured, and many
deserters. He no longer believed he would be able to return
home before Christmas, as it would take months before he
could regain order.

At least she has some good news for him. She can no
longer doubt she carries his child. She risks his disappointment
by telling him she believes it must be another boy. In her note
she writes that a mother knows such things, and asks him to
choose a name for their unborn son.

Gelly Meyrick has a glint in his eye as he delivers a letter for
Penelope, who says a silent prayer as she breaks the red wax
seal. She holds her breath as she reads it, then calls for Frances.
'Her Majesty has decided my brother is no longer to be held
under arrest.' She hands the letter to Frances, who reads it with
a frown.

'He complains that banishment is a cruel punishment for a
man like him.' She looks up at Penelope. 'He should be glad to
be let off so lightly, but his life at court is all he knows. I don't
know what he'll do now he's banished.'

Penelope agrees. 'The queen showed my mother how long
she can bear a grudge, and Sir Robert Cecil has achieved what
he wants. Let us pray we can finally put this behind us.'

Frances folds the letter and hands it back. 'Robert invites us
both to a party for his friends and supporters at Essex House.'
Frances frowns. 'He seems to forget I am here for my lying in,
expecting *his* child.'

Penelope hears the note of bitterness in her voice. 'You

know what he is like, Frances, and I doubt he will ever change.' She smiles. 'My mother will be there with my stepfather, as well as my sister Dorothy. This will be the first time we have been together for a long while.'

Despite the event being a celebration of his freedom, Robert's mood is pensive. He has lost weight, allowed his hair to grow to his shoulders, and his reddish beard to grow thicker than is fashionable. He wears a fine silver doublet and hose with a blue sash, and carries Philip Sidney's best sword at his belt once more.

'I see you are with child again, dear sister.' He grins. 'I'll wager I can guess the father.'

Penelope can tell he is a little drunk as she hugs him. 'I've seen that look before, dear brother. I can tell you are planning something.'

He takes a deep drink of ale. 'I would like to have revenge on that accursed hunchback Robert Cecil and his cronies, who delight in misleading the queen for their own profit.'

'Take care not to provoke him further, Robert. We all feared you would end up in the Tower dungeons, and too many people never leave there. Remember what happened to Dorothy's father-in-law.'

He nods. 'I know Charles and our stepfather had plans to free me from York House, as did Gelly Meyrick, but they were risky, and could have seen us all locked up in the Tower, so I thank the Lord they never had to try.'

'How did you manage to convince the Star Chamber of your innocence?'

He stares at her for a moment, as if deciding how much to tell her. 'There were eighteen men at my hearing, yet the only ones I would call a friend were the old master of my college in

Cambridge, Archbishop John Whitgift, and our uncle, Sir William Knollys. Neither said *one word* to defend me.'

'It seems there would be little question of the outcome when it came to a vote, regardless of anything you said.'

'The Attorney General, Sir Edward Coke, has never forgiven me for proposing Francis Bacon for his post. He'd decided I was guilty before the hearing began.' He takes another deep drink, draining his tankard of ale.

'So, what did you say to them?'

'I fell to my knees and begged forgiveness for my actions, and explained I am the queen's most loyal servant. That seemed to persuade most of them, except for Coke. He read aloud from your letter to the queen, as if I was somehow to be blamed for it. He said the letter was proof of our disrespect for the queen and the loyal members of her council.'

Penelope frowns. 'I regret my choice of words in that letter, but despite all the trouble it caused, it allowed me to send my private apology directly to the queen. I named those she must not trust on her Privy Council, so it served its purpose.'

Her brother's eyes narrow. 'They deserve to be thrown out.' He cursed. 'They spoke as if I'd committed treason, yet any of them might have done the same in my position – if they'd been brave enough to set foot in Ireland in the first place.'

'What are you going to do now?'

'I will write to King James, confirming my support for his accession, and denouncing Robert Cecil and Walter Raleigh as men who should not be trusted.'

'Be careful, Robert. That sounds like treason.'

'They leave me with no choice, Penelope. We must face the facts: the queen is growing old and frail, and her advisors circle her like carrion crows, waiting for easy pickings. We need to look to the future, and promote the interests of her successor.'

Her child is a healthy boy, as Penelope had somehow sensed he would be. Born in the middle of the night, he wails loudly enough to wake the entire household. Penelope lies back exhausted but happy as her midwife cleans her new baby with a towel.

'It's some time since I've seen a boy so eager to come into the world before his time, my lady.' The midwife sounds reassuringly cheerful at her work, yet Penelope's instinct alerts her.

'Before his time?'

'Yes, my lady, unless there was some miscalculation.' She smiles. 'It happens often, and easily enough.'

She hands the swaddled baby to Penelope who kisses him on the forehead for luck, and to begin the special bond between them. Her new son stares up at her, his eyes sparkling in the candlelight.

'He is to be named St John.'

The midwife looks curious. 'After the saint, my lady?'

Penelope shrugs. 'I asked his father to choose the name. He gave no explanation, but we shall all call him John.' She smiles. 'Graced by God.'

24

THE REBELLION
FEBRUARY 1601

Charles Blount was ordered to remain in Dublin, as he'd feared, so Penelope spends New Year at Leighs Priory with her children. Frances writes to tell her she's been graced with a daughter, so Penelope makes the journey to Barn Elms as soon as the weather allows, and finds the house full. As well as Frances' mother, Lady Ursula, her daughter Elizabeth is there with Wat's young widow, now Lady Margaret Hoby.

Frances welcomes her, and calls for the nursery maid to bring her new daughter. 'I've decided to name my daughter Dorothy, after your sister. She seems to be thriving, despite the freezing weather.'

Penelope smiles as she sees the new baby. 'Has my brother seen her?'

'I sent one of my grooms to Essex House to tell him, and he returned with news of rowdy Welsh soldiers guarding the gates.' She frowns. 'It's a worry, as there are rumours of insurrection in the city, and of bands of drunken soldiers in the taverns.'

'What *is* my brother up to now?'

'I'm not sure, but he needs to take care, or he'll find himself in the Tower, after all we've done to prevent it.'

Penelope agrees. 'I will have to go and see for myself, but let us pray it's not too late.'

Penelope finds Essex House busy with men building barricades and preparing weapons. She is welcomed by the Welshman, Sir Gelly Meyrick, who wears a breastplate over his doublet and a sword at his belt. His usual jovial manner is replaced by a serious frown.

'Your brother is here, Lady Rich. He will be glad to see you, but it would be best if you stay with Lady Essex, as we're expecting trouble.'

'What sort of trouble?' She watches as the guards secure the gates behind her with iron chains. Several carry muskets and some wear pistols at their belts.

Gelly shows her to the front door. 'Your brother refused a summons from the Privy Council, my lady. We believe they could send armed men to take him by force.'

Penelope looks up at the house, where candlelight flickers in every window. 'I'll speak with him. This will only be worse if we turn the queen's guards away.'

Her brother sits at the dining table in the great hall, flanked by their stepfather, Sir Christopher Blount, and his step-daughter Elizabeth's husband, Sir Roger Manners, Earl of Rutland. They seem to be arguing about what to do. The table is littered with wine bottles, flagons of ale, and maps of the streets of London.

She is surprised to see her uncle, George, who must be close to sixty. His once dark beard is now grey, and his face looks tanned and weather-beaten. He smokes a pipe of tobacco, and stands when he spots her. 'It's good to see you looking so well, Lady Penelope.'

She smiles. 'And you, Uncle. I've been meaning to visit you in Lamphey.'

'I've ridden from Wales with two dozen armed men.' He glances at her brother. 'I know I wouldn't be called to London without good reason.'

Her brother nods. 'Welcome, Sister. He gestures towards a dark-eyed man at the table. 'This is Sir Ferdinando Gorges, Governor of Plymouth, who fought with me in France.'

Sir Ferdinando smiles. 'It is my honour to meet you, my lady.'

'It seems you have also travelled some distance, Sir Ferdinando.' She looks down at a map of the roads around Whitehall Palace on the table, then into the eyes of her brother. 'I am intrigued to know the reason.'

Her brother glances at his companions. 'Robert Cecil won't rest until we are all ruined. He poisons the mind of the queen against me, as well as others on the Privy Council. We must deal with him – and soon.'

Penelope's eyes widen in alarm. 'How do you propose to do that?'

'We will choose our moment, when the queen is at the Palace of Whitehall. The royal apartments are relatively unprotected.'

'Sir Walter Raleigh commands the queen's guards. He will have you arrested if you march on the palace.'

'We have some three hundred men armed and ready. I hope as many again will join us when we show our hand, including the Mayor of London's militia.' He grins. 'The people are on my side. They tire of our government, and more men are arriving every day. I sent a message to Charles Blount to bring back his army from Ireland, and King James is sending men from Scotland. Robert Cecil's time is over.'

She stares at him. She doubts Charles will wish to be drawn into his plan, but his army of experienced fighting men would make all the difference. The wildness in her brother's eyes unsettles her. He has the haunted look of a man with nothing more to lose.

More armed men arrive at Essex House, and as night falls Penelope takes Gelly Meyrick's advice and returns to join Frances at Walsingham House in Seething Lane. Now she has had a chance to think, she shares her concerns with Frances.

'I worry about my brother. He places too much faith in his ability to persuade the queen to replace the Privy Council with his own supporters.'

Frances agrees. 'I fear he's already past the point of no return. Robert Cecil will have spies at Essex House, and they'll report his talk as treason.'

The word hangs in the air. They sit in silence for a moment before Penelope speaks. 'We must support my brother. He leaves us with no choice, and if Charles supports him—' She can't bear to think through the consequences.

Frances gives her a sympathetic look. 'We will take this one day at a time. You need a good night's sleep, and if you feel the same way in the morning, I'll come with you to Essex House, and we'll see if we can talk sense into him.'

Bells ring in the chill morning air, calling the faithful to church. Penelope has forgotten it is a Sunday, but after a restless night decides to ride back to her brother with Frances. They arrive to find the streets full of soldiers, many on horseback, and Essex House has become a barricaded fortress.

Gelly Meyrick curses when he sees them, but orders his guards to let them pass. 'Have a care, my ladies, and keep well back from the windows.'

They find much the same confusion inside the house, with

armed men shouting to each other, and the rooms in disarray. There is an air of anticipation, and Penelope senses something else … a look of desperation. They find her brother, who seems surprised to see them.

Frances kisses Robert on the cheek. 'Mother is caring for our daughter, so you will understand I can't stay for long. Come back to Barn Elms with me, Robert, at least until this all dies down.'

He stares at her in surprise. 'I cannot.'

'For the sake of our children, if not for me, I beg of you.'

'This has gone too far—'

'It has *not*, not yet, but I know what you plan to do.'

'You can't know.'

'You plan for your men to infiltrate Whitehall Palace and seize control on a signal.'

He stares into her eyes. 'Where did you hear of this?'

'Penelope told me. You call the queen's advisors traitors, but most people would say it is *you* who are the traitor.'

'You're wrong, Frances. The people love me, and are tired of our vindictive queen.'

'You're a fool, Robert.' She steps back from him, and glances at Penelope. 'You could have had anything you wanted, but you're throwing it away. For what? To prove you are a better man than Robert Cecil, with his crippled back, or that arrogant peacock, Walter Raleigh?' Her raised voice reveals a new side to her.

'It's too late.' He no longer has the bravado of the previous day, and will not look them in the eye.

Penelope puts her hand on his arm. 'It's *not* too late. Ride back to Lamphey with our uncle, and stay there until King James is on the throne. The queen is soon for the grave, and is not forgiven for the way she's treated our father, our mother, and now you.'

He scowls. 'She sent Lord Keeper Egerton, with our uncle,

Sir William Knollys, Sir Edward Somerset, and Lord Justice Popham. They said if I have a grievance I should raise it in the proper manner and allow the law of England to take its course.'

'What did you say?'

'I told them I don't trust their justice. The men wanted to throw them out, but I put them under guard in my study, and will hold them as hostages until this is all over.'

Penelope cannot believe his foolishness. 'Even our uncle?'

Her brother nods. 'Our uncle threatened that detaining them will have serious consequences.'

Penelope frowns. 'They can't know what you are planning, or they would have come here with an armed escort.'

Gelly Meyrick calls from the doorway. 'The men are assembled and ready, my lord.'

Robert looks from Frances to Penelope, and tucks a pistol into his belt. 'There's been no word from Charles in Ireland, but I shall leave enough men here to ensure you are safe. Wish me luck.'

Penelope says a prayer for him as she watches him go. A group of armed men chain the gates behind him, and she hears a rousing cheer from the men waiting on the road. Her brother raises Philip Sidney's sword in the air, and calls out, 'To the queen! To the court!'

Frances joins her at the window. 'We should leave. The people will *say* they support him, but few enough will be prepared to risk their lives to prove it.'

The door opens and Sir Ferdinando Gorges enters with two men carrying pistols. He nods to Penelope and Frances. 'The Earl of Essex ordered me to release the hostages. I have a boat waiting by the watergate. You should both accompany us, my ladies.'

His voice has a note of urgency, and Frances nods, but Penelope hesitates. 'Take them while you can, Sir Ferdinando. I shall stay. Whatever happens, I expect my brother will have need of me.'

The doors burst open as the men return. Several are bleeding from serious wounds, including Penelope's stepfather, who holds a blood-soaked cloth to his head. Her brother has a bandage over his hand and seems surprised to find Penelope and Frances still there, and his study door open and unguarded.

'Where is our uncle, and the others?'

Penelope gives him a puzzled look. 'Sir Ferdinando Gorges said you ordered them set free.'

Robert curses. 'Ferdinando Gorges has betrayed me. I gave no such order. He must have been Robert Cecil's man the whole time, a viper in our midst, discovering every detail of our plans.'

She glances at their stepfather and frowns. 'I can see your plans did not work out.'

Her brother scowls. 'They chained the Ludgate. Our only choice was to escape by river, and now they surround us. He takes a key from a cord around his neck. 'The queen's men will be here any moment. I must burn the letters from King James. Could you help tend to the wounded?'

At dusk, the iron gates are smashed open and soldiers burst into the courtyard. Shots echo, and men swarm in, taking firing positions where they can. A bullet cracks a pane of leaded glass, killing one of Gelly's Welsh lookouts, and another thuds into the barricaded door, splintering the wood.

Men armed with muskets, accompanied by Sir Robert Cecil and Sir Robert Sidney, call for their surrender. 'Culverins have been sent for from the Tower and we will reduce Essex House to rubble if necessary!'

One of the men calls back. 'We'll never surrender. We will die first.'

After a silence, Robert turns to Penelope and Frances. 'I shall have to send you out. We cannot surrender.'

He embraces them in turn as they prepare to leave. Frances looks pale and frightened. She leans forwards and kisses him on the cheek. 'You *must* surrender. You are outnumbered and they have the house surrounded.'

'I've escaped from tricky situations before.' He forces a brave smile. 'Thank them for freeing you – and be sure to tell them you were held against your will.'

Penelope has tears in her eyes as she says farewell. 'Beg for their mercy. I will pray for you.' She kisses him one last time and bows her head, doubting she will ever see her brother again.

Life under house arrest takes on a dull routine. Penelope is not allowed visitors, or to write or receive any letters. Taken from Essex House by carriage in darkness at midnight, she is not even sure where she is. Her door is guarded night and day, the windows are kept shuttered, and she has no servants of her own.

She passes the long days reflecting on the events that led her there, not daring to think about what the future holds for her, or her brother. She can imagine Robert Cecil has made sure the queen has no choice but to declare them all guilty of treason.

The elderly serving woman who brings her meals says nothing, and watches her warily, as if she fears she might try to escape. On the second day Penelope asks her name, but she bows her head and leaves without answering.

On the next day a young maid brings her food, with a silver goblet of wine instead of the cup of ale usually served. She gives Penelope a curious look, perhaps intrigued by stories she's heard. She doesn't speak, but doesn't seem wary, or in such a hurry to leave.

Penelope sees her chance. 'Tell me, what is your name?'

'I've been told not to speak to you, my lady.'

Penelope pulls the diamond ring from her finger and holds it up for the girl to see. 'I will give this to you, if you deliver a message to my lawyer, Master Richard Broughton, at the Inner Temple.'

The girl stares at the ring, her eyes widening, and hesitates. 'What do you wish me to tell him, my lady?'

Penelope keeps her voice low. 'Tell him where I am, and that he must find a way to see me.' She sees the doubtful look in the girl's eyes. 'You can also tell him I said he is to give you ten pounds for your trouble.' She smiles, to put the girl at ease. 'Now, what is his name?'

'Master Richard Broughton, at the Inner Temple, my lady – and I am to tell him you are in the household of Sir Henry Seckford, Keeper of the Privy Purse, in St John's.'

The next day passes more slowly, and Penelope does not see the young serving maid. An older woman brings her a bundle of her clothes from Essex house, and sets them down on the table. Penelope's heart misses a beat when she recognises her friend, Anne Broughton, dressed as a servant with a linen coif over her greying hair.

Anne gives her a cautionary look. 'I do not have long. I've told them I'm your servant, sent by your husband, who is concerned for your welfare. I'm afraid the news I bring is not what you will wish to hear.'

'Thank you for coming, Anne. You must tell me. I am prepared for the worst.'

'Men died at the Ludgate rioting, and your brother is imprisoned in the Tower. He's charged with treason: conspiring to depose the queen and change the government. He faces trial in the great hall of Westminster, and will present his own defence.'

Penelope listens with rising concern. 'He believes he can have a fair trial, despite everything that's happened.' She frowns. 'Do you know what is to become of me?'

Anne frowns. 'You are also accused of treason. Lord Chief Justice Popham says you told the men guarding him you would have his head if he caused trouble.'

Penelope stares at her in disbelief. 'I would *never* say such a thing.' Her pulse races as she thinks of the consequences. 'Lord Popham knows it's untrue, but my word will count for little against his.'

Anne nods. 'They spread such rumours to undermine your case, but we must hope the Lord Chief Justice will not commit perjury in a court of law.' She glances at the door. 'I must go, but my husband is attending your brother's trial. He told me Lord Rich is among the jurors.'

Penelope looks at her in surprise. 'My husband? It makes no sense, unless—'

Anne nods. 'Like Francis Bacon, he has turned against your brother to protect himself.' Anne gives her a look of sympathy. 'I will return when I can to tell you what has happened.'

More than a week passes before Anne returns. She seems unsure how to begin. 'I am sorry to tell you this, my lady, but your brother has made a full confession, and was found guilty of all charges.'

Penelope bows her head. 'I expected as much.'

'The queen commuted his sentence from a traitor's death to a private beheading on Tower Green.'

'My brother is dead?' Penelope cannot cry. Her voice is cold, as if part of her has frozen, as icy as the Thames in the worst of winters.

Anne has tears in her eyes. 'I heard he was buried in the Chapel of St Peter ad Vincula, close to the queen's mother, Anne Boleyn.'

Penelope kneels on the cold floor at the side of her bed after Anne leaves. She prays for her brother's soul, finally at peace. She prays for his widow, her good friend Frances, for little Robin, who she hopes will become the third Earl of Essex, and his infant sister Dorothy, who will never know her father.

She says a prayer for her stepfather, who she last saw at Essex House, and remembers his gratitude when she tended to his head wound. Her mother will lose a second husband, as he will surely be executed for his part in the failed rebellion.

Penelope thinks of all the others caught up in her brother's wild adventure, like the cheerful Welshman, Gelly Meyrick, who tried to persuade her to stay away from Essex House. He will suffer the worst punishment: a traitor's death at Tyburn.

Last of all, she prays for Charles Blount, forced by their vindictive queen to lead her unwinnable campaign against the Irish, at great risk to his own life. She says a prayer for each of her children. She fears she will never see them again, and falls sobbing to the floor, surrendering to her grief and despair.

25

THE SUCCESSION

MARCH 1603

'The queen is dead. Long live the king!' The shout echoes in the streets of London, accompanied by a cacophony of church bells. Even while the queen lies in state at Whitehall, the people look to a new future under King James. Penelope is not sorry she never returned to court. She cannot grieve the old queen's passing, and only feels relief her long ordeal is over.

Her fortieth birthday was celebrated at Wanstead with her children and her mother, as Charles Blount remained in Dublin. His success in Ireland is the reason she's escaped her charge of treason without a trial, or even a fine. Brought before the Privy Council, Penelope had feared she would not have a fair hearing.

They said her brother blamed her in his confession, and told them she'd urged him on. She explained her involvement was no more than that of a loving sister, and refused to confess to their accusations. She guessed no one on the Privy Council wished to risk Charles Blount's loyalty. He held the Pale as far as Dundalk, against the odds, and had fought off a landing by the Spanish to the south.

It seems from his letters he's paid a high price. He was injured when a rebel shot his horse from under him, and he suffered the flux and a fever, yet the queen refused to grant him leave to return. Penelope has no idea what the new king will do about the Irish, but prays for Charles Blount's safe return to her.

She visits Essex House for the first time since her brother's death. Seized by the Crown, along with all his assets, Frances has taken the lease, and now lives there . Penelope finds it strange to enter the great hall, scene of so many memories, and is greeted by her brother's son Robin, who will soon be twelve.

'Good heavens, Robin. You are the image of your father when he was your age.'

He gives her a boyish grin, and takes it as a compliment. He has the same mischievous glint in his blue eyes, and wears a silver doublet and hose with pearl buttons. All he needs is Philip Sidney's best sword at his belt, but it was taken by the royal armoury.

Frances shakes her head. 'I pray he follows me, and *not* his father in temperament.'

'You cannot still be bitter towards him, Frances.'

'I can never forgive what he did, or understand him.' She looks at Penelope with cold eyes. 'He said you encouraged him by calling him a coward, and persuaded others to follow. When I heard, I feared you would share his fate.'

Penelope glances at Robin, aware he is listening to every word. 'I forgive him.' It is the truth, yet Penelope cannot forgive her brother's attempt to incriminate Charles Blount.

Frances accompanies Penelope to Whitehall Palace, curious to see the queen lying in state. They wait in line, in a queue which trails down the palace corridors. When their turn comes, Penelope stares at the effigy of the queen, dressed in her parliamentary robes, lying on top of her coffin.

The dark eyes of the painted wooden face stare into space. With a sceptre in her hands and a gilded crown on her head, the effigy is intended as the symbol of her monarchy, yet the faded, reddish wig seems to mock her memory.

Penelope stands before the velvet-draped coffin, conflicted with memories. Their vindictive queen showed no mercy to her brother, yet chose to spare her own life. She bows her head and says a prayer that Elizabeth finally rests in peace. This woman will trouble her no more.

Penelope studies the unfamiliar royal seal on the letter before she dares to open it. King James sits astride a horse, brandishing a sword over his head, more like a Scottish invader than their new sovereign. The letter was delivered by a royal messenger in the livery of the late queen, a sign not everything has changed.

Breaking the seal, she unfolds the letter. She is appointed a lady of the bedchamber to Queen Anne. In an instant, all the doubt and worry falls away. Her plan to declare support to King James is vindicated. For the first time in years, she will have influence at court, not as a naive maiden, but as a senior member of the new queen's closest circle.

Penelope makes the long journey north with the others chosen by the Privy Council to escort Queen Anne to London. She rides at the side of Lady Frances Howard, who she's known since they were maids of honour, living in the maidens' chambers. She doesn't trust Lady Frances, who her brother called *the spider of the court* for her meddling.

Penelope thinks her an odd choice by the Privy Council. Her second husband, Henry Brooke, Baron Cobham, is a supporter of the Lady Arbella Stuart, and an outspoken critic of their new king.

Lady Frances turns to Penelope as they ride. 'I heard young Lucy Russell, Countess of Bedford, has ridden to Scotland to be first to see the new queen, and hopes to win her favour.'

Penelope smiles at the note of envy in her voice. Lucy Russell is two years younger than her own daughter, and a friend of the family. 'She is a bright girl, and right to make the most of this opportunity. Did you know she speaks fluent French, Spanish and Italian?'

'Our new queen is from Denmark.' She sounds scornful. 'I expect she struggles to speak English.'

Penelope doesn't warn her not to underestimate their new queen. She's learned that Anne of Denmark is well educated, and fluent in French and Italian. 'She married King James at the age of fourteen, so has spent half her life surrounded by Scots. She will have need of women she can trust to explain our strange English ways.'

Lady Frances laughs. 'They say the queen is with child. Do you think we shall have to wait in Berwick until it is born?'

'I would not be surprised. King James seems in no hurry to be crowned, and three servants died of the plague in a day at Hampton Court. It suits Sir Robert Cecil to keep him entertained at Theobalds, where he can ensure his own future in the new court.'

Lady Frances gives her a conspiratorial look. 'I have been thinking of my own future at court, and will ask to be governess to Princess Elizabeth. She is seven years old, and my own daughter Elizabeth will be six this year, so they will be good company for each other.'

Berwick Castle dominates the garrisoned border town. Armed soldiers guard the gates, even though Scotland and England are now united under the same king. Penelope is accommodated in an ordinary house, where rushes crackle under her feet, and she must share a room with other ladies. Like all those who are chosen to serve the new queen, she is forbidden to continue into Scotland.

They dine in an oak-beamed hall, and the talk is all speculation about what they might expect from Queen Anne. When, at last, the queen arrives, they are told she is not well enough to greet them. Penelope finds Lady Lucy Russell, who has been with the queen for the past two weeks, and asks to speak to her in private.

'I'm sorry to hear the queen is unwell.'

Lady Lucy nods. 'I regret to tell you she lost her child.' She frowns. 'I also lost a child, and know you have. I can never forget that time.'

'I am surprised she feels well enough to travel.' Penelope pushes away the painful memory of her little daughter Elizabeth, taken too soon. 'I suppose she has little choice.'

'I'm afraid I have more bad news for you. The queen has brought her Scottish ladies-in-waiting, and says she has no need of more ladies at court.'

Penelope sees her prospects sink like a stone dropped into a well. Her appointment means nothing without the queen's approval, but she can't face the prospect of returning to obscurity. Her only hope is that the knowledge her informers gathered about the queen can somehow be turned to her advantage.

She leads Lady Lucy back to her room and takes a small, leather-bound book from her travel chest. 'This is *La Semaine*, a poem in French by Guillaume de Salluste, about the creation of the world.' She hands it to Lady Lucy. 'Please give it to

Queen Anne for me, and tell her it's one of my most cherished books.'

Lucy smiles. 'I shall do my best to recommend you to the queen, as well as your sister Dorothy.'

'Thank you. I am sorry about how your husband was drawn into my brother's revolt.'

'My husband was fortunate to be pardoned, and supported your brother through his own free will, so you cannot blame yourself.'

Queen Anne sits with Lucy Russell at her side. She wears distinctive pendant earrings of large, pear-shaped pearls which Penelope remembers were looted from a Spanish treasure ship by Drake. She has another large pearl in her reddish hair, worn piled high, and an upstanding lace ruff frames her face. Her pale green gown is decorated with marigolds and pink rosettes, set with dark jewels.

Penelope feels her age, and looks down at her own gown. It is one of her best, a rich brocade, yet the frayed hem is repaired and the style is that favoured by the old queen. Queen Anne is not yet thirty, and will bring more than new fashions to England. She curtseys, and looks into the intelligent brown eyes of her new queen.

'Lady Penelope Rich at your service, Your Highness.'

'Welcome, Lady Rich.' She has a soft voice, with a trace of a Scottish accent. 'Thank you for the copy of *La Semaine*. I look forward to discussing it with you, as few of my ladies share my interest in poetry.' She glances at Lady Lucy. 'The countess tells me you are a baroness, and skilled with the lute. Will you play for me?'

'I regret I have not brought my lute, Your Highness.'

'Then you shall have the use of mine, a fine instrument

from Bologna.' She gestures to a maidservant, who hurries away and returns carrying the lute.

Penelope tunes the strings and sings one of the Huguenot songs taught to her by Jeanne, long ago, and sees the queen's nod of approval. She senses a special bond of shared interests between them and, when she finishes, Queen Anne looks thoughtful.

'You have a beautiful voice, Lady Rich, and play well. Do you have masques in England?'

'Indeed we do, Your Highness. We celebrate feast days with masques, as well as plays and pageants.'

Queen Anne nods. 'I did not look forward to this journey to England, but the Scots can be dour, and I will be glad of your help to arrange entertainment fitting for a new court.'

Penelope smiles. 'I am honoured to be at your service, Your Highness.'

It takes their slow-moving procession more than a week to reach York, where the new queen is welcomed by the Council of the North. Penelope's uncle, Henry Hastings, Earl of Huntingdon, is long gone, and Countess Catherine has retired to a nunnery, but King's Manor feels like home, even after all these years.

While the others rest after the long ride, Penelope walks in the sunshine down the long garden towards the river. The oak bench in the shade of a willow tree, once her sanctuary, is replaced with a newer one. She sits and remembers her brothers, both so keen to throw away their lives fighting for their family name. She misses them, and clasps her hands together to say a prayer.

She also prays for Charles Blount, who hopes to return to her after more than three long years. Penelope hasn't seen her husband since he sat in judgement on her brother, but heard he was one of the twelve barons marching at the side of the late queen's coffin. When the time is right she will ask him to end their marriage.

They finally reach Windsor Castle on a warm June afternoon. Penelope is now a firm favourite of Queen Anne, which has many privileges, including her own private bedchamber, close to the royal apartments. She is writing a letter to her sister, reporting her progress, when there is a knock at the door, and her servant announces that the Earl of Devonshire wishes to see her.

She finishes the sentence she is writing and tells her maid to make him wait. If she has ever met the Earl of Devonshire, he made no impression on her, but she is curious about why he visits at so late an hour. She lays down her pen, and smooths the creases from her gown before telling her maid to admit her visitor.

The door opens and she gasps, tears welling in her eyes. They stare at each other in silence for a moment, then Penelope dismisses her maid. Charles Blount is rugged and tanned from his years in Ireland. His hair is greying, yet his eyes study her with the same longing she remembers. They embrace, and he kisses her, holding her tight in his strong arms, as if she might escape.

'How long have you been back?' She speaks in a whisper, struggling to believe he is here.

'Long enough to win the favour of our new king. Who would have thought I'd be an earl, and a privy councillor?'

Penelope smiles. 'You deserve to be an earl, but are no politician.'

'The war in Ireland has made me one. I've had to deal with

far worse than anything Robert Cecil is capable of.' He looks into her eyes, as if seeing her for the first time. 'I've been told you are chosen as one of the new queen's ladies of the chamber.'

'I like her. She has shown me great kindness, and we share many interests.' She kisses him. 'Tell me, what do you make of our new king?'

Charles thinks for a moment. 'He's not to be underestimated. Raleigh and Cobham made that mistake while you were in the North, and are locked up in the Tower, charged with conspiring to kidnap the king and put Lady Arbella Stuart on the throne.'

'My brother always thought of Sir Walter Raleigh as his enemy, but I feel sorry for his poor wife Bess, and her son Walter.' A thought occurs to her. 'Lady Cobham is here in Windsor, and hopes to be Princess Elizabeth's governess.'

'That seems unlikely now, but I have good news about your brother's reputation. I told the king he did not have a fair hearing. He agreed to grant his children their rights and titles, and that Robin shall be the third Earl of Essex.' He smiles. 'The king also places you above the other baronesses, as a senior lady of the court.'

Penelope stares at him in amazement. 'Thank you, Charles, that means a lot to me. I never thought I would live to see our family name restored.'

His face turns serious. 'There were times in Ireland when I feared I would never see you again, Penelope. In case you are wondering, I have always been faithful, and prayed for you every day.' He crosses to the door and slides the bolt across, then pulls her close. 'From now on, we must make the most of every moment.'

~

The angelic singing of the choir echoes through a half-empty Westminster Abbey, where only the most favoured wait to witness the coronation. Sixty thousand people have died after the spread of the plague, so there is no procession from the Tower, and no grand banquet.

The citizens are banned, by royal proclamation, from coming to Westminster, yet crowds gather in defiance of the order. Penelope feels sympathy for the ranks of yeomen, armed with halberds. Tasked with standing outside to protect those attending from the danger of infection, they suffer a soaking in heavy rain.

Penelope finds her wide gown is not the most practical in the narrow stalls but, like all the queen's ladies, she follows the new fashion. Her red-gold hair is piled high, like the queen's, and she has an upstanding ruff of delicate starched lace, open at the front.

Charles escorts her, wearing his earl's robes of crimson velvet, with his gold coronet and blue Garter ribbon. The king keeps him busy, and has appointed him Lord Lieutenant of Ireland, with generous grants of land. He is also Master of the Armouries and, as a favour to Penelope, ordered her brother's best sword, once owned by Philip Sidney, to be returned to his son, Robin.

A fanfare of trumpets announces the entry of the king and queen, who've arrived at Westminster steps by royal barge. King James walks under a canopy of state, followed by members of his household and his royal guard, armed with gilded halberds.

Twelve countesses in scarlet dresses, including Lady Lucy Russell, Countess of Bedford, lead Queen Anne, under another canopy, in crimson velvet robes lined with ermine. Penelope is surprised to see Lady Arbella Stuart walking at the queen's side, a sign she is not held responsible for the plotting to place her on the throne.

King James and Queen Anne wear crimson velvet cloaks over velvet coats lined with ermine, and sit before the high altar. Penelope watches as the elderly John Whitgift, Archbishop of Canterbury, anoints them, before placing Saint Edward's crown on the king's head. At last, she can begin a new chapter of her life, and cannot recall a time when she has been happier.

26

THE TWELVE GODDESSES
JANUARY 1604

The great hall of Hampton Court Palace echoes to the sound of laughter and chattering as guests gather for the late evening's special entertainment. Penelope is surprised to see the group of Spanish envoys, who Charles tells her are invited as a first step in negotiating a peace treaty.

The new queen spares no expense on her masques, although she scandalises the older ladies of court by ordering the cutting up of the old queen's precious gowns to use as costumes. Penelope is amused, and provokes them further by pointing out there are over five hundred dresses, many worn only once by the queen.

Seating for spectators is arranged on both sides of the great hall, rising in tiers. The royal craftsmen have built a mountain path and a magnificent temple of peace at one end of the hall, with stained-glass windows and a roof with carved beams. The backdrop of mountains flickers with little lamps, like stars twinkling in the sky.

At the other end of the hall is a mystical cave, made to look surprisingly realistic with large rocks, trees and bushes. In place of Queen Elizabeth's aging court minstrels, Queen Anne has brought Master Alphonso Ferrabosco with an orchestra of thirty skilled musicians from Italy.

At ten in the evening, when everything is ready and all the company assembled, the doors of the great hall open. The royal heralds announce the arrival of the king with a shrill blast of trumpets. He enters to cheering and applause, and takes his seat under a cloth-of-gold canopy of state, near the south oriel window.

Haunting music plays as the shadowy figure of Night, dressed in black velvet covered with glittering stars, rises from a hidden trapdoor in the middle of the floor. She approaches the cave, where she wakes her son, Somnus, with the words, 'Awake, dark sleep.' Her son summons a vision for the audience, by incanting a spell and waving a magic wand, and then returns to sleep.

Iris, messenger of the goddesses, appears at the top of the mountain in a rainbow-coloured robe. She descends the winding path to the temple of peace and announces the approach of the goddesses. 'I, the daughter of wonder, am here descended to signify the coming of a celestial presence of goddesses, determined to visit this fair temple of peace, which holy hands and devout desires have dedicated to vanity and concord.'

The first to appear are the Three Graces in silver robes, coming down the winding pathway hand in hand, to the sound of a stirring march. Next come the twelve goddesses, three abreast, in brightly coloured dresses, each followed by a young page as torchbearer, in flowing white robes studded with gold stars.

The procession wends its way down the mountain until all twelve goddesses can be seen. The first is Juno, represented by Lady Catherine Howard, Countess of Suffolk. In a sky-blue gown, embroidered with gold, and decorated with iridescent peacock feathers, the countess wears a gold crown and carries a sceptre. Like Penelope, a gilded mask hides her scars of the smallpox.

'First here, imperial Juno, with sceptre of command for kingdoms large, defends all clad in colours of the air, crowned with bright stars, to signify her charge.'

The audience gasp as they recognise Queen Anne as Pallas, goddess of wisdom, in a bright blue mantle, embroidered with weapons. Jewels flash in her helmet, and her costume is cut scandalously short at the knee, revealing her legs. She brandishes a lance and says, 'Next, war-like Pallas, in her helmet dressed with lance of winning, in whom both wit and courage are expressed, to get with glory, hold with providence.'

Penelope, as the goddess Venus, in shimmering cloth of silver embroidered with doves, carries the girdle of amity. She says her well-rehearsed speech, looking across the hall into the eyes of the king. 'There lovely Venus, in bright majesty, appears with mild aspect, in dove-like hue, with all combining amity, to gird strange nations with affections true.' She cannot resist a smile for the watching ambassadors of Spain.

The next three goddesses are Diana, Vesta, and Proserpine, represented by Lady Hertford, Lady Lucy Russell, Countess of Bedford, and Lady Derby. Then follow Macaria, Concordia, and Astrasa, played by Lady Hatton, Lady Nottingham, and Lady Walsingham.

Lastly, Lady Susan Vere, granddaughter of William Cecil, Lady Dorothy Hastings, and Countess Catherine's daughter, Lady Elizabeth Howard, represent the goddesses Flora, Ceres, and Tethys. When they reach the foot of the mountain, they march to the centre of the hall and the temple of peace, while the Three Graces sing.

Desert, reward, and gratitude,
The Graces of Society do here
With hand in hand

Conclude the blessed chain of amity,
For we deserve, we give, we think,
Thanks, gifts, deserts, thus join in rank.
We yield the resplendent rays of light,
Unto these blessings that descend
The grace whereof with more delight.

The serene music to accompany them is from musicians hidden within the dome of the temple. The goddesses place their gifts, one by one, on the altar of the temple of peace and return to the middle of the hall. They dance measures together, as the Italian musicians play, moving in elegant squares and triangles, before forming a circle for a pavan with linked hands.

The Three Graces call on the goddesses to choose lords, and they dance galliards and fast-paced corantoes. Penelope sees the king stand to applaud – a rare thing. Queen Anne told her he tolerates these extravagant masques, in return for her tolerating his private entertainments with young gentlemen.

As the dancing ends, Iris appears again and announces that these divine powers are about to depart. Penelope makes her final bow to the applauding audience, and follows the queen up the mountain in the same order as they came down. At the stroke of midnight, they all return unmasked, still wearing their impressive costumes.

Penelope joins Charles for the royal banquet with the king and Spanish ambassadors, but he cannot relax and enjoy the festivities. 'The king has put me in charge of peace negotiations with Spain, alongside Robert Cecil – for my sins.' He gives her a wry look. 'I'm as pleased as anyone to see an end to war with Spain, but it will mean more time apart.'

Penelope frowns, his news spoiling her good mood. 'Do you think there is any chance of a lasting peace?'

He sips his wine, then nods. 'Like us, Spain has been

ravaged by famine and plague, and many good men have died. They cannot afford to be at war, but the real prize for us is access to the West Indies, where there are fortunes to be made in trade.'

She studies him with growing concern. 'I trust you're not planning to go to the West Indies, after all the time we've had to be apart?'

'I promise you, Penelope, my only wish is to be with you and our family at Wanstead.' He looks at the drunken courtiers with a frown of disapproval, then smiles at her. 'Who would wish for any of this, when they can be with the goddess Venus?'

The whole of London comes to a standstill for the first coronation procession in forty-five years. Delayed from the previous July due to the plague, the king is to process through the city streets from the Tower to the Palace of Westminster to attend his first Parliament.

Penelope calms her palfrey at Tower Green and stares at the spot where her brother was executed. She says a silent prayer in his memory as she takes her place behind the queen's carriage, and thinks how different everything could have been. If only they could have known the queen would be dead just two years and one month later.

A fanfare of trumpets marks the start of the slow procession, which stretches ahead of Penelope as far as she can see. The king's messengers lead the way on horseback, followed by the chaplains and deacons of the king's chapel. The sergeants, lawyers of the courts, and chancery officers ride before the knights and gentlemen, secretaries of the queen and council of state.

Fourteen trumpeters of the king lead the Knights of the Bath, marching on foot, one after the other. Then ride the barons, including Robert Cecil, now made Baron Cecil of Essendon, doing his best to sit upright, his crooked back under a cape embroidered with pearls.

Twenty bishops and archbishops in their colourful capes lead the counts, all dressed with brocades and pearls. The harnesses of their horses shine with gold and silver, and rattle and tinkle as they ride before the king's mace bearers, who lead the Mayor of London and the city magistrates.

Fifty gentlemen pensioners march with gilded halberds before Prince Henry, the king's eldest son, on a fine black horse. Seen for the first time in public, the ten-year-old heir to his father's thrones of England and Scotland grins as he waves to the cheering crowd.

The Count of Worcester carries the sword of state before the king. Glittering with jewels and pearls, King James rides a white horse, a gift from the King of Spain, under his canopy of state, held by sixteen gentlemen of his chamber. Queen Anne confided to Penelope that he fears assassination, and will be glad when the day is over.

Behind the king rides Charles, the new Earl of Devonshire, at the side of Henry Wriothesley, Earl of Southampton. Released from his long imprisonment in the Tower for his part in the Essex rebellion, Sir Henry is rewarded with the post of Master of the Horse.

The queen rides on a silver and crimson open litter, dressed in white silk sparkling with jewels, followed by four countesses on horseback. Lady Arbella Stuart follows the queen in a gilded open carriage with her cousin, Lady Alethea Howard, Countess of Arundel.

Penelope leads the queen's ladies-in-waiting. At forty-one, she is the eldest and most experienced. She is also a confidante of the queen, and spends the most time with her. This means she needs the queen's permission to leave court, even to see her children, but has more influence than she could dream of.

The captain of the king's guard, Sir Thomas Erskine, brings up the rear of the long procession with one hundred and fifty armed halberdiers. A lifelong friend and companion of the king, Sir Thomas is one of those who supported Penelope's early correspondence with the king, and she counts him as a useful ally.

They ride west to the stirring beat of drums with a clatter of hooves on cobbles. The street is lined with the guildsmen, arranged according to their crafts. Penelope is deafened by the cheering of the crowd and the bells of one hundred and twenty-three city churches clanging in celebration. At Fenchurch Street they pass under the first of eight celebratory arches, built by over two hundred craftsmen, where a pageant is performed.

The arch is fifty feet high, with models of the houses, turrets and steeples of London decorating the roof. Speeches are made about the virtues of their new king, yet few can hear what is said over the roar of the crowds and the clanging bells as they continue down Gracious Street, then Cornhill and into Cheapside, past the cathedral of St Paul's.

The theme of the towering Londinium arch is the London of ancient times. The most finely crafted, it is topped with a model of the old cathedral as it might have once looked, with models of the most important churches, identifiable by their steeples and Latin inscriptions.

The slow-moving procession continues under the arch at the end of Soper Lane in Cheapside, representing the fountain of virtue, which dried up at the passing of Queen Elizabeth and is brought to life again by the accession of King James. Penelope slows to hear a rousing speech where the king is called *the new phoenix*, risen from the ashes.

After the best part of six hours, they reach the Temple Bar and, finally, Whitehall Palace. The king and lords depart for a sitting of the new Parliament, delayed, like the procession, by the plague. Penelope follows the queen and her ladies for a banquet with the ambassadors. Her fluent Spanish proves a great asset, and with the queen, she helps prepare the way for peace.

The warm summer at Wanstead with the children is idyllic; a peace treaty is agreed, and Charles returns, with a generous pension from the King of Spain as his reward. Penelope is glad to spend time with her daughter Essie, now a grown woman, soon to be nineteen years old. Essie has her father's dark hair and the same dark eyes, leaving no doubt about his identity.

They walk together in the sunshine through the same rose gardens Penelope once walked with her mother. She turns to Essie, who dresses in the sombre Puritan manner of her father, with a high neckline and wide, starched collar. Her only jewellery is a small crucifix on a silver chain around her neck.

Penelope stops to smell the fragrant roses, which flower in profusion. 'We must talk about finding you a suitable husband, Essie, before your father marries you off to the highest bidder.' She hears the trace of bitterness in her voice. Her daughter Lucy *seems* content with her old Devon squire, yet rarely writes.

'At least my father cares for me. I cannot recall the last time you came to see us at Leighs.' Essie gives her an accusing look. 'In truth, Mother, I suspected you had forgotten about us.'

'I pray for you all every day.' Penelope stops and takes Essie's hand in hers. 'I've never told you, but I thought I'd lost you when you were born. Your cord was around your neck, and my midwife struggled to save you.'

Essie stares at her in silence for a moment. 'There were times when we needed a mother.'

Penelope feels a stab of conscience. It's no use explaining how busy she's been, or that she had to stay in London. Her sons Robert and Henry are completing their education, but her three children by Charles are at Wanstead with them for the summer. Penny, now twelve, is good company and helps to look after Isabella, now nine, Mountjoy, a lively boy who will soon be seven years old, and St John, who is the image of his father.

She gives her daughter's hand a gentle squeeze. 'It's not been easy for me, Essie. I feared I would end up in the Tower, or worse, after what happened, but the future looks brighter now, and I promise to be a better mother to you all.'

Charles spends his time overseeing improvements to the house and estate, and restoring the ornamental gardens with long walkways. He had the old fishponds cleaned and restocked, and they've become a favourite place for the children to paddle and play, and escape the heat of the sun.

Penelope laughs as they splash each other and try to catch little fishes in the murky ponds. She's reminded of her happy childhood at Chartley, but saddened to think only Dorothy remains. Although her sister has at last had a son, her husband Henry Percy opposes the persecution of Catholics, and seems unconcerned about angering the king.

Penelope's mother pays them an unexpected visit. Her red hair, of which she was so proud, is turning grey, and she worries about her future. 'That scoundrel Sir Robert Dudley has filed a claim in the courts against my estates.' Her mother scowls. 'He says his mother was legally married to my Robert, which is an outrageous lie. He's also claiming his late father's title of Earl of Leicester.'

Penelope frowns. 'He would never have stood a chance

during the old queen's reign, but who can know who has influence in the courts now?'

Her mother's eyes flash with anger. 'Baroness Sheffield swears she was married in secret to Robert. She claims he pleaded with her to disavow the marriage, offering her seven hundred pounds a year, or threatened to leave her penniless.'

'That means nothing if she has no proof, and it would mean her marriage to Edward Stafford would be bigamous.'

Her mother nods. 'He cannot be allowed to succeed with this claim. I could be left with nothing, and he will also have a claim on Essex House – and even Wanstead.'

Penelope stares at her in alarm at the thought of losing her beloved Wanstead. Her mind races with the consequences. 'Does she have any witnesses, a chaplain or minister?'

'How can she? Her claimed marriage never took place.' Her mother gives her a questioning look. 'I hoped your husband, Baron Rich, would be able to help me. He has influence in the courts.'

'My so-called husband condemned my brother at his trial, to defend his own reputation. He's married my Lucy to George Carey, against my wishes, and has abandoned me since.' She sees her mother's look of concern. 'I shall not rest until this is resolved in our favour. We shall produce so many witnesses no court could be in any doubt.'

Her mother looks deep in thought as she remembers. 'Our marriage was here at Wanstead, and Robert's chaplain, Humphrey Tindall, officiated. He became Dean of Ely Cathedral, and will testify in court.'

'Grandfather took the trouble to be certain your marriage was properly conducted, so you need not worry.'

Her mother's eyes begin to fill with tears. 'My father would have been an ideal witness. I miss him, Penelope, and can hardly believe he's been dead eight years, as has my brother

Richard, who was also a witness, and Robert's brother, Ambrose Dudley.'

She holds her close for the first time in years. Her mother is now past sixty years old, and seems vulnerable and lonely, even frail. Once again, Penelope understands she must be the strong one in the family. It is time to put her influence to the test, and defend their land and property.

27

THE GUNPOWDER PLOT

MAY 1605

Penelope smiles at the sight of her sister holding the train of the new princess. She decides not to say it was she who recommended Dorothy to the queen. It would have been easy enough to take the honour of becoming godmother to the little princess herself, but from now on she's vowed to put her family first.

The birth of the first royal child in sixty-eight years was celebrated with the church bells of London ringing all day, and great bonfires lighting up the night sky. King James shows no sign of disappointment at the birth of a daughter, and the queen is exhausted, but in good spirits.

The christening is held at the Chapel Royal in Greenwich Palace. The queen's doctors had recommended moving her court to Greenwich to have the baby, after one of her Scottish maids of honour caught the smallpox, and reports of increased cases of the plague in the city.

The child has a long train of purple velvet, trimmed with ermine and embroidered with gold, carried by Countess Elizabeth de Vere and Penelope's sister. The Archbishop of Canterbury, Richard Bancroft, one of the few present at the death of

Queen Elizabeth, begins the service with overlong prayers. He makes the sign of the cross, and names the child Mary.

Penelope sees the mischievous nod from the queen's handsome young brother, Ulrik of Denmark, who is dressed in robes of crimson velvet. Outspoken in his opposition to the peace treaty, he seems a poor choice as a godparent. He has a reputation for using his limited English to tease his hosts, and she finds his contempt for protocol amusing.

The other godparent is the king's cousin, Lady Arbella Stuart, who, as a princess of the blood, represents the queen, absent by tradition until she is churched. Penelope dislikes Lady Arbella, rumoured as a match for Charles. She complains of the queen's extravagance and calls her masques childish singing and games.

After the ceremony Penelope takes the opportunity to speak in private with her sister. Dorothy looks happier than she's been for ages, and wears a velvet brocade gown with a high lace ruff, decorated with pearls. They walk through the royal gardens until they find a secluded spot with a good view of the river.

Dorothy smiles. 'I've been meaning to thank you for helping our mother.'

'All I did was encourage her to ask for the matter to be heard in the Star Chamber. It helped that Dudley's mother couldn't recall the name of her minister, or the date of her alleged marriage, and that her key witnesses are long since dead. It's too early to celebrate, though. The final judgement has yet to be pronounced.'

Dorothy gives her a knowing look. 'You have put your new influence to the test, dear sister.'

'I worried the hearing would put a great strain on our mother but, in truth, she enjoys being the centre of so much attention, *and* having her revenge on Baroness Sheffield and her troublesome son.'

'Mother told me Sir Robert Sidney is a great help to her. He feels he owes it to his brother's memory.'

Penelope nods. 'He's a good man, and liked by the king. Our mother also has a surprising ally. Sir Robert Cecil decided to support her appeal. He spoke in the Star Chamber of her affection for Earl Leicester, and how she was long disgraced by Queen Elizabeth.'

'That's not much of a compliment.'

Penelope smiles. 'We will take whatever we can get from Robert Cecil.'

'I heard Sir Robert Dudley is planning to leave the country, to work in the service of the dukes of Tuscany.'

'Well, let us pray that's true. Where did you hear of it?'

'My husband told me it's not the action of a man who thinks he's going to win his case.'

'Charles said your husband annoys the king by speaking out in favour of the Catholics. He's fortunate the king is tolerant, but can you persuade Henry to be more discreet?'

'I wish I could. You know what he's like, Penelope. I worry he's spending too much time with men like Robert Catesby, and his cousin, Thomas Percy, who encourage his outspoken views.'

'I remember Robert Catesby. His wife is Bess Raleigh's cousin. Our brother called him Robin, and he was wounded in his rebellion. He was one of those who escaped execution, but lost everything to the Crown. I've never heard of Thomas Percy.' Penelope frowns. 'I presume he's one of the more radical Catholics?'

'He's really a second cousin, a distant relative. Thomas Percy looks after my husband's estates in the North, but he's started bringing men to the house late at night. They lock themselves away and Henry says they are not to be disturbed.' Dorothy looks at Penelope with concern in her eyes. 'I worry they are up to something.'

Penelope puts her hand on Dorothy's arm. 'I will ask Charles to have a word with Henry. With God's grace, and the help of Robert Cecil, our family will soon be out of one crisis, and we must *not* be drawn into another – particularly now I have another child on the way.'

Charles returns to Wanstead in an unusually dour mood, and Penelope fears the worst. She waits until the children are off to bed, then dismisses the servants and pours him a glass of their best Rhenish wine. He sits staring at the fire for a moment, then turns to her.

'There has been a Catholic plot to murder the king.' He takes a sip of his wine. 'If their plan had succeeded, I could also have been killed.'

'Dear God.' Penelope stares at him, her eyes wide in alarm. 'What happened?'

'Sir Robert Cecil's agents discovered the plot through a letter sent to Lord Monteagle. He told me they'd been watching the conspirators, waiting for them to make their first move.' He takes another deep drink of his wine and looks at her, his face grim. 'A man named Thomas Percy secured the lease to the undercroft beneath the House of Lords. Robert Cecil ordered a thorough search before the state opening of Parliament. They found thirty-six barrels of gunpowder, more than enough to kill us all.'

Penelope holds her untouched glass of wine, hardly daring to ask what she suspects. 'Thomas Percy is a relative of my sister's husband. Is Henry Percy involved?'

'I'm afraid Robert Cecil accuses him of helping to fund the conspirators. Henry's been taken into custody at Lambeth Palace as a precaution while enquiries are made.'

'I shall have to send a message to my sister. Can I invite her to come here? She will be good company during my lying in.'

Charles takes his pipe, a habit since his time in Ireland, and fills the bowl with a little black tobacco from a leather pouch, then looks up at Penelope. 'I'm afraid you cannot. It could put me in an impossible position. You need to know the conspirators planned an uprising in the Midlands, and were going to kidnap Princess Elizabeth.'

'As a hostage?' Penelope struggles to understand. 'How does that affect my sister, or her husband?'

He takes a taper and lights his pipe from the fire before answering. 'Robert Cecil's informers claim they planned to put Princess Elizabeth on the throne, with someone like Henry Percy acting as regent until she comes of age. He also believes Percy was to stay in London and lead the capture of Prince Henry.'

Penelope stares into the crackling fire as a draught makes the flames flare and find the sap in the unseasoned logs.

'Our family seems to have a talent for being implicated in these conspiracies.'

'I'm afraid we must take care, and I must distance myself from your sister. A good number of the accused, including Robert Catesby, are known to have been close to your late brother.'

'Does that mean we are under suspicion of somehow being involved?' The thought sends a chill through her.

Charles sucks on his pipe and blows out a puff of grey smoke. 'I doubt it. The king has appointed me as one of the commissioners, to sit in judgement over the conspirators.'

'You could be the one who sends my sister's husband to the scaffold.' Her voice is flat as she thinks of her sister. 'Unless Henry can prove his innocence, Dorothy will lose her husband, her children's titles and inheritance. His fortune and all property and estates could be seized, including Syon House, and she would be ruined.'

'Henry Percy brought this on himself. He's spent his time since the coronation making enemies at court, not least of the one man who could save him, Robert Cecil. I tried to talk some sense into him, as you asked, but he accused me of being the king's lapdog.'

Penelope knows him well enough to tell from his tone that he holds out little hope for Henry Percy. 'What is to happen now?'

'The Lord Chief Justice, Sir John Popham, is questioning the man they captured in the undercroft. Most of the other conspirators fled to a house on the border of Staffordshire, where they were besieged by the pursuing sheriff's men. Robert Catesby and Thomas Percy were both shot and killed in the fighting.'

'I suppose this means you'll have to stay in London?'

'Worse. I have orders from the king. He's concerned there could be a Catholic uprising, so I've been told to take an army north.'

He does his best to keep it from her, but she suspects Charles has not been well since his return from Ireland. She fears he's haunted by the memories of what he had to do there. He's become a restless sleeper, and often wakes at dawn. His face looks pale, and his hair is thinning.

She worries about him riding north. There has always been talk of a secret Catholic army, awaiting its chance, and the failed plot could tip the balance. Penelope looks him in the eyes, and sees he's waiting for her response.

'Do you think this could lead to civil war?'

He takes another puff of his pipe. 'I pray it does not, Penelope. My orders are to encourage the good, and terrify the bad.' He frowns. 'God knows my experience with the Irish prepared me well, but I confess I don't relish such a task, and will take care not to endanger myself or my men.'

Penelope looks around the faces of the ecclesiastical court, conscious of the growing bulge in her middle. They are all men of a certain age, wearing black, and she feels their unblinking eyes judging her before she speaks. Most are strangers to her, but she recognises the dour face of the Archbishop of Canterbury, Richard Bancroft.

They last met in the Chapel Royal at Greenwich Palace under happier circumstances – the christening of Princess Mary. She wishes she'd taken the trouble to speak to him, but now it's too late, as he must decide her future, and the future of her children.

She can imagine some of these devout clergymen took unwholesome pleasure in the lurid tales they no doubt shared about her marital conduct. For many years, she's made no pretence of fidelity, openly living with Charles as if they were husband and wife, and now it seems she might pay the price.

The clerk calls the court to order, and Archbishop Bancroft studies the papers in front of him, as if seeing them for the first time. Penelope expects a reproach from him. She wonders if it is possible to have a fair hearing from men like these, who've never been forced into an arranged marriage, or even taken a wife.

The archbishop looks up at her and clears his throat. 'Your husband, Baron Robert Rich, has sued for a divorce on the grounds that you committed adultery with a stranger.' His eyes stay on hers, and she sees what might be pity in them, although it is hard to tell. 'Do you admit or deny this accusation, Lady Rich?'

Penelope hesitates. It could help her case if she tells them

Charles is no stranger, but Charles's lawyer, Joseph Earth, told
her to say as little as possible, and show the court humility. She
misses the advice of her own lawyer, Richard Broughton, who
died the previous year.

'I confess, Your Grace, and beg the forgiveness of the
court.' She bows her head and holds her breath. Her life will
be complete if she is free to marry Charles. As well as her
promise to him, it is important to legitimise their children.

Archbishop Bancroft nods. This seems to be the answer he
expects, yet he looks back down at his papers.

'Baron Rich states that the adultery was not an isolated
incident, but took place over many years, at several locations. Is
that correct, Lady Rich?'

'It is, Your Grace.' She bows her head again, but her pulse
races as a new concern occurs to her. She wishes she had found
out whether there is some sort of punishment for what she's
done.

'Then I shall adjourn the hearing until you have provided
details of the dates and places in writing. In the meantime, we
will establish whether your marriage to Baron Robert Rich was
properly conducted.'

A long week passes before Penelope is summoned back to
appear before the court. With help from Joseph Earth, she
confessed in writing to adultery at Essex House, as well as
Wanstead, providing dates to convince the court. Charles had
given his consent for her to name him, but her lawyer advised
against risking his good reputation.

The same grim faces study her, offering no clue to their
verdict. At the last hearing Penelope chose a dark gown, with
no jewellery. Now she wears an azure-blue gown, but doubts
any of them will know it is the colour of love, fidelity and trust.

Archbishop Bancroft studies her for a moment, then reads

from his notes. 'Before I pronounce the judgement of this court, I will say the conduct of both parties to this marriage leaves much to be desired.' His dark eyes scan the faces of those present, and several nod in agreement. 'Baron Rich has revealed his Puritan meanness of spirit, and is guilty of hardness to this noble lady, his wife, who it is said was married to him against her will. Lady Rich is from a good Protestant family, and has raised her children in the faith.'

Penelope stares at him in surprise, but recalls how, when Bishop of London, he preached a controversial sermon at St Paul's Cross, which became a passionate attack on the Puritans. She hardly dares to hope she has an unexpected ally in this court.

The archbishop continues. 'A marriage which is not agreed by both parties is not recognised by the Church.' He pauses, and looks up at Penelope. 'Unfortunately, there is no evidence, other than hearsay, and the minister who conducted the ceremony is dead.'

Penelope sees her chance, but knows there will be consequences if the court is persuaded her marriage is unlawful. Her son, Robert, is heir to her husband's fortune. Married to Frances, daughter and heiress of Sir William Hatton, he could be declared illegitimate if she speaks out, his life ruined.

Archbishop Bancroft takes her stony silence as acknowledgement. 'This court grants a divorce between Baron Robert Rich and his wife, Lady Penelope Rich, on this fourteenth day of November, 1605, on the grounds of Lady Rich's adultery with a man whom she refuses to name.'

Penelope struggles not to smile as the great weight of her twenty-two years of marriage is lifted from her. At last, she is free to live her life without the shadow of Robert Rich. It feels like a fresh start, and her mind whirls as she begins to plan her new life as Countess of Devonshire.

Archbishop Bancroft takes a deep breath and looks as if he

is about to close the hearing, but then looks Penelope in the eye. 'This divorce is declared *a mensa et thoro*, from bed and board, and is not an annulment, which requires an Act of Parliament.'

Penelope's mind whirls with the consequences of his words for Charles and their children. 'Then I cannot remarry, Your Grace?'

He frowns. 'The Church of England does not permit remarriage during the lifetime of the other partner, and both you and Baron Rich are ordered by this court to live celibate lives.'

Charles curses, a rare thing, when he finally returns and hears the news. 'All Baron Rich has achieved is to make matters worse for us all.'

Penelope must agree. 'The divorce is granted, but we are forbidden to marry, and I see no way to legitimise our children without an Act of Parliament, which my lawyer advises would be refused.'

Charles looks sullen. 'Your lawyer is right. Trying to obtain the consent of Parliament would drag our reputations through the mire, and your husband's as well.' He reaches for his pipe and fills the bowl, lighting it with a taper before puffing on the stem.

He's told Penelope that smoking helps him to think, and she sees from his furrowed brow he is deep in thought. His habit is more frequent now, and he looks older and thinner since helping to deal with the conspirators. She suspects the king is right in declaring tobacco smoking loathsome to the eye, hateful to the nose, harmful to the brain, and dangerous to the lungs.

Charles seems to reach a conclusion. 'Will you marry me,

Penelope, and say to the devil with the orders of the ecclesiastical court?'

Penelope smiles, glad to see his old spirit return. 'I will gladly marry you, whatever the consequences.'

'You realise the king will object, and you could be banished from court?'

'I made you a promise, before you went to Ireland, and cannot think of anywhere I would rather be than here at Wanstead, with you.'

The steady contractions begin at dawn, but now a bright shaft of sunlight lights the room, and a blackbird sings outside her open window, helping her feel at peace. Twenty-three years have passed since the birth of Lucy, her first child.

She's learned to trust her midwife more than any doctor, and her prayers are usually answered. She longs for her aching body to return to normal, and to fit into her fine silk gowns before they go out of fashion. The midwife gives her a nod, as they both know the well-rehearsed routine.

Penelope closes her eyes, and listens to the blackbird's carefree song, waiting for a phrase to repeat, yet they are never quite the same. She tries not to fight the pain as her child is pulled free, and breathes again, shedding unexpected tears of joy as she hears the first cry.

'Another fine little boy, my lady.'

She thanks God her child is a boy, as she'd hoped, and doesn't hesitate to name him Charles, after his father.

Few notice the absence of Penelope or Charles from the extravagant Christmas festivities at Whitehall Palace. Much of the work of interrogating the surviving conspirators of the Gunpowder Plot is done, and Charles tells the king he needs to be permitted a well-deserved rest, which is the truth.

Penelope sees it as a small sacrifice to forgo the excesses of another Twelfth Night masque to spend a quiet Yuletide with their children, her mother, and sister Dorothy, and have a special celebration of their own. Dorothy's husband is still in the Tower, but Charles reassures her there is no evidence to convict him.

On Boxing Day, they gather in the Wanstead chapel, where Charles's young chaplain, William Laud, is persuaded to conduct the simple private ceremony. Penelope is close to tears when the chaplain asks if she will have Charles as her husband, and she says, 'I do.'

28

THE CRUELLEST BLOW

JANUARY 1606

Penelope stares at the brief letter from her eldest son. She has become a grandmother to his daughter named Anne, after the queen. She should be elated, yet the next line breaks her heart. Writing from Leighs Priory, he tells her she is not allowed to see her granddaughter, as she is to be raised in the Puritan faith.

She folds the letter and recalls the words her brother said when he saw her eldest son for the first time. *The future Baron Rich. One of the wealthiest babies in the country*. Too late, she knows she should have spent more time with her son, and made him a good Protestant. It's no surprise his father groomed his heir in his own image. She can imagine how he treats his sixteen-year-old wife.

Charles scowls as he reads the letter. 'You have a right, as her grandmother. There is nothing to stop you going to Leighs Priory, and demanding to see the child.'

Penelope shakes her head. 'In truth, I never wish to set eyes on Baron Rich again, even if this is the price I have to pay.' She forces a smile. 'Little Anne is one quarter Devereux, and always welcome to come and see me when she is old enough to. I must learn to be patient.'

'I met Baron Rich in the corridor in Whitehall.' Charles frowns. 'He called me a liar.'

'I'm sorry, Charles. What did you do?'

'I counted to ten, then wished him good day.' He gives her a wry smile. 'In truth, I have to admire his tolerance all these years, although I can't pretend to understand it.'

'Have you spoken to the king since your return to court?'

He nods. 'The king is displeased with your divorce, and says I deserve to be punished for defying the law. I hoped he would show more understanding, but he told me I have won a fair woman with a black soul.'

'Then I am not welcome back at court?'

'Would that trouble you?'

'I wasn't going to tell you until I was certain, but I am with child, so will have plenty to distract me from the gossipers of court.'

Charles brightens, a glint in his eye. 'Then you provide me with one more good reason to persuade the king our marriage is valid.'

'What are you planning, Charles?'

'I will write to King James and explain you did not consent to your marriage to Baron Rich of your own free will, which is a requirement for valid matrimony.'

Penelope stares at him for a moment. 'Will you allow me to see your letter, before you risk your future for me?'

'Of course. I'm not only doing this for you. I do this for us, Penelope, and for our children's future inheritance.'

She hears him coughing as he works on his letter, late into the evening, and worries that his chest suffers from so much smoking. It is close to midnight before he brings his draft to her bedchamber, and hands it to her to read.

A lady of great birth and virtue, being in the power of her friends, was by them married against her will unto one against whom she did protest at the very solemnity and ever after; between whom from the first day there ensued continual discord, although the same fears that forced her to marry constrained her to live with him.

Penelope looks into his eyes. 'I could lie low, keep to myself until our child is born.' She smiles. 'My mother says out of sight is out of mind, and you can work to rebuild your reputation at court, and win back the king's support.'

Charles shakes his head. 'I want you to read the rest, and give me your true opinion. The king refers to holy canon law, yet as far as I know this is the first time the new laws against remarriage have been put to the test.'

Penelope is not sure, but the worst that can happen is they are both banished from court. Charles often says how tired he is of the politics of court. She will be glad to see him recover his good health with her and their children. She holds the letter closer to the candle at her bedside, to read the rest.

He did study in all things to torment her; and by her fear did practise to deceive her of her dowry, and though he forbore to offer her any open wrong, restrained with awe of her brother's powerfulness, yet, as he had not long in time before in the chief duty of a husband, used her as his wife. He did put her to a stipend and abandoned her without pretence of any cause but his own desire to live without her, he did by persuasion and threatening move her to confess a fault with a nameless stranger, without which such a divorce could not by the laws of practice proceed.

Charles complains of the headache he calls his *old fury*, but must attend the hearing at Westminster Hall, where the conspirators who remain alive are to be tried for high treason. He returns after two days, grim-faced, and reluctant to talk about it, until they retire to bed for the night.

'They were all convicted and sentenced to a traitor's death.' His voice is flat in the darkness. 'The man discovered in the undercroft, named Fawkes, escaped the worst by jumping from the gallows once the rope tightened around his neck. Others cried out, begging for mercy.'

Penelope tries not to think about the horrific scenes Charles has been forced to witness. 'They would have killed the king and all of Parliament, including you, if their plot had succeeded.'

'The king says he was spared by God, but he should thank Robert Cecil and his agents.'

'Has the king said anything about your letter?'

'I fear it has done little good. We've made no secret of how we live together, yet now I'm taken to task in public by the king. He says I've broken a holy contract, and shown contempt for the law.' His voice has an edge of anger at the injustice.

Penelope takes him in her arms. 'Is there nothing we can do?'

'I've decided the time has come to retire from public duty. I have one more hearing to attend, and I'm meeting my lawyer, Joseph Earth, at my London house to make sure our children inherit.' He lies in silence for a moment. 'I look forward to living here in peace with you.' His voice brightens. 'I will have the library improved, and collect rare books.'

Penelope kisses him. 'I would like that, and so would our children. You have enough income from the rents on your estates and, if the king allows you to keep your revenue from imported wines, you will never have to work again.'

Penelope's maidservant tells her that Fynes Moryson, Charles's personal secretary, has returned early from London and wishes to see her. Penelope sees the mud spattering his black riding cape. His eyes have the wild look of a man who has ridden hard, despite poor roads.

'Whatever is the matter, Master Moryson?' She knows Fynes Moryson disapproves of her, and suspects he blames her for his master's fall from grace with the king.

'Sir Charles asks you to come to the Savoy in London at once, my lady, and bring your son, Mountjoy.' He glances at her waiting maidservant. 'I came back to escort you.'

Penelope senses the urgency in his voice, and her pulse races with concern. 'Did he say why? Why the Savoy, and why does he want me to bring Mountjoy? He is only nine.' She stares at him. 'I'm sorry, Master Moryson, but I feel there's something you're not telling me.'

Fynes Moryson lowers his voice. 'I regret to tell you Sir Charles's old trouble from Ireland has returned. The Savoy is used as a hospital and has the best doctors in London.'

Penelope turns to her maid. 'Tell the grooms to have my carriage made ready, pack my bags – and bring the children here. I need to speak to them.'

A bright full moon lights their way by the time they reach the Strand, where Penelope is met at the Savoy by a well-dressed man she's not seen before. 'I'm Doctor Turner, my lady. The Earl of Devonshire has a fever. I've given him a tonic, and let blood, but I regret to tell you he weakens by the hour.'

Penelope cannot believe him. 'He was in good spirits when he left yesterday. How can he have become ill so soon?'

Doctor Turner looks apologetic. 'He told me he's been

unwell for some time, my lady, but you had better see the earl for yourself.'

Penelope asks Fynes Moryson to arrange a meal for Mountjoy, and follows the doctor up creaking wooden stairs. She hears the familiar coughing before they open the door and realises she has been refusing to accept the truth. Charles has not been well since his time in Ireland.

He sits in bed, propped up on pillows. The shutters are closed and a single candle glows at his bedside. His eyes meet hers as she enters. 'Thank you—' He gasps for breath. 'I'm glad you've come.' His body shakes as he coughs, and when he speaks his voice is a rasping whisper. 'Have you brought our son?'

'I have, but why do you need to see him?'

Charles tries to raise himself, but falls back on his pillows. 'I've been through my will with my lawyers.' He has another fit of coughing, and struggles to recover his breath. 'I must tell our son about his inheritance.'

Penelope puts her hand to his forehead and feels the warm sweat. 'Mountjoy is having his supper, but I'll bring him to you before he goes to bed.' She takes his hand in hers and gives it a gentle squeeze. 'You must fight this, Charles. I need you, and so does our unborn son.'

He manages a weak smile. 'Another boy?'

'I've told you before. A mother knows these things.' She tries to make light of it as she pushes away a deepening sense of despair.

'You must rest, but I will sit with you.'

Charles closes his eyes and lies back, breathing heavily. Sweat glistens on his brow, yet he shivers, as if cold. Penelope holds his hand until he falls into a fitful sleep, then sends for Doctor Turner.

'Has he eaten?'

Doctor Turner shakes his head. 'It's best to starve a fever, my lady, but I can bleed him again.'

Penelope looks back at Charles. He seems to be sleeping. 'He should rest for now, doctor, but he might have something to drink when he wakes.'

A week passes, and Penelope settles into a routine of caring for Charles and fending off his visitors. Some are well-wishers and family friends like Henry Wriothesley, Earl of Southampton, who'd supported her brother. She suspects others, like Sir William Godolphin, are curious to see if the rumours are true.

She is encouraged when Charles recovers enough to see Mountjoy. He tells him his estates are in trust for when he comes of age, and he must guard against those who would trick him out of them. His lawyer, Joseph Earth, brings more papers to be signed, and Penelope is alarmed to see Charles's chaplain, William Laud.

Joseph Earth seems to notice her concern. 'The earl asked to sign a revised copy of his will, my lady, and his chaplain is one of those I've invited as a witness.'

'Why does he need to change his will?'

'To make provision for his unborn child, my lady, and as a beneficiary, it's best if you are not present at the signing.' He frowns. 'If I may, you look tired, and should rest.'

Penelope agrees. She's not had a full night of sleep since coming to London, and returns to her apartment, where she finds Mountjoy reading a book. She wishes she'd ignored Charles's request to bring their son. He looks up at her with Charles's questioning eyes.

'How is Father?'

'With God's grace, he will soon be better. We must pray for him, Mountjoy, and then we can all go home to Wanstead.'

．　．　．

One of the Savoy maidservants wakes her at dawn, her face pale in the early light. 'The Earl of Devonshire asks for you, my lady.'

Penelope dresses as fast as she can, fighting a growing sense of panic, and rushes to Charles. He lies back in bed on his pillows, his body shaking with each cough. His breathing is too fast, as if he fights for each breath. She puts her hand on his brow and feels the feverish heat.

He stops coughing and looks up at her. 'I'm thirsty.'

Penelope hands him the cup at his bedside, and watches as he takes a drink. 'Doctor Turner said the fever will worsen before you recover.' She forces a smile. 'Mountjoy asked after you, and prays for you to be well.'

Charles reaches out a hand. 'Hold me close, Penelope.' His voice sounds breathless, yet his eyes shine. 'I want to tell you—' He gasps for breath. 'I have loved you since the first day we met.'

She climbs on to the bed and takes him in her arms. His nightshirt is damp with sweat, but his breathing steadies, becoming less shallow. 'I remember the first time I saw you, at a New Year's dance at Richmond Palace.' Penelope kisses his cheek. 'You had me at a disadvantage. I didn't know who you were.'

'I knew of you—' He gasps for another breath, his chest heaving with the effort. 'They all talked of Lady Rich—' His face is pained as he battles to breathe. He makes a wheezing sound and lies back on his pillows. 'The most beautiful lady at court.' His voice is a whisper. 'The goddess Venus.'

She holds him close, remembering the happy times, and making plans for their future. Charles is right about retiring from public life. He must put their family before the demands of court, and they will spend more time together as a family.

She rocks him back and forth, as she did to send her children off to sleep, and kisses him on the cheek.

His eyes flutter open and he begins coughing again, a strange, wheezing cough that worries her. She sees a look of fear in his eyes as he fights to take a breath. It's not a look she's ever seen before, and her heart races with alarm. She calls out for the doctor or a servant but no one comes.

His breathing slows, and he takes his last breath. She senses he has gone. His eyes are closed, his face is at peace. She puts her hand to his forehead, already growing cooler. Tears run down her face as she weeps. She cries for their children, who need a father, and for the man she wished to spend the rest of her life with.

The wetness wakes her. She is back in her own room, and she feels with her hand, knowing the reason. There is blood on her fingers. She pulls back the silk coverlet to see the bright red stain spreading over the white linen sheets.

In a rush, she remembers the maid staring wide-eyed at the sight of her crying with Charles in her arms. The doctor came soon enough, a coat over his nightshirt, but had no need to hurry. His tonics were no use to Charles, and now he was too late. She'd begged to stay for one more moment, but they took her to her room, where she cried for hours before falling into exhausted sleep.

She staggers from her bed and collapses to the floor, calling out in a wail of anguish that echoes like the cry of a wounded animal. She lies where she's fallen, still bleeding, her body shaking with her sobbing. Her child is gone, before he had a name. She wishes she were dead.

Penelope opens her eyes at the sound of her sister's voice. 'Dorothy?' She blinks as her eyes become accustomed to the light, and is confused to find she is in her black silk and velvet bed at Essex House. 'How did I get here?'

Dorothy studies her with concern. 'They found you on the floor in your room at the Savoy, and brought you here.' A single tear makes its journey down her cheek. 'I'm sorry, Penelope—' She struggles to compose herself. 'I'm so sorry about Charles.'

Penelope can't find any words. Some part of her hopes she's woken from a bad dream. 'And my baby?'

Dorothy shakes her head, and reaches out to take Penelope's hand. 'I'm afraid you lost your child. The doctors think it must have been the shock. They say you must rest.'

Penelope stares at her sister. 'Where is Mountjoy? Is he still at the Savoy?'

'He's here, with my children. Frances has gone to live with her husband, and passed the lease to me.' She gives Penelope's hand a squeeze. 'You are welcome to stay here for as long as you wish; I am glad of your company, and you have to rest.'

Penelope agrees. 'Thank you, dear sister.' She closes her eyes, and surrenders to her exhaustion.

Penelope is with her mother and younger children at Drayton Manor when Charles's lawyer, Joseph Earth, visits to offer his condolences. 'A date has been set for the funeral, my lady. The earl is to be honoured with a state funeral. He is to be interred in St Paul's Chapel in Westminster Abbey on the seventh day of May.'

'He would have thought it quite an honour.' Her voice sounds flat, although she knows Joseph Earth is trying to help.

'Do you feel well enough to discuss legal matters, my lady?'

'I must.' She looks up and sees the concern in his brown eyes. 'I'm sure you know how difficult this is.'

He nods in understanding. 'The earl made provision for you, as well as dowries for your daughters, with the estates, including the house at Wanstead, in trust for his son, Mountjoy, when he comes of age.' His face turns serious. 'I regret to tell you a number of claimants challenge the will, as the earl expected they would.'

'What can we do?'

'We are well prepared to contest any claim, but there are certain issues I would rather not share, my lady.'

'Charles would have wished you to tell me everything.'

Joseph Earth remains silent, then agrees. 'They question whether the earl was of sound mind, and say he was delirious when he signed the will. They also accuse you of persuading him to make you and the children the beneficiaries, my lady.'

'That's an outrage!' Penelope's pulse races in anger. 'Why would they say such a thing?'

He frowns. 'The earl became a wealthy man, with considerable estates in more than six counties. Those who challenge his will have little to lose, and much to gain by proving his marriage invalid.'

'And his children illegitimate.' The bitterness echoes in her voice.

'I am not a specialist in inheritance law, and will need help to defend against all challenges, but I have to tell you, if I fail you could lose everything.'

Penelope understands. 'I see why you had so many witnesses. They can all testify that Charles was of sound mind. I can pay for a specialist lawyer. Is there someone you would recommend?'

'Sir Francis Bacon, my lady. He will be expensive, but there is talk he is being considered as Solicitor General.'

'Francis Bacon helped to see my brother executed!' Her voice is raised in protest.

'That is why he will help you, to the best of his ability.'

'Then we have no choice. I agree, for the sake of my children.'

29

THE SETTING SUN

JUNE 1607

Her mother makes the long journey to Wanstead in her fine coach from Drayton Manor. She arrives with her own servants and enough luggage to last a month. She takes control of running the household, and orders Penelope to bed. 'I have sent for Doctor Layfield to come from Westminster. His potions can cure a fever.'

'I cannot go to bed. I have too much to do.' Penelope raises her voice in frustration as she tries to explain. 'We are close to settling the final challenges to Charles's will, and I must attend the court hearings.'

Her mother looks unconvinced. 'Your lawyers can represent you in court. Is that not what you pay them for?'

'I need to look the judges in the eye, so they see I speak the truth. My children's future depends on it.'

'Your children's future depends on them having a mother.'

Her stern words take Penelope by surprise. She cannot forget Charles is gone, but is not yet used to the burden of responsibility. 'I struggle with the strain of these hearings, on top of everything that has happened.' She frowns. 'I'm grateful for your help, but I refuse to take any doctor's potions. They were no use to Charles.'

Her mother seems as if she disagrees. 'You need to rest. Dorothy is at Essex House, and I will look after your children until you are well again.' She smiles. 'It will be good for us all.'

'You are right, Mother. In truth, I have been unwell since I lost my child, and feel tired all the time. I'm sure I'll be a lot better after a few weeks with Dorothy.'

Her maidservant announces the arrival of the Countess of Clanricarde. Penelope is pleased to see Frances, but wishes it could be under better circumstances. Frances wears a wide ruff with an open-fronted gown of shining silk, revealing a rich brocade bodice with a necklace of gleaming pearls.

Her intelligent eyes study Penelope. 'I heard you were in bed with a fever. Should you not be resting?'

Penelope embraces her friend, who looks older than her forty years. 'Events of the past year have taken their toll on me.' She manages a smile. 'I feel better for seeing you again.'

'I thought it best to visit before we return to my husband's estates in County Galway. He's having a house built there, but I've seen his plans, and it looks more like a castle.'

'You deserve a castle, Frances, fit for a countess, after those years in your father's draughty house in Seething Lane.'

'Where should I write to you, when we go to Ireland?'

'I plan to stay here at Essex House until my sister Dorothy returns to Syon, then I must return to Wanstead. I fear the children can only face a few weeks of my mother's care.'

Frances smiles. 'I'm sure my Robin says the same of me. He is off to travel the continent with his friends, rather than come with us to Ireland.' She sounds disapproving. 'He is worryingly like his father, always ready for a new adventure, regardless of the cost or consequences.'

'I thought Robin was only recently married?'

Frances nods. 'I see now they were both too young. He was only thirteen, and Lady Frances Howard fourteen, when they were married. He's sixteen now, and much changed.'

Penelope agrees. 'My Henry is seventeen, and although he seems a grown man, I've tried my best to stop his father marrying him off until he is of age.' She smiles. 'Henry is a true Devereux, and I'm sure he deliberately infuriates his father.'

Frances takes Penelope's hand in hers. 'There is much talk about Charles Blount's will. I heard the lawyers joke that his kinsmen will argue until they have used every penny in costs.'

'It has been difficult for me, Frances, but Charles prepared well for this day, and I live in hope our children will have what is due to them.'

Dorothy looks troubled when she comes to see Penelope, resting in the black silk and velvet draped bed. As usual, she comes straight to the point. 'There is a rumour my husband has a lover.'

'How can he?' Penelope knows her sister better than anyone, and sees Dorothy is hurt. 'Is your Henry not still confined in the Tower?'

'He bribes his jailors to keep him on the best conditions. He has a whole apartment, and they allow entry to such visitors as he wishes.' Dorothy frowns. 'I've seen how lax his warders have become.'

'Then I can offer some comfort, Dorothy. When the will was first disputed, they started cruel rumours, and seemed happy to repeat them in a court of law. They called me a harlot and a whore, and accused me of forgery. It is a trick they play, to weaken reputations, and God knows your husband has enough enemies, yet the truth always wins such a game.'

'In truth, I've been happier without Henry.' She gives Penelope a wry look. 'At least I know where he is.'

'You should reclaim Syon as your family home, before it is too late. I will be well again soon, God willing, and you will be able to visit whenever you wish.'

Lucy reminds Penelope of herself at twenty-five. Her plaited hair is the deep, coppery red her grandmother calls her Tudor heritage. She wears her simple gown with natural style and grace and her bright eyes flash with concern.

'I came as soon as I had your letter, but it's over a week's ride from my home in South Devon. I'm sorry it has taken me so long.'

'I'm the one who should be sorry, Lucy. All that time your husband was away in Ireland I never made the time to visit you.' Penelope gestures to the comfortable chair at her bedside. 'Please sit with me. I have something important to tell you.'

Lucy sits in the chair, and frowns as she studies Penelope's face. 'You said in your letter you have a fever?'

Penelope sighs. 'Doctor Layfield tells me to rest, but is annoyed I won't take his tonics, or let him bleed me.'

'You should listen to him, Mother.'

'You sound just like your grandmother, but the doctors were little enough help for Charles.'

Lucy shakes her head. 'I thought I would see you at his funeral. My husband was a good friend to Charles.'

Penelope nods. 'I'm sorry I opposed your marriage, Lucy. Like a typical mother, I thought George Carey not good enough for you, but he's proved me wrong.'

'George is a good man, and I am well provided for, but he has been away a great deal.'

Penelope nods. 'Charles was away in Ireland for the best part of three years.'

'That seems to be the price we must pay for marrying such men.' Lucy's voice has a note of sadness, a hint of other troubles she won't speak of. 'You said you have something important to tell me?'

Penelope takes a small book, with a monogram of an interlinked *A* and *S* in gold, from the table at her bedside. Opening it, Lucy reads the first page. '*Astrophel and Stella*, by Sir Philip Sidney.' She smiles, for the first time. 'It's no secret that you are his Stella.'

'But I do have a secret for you, Lucy. I cannot be certain, but I've always wondered if you are Philip Sidney's daughter. I saw you as a girl with his daughter Elizabeth. You were like twins.'

Lucy stares with wide eyes. 'Why did you not tell me?'

'For the sake of Baron Rich. For all his faults, he did provide for you – and it's impossible to be certain.'

'It would explain why I have little in common with Essie, or Robert.'

'I'm sorry I kept my secret for so long. You deserve to know, and I want to show you this. She reaches behind her neck to unfasten the clasp of her gold locket, and hands it to her daughter. 'Philip Sidney gave it to me, before you were born.'

Lucy opens the locket and reads the words inscribed inside. '*Omnia Vincit Amour*. Love conquers all.'

Penelope opens her eyes. It takes her a moment to realise her daughter Penny sits at her bedside. 'Thank you for coming.'

Her voice sounds weak, and the effort of those few words exhausts her.

'Grandmother allowed me to ride from Wanstead in her carriage with the chaplain, William Laud.' Her daughter wipes a tear from her eye.

Penelope understands. Her mother hopes Penny, as the eldest, can be some comfort to her. 'How are your brothers—' She makes a conscious effort to take a breath. 'And your sister, Isabella?'

'Mountjoy thinks he is the Lord of Wanstead.' Penny manages a smile. 'We are all well, but we miss you, Mother, and pray for you to be well soon.'

'Come closer, Penny.' Her voice is a whisper. 'There is something I wish to explain.'

Penny brings her chair as close as she can, and takes her hand. 'You think it's time I was married?'

Penelope smiles. 'You are fifteen.'

Her daughter nods. 'Grandmother says I will marry soon enough.'

'Then you need to know—' She lies back on her pillows.

'What are you trying to say, Mother?'

'You must refuse—' She gasps for breath. 'If they try to marry you—' She rests for a moment. 'To a man not of your choosing.'

Penny gives her mother's hand a squeeze. 'You have my promise, Mother, and I won't marry until you are well enough to be at my side.' A tear runs down her cheek.

There is a tentative knock at the door. Dorothy enters with the black-robed chaplain, William Laud, who carries a prayer book. Penny stands at their side, her hands clasped in prayer, her head bowed.

Motes of dust sparkle in the warm glow from the setting sun, streaming through her open windows. Penelope listens as the church bells ring to call the faithful to evensong. She hears distant happy laughter and the clip-clop of horses on the cobbled streets.

She hears William Laud's prayer. 'Almighty, eternal God, heavenly Father, comfort and strengthen this your servant, and save her through your goodness.'

Penelope's mind wanders. She will visit Westminster Abbey and light a candle for Charles. She smiles as she imagines what he would say if he knew he'd had a state funeral, and will spend eternity with the kings and queens of England. When the arguments over his will are over she will commission a monument in his memory.

William Laud is still praying. 'Deliver her from all anguish and distress, release her in your grace, and take her to yourself in your kingdom; through Jesus Christ your dear Son, our only Lord saviour, and redeemer.' He closes his prayer book, and they all say, 'Amen.'

The orange glow fades as the sun slips below the far horizon, casting lengthening shadows across the room. The church bells fall silent. Her breathing slows, and Penelope closes her eyes. A familiar voice whispers to her. *I have loved you since the first day we met.* She smiles one last time, and surrenders to the stillness, finally at peace.

EPILOGUE

Be still, my soul; when dearest friends depart
and all is darkened in the vale of tears,
then you will better know his love, his heart,
who comes to soothe your sorrows and your fears.
Be still, my soul; your Jesus can repay
from his own fullness all he takes away.

Be still, my soul; the hour is hastening on
when we shall be forever with the Lord,
when disappointment, grief, and fear are gone,
sorrow forgot, love's purest joys restored.
Be still my soul; when change and tears are past,
all safe and blessed we shall meet at last.

Katharina Von Schlegel, 1752

AUTHOR'S NOTE

Lady Penelope died on the 7 July 1607, aged forty-four. One of my sources, Sylvia Freedman, author of *Poor Penelope*, found an entry dated 7 October 1607, in All Hallows Church, close to the Tower, where Penelope's brother is buried in the Chapel of St Peter ad Vincula. The ledger entry is, 'A Lady Devereux', but there is no evidence of Penelope's final resting place.

Sir Charles Blount, Earl of Devonshire, was buried in St Paul's chapel in Westminster Abbey on the 7 May 1606. There is no gravestone or monument for him, but his efforts to ensure the legitimate future of his children succeeded.

Sources vary regarding the names and dates of Penelope's children, partly because of controversy about their fathers, and deaths at early ages. I therefore rely on those which are consistently documented in the most reliable sources.

Penelope's mother, Countess Lettice, outlived them all, and died on Christmas Day 1634, at the age of ninety-one. She has been called one of the last great Elizabethan women, although Queen Elizabeth never forgave her for marrying Robert Dudley.

Penelope's sister Dorothy died in August 1619, aged fifty-five, and was buried at St Mary's Church, near the Percy home, Petworth House. Her husband, Earl Henry Percy, was not released from the Tower until 1621.

Baron Robert Rich bought the title Earl of Warwick for ten thousand pounds in 1618, but died the following year. He'd married the daughter of Sir Christopher Wray, Lord Chief Justice to Queen Elizabeth I, Frances, who became one of the richest women in Lincolnshire.

Penelope's daughter Lettice, known as *Lucy*, lost her husband Sir George Carey in 1616. She was married again, to Sir Arthur Lake, and in April 1619 gave birth to a son, but died shortly after, aged thirty-seven, having been 'grievously tormented a long time with pains'.

Penelope's son Robert Rich inherited his father's title of Earl of Warwick, and became an English colonial administrator, Admiral of the Parliamentarian Navy, and a leading Puritan. He joined the Guinea, New England, and Virginia companies, and invested in ships involved in what became the American slave trade.

Henry Rich was a close friend of King Charles I, and a favourite of his queen, Henrietta Maria. He was made the Earl of Holland, and tried to end the English Civil war with a peace treaty. After being captured fighting for the Royalists, Parliament sentenced Henry to death by thirty-one votes to thirty. Despite his brother Robert's protests, Henry was executed on the 9 March 1649.

Mountjoy Blount became a member of King James I's court, where he was a royal favourite. Made Earl of Newport, he held several positions under King Charles I of England, and fought for the Royalists in the Civil War.

Her daughter Penny married Sir Gervase Clifton, who King James made one of the new baronets, and Penny a baroness. She died aged only twenty-one, soon after the birth of their son, named Gervase, on 26 October 1613, at Clifton Hall in Nottinghamshire.

Writing this series has taken me on quite a journey, which began when I decided to write the story of Henry Tudor (who, like me, was born in Pembroke). I found I had enough material for a trilogy, where Henry could be born in the first book, come of age in the second, and become King of England in the third.

After the Tudor trilogy, I continued following the Tudor line with the Brandon trilogy, and my Elizabethan series brings the story of the Tudors to a close. I decided to continue the series by writing about three of Queen Elizabeth's ladies, of which Penelope is the first.

I would like to thank my wife Liz, and my editor Nikki Brice, for their support during my research and writing about Penelope's eventful life. If you enjoyed reading this book, please consider leaving a short review. It would mean a lot to me. Details of all my books can be found at my author website, which also has links to my podcasts about the stories of the Tudors.

Tony Riches, Pembrokeshire
www.tonyriches.com

The Tudor Trilogy

THE TUDOR TRILOGY

England 1422: Owen Tudor, a Welsh servant, waits in Windsor Castle to meet his new mistress, the beautiful and lonely Queen Catherine of Valois, They fall in love, risking Owen's life and Queen Catherine's reputation, but how do they found the dynasty which changes British history – the Tudors?

1461: King Edward of York has taken the country by force. Jasper Tudor, Earl of Pembroke, flees to Brittany with his nephew, Henry Tudor. But dare they risk a reckless invasion of England?

Henry Tudor's victory over King Richard III at Bosworth in August 1485 is only the beginning. Can he end the Wars of the Roses through marriage to the beautiful Princess Elizabeth - and unite the warring houses of Lancaster and York?

Available as paperback, audiobook and eBook

The Brandon Trilogy

THE BRANDON TRILOGY

The story of the Tudor dynasty continues with the daughter of King Henry VII. Mary Tudor watches her elder brother become King of England and wonders what the future holds for her.

Everyone has secrets... but will Charles Brandon's cost him everything? He's fallen in love with King Henry VIII's sister, Mary Tudor, the beautiful widowed Queen of France. Will he dare to marry her without the king's consent?

A favourite of King Henry VIII, Katherine knows all his six wives, his daughters Mary and Elizabeth, and his son Edward. She becomes the ward of Sir Charles Brandon, and when his wife Mary dies, he ask her to marry him and become the Duchess of Suffolk.

Available in paperback, audiobook and eBook

The Elizabethan Series

THE ELIZABETHAN SERIES

Francis Drake sets out on a journey of adventure, and risks his life in a plan to steal a fortune. Queen Elizabeth secretly encourages his piracy, and Drake becomes a hero, sailing around the world and attacking the Spanish fleet.

Robert Devereux, Earl of Essex, is one of the most intriguing men of the Elizabethan period. Tall and handsome, he soon becomes a 'favourite' at court.

Walter Raleigh has been called the last true Elizabethan. He didn't come from a noble family, so how does he become a favourite of the queen, and Captain of the Guard?

Available in paperback and eBook

Printed in Great Britain
by Amazon